THE LAST SECOND CHANCE

BLUE MOON #3

LUCY SCORE

That's What She Said Publishing,Inc.

The Last Second Chance

Copyright © 2016 Lucy Score

Cover by Kari March

ISBN: 978-1-945631-41-2 (ebook)

ISBN: 978-1-945631-42-9 (paperback)

lucyscore.com

060122

To Jennifer, my friend, my soul sister, my third-grade partner in crime.

To Sunshine, my furry soulmate. In your short time with us you taught me what unconditional love looks like … and to never leave a dog alone in a car with a tuna sandwich.

We must be our own before we can be another's.
— Ralph Waldo Emerson

PROLOGUE
EIGHT YEARS AGO

*J*oey Greer let the night wind from the open car window whip over her bare arm. She was three days away from turning eighteen and five from graduation. The freedom looming on the horizon burned like embers inside her. Or maybe that smolder came from the driver whose hand rested possessively on her bare thigh just below her ragged cutoffs.

She shot a look at him in the dark. He looked like one of the gods in the Greek mythology section of her World Cultures book.

Jackson Pierce's profile was just as fine as the rest of him. The perfect blade of a nose over lips that were either spread wide in a mischievous grin or attached to Joey's mouth. His square jaw and high cheekbones gave him the same warrior-like look his older brothers shared. He was leaner than them, and his gray eyes had a hint of icy blue to them. But there was no mistaking him for anything but a Pierce.

Jax was six months older and miles more experienced than Joey. But it wasn't his fault he hadn't fallen for her in kindergarten as she had for him. He was making up for it now.

In the end, all it had taken was for Joey to accept Bannon Bullock's invitation to Homecoming last year. One look at the basketball captain's wandering hands on the dance floor, and Jax had finally laid claim. Joey's virginity had lasted all of a week after that.

She loved him completely, simply, unconditionally, and she knew that, as surely as her heart beat, he felt the same about her.

She felt the purr of the engine ride up her spine as Jax accelerated toward her home to meet curfew. The '68 Camaro had been Jax's first love, until Joey.

Everything about him—about them—was fast, dangerous. She wouldn't have it any other way.

"I'm serious, Jojo. Think about it," he said, his voice low and smooth. "Forget college. Let's see what's out there."

Joey laughed as she always did when Jax pitched his see-the-world quest. "College *is* seeing what's out there. I've got plans. You've got plans."

Those plans included partial rides to Centenary where Joey couldn't wait to try for a spot on the equestrian team. Jax was already guaranteed to start on the Cyclone's lacrosse team.

He gripped her thigh tighter, and she felt the thrill she always did at his touch. "Come on. There's got to be more to the world than Blue Moon and college."

Joey rolled her eyes and calculated how far they were from home. Her curfew was non-negotiable, set in stone. Her father didn't like Jax. Thought he was too smooth, too charming, too rebellious. Joey's mother, on the other hand, adored him... and had insisted on scheduling a doctor's appointment for birth control as soon as Joey told her they were dating.

"Okay, where would we go?" Joey said, spreading her fingers as if to caress the night air. His answer was always different. One night they'd build a cabin in the hills of Montana. Another and they'd backpack their way down to Florida where they'd set sail for the Caribbean.

"West," Jax decided. "We'll just drive west. Pick up odd jobs wherever we stop."

"And then what?" Joey asked, hiding her smile. A chorus of frogs serenaded them as they sped past Diller's pond.

"L.A."

Joey shot him an incredulous look. "You want to live in Los Angeles?" As far as she was concerned, L.A. was a horse-less wasteland of boob jobs and overpriced real estate.

"Why not, Jojo? I wanna be someone. I'm not going to be anyone but John Pierce's son or Carter and Beckett's brother here."

Joey reached out and put her hand over his t-shirt. She could feel his heartbeat strong and steady under her palm. "Jax, you're never *just* going to be a Pierce."

"That's all that's here for me." He said the words quietly, heavily.

Her mood shifted from quiet amusement to pissed off like the flip of a switch. She dug her nails into his chest. "That's *all* that's here for you? What the hell am I, jackass? Some high school distraction for you until you can start living your real life?"

Jax was used to her flares of temper and was practically immune to them by now. He squeezed her thigh hard enough to leave fingerprints until she quit stabbing him in the chest.

"Joey." Her name on his lips had the effect it always did— goose bumps on her skin and a warm, melty feeling in her stomach... like drinking hot chocolate on a cold night.

She crossed her arms over her chest, trying to hold on to her mad.

"You're everything to me. There's no future without you."

"You know I'm not going to throw away college and all my dreams to live out of a car with you and take showers in gas station restrooms, right?"

Eyes on the road, Jax grinned. "I know. And I'll be right there with you."

"Promise?"

"I promise you." He brought her hand to his mouth and kissed her knuckles. "But maybe we could take a road trip this summer? Just the two of us. No parents, no brothers, no school."

Placated, Joey relaxed in her seat. Her horse fund could probably spare a few hundred dollars for a road trip with Jax. She'd be eighteen, an adult. She would find a way to smooth things over with her dad, who'd hate the idea. Anything would be worth spending her nights wrapped in Jax's arms, waking up to that sexy-as-hell face.

"Let's do it," she said.

"Seriously?" He was back to her lighthearted Jax again.

"Yeah. Let's figure it out. Maybe we could leave right after graduation."

"I love you, Joey." He laid a hand on his chest over his heart.

"I know." She smirked at the dark outside her window, and he gripped her leg again.

A flash of brown on the side of the road caught her eye. It was moving fast, too fast for her to get Jax's name out of her throat.

The headlights caught the glow of the deer's eyes as it burst through the trees onto the road. Jax braked hard, cutting the wheel to the right. And for a split second, as the deer bounded safely across the road, Joey thought they were out of danger. But the gravel sent them fishtailing.

She had less than a second to feel the sick, icy fear in her gut as the colossal oak loomed before them. Jax's name exploded from her in a scream of dread. His arm slammed against her chest pinning her to the seat just before the sickening crunch of metal and glass.

And then her world went dark.

~

PAIN WOKE HER. And with it dread.

"Jax?" In her head it was a scream, but somewhere between her head and her lips it came out as a strangled rasp.

"He's not here, honey. Remember?" Her mother's voice and the scent of her Vanilla Fields came to her, floating on the fog of fluorescent lights and grief.

She went under again trying to remember why Jax wasn't with her.

~

JOEY WAS DISCHARGED on her birthday with seventeen stitches running from wrist to elbow and fifty units of a stranger's blood coursing through her veins. Her chest and stomach were a mottled purple from the seatbelt that had saved her life.

But there was no celebration.

Jackson Pierce was gone.

She'd heard her mother and Jax's mom, Phoebe, talking in hushed whispers at the foot of the bed when they thought she was asleep.

He'd vanished from the farm in the middle of the night, leaving behind a note and most of his possessions.

He was heading west, the note said.

Joey's father said in no uncertain terms that he preferred to think the boy who put his precious daughter in the hospital was dead.

So did Joey.

1

*J*ackson Pierce watched his brother Beckett straighten his tux-clad shoulders and take a deep breath. The man was nervous as hell and not doing a good job of hiding it.

The popsicle-stick-width stage of the Take Two Movie Theater was getting crowded, but then again, so was the theater itself. Beckett and Gia's wedding turned out to be the premiere no one in Blue Moon Bend wanted to miss, and the theater was the only venue big enough to hold all of them.

Jax's oldest brother, Carter, elbowed him in the kidney with newlywed pride when his wife, Summer, floated down the aisle. Even edging close to six months pregnant with twins, she was a glowing vision in the short, rose gold dress.

Jax meant to wink or at least smile at Summer as she carefully climbed the stairs, but he couldn't tear his eyes away from the next bridesmaid. Joey Greer, his heart and soul for as long as he could remember, strutted down the aisle. Her long legs had no patience for the slow beat of the processional and ate up the space that separated them.

He willed her to look at him. He needed that glimpse to know that walking down an aisle make her think of him.

She was halfway to the stage before those coffee-colored eyes found his and held. It wasn't a look of love that she was shooting at him. There was more dagger than Cupid's arrow, but it was enough.

She was incredible. Her rich brown hair hung down her back in thick waves. Gia must have talked her into letting a stylist get her hands in it because it was partially pulled back with braids and secured with a sparkling clip. She'd given up her riding boots for heels that looked as if they were made out of tiny glints of snow. They matched the sequins on the dress —which, given her height advantage, was even shorter on her than it was on Summer. She was the perfect homage to New Year's Eve.

Her full lips, slicked with a dark gloss that made him want to sample them as he'd done so freely years before, frowned. Jax put his hand over his heart, and he watched her eyes widen, those lips part.

It was a gesture they'd developed in high school. A secret "I love you" across the classroom or the dinner table. Something that was just theirs.

And he was determined to earn it back.

JOEY GREER WAS BUZZED. Pleasantly, enjoyably buzzed. She took an energetic turn around the dance floor with Donovan Cardona, who quizzed her about Gia's gorgeous younger sister and, pulling out his figurative sheriff's cap, made her promise not to drive home.

Beckett sailed past them, his bride in his arms. Gia

sparkled as she gazed up at her husband, laughing at some private joke. A private dirty joke, judging by the blush on her friend's fair cheeks.

The band slowed it down, and Joey slipped out of Donovan's arms and headed for the bar. She was looking for fun tonight. Fast and bright.

She had no intention of starting off the new year slow dancing in the arms of a friend. Maybe, just for tonight, she'd step a toe over the line, she thought. What harm could it do? A few hours of debauchery before shifting gears into a brand-new year.

She ordered a beer from the adorable, attentive bartender and surveyed the scene. The reception hall was a literal circus tent. With the entire town turning out, Beckett and Gia had decided to host a massive New Year's Eve blow out that would have Blue Moon talking for years.

The tent was erected in One Love Park and ringed with outdoor heaters to protect the guests from the icy December chill. The open bar and crowded dance floor were also doing their part in keeping spirits and temperatures high. Fran from Blue Moon's gym Fitness Freak was rocking out on her bass with her band the Wild Nigels. Gia's ex-husband Paul had been invited to play with them.

It said something about a woman who was confident in her new marriage to invite the ex to the party. It also said that Beckett was out-of-his-mind happy to be locking down Gianna Decker and the newest Mrs. Pierce and didn't bother making a fuss about Paul's presence. He was harmless, of course, but during their courtship had been a thorn in both their sides.

Joey accepted the beer and the wink from Blond Bartender Bailey.

"Some party," he said.

"You got that right," Joey said wryly. Weddings creeped her out. The whole crowd of people staring at you as you said some very personal things to your significant other. The months of planning all wasted on a few blurry hours of chaos. That's not how she'd do it. If she did it.

She'd watched Summer and then Gia stress out over napkins and appetizers and the all-important white poufy dress. Although, Gia's dress wasn't overly poufy. The ivory lace overlay was cut straight across her friend's chest. It would have looked almost demure if it hadn't been for the racy open back. And judging from the way Beckett was looking at her, the dress wasn't going to survive the night.

Summer appeared at her side and hefted herself onto a barstool. "Please let me smell your beer," she begged, pulling Joey's cup to her nose. "No one ever tells you how much you'll miss alcohol when you're growing human beings."

Joey let her take a deep sniff before confiscating the cup. "Watch it. I don't want the twins getting drunk on the fumes of Gia's Red." It had become a tradition in the Pierce family to name the brewery's new beers after their brides. And with the grand opening two days away, the smooth, malty ale inspired by Gia was a nice addition to the taps.

Speaking of the bride, Gia glided up to the stool on Joey's left.

"Hey there, blushing bride," Summer greeted her friend.

"Hey there, glowing mama," Gia laughed.

Joey rolled her eyes. Being flanked by the archetypes of womanhood reminded her that she had no idea where she wanted her life to go beyond work. She didn't even know if she liked the idea of marriage and kids. And if she did, who in the hell would she ever want to settle down with?

Jax. The quiet whisper in her head pissed her off.

Jackson was the last man she'd trust with her future. Everyone else might be impressed with his Hollywood bank account and his follow-through with the brewery, but not her. She would put money on him leaving town in the next six months. Where others would say he'd already stuck it out in Blue Moon for six months, she knew that just put him that much closer to leaving again.

He was a wanderer, a sampler in places and in women. And he would keep on wandering and sampling until the day he died.

She, on the other hand, knew where her heart and her home were. And that was here in Blue Moon.

"So, Joey," Gia said, drawing her back to the conversation. "I couldn't help but notice Jax's attention during the ceremony."

Summer raised her glass of water. "He was mouthing something to you, wasn't he?" she asked innocently.

Jax's perfect lips had mouthed every word of Beckett's vows, his gaze never leaving Joey's face. She didn't know what kind of game he was playing. First his hand over his heart when she walked down the aisle and then the vows. And when he took her arm during the recessional, he'd leaned in so close his lips brushed her ear.

"It's going to be us next, Jojo. You can fight it all you want, but you know as well as I do that we're going to happen."

She'd been so startled by the unguarded touch and his words that she'd nearly stumbled. Jax used the opportunity to pull her in against him as they hurried the rest of the way down the aisle.

He'd thrown her, and she needed to get back in control, back on top. Maybe a night of no strings sex would do just that.

Joey held up a hand to catch Bailey's attention. "Can I get a shot? A really big, strong one?"

"Make that two," Gia added.

"You remember what happened last time we did shots together?" Joey warned Gia.

"Ugh, Ed's Erasers. Don't remind me. I ended up giving Anthony Berkowicz a *Monthly Moon* cover story about how dumb I thought Beckett's face was."

Joey grinned. "On second thought, maybe we should have some Erasers."

She felt a tingle at the base of her spine and knew that Jax was watching her. Whether he was joking with his brothers or taking his mother for a spin around the dance floor, his gaze always returned to her.

Joey bided her time until just before midnight. Without looking in his direction, she sauntered outside, leaving the liveliness inside.

It was a night so crystal clear and cold that she could see her breath. Thankfully the perfect amount of booze in her system kept her warm. She hadn't drunk enough to make any bad decisions, just enough to loosen a few inhibitions.

She carefully followed the side of the tent looking for a quiet, secluded spot. Joey felt him before she heard him. That awareness of his presence she'd always had. His return to Pierce Acres had woken her from a sound sleep. It was as if the shadow had slipped off the face of the moon, finally bringing the light. But in the last eight years, Joey had grown accustomed to the dark.

"You're not leaving without dancing with me." It wasn't a question or a request. Jax didn't ask for permission.

Joey turned to face him, bracing for the familiar hum that vibrated through her blood every time she looked him in the eyes. She'd avoided him for months when he came back, not certain she could resist her body's baser instincts.

Looking at him now, she knew the caution had been warranted. Even in her painful, pinching heels, he still had a couple of inches on her. His hair, dark and thick, curled a bit at the top. The ever-present stubble, something she'd always found irresistible, had been shaved off for the day. At one time, she'd been convinced that fallen angels had carved his face. Now she was fairly certain those dangerous planes were the work of the devil.

His gaze, despite a color akin to icy seas, warmed her blood to a simmer.

Even after all this time, she still remembered what if felt like to have his hands on her. She'd told herself that it was puppy love, that her sex life couldn't peak during her teenage years. But, so far, her carefully selected ventures into the physical since then had held none of the thrill she'd experienced with Jax.

She walked to him, thankful that she didn't trip on the uneven sidewalk, and put her hands on his shoulders.

Joey almost smiled at the suspicion that lit his eyes. He probably thought she was going to kick him in the balls. But she had something more mutually satisfying in mind. A fling. A one-night stand. She could enjoy scratching an itch and putting him back in his place, reminding him of what could have been his had he stayed.

"What are you doing?" he asked on a gravelly whisper.

"You wanted to dance." She smiled slyly.

Jax hesitated for a beat before shrugging out of his jacket and draping it over her shoulders. She felt claustrophobic surrounded by his heat, by his scent. But two could play at that game.

Joey let him bring his broad palms to her waist. She wound her arms around his neck and let her hips sway to the beat of the slow rock ballad the Wild Nigels were playing the hell out of.

She felt his hesitation and relished it. Back in control. God, it felt good. And so did being in his arms again. But she wouldn't dwell on that. Joey shook her hair back and wet her lips. She wasn't going to lose her nerve now.

As if he read her mind, Jax's fingers tightened on the curves of her hips. He pulled her in closer so they were touching everywhere. The heat that pumped through his crisp white shirt should have scalded her hands, but instead it just drew her in.

Her breasts were flattened against his chest, and she felt his belt buckle digging into her stomach. It wasn't the only thing hard against her. Somewhere between exiting the tent and pulling her in, Jax had gone raging hard.

She swallowed a heady combination of desire and fear. She could control this, couldn't she? She could be the one to walk away this time.

His breath was hot against her face. They were too close. Her heart was thumping like a hammer, and she hoped he couldn't feel it.

"Joey." There it was. Her name on his lips. A prayer and a curse.

She was saved from responding by the crowd in the tent.

"Ten, nine, eight, seven ..."

She tried to step back and get an inch of space to breathe, but Jax wasn't having it. One hand trailed up her back to cup her neck, the other slid dangerously low on her hip.

"Six, five, four ..."

Her heart was pounding out of her chest now. She could still win, just needed to keep her head.

"Three, two, one!"

She didn't hear the roar of the crowd. She didn't see the fireworks display happening at the front of the tent. The only thing that existed to her at midnight was Jax's mouth. There was nothing soft or sweet about the kiss. There was a repressed violence about the way his lips moved over hers, crushing, bruising.

The years apart had mellowed nothing. Joey dug her fingers into his shoulders, holding on for dear life as her mouth voluntarily opened to him. His tongue breached her lips and invaded with aggression.

He was using the kiss as a brand, reminding her who she belonged to. But Joey Greer belonged to no man. She stole back the lead, only partially aware of what she was doing. She pushed them away from the white walls of the tent, the only thing separating them from the merriment of a few hundred people, until his back met a tree.

Joey shoved her knee between his legs and felt him tense. She smiled against his lips when he flinched.

His hands were roaming now. One slid around to cup her breast through the fabric of her dress. She purred, and he growled.

"Be with me tonight." She bit his lower lip and sucked it into her mouth. He wasn't the only one who could make demands.

"How much have you had to drink?" He groaned out the words as she pressed her hips into him. She felt him flex into her, grinding his erection against her lower belly.

"What?"

He pulled back from the kiss, fisted his hand in her hair.

"How much have you had to drink?" he repeated.

"What are you, my mother?" she asked, trying to get her

body under control. She shoved against his chest, but he didn't loosen his hold on her.

"You're drunk." He sounded out of breath and accusatory.

"I'm not drunk. I have a nice little buzz going. I know what I'm doing," she told him.

"We can't do this, Joey." He was pulling her hands away from him. "You've had too much to drink."

"I'm giving you permission."

"Not like this." Jax's tone left no room for argument, and it pushed her over the edge.

All of the heat from their kiss evaporated into the bitterest of anger.

She bit her tongue and spun around, intending to march off, leaving him and his spectacular hard-on alone. But his hand snaked out and grabbed her by the elbow. "Joey, I'm trying to be the good guy here."

"Have fun with that." She bit off the words. "You don't want me. I'm sure there's someone else inside who won't have any problems going home with me tonight."

She'd gone too far, hadn't actually meant it. But before she could take the words back, which she wouldn't have anyway, he was whirling her around. Now it was Joey who had her back to the tree. Jax stepped in on her, robbing her of her personal space. His hands gripped her arms hard.

"Don't ever say that again." The tic in his jaw, once only visible on the lacrosse field, flared to life. He gave her one good shake. Rather than fear, Joey felt fury race through her system.

"You have no say in what I do with my life. You lost that privilege a long time ago."

"I'm back, Joey." He gritted it out. "And I *will* fix this."

"Not this way, Ace." Joey stomped on his foot and shoved away from him. She thought about running back to the party, but that would only result in two broken ankles from the ice picks on her feet. At least they served her well on Jax's foot. She settled for a steamed stomp toward the tent. But it wasn't fast enough. She heard him coming and barely had time to brace for the impact. He was on her like a freight train, manhandling her over his shoulder. She landed hard enough to knock the wind out of her, if not the fight.

She got in a half-assed punch to his kidney and a weak kick to his stomach before he slapped her on the ass hard. Handprint hard.

Joey gasped in shock. Her dress had ridden up scandalously high, showing off her very small underwear. Jax's hand settled over her ass, and she froze, not willing to move a millimeter in case it would make his palm press even harder against the part of her that, a minute ago, had been a rainforest of lust.

"Where are you—"

"I'm taking you home."

"I'm not ready to go home." She was pouting. She was hanging over a man's shoulder and pouting. Maybe she had had a little too much to drink. Joey Greer didn't pout. She punched.

Jax set her on her feet next to his car. "Get in."

"No!"

He yanked the passenger door open so hard she thought he might rip it from the frame. "Get in the fucking car, Joey."

She took a page from Summer's book and primly slid onto the seat, refusing to look at him as he slammed the door shut. It wasn't the first time she'd been in Jax's car. The Nova was a sweet ride. He'd even let her drive it once after Summer had stupidly broken up with Carter and they all convened at his house to cheer Carter up with greasy food and zombie TV.

Jax certainly wasn't going to let her take the wheel this

time. He slid into the driver's seat and slammed his door. The tic in his jaw was pulsing.

"You know, it's rude to leave without saying goodbye to the bride and groom," she said icily.

Jax didn't bother sparing her a glance.

"Shut up, Joey."

2

———————

*S*he woke up the next morning with a mouth dryer than the sawdust floor of the stable's riding ring and a marching band of a headache. Goddamn that Jax. She hated when he was right. She'd had too much to drink and humiliated herself with the one man she was determined to never let see her vulnerable again.

And that asshole turned her down.

How dare he? Joey started to stomp downstairs until she realized her head was about to snap off her neck. Carefully, she made her way into the airy kitchen that was way too bright. She intended to keep her head on straight enough to start the coffee. Only the coffee had already been started. Next to the machine sat a horse-covered mug that she'd tucked away in the back of her cabinet out of stupid sentimentality. It was the mug Jax had bought for her at their first date at Overly Caffeinated. There was a bottle of aspirin next to the mug.

Jax.

Last night, she'd busted through her front door the second his car came to a halt out front. He must have come inside after she stormed upstairs.

She had offered him a night of no-strings-attached fun, and he had the audacity to lecture her on alcohol consumption. What she wouldn't give to throw this horse mug at his head right now.

She settled for putting her head in her hands to block out the annoying light of dawn that was beginning to invade the front windows of her house. She had work to do. Plus, it was launch day for Summer's online magazine. She had to slap on a not-hung-over supportive face for her friend.

Her groaning must have drowned out the purr of the engine because she jumped when she heard the knock at the front door.

"Go away if you value your life," she said in a half-yell, half-moan that had her head splitting open again.

She lowered her forehead to the cool granite of the island.

The door opened. *Damn it. She was going to have to start locking up.*

The smell of warm, deep-fried goodness had her peeking over an arm. Jax stood just inside her door grinning and holding a grease-stained paper bag.

"Get out," she rasped.

"Not feeling so friendly this morning, huh?" Jax smirked.

She hurled the coffee mug at him showing off her Little League arm. She would have nailed him too if he hadn't ducked. The ceramic shattered against the doorframe, sending red splinters everywhere. Unfazed, Jax crossed to her.

He dumped the bag on the counter and handed her a sports drink. He reached around her, caging her against the island.

"Listen, Ace, last night was a one-time offer. There's no second chances," she told him, trying to shove past him.

He handed her two aspirin and looked her dead in the eyes.

"I didn't turn you down, Joey. I took a rain check."

Desperate for relief, she washed down the tablets with a glare and the never-found-in-nature blue liquid.

She tried not to pay attention to the fact that he looked entirely too good in jeans and a tight thermal shirt. It made her nauseous.

"No rain checks, Pierce." She tried shoving him back a step, but the man was a mountain. Immovable and impressive.

"We *will* happen, Joey. There's no point fighting it." He tucked a clump of hair behind her ear, and before she could react, he leaned in for a hard, fast kiss.

He pulled back before she had time to respond... or kick him.

"I'll see you around." And with that, he was gone, whistling his way out the front door leaving Joey wishing that she had something else to throw at him.

She waited until she heard him drive up toward the brewery before sneaking a peek in the bag. Three hash browns, glimmering in their own oil, beckoned her unsettled stomach with the promise of carbs and grease.

"Bastard," she muttered as she took a healthy bite of the first one.

JAX WAS STILL WHISTLING when he got to the brewery. He'd beat Carter and didn't expect Beckett until well after lunch seeing as how his brother was probably still in bed with his new bride.

He tried not to think about how long it had been since he'd been with a woman. *Great, now he was thinking about it. And about last night. And, great. Now he was hard.*

Jax took a few deep breaths and concentrated on his

surroundings, willing the blood to return to his head. The day before the grand opening and the construction work was finally complete, leaving only the chaos of dressing and outfitting the place to be ready to serve a few hundred beers and plates of farm-to-table goodness.

The tables and chairs had been set in the Summer-approved layout, which he had to admit was a much better use of the space than the haphazard jumble he and his brothers had originally planned.

The bar was stocked with a shiny new tap system and shelves of full liquor bottles. There was another box of glassware ready to run through the washer, new towels ready to sop up the inevitable spills. The barstools were a work of art. They'd been a stretch for the budget, but the metal bodies and rustic wood tops fit the space perfectly.

He could see it all in his head. His family clustered around a table while half of the town bustled in and out, sampling, laughing, gossiping. His brothers and their wives would raise their families here with the solid pine floors beneath their feet. He'd win Joey back here, and their story would begin again.

He always had a knack for seeing stories. That was the appeal of screenwriting to him. And his story in Blue Moon was just getting started. As an idiot teen, he'd been convinced that he needed to go somewhere to be someone. As John Pierce's son, he had already been defined, already had expectations. And as the brother of an Army Ranger and a lawyer, he was already fucked.

It hadn't bothered him really. Until Joey.

She deserved more than a jock and a teenage screw up. She deserved a man. One successful in his own right. And if Blue Moon was her home, well, then it would be his too.

He'd doggedly pursued a career in Hollywood, slowly

crawling up the food chain until one of his pet scripts hit it big. It could have been enough, probably should have been enough. He could have come home flush with success and cash. A real somebody. Jax felt the familiar stab of guilt when he thought what his selfishness had cost his family. He hadn't been here when his dad got sick or when Carter was discharged with bullet holes.

But more doors had opened for him. More opportunities arose. He'd carved out a comfortable life for himself on the west coast. A nice house in the hills, the phone numbers of several aspiring actresses and models, invitations to the hottest events. But it hadn't been enough.

No matter how fat his bank account or who was on his arm on the red carpet, something was always missing.

When he found the picture of Joey—all cocky grin and long, long legs—that Summer had posted on her blog last June, he'd booked a red-eye home. Nothing would ever be enough without her. So he'd plant roots here with his brothers on the land his father had loved. And he would make it all up to them. Especially Joey.

She'd kissed him last night. A smile tugged at the corner of his lips. It had been a power play on her part, but it still counted. Joey didn't do things she didn't want to do. And for the first time since he'd come home, Jax felt hope. She still wanted him.

And now that he'd had a taste of her, he wasn't going to stop.

A commotion from below had him snapping back to reality and shoving thoughts of Joey and her wicked mouth aside.

He found Franklin, his mother's fiancé and Gia's father, directing a symphony of chaos on the lower level. He was a bear of a man, broad shoulders and generous proportions.

Today he was wearing a long-sleeve Hawaiian shirt with hula girls and sharks on it. He held a cell phone to his ear while carrying on a conversation with a delivery guy and rolling silverware into paper napkins.

Jax sighed with relief. Franklin, Blue Moon's most successful restaurateur, had volunteered to help the brothers set up for the opening. And thank God for that because Jax was just starting to realize that they were dangerously close to being in over their heads.

"Morning," Franklin greeted him from the center of the chaos.

"Morning. I thought you'd take a few hours off this morning to recover from the festivities last night." Not only had he walked Gia down the aisle, but Franklin also sang a convincing Sinatra tune with Fran's band.

"I've been thrown out of my own house," he lamented with a chuckle, signing the delivery slip. "Eva and Emma commandeered Phoebe and the kids."

"Poor Evan," Jax said, thinking of Gia's twelve-year-old son trapped in a house full of women. "I'll have Beckett swing by and pick him up before he comes in this afternoon."

"My grandson will be eternally grateful."

"Yeah, especially if I let him hang out with Joey for a while today," Jax said, whipping out his phone and firing off a quick text to Beckett.

Franklin chuckled. "He's got good taste. Seems like you do too."

"All of us Pierce men do," Jax said evasively.

"Do what?" his older brother Carter said strolling through the downstairs door.

"Have good taste in women." Franklin grinned.

Carter lit up as he always did at the thought of his wife. "You know, I seem to recall Jax and Joey disappearing from the reception right around the same time," he said stroking his beard.

Franklin's eyes sparkled. "That's right. The photographer was looking for you two for the countdown to midnight."

Jax looked at his feet. He sure as hell wasn't about to give his family any ammunition over him and Joey, not when he finally felt like he had a shot.

"What are you doing here so early?" Jax asked Carter, ignoring his brother and Franklin's speculation. "Shouldn't you be hovering over Summer for launch day?"

Carter shrugged and shoved his hands in his pockets. "She kicked me out. Said I was driving her nuts. She's being eerily calm."

The brothers knew from experience that a calm Summer was a dangerous Summer. It meant she was burying all her stress and pretending everything was just fine. Jax decided then and there that he'd swing by Summer's office a little later in the morning to see for himself how close to the deep end his sister-in-law was.

"We still on for the celebratory dinner tonight?" he asked Carter.

"Yeah. I was thinking maybe we should have it here? Kind of a family-only grand opening."

Jax nodded. "I like it."

AFTER HELPING with the feeding and turning out the horses, Joey was feeling marginally better. Not good enough to tackle the thirty pounds of paperwork that had piled up while she helped Gia and Summer wrangle wedding plans—did anyone really care what color the napkins were on the damn table? You were just going to smear food on them anyway. So as long as *storm cloud gray* absorbed cake the same way *pewter* did, Joey couldn't understand the fuss.

She decided to pay Summer a visit to see how the launch was going. Joey found her friend in her office on the second floor of the farm's smaller barn. Clad in leggings and a thick sweater, she was obsessively hitting refresh on her screen.

"Load, damn you!" Summer yanked her blonde hair back into a low ponytail with a frown.

"I was going to ask how the launch is going, but judging from your angry face, it sucks and you're going to have to find a day job."

Summer snorted. "I'm just trying to look at the web traffic stats and the idiotic, moronic, freakishly perverse page won't load."

"I'm glad to see you're handling stress so well during your pregnancy," Joey quipped.

Summer shoved back in her chair and took a deep breath. "Fine. We'll try patience and see where that gets us. Now, distract me from my obsession."

"You can take me to pick up my truck this afternoon," Joey offered.

Summer came out of her chair awfully fast for a woman nearly six months pregnant with twins. "Did you go home with someone? Oh my God! Did you go home with Jax?" She paused, and Joey could see her wheels turning. "Wait, Jax was home last night. Did you go home with someone who isn't Jax?"

Joey rolled her eyes at the interrogation. Summer was famous for weaseling information out of reluctant people. "Jax drove me home after I got slightly shit-faced."

"Damn it. I was hoping we could all exchange hot sex stories from last night."

"Don't rub it in," Joey sighed. It had been too long since she had a hot sex story to share.

"I wondered where you disappeared to. Did he at least make a move on you?" Summer asked.

The dredges of her hangover came racing back, and she dropped down into one of the vibrant floral print chairs in front of Summer's desk. "There was a move," she confessed. "But Jax didn't make it."

"What?" Summer shrieked.

A disheveled red blur dashed through the door. "There's screaming! What did I miss? What's the traffic look like?" Gia demanded.

Joey and Summer blinked. Gia's hair was falling out of the sloppy knot she'd shoved it into. She was wearing pajama bottoms and one of Beckett's law school sweatshirts. Her cheeks were flushed and her eyes bright.

"Jesus, I can almost smell the sex on you," Joey groaned.

"My husband is insatiable." Gia grinned wickedly. She took the seat next to Joey. "Now fill me in."

"Well the page with the site stats won't load, and Joey here went home with Jax last night after she made a move on him."

"Have you tried contacting tech supp—" Gia's head swiveled so fast in Joey's direction that Joey was surprised she didn't hear a snap.

"You and Jax? On my wedding night?" Gia's slim hands fluttered. "This is the best, most amazing—"

"Hold your horses," Joey cut her off before Gia could start levitating with joy. "I had too much to drink."

"And?" Summer prompted.

"And I kissed him."

"Where and where?" Summer demanded resting her chin in her hands.

"Don't you have some numbers to freak out over?" Joey asked her.

"Nice try. Now answer the questions."

"Yeah, did you get to see his meat stick?" Gia jumped in.

Joey's jaw dropped. "Married to Beckett for five seconds and look what happens," she said, ignoring the fact that she'd asked Gia that very question about Beckett early on in their relationship. "You used to be so polite and reserved. Now you're shoving your nose in places it doesn't belong."

"I'm a Mooner now," Gia reminded her. "Nosiness is a town ordinance here."

"Joey, quit stalling," Summer ordered.

"I should have kept my big mouth shut," Joey lamented.

"You mean, of course, when you kissed Jax? Did you use too much tongue?" Gia teased.

"These questions and this hangover are making me hate you two. I need to make some new friends."

"Yeah, yeah, yeah. After you spill, you can start auditioning new BFFs." Summer waved away her threat.

Joey let out a tortured sigh. "Fine. I lured him outside, and I kissed him. Happy now?"

"Yes!" Gia crowed.

"Nope."

Joey glared at Summer.

"You are shockingly light on details," her friend said. "When you say lured..."

Joey reluctantly recited a high-level overview of the kiss.

"Wow," Gia said, fanning herself when Joey had finished. "Did your underwear melt off at that point?"

"Almost. But it would have unmelted immediately after he got done turning me down."

"He turned you down?" Gia and Summer shouted the question together, and Joey wondered if there was a surgery for reinserting eyeballs after they catapulted out of their sockets.

"Wait, wait, wait," Summer said it fast, holding up a finger.

"Jackson Pierce turned *you*," Gia waved a hand in front of Joey's face and chest, "down?"

"Yep."

"That son of a bitch," Summer muttered, rubbing her rounded belly.

"Thank you!" Joey jumped out of her chair and started to pace. "*Exactly!* He just waltzes out of my life after promising me a future, and then he has the nerve to show up here and lay one on me like I should be happy about it?" She was in full-on rant mode now.

"And then he gets in my face for six months. *Six months!* Hinting and flirting and looking at me like he wants to take a bite out of me. And *then* when I offer him a night of no-strings fun, he's all Mr. Thanks But No Thanks?"

"I believe what I actually said was that I'd take a rain check."

Joey froze mid-pace. Judging from the expressions on Summer and Gia's faces, the amused tone from the door belonged to Mr. Thanks But No Thanks himself. She whirled around. Sure enough, Jax was leaning against the doorframe, arms crossed, enjoying the show. He shoved away from the door and crossed to her.

"You were drunk," he said when they were toe-to-toe. "Phoebe Pierce didn't raise boys who would take advantage of that. And April Greer didn't raise girls who would threaten to go get what they wanted from someone else when they didn't get their way." Those gray eyes were anything but icy now.

Joey crossed her arms and set her jaw to ward off the shame. Summer and Gia whistled innocently and avoided eye contact.

"Let me make one thing clear," Jax said, slipping a hand behind her neck. His voice dropped to a low, commanding whisper. "When it does happen, when I'm touching you, I want you to be completely present, stone sober. Because there's nothing that's going to come between us. And there will be no regrets."

She fought him, but Jax used the hand gripping her neck to drag her in for a hard kiss on the mouth.

He pulled back and grinned. She stomped on his foot. "Stop doing that!"

He released her and turned his attention to her friends. Jax threw an arm around Gia's shoulders. "Welcome to the family, sis."

Gia grinned up at him, totally falling for his Pierce charm. Joey rolled her eyes. *Amateur.*

"And as for you," Jax said, pointing at Summer. "I know what you're up to."

"Whatever do you mean?" Summer asked innocently.

"You're freaked out about this launch, worrying about how it's gonna go and what it's gonna mean. So you kick Carter out so he doesn't worry about you worrying, and then you try to drag your friends in here as distractions."

Summer's pretty face was working its way into a frown.

"Don't even try it," Jax warned. "You didn't fool Carter either. He's just legally required to tip-toe around you."

Gia snickered.

"Now that that's out of the way, let's look at the site traffic so I can report back to my brother before he paces a trench in our nice new floors at the brewery."

Summer sighed. "The page wasn't loading."

"Well, try it again," Jax ordered, leaving no room for discussion.

"I see all Pierce men inherited the bossy pants gene," Gia said, from the safety of the sidelines.

Joey smirked. That was certainly true. The funny thing was, the brothers didn't get it from their father. The brothers' unwavering loyalty, their love of land and family, that was John's influence. But their tenacity and hard-headedness was all Phoebe.

Summer punched a few keys, and quiet descended on the room.

"It's loading," she murmured, squinting at the screen.

Joey flopped back down in the chair and tapped her fingers on her knees. She didn't make time for things like stats and technology. The traffic she worried about was the four-legged kind as it trotted around the indoor riding ring. But she knew this launch was important to Summer, and that made it important to her.

Summer's eyebrows skyrocketed up.

"Well?" Joey demanded, leaning forward.

A sound like a beach ball deflating emanated from behind the monitors.

Gia's fingers dug into Joey's arm.

"Twenty-three thousand."

"What?" Gia's voice was an octave higher than usual.

Summer was frozen halfway out of her chair. "Twenty-three thousand visitors."

"What?" Gia was shrieking now.

"If you get any louder, I'm going to lose an ear drum," Joey warned her.

"Twenty-three thousand visitors, and its only eleven!" Summer was all the way out of her chair now and yelling. She came around the desk, and there was more yelling and grabbing and some jumping.

"Are you allowed to bounce? Won't the babies fall out?"

Joey asked, grabbing Summer's shoulder to keep her grounded. Carter and Beckett burst in. "What the hell, Jax?" Carter yelled over the noise and made a grab for Summer. "What's wrong? Are you hurt?"

Summer threw herself into her husband's arms. "Twenty-three thousand, Carter!"

"Don't let her start jumping again," Joey warned him.

Beckett, wearing sweatpants and a big, fat smile, pulled Gia in to him. He tucked her head under his chin and held tight. It was such an intimate moment that Joey had to look away.

Carter was still searching the room for a threat. "Twenty-three thousand what, honey?" He brushed her hair back from her face.

"That's how many people have been to the site so far today. We were hoping for maybe fifteen thousand all day."

"Holy shit!"

There was more jumping and yelling, and even Joey bounced a little in her riding boots. She snuck a glance at Jax and found him watching her. Summer grabbed for Joey and Gia, pulling them in for a hug before dragging the brothers in.

"We're really doing this, guys."

Carter dropped a sweet kiss on the top of her head and closed his eyes in the bliss of pride and love.

3

Cold and a little cranky, Joey dragged her boots off and left them on the porch. She pushed her front door open and dropped down in front of the fireplace in the living room. With the push of a button, the gas fire wooshed to life. She leaned in, determined to absorb every degree of heat the flames threw off.

January in Blue Moon meant long, frigid days. The barn and indoor riding ring were warm enough, but she'd spent the last hour and a half fixing fences in the northern pasture. The winter wind had meticulously picked apart her defensive thermal layers until her ass was officially frozen.

She glanced up at the clock on the mantel. If she wanted to make it to the brewery's grand opening tonight, she was going to have to drag her frozen ass away from this very cozy fire and into a hot shower upstairs. At least she was a few days removed from her New Year's Eve hangover, so the thought of a beer didn't make her want to vomit.

She'd begged off from the Pierce family dinner celebrating Summer's magazine launch, but she knew there'd be no missing the brewery opening. The Pierces were meeting at

4:30 for a private toast. She was going to have to choose between washing her hair and shaving her legs. She was just trying to talk herself into prying her ass off the floor when her cell phone rang.

Mom.

The familiar wave of guilt, as comfortable as an old pair of shoes, settled over her. She heaved a heavy sigh. Joey had been busy or ignored the last two calls, and if she dodged again, she'd have her parents showing up on her doorstep in a panic.

"Hi, Mom."

"Well thank God." Her mother's voice filled with relief. "Your father and I were getting worried."

"Everything's fine. I'm fine," Joey said, trying to keep the annoyance out of her tone. Ever since the accident, they'd been overly protective, easily concerned. Thank God for her sister's kids. Otherwise April and Forrest Greer never would have moved away from Blue Moon. When she'd waved off that moving van two years ago, it was the first deep breath she'd been able to take in Blue Moon since before the accident.

She'd spent every day since the hospital trying to distance herself from the pain and the pity. Sure, in the ensuing years, she'd had friends—well, acquaintances—and there had been other men, carefully selected so as not to puncture her shiny new armor. But she'd spent her time in college and since building a private, independent life. She made the decisions, and she was responsible for the outcomes. It was a quiet existence, but that's how she wanted it.

"How was Beckett's wedding?" her mother was asking, but she plowed on ahead without giving Joey the chance to answer. "Your father was so disappointed you couldn't spend New Year's Day with us."

"Tell him I'm sorry I missed the festivities," Joey said, rolling with the guilt trip. Her mother always played the "your father" card. That relationship had been strained years ago when Joey accepted Carter's job offer. They had never quite recovered. In Forrest's hardheaded mind, his daughter working for Jax's family was Joey choosing the Pierces over her own blood. He'd spent every interaction since trying to convince her to move on.

"How is Dad?" Joey asked.

"Oh, you know your father," her mom said airily. "Are you seeing anyone?"

Joey leaned over the island and put her forehead in her hand. "No, Mom."

"I just wanted to check. Jax has been back for a while now. And I didn't know if you two—"

"I'm not seeing Jax. I'm not seeing anyone, Mom. I don't have much time for a social life these days."

"Those Pierces work you too hard. They take advantage of your work ethic," a deep voice bellowed from the background.

"Hi, Dad," Joey said, cursing her parents' use of speakerphone.

"Oh, Forrest. Don't start picking," her mother sighed.

"All I'm saying is you could have your pick of jobs if you'd be willing to leave Blue Moon. Hugh's son works for the place that owns the horse that came in second in the Preakness last year. What was his name?"

"Joel?"

"No, not the son. The horse."

"Sunday Squall."

"That's the one."

April ignored their conversation and plowed ahead with her own. "So listen, sweetie, since you missed Christmas Eve and New Year's Day with us..."

Phone calls with her parents were like a lopsided tennis

match, and she knew her mom was going to serve up an ace here. Joey silently willed her mother to get to the point.

"We were hoping you could come out Sunday for Isaac's birthday."

The last thing Joey wanted to do on her one day off was drive an hour one-way to watch her two-year-old nephew pick his nose and smash his face in a fire truck cake that tasted like paste.

"Uh-huh," Joey said, her tone noncommittal.

"If you're busy," her mom continued, "we'll just have to bring the party to you. Rosemarie would be devastated if you missed Isaac's birthday."

Joey and her sister exchanged the equivalent of one email a month and made small talk at family gatherings. The only devastation if Joey didn't attend the birthday party would be on the part of her parents. It wasn't that they didn't get along. It was that they had absolutely nothing in common. Rosemarie was up to her eyeballs in diapers and repainting her kitchen. Joey was buried in vet appointments and researching a new horse trailer.

"I guess I can make it," Joey said, mentally kissing her quiet day of trashy novel reading and baking goodbye.

"Good," her father said gruffly. "Family first, I always say."

And the Pierces weren't family. Joey got his message loud and clear.

By the time she hung up, she had just enough time to rinse off and head up to the brewery. But still she couldn't force herself away from the fireplace. The more she thought about it, the less enthusiastic she felt about going up for the pre-party party.

It was a family thing. And, as often as Joey let herself get sucked into Pierce family gatherings, maybe it was important to start remembering that she wasn't one of them.

WHEN JOEY DIDN'T SHOW up to the brewery with the rest of the family, Jax started to worry. He'd even held off on the toast, just in case she was running late. When he texted her to see where the hell she was, her response took him from worried to pissed.

Joey: Be there later.

Didn't she realize that all of this was for her? She should be here, holding a glass with the rest of the family. But Joey couldn't be bothered to show up for it.

She should be here, nervous and excited like everyone else. He glared out the window in the direction of her house, the dozens of cars that were lining up in the parking lot meant nothing without that cherry red pickup.

He turned away from the windows, a dark cloud hanging over the festivities. He had work to do, but talking some sense into Joey would be at the top of his list.

By the time she waltzed in at six, Jax had moved beyond pissed to fucking irate. The woman was born to make him insane. She came in the door behind Dr. Delvecchio and Mrs. Nordemann. Her hair was long and loose. Jeans that went on for days hugged her slim curves. Knee-high boots in a gray suede matched her soft, off-the-shoulder sweater. Her cheeks were rosy from the cold, her lips glossy.

Jax was starting to realize that no matter how long he knew her, he would always get this kick-start to his heart every time she walked in a room.

Her gaze found his in a silent connection thick with tension.

Jax ducked his head and dumped another batch of glasses

into the rotating washer. It was two-deep at the bar. Carter was helping get the food out while Mr. Mayor double-teamed the host stand with Phoebe. Summer and Gia flitted from table to table.

It was a family affair. The entire town—since recovered from their wedding hangovers—had turned out to help them celebrate. And it still wasn't enough. Not without her.

"Fuck it," Jax muttered. He stormed out from around the bar and grabbed her by the arm.

"What the hell, Jax?"

"Come with me."

She started to wrestle out of his grip. It was yet another thing he loved about Joey. She wasn't afraid of causing a scene. And neither was he. He dragged her down the stairs, past the kitchen, and into the taproom.

"What is your problem?" she demanded, wrenching free.

"My problem is you. Where the hell were you? You were supposed to be here early."

"That was a family thing."

"You're family."

"No, I'm not! And if I were, that would make what we did in high school illegal," she shot back.

"I wanted you here," Jax said, pacing now. Why couldn't she see it?

"Oh for fuck's sake. Why didn't you just say so? I'm not family, Jax. I'm not going to show up for every freaking Pierce occasion."

"You damn well should have showed up for this," he said, his voice grim.

"Why?"

"Because it's for you," he exploded. "It's all for you. I came back for you."

Well, that shut her up. She was gaping at him like a fish on the line before she let out a noise somewhere between a screech and a growl.

"You drive me insane!" She threw her hands up in the air.

"Right back at ya, Jojo."

She crossed her arms and kicked at a keg. "Why do you want to be with me?"

Jax stopped and stared at her. "Why?" he laughed. "You seriously don't know?"

Joey just stared at him.

"Joey, I love you. There hasn't been a time in my life when I haven't loved you."

She was staring at him, her expression unreadable.

"Say something," he said quietly.

"I don't think we know what love is," she said finally.

"How can you even say that?" He shoved his hands through his hair.

"You hurt me, Jax."

He stared at the floor, shoved his hands in his pockets. The guilt clawed at him. "I know I did. I was reckless and careless, and you got hurt. I can still see you in that car."

"In the car?" I'm not talking about the accident, you idiot. I'm talking about you leaving."

"I almost killed you!" His voice echoed off the metal of the kegs.

"Oh, sweet Jesus. A deer almost killed me. *You* almost destroyed me when you left without a word."

"The accident—"

"Was an accident," she said, enunciating each word like he was an annoying toddler. "You leaving was on purpose. And I don't know how to forgive that."

"You have to." She did. There was no way around it. Joey had to forgive him so she might as well accept it.

39

"Maybe it would go a little better if you'd at least, oh I don't know, *apologize*?"

Jax cringed. "I don't know how." He said the words quietly. "How do I say I'm sorry for something that big? You almost died because of me."

"Are you not listening?" Joey threw her hands up as if she was appealing to a higher power. "You don't owe me an apology for the accident. You owe me an apology for abandoning me. How am I supposed to move past that if you won't tell me why you did it?"

"Because I hurt you!" he shouted.

"I'm about to hurt you," she yelled back. "Get it through your thick, stupid skull. Until you can make me understand why you felt like you had to disappear without a word, or a call, or an email for eight years, there is no chance for us. Now, I'm going back upstairs to have a beer."

She stormed out, the slim heels of her boots clicking on the concrete floor.

She was right, and Jax knew it. But he also knew the answers would only push her further away.

4

"I need you and your house," Gia announced, hovering over Joey's head as she lay in a puddle of her own sweat on a borrowed yoga mat. Joey's head lolled to the side. A chipper Summer was sitting cross-legged and staring at her expectantly. The rest of the yoga studio was empty except for Gia's sisters. Emma was frantically typing away on her smart phone while Eva lounged on her mat staring out the front window.

Summer had dragged her along to class again. Joey had to admit, it wasn't awful. Especially not after spending the morning wrestling horses for vaccinations with the vet. Gia's class had helped work the kinks out. Plus, it gave her the perfect excuse to avoid the two dozen red roses and apology card from Jax that arrived at the stables from Every Bloomin' Thing.

They had tangled at the brewery the night before, but it felt good to finally say a few of the things that had been running laps in her mind for the past several years. She hadn't actually expected him to apologize.

Joey could only imagine the Blue Moon gossip mill

warming up with this little tidbit. Anthony Berkowicz, editor of *The Monthly Moon,* would be knocking at her door asking for a copy of their wedding announcement.

"Why do you need me and my house? You haven't murdered your husband and need help with the body already, have you?"

"No, but if he pulls the whole 'I took care of your cell phone bill because I thought you forgot' thing again I may maim him." Gia winked.

"Did you forget?" Joey asked.

"Well, yeah, but Beckett didn't know that. I would have remembered eventually. I have a reminder in my phone."

Summer snickered. "Ah, the joys of married life."

"Said the experienced wife," Gia quipped.

"I've got a month on you. I'd be happy to tutor you on the ins and outs of marriage," Summer offered.

"Back to needing my house," Joey shoved the conversation back on course.

"I was thinking girls night in. Tomorrow's my sisters' last night in town, and your place is the only one not crawling in children and men."

Oh goodie. More socializing. Joey sighed and flopped back down on her mat.

"C'mon. Please?" Gia loomed over her batting her long lashes at Joey.

"I don't have the genitalia that look works on."

"Beckett and I are leaving on our honeymoon soon. It might be our last chance to hang out," Gia said with a sad puppy face.

"Crap," Joey sighed.

"I'm so pregnant the twins could get here at any time, and you may never see me again until their high school graduation." Summer leaned in and gave her best pleading face.

Eva and Emma popped into her line of sight looking hopeful.

"Ugh, fine," Joey said, sitting up. "But I'm not cooking, and it can't be before seven. I have a lesson."

The celebratory cheers brought Aurora out of the smaller studio where she'd been entertaining herself with a tablet, four of her favorite stuffed animals, and strict instructions not to come out until after class was over.

"Can I come out now, Mama?" the little redhead asked in a five-year-old's whisper.

"All done, kiddo." Gia held her arms open and Aurora rushed into them. The little girl gave her mom a noisy kiss before flopping down in Joey's lap.

"Hi, Joey," Aurora said, smashing the blue bear she held into Joey's face. "'Dis my bear."

Joey spit the blue fur out of her mouth. "Nice. Does your bear have a name?"

"Mr. Fur Face."

"Well, that's accurate," Joey said wryly.

"Can I come to your party, Joey?"

Joey looked at Gia for guidance. "Uh, sure?"

Aurora bounced out of Joey's lap and exploded across the studio. "Woo! I love parties!" She paused mid-spin with Mr. Fur Face. "Can I have cake?"

Again, Gia and Summer were no help. "Um, okay?" Great. Now she had to bake a cake in addition to scrubbing the toilets and dusting.

Aurora was celebrating again, doing somersaults on Gia's mat while chanting "cake."

"Aurora, you can come for cake, but then Beckett is going to take you home."

"Cake! Cake! Cake!"

Gia rolled her eyes. "I swear this kid would build a house

out of sugar if we let her. I'll have Beckett come get her after his errand with Jax."

"I wonder what they're up to?" Summer mused. "Carter said he's helping Jax with something tomorrow too. I'm suspicious."

"Well, whatever it is, it's probably better that we don't know," Gia sighed.

Joey wasn't so sure.

⁓

SHE BAKED A CAKE.

And since she already had all of her baking weapons out, Joey made three-dozen peanut butter cookies with chocolate chunks and two loaves of rosemary olive oil bread.

Baking was her yoga. The step-by-step process, the measuring, the transformation of simple ingredients into edible art. It calmed her, cleared her mind, and fed her carb obsession.

She stared at the cooling cookies. They were Jax's favorite, and as a kid, once she realized that, she always made sure to set aside a bag just for him. She bit her lip, considered. What harm would setting aside one baggie do? It would be her secret stash in case the girls inhaled the rest of them. Or she could save them and give them to Jax.

Their fight at the brewery played in her head on a constant loop. And so had the feelings that it had dredged up. She'd gotten so used to her simmering animosity and unavoidable, uncontrollable physical attraction. But she'd forgotten about all the other long-buried feelings associated with Jackson Pierce.

It's all for you. I came back for you.

His words, earnest and angry, rolled through her head.

What the hell had changed? And why now? She'd spent the last eight years moving on, building a safe, manageable life. Sure, she'd refused on principle to watch any of the movies he'd written. She'd done her best to put Jax out of her head and heart. Of course, she'd slipped a few times over the years and did a little online research. He'd certainly moved on, many times over. A different woman on his arm at every event.

She bit violently into a cookie, remembering the blonde with the watermelon-sized rack.

The idea that he'd come back for her was... unsettling, confusing.

They'd gone eight years without contact. When he came home for sporadic, infrequent visits, she made herself scarce. And that included John Pierce's funeral. Joey's father had taken her decision not to attend the services as a sign that she'd finally gotten over it all.

What her father didn't know was that while everyone else in town was at the funeral, Joey snuck into the farmhouse and cleaned it from top to bottom, leaving behind a few million calories of baked goods to help feed the flood of visitors that Phoebe would face in the following days.

But things were different now. Phoebe was happily engaged to the charming Franklin. Carter and Summer had made the farmhouse their home. And Jax was back, professing the things that her heart had yearned for years ago. But it was too late.

Wasn't it?

Too little, too late. And without answers to her whys, there was no altering her course. Her heart would remain closed where Jax was concerned, she decided, even as she bagged up four cookies and tucked them away.

Joey took one last sip of precious coffee and willed herself to put him out of her head. She shrugged into her down field jacket and stomped off to the barn to focus on her Wednesday night lesson. This was her more intermediate group. Six of them, each with their own care horse. They were still young enough to enjoy the easy repetition of grooming and tacking up.

"Nice seat, Alesha," she called out to a lanky girl with braces and pink jodhpurs. Their neat little circle trotted around the indoor ring, inches of sawdust muffling the hoof beats.

Evan, Gia's son, posted nicely on the ten-year-old bay, Tucker. "Okay, Evan, switch over to a canter and lead off a figure eight," Joey ordered.

Beneath his riding helmet, she saw the spark in his brown eyes. He'd started lessons just two months earlier and was clearly a natural.

Colby, one of the helpers she shared with Carter and the farm, sauntered up. "Kid looks good," he said, nodding at Evan. He took his hat off and shoved his hand through his corn silk hair.

"Picking it up fast," she agreed. "Watch your hands, Aliya."

The girl on the strawberry roan corrected her grip on the reins and earned a nod from Joey as she passed.

Joey patted Colby on the shoulder and let him take over the instruction. She wandered over to the edge of the ring and ran her hand over a hoof-sized ding in the wall. Romeo had been feeling spunky when he decided to kick the shit out of the boards.

She took a deep breath of horses and sawdust. The creak of the saddles, the occasional giggle from the kids. It was all home to her. Home and heaven.

God, she loved this place. Even the long days, the never-ending maintenance. Maybe especially them? When she committed to something, it was whole-heartedly. And she found a steady, comforting peace in the chipping away at the daily list of chores.

This time of year, while the farm lay dormant, Joey did her planning. She had more hands available to her with Carter and his crew of part-time help.

She'd grown this operation from six horses and twice weekly lessons to thirty mounts and a comprehensive equestrian program for all levels of ability. They had two beefy Clydesdales that pulled Santa's wagon in the Christmas parade. She was a certified therapeutic riding instructor and taught weekly group classes for a handful of students with physical and mental challenges. And their regular weekly class schedule was bursting at the seams.

She had plans. It was time to think about the next step. A breeding program. They had a few solid mares. The next step would be to find the right stud. She'd start small, build a solid program, and expand selectively.

It would mean more equipment, more hands, more damn paperwork. But it was a smart move, and if the stock was good enough, the profits would be pretty freaking great.

She'd started a proposal to give to Carter with projections and timelines. Started it but hadn't finished it. She wanted to do some research into studs first before she sprung it on him. It was harder for the man to say no to deep brown animal eyes. And if he dragged his feet, she was prepared to call in the big guns—Summer.

It wasn't that Carter had ever actually said no. He was smart enough to know that she knew what she was doing. But that didn't stop Joey from dotting the i's and crossing the t's. She knew Carter liked to have all the information at his fingertips, mainly so he could dump it all off on Beckett's desk when his brother asked too many questions.

She wondered if Jax would also be playing a role in the decision-making now that he was home.

And just like that, he was back on her mind.

"Hey."

And back in her barn. At least he was on the other side of the fence.

"Hey," she said, keeping her eyes trained on the riders. But it didn't make her any less aware of his presence.

"I'm here to pick up Evan," he told her. "You almost done?"

Joey reached over and turned his wrist so she could see the face of his watch. "Yeah, we're finishing up here." She started to push away from the fence and paused. "About the flowers."

Jax cocked an eyebrow.

"They're beautiful." She spotted the beginning of a cocky grin. "But you're going to have to do better than that."

"Jojo, I'm just getting started."

"OKAY, WE'RE HERE," Beckett announced, bringing his SUV to a halt in the parking lot of Furever Home Animal Rescue. "What's the plan?" he asked Jax.

"We're getting a dog," Jax announced.

"Awesome!" Evan squealed from the backseat.

"Whoa, hang on there." Carter leaned between the front seats. "You live in my house, and you didn't think to mention that you're getting a dog?"

"I'm not getting a dog for me. It's for Joey."

Evan squished under Carter so he could lean between the seats too. "You're getting Joey a dog?"

"It's part of my multi-tiered apology plan," Jax explained.

"What are you apologizing for?" Evan wanted to know.

Jax ignored the smirk that passed between his brothers.

"Kid, you'd be driving age by the time I got done explaining. Let's just say I screwed up a long time ago."

"And you're just now apologizing?" Evan asked.

"Yeah."

Evan shook his head. "Man, there better be a lot of tiers to that apology."

No kidding, Jax agreed.

"Okay. Let's find you an apology dog," Carter sighed, opening his door.

"COME ON, EVAN!" Carter grumbled. "I told you to keep a good grip on that leash."

"Sorry! Diesel just wants to get to know Tripod Jr. better," Evan said, reeling the fat, fluffy puppy back in. Tripod Jr. meowed mournfully from his carrier on the seat between Evan and Carter.

"For the love of God, who the hell is howling?" Beckett yelled over the racket.

"I think it's Meatball," Evan said, peeking into the hatch. "Waffles just sat on him."

"No, I have Waffles up here," Jax said, pointing to the black and white hairball that had his head out the window.

"Oh, then Valentina sat on Meatball."

Waffles shifted in Jax's lap and stepped on his balls.

"Ow! Fuck!"

"I'm telling Mom," Beckett threatened with a grin.

"Is anyone else thinking this might have been a bad idea?" Jax asked.

"There's no point in asking that question. We're committed, and we have to deal with the fallout," Evan said, squishing Diesel's little face in his hands. "Right boy?"

The puppy licked him in the face. And then bit his nose.

"Ow! Damn it!"

"I'm telling Gianna," Beckett snickered.

Evan wiped the puppy's slobber off his nose. "I don't think she's going to care about me saying 'damn' when we show up with a three-legged cat and a puppy with razor blades for teeth."

"At least we didn't get the elderly, obese howler and Marmaduke Jr. Summer is going to lose her sh—crap when she sees that duo," Beckett said, jerking his thumb toward the back of the SUV.

"For your information, Meatball is only nine, and it's an easily manageable thyroid condition," Carter retorted. "And Valentina is named after one of Summer's favorite designers, and I couldn't say no to those big, bloodshot eyes."

"I'm just glad you didn't adopt another damn goat," Jax said, pulling Waffles off Beckett's lap. "Mrs. Penskee told me it's the most successful day the rescue ever had."

"That's because the only animals left are the ones with pending adoptions," Beckett said dryly.

"And that wrinkly pug dog with a sinus infection," Carter said. Jax thought he detected a little wistfulness in his brother's voice.

"Mr. Snuffles?" Evan asked. "Poor guy. Can't we—"

"No!" All three Pierces yelled, which only encouraged Meatball to start howling again. The human passengers sat in silence for a few minutes, each pondering Mr. Snuffles's unfortunate predicament.

"You know, Mom and Franklin are going to need a dog to go with their new house," Jax ventured.

Beckett was already making a U-turn. "Fine, but Mr. Fucking Snuffles better not get his green snot all over the leather."

Evan hooted, and Valentina turned Meatball's solo into a duet. Tripod Jr. added a sad meow chorus.

"Well, Waffles," Jax murmured to the furry mop in his lap. "I'm counting on you to soften your mom up for me."

The dog turned to look at Jax with one brown eye and one blue. He blinked.

"I feel like you understand what I'm saying."

Waffles blinked again.

"Huh," Jax said.

Carter sniffed the air. "Please tell me that came from one of the dogs."

Evan pulled his shirt over his face. The smell wafted its way up to the front seat. Beckett gagged, and Jax buried his face in Waffles's wiry fur.

"Did someone just shit themselves in my car?" Beckett demanded, rolling down all the windows.

They pulled back into the rescue's parking lot. Mrs. Penskee was casually walking Mr. Snuffles around the front porch on a leash. "Back so soon?" She greeted them with a cheery wave. Mr. Snuffles sneezed, sending a green shower in a two-foot radius.

"We'll take the four-legged sinus infection, Mrs. Penskee," Jax said, handing his credit card out the window.

"Oh, how exciting!" she said, patting her silver-streaked curls, eyes sparkling behind her wire-rimmed spectacles. She looked like an energetic Mrs. Claus. "I'll just hand him over and bring you a receipt," she said, shoving the dog into Carter's arms through the back window.

"She's running as if she's afraid we'll change our minds," Carter muttered.

"She had him out here on a leash. She knew we'd be back for him," Beckett said, massaging his temples.

"How'd she know that?" Evan asked, unwrapping Diesel's

leash from his wrist and ankle.

"Because we have 'suckers' stamped on our foreheads," Jax grumbled. Waffles gave a happy little yip.

Mrs. Penskee reappeared waving Jax's credit card and receipt.

"Thank you boys so much! Are you sure I can't talk you into posing for a group picture for our Facebook page?"

"No!" They answered in unison.

"Remember, no posting on social media until tomorrow, right, Mrs. Penskee?" Beckett said, flashing her his best mayoral grin.

"All right. Well, you boys have fun surprising your girls," she said with a wink.

Beckett rolled up the windows and pulled away before they adopted anything else.

"Okay, we've got a problem," Jax announced.

"I don't smell it, yet," Carter said, sniffing.

"Not that kind of a problem," Jax said, exasperated. "Waffles here is supposed to help me sweep Joey off her feet. With the rest of you and this rolling fart circus, you're gonna steal my thunder."

"Fart circus," Evan snickered.

Valentina chose that moment to vault over the backseat, knocking Tripod's yowling carrier into the console. She lunged forward, her giant tongue colliding with Beckett's face. He swerved across the double line and back, but the overcorrection took them onto the berm before Beckett was able to get them back between the lines.

They all heard the sirens at the same time.

When Beckett managed to pull over and roll his window down, Valentina shoved her head out and gave Sheriff Cardona a face full of tongue.

"Is there a problem, officer?"

5

_____

The fire crackled merrily, casting a cozy glow around the room while the blender mixed up margaritas in the kitchen. Joey's house was full of women and food. And it wasn't awful. Gia's sister Emma, in a fitted black turtleneck, had made herself useful mixing drinks and plating food at the island. Eva and Summer snuck cookies and antipasto while discussing the pitfalls of freelance writing.

Gia lounged in front of the fireplace with Aurora who was on her second and last piece of cake. Phoebe relaxed on the sofa with a glass of wine.

"I love your house, Joey," Emma said, handing her a frosty margarita.

"Oh, uh, thanks," Joey said, wiping her hands on her jeans before accepting the glass.

"Did you see the claw foot tub she has on her deck?" Summer called from the kitchen.

"You have an outdoor tub? Does it work?" Emma asked, eyeing her speculatively.

Joey nodded and flipped on the outdoor lights so she could see for herself.

She liked Emma about as well as she could like anyone new. She was direct, a little cool, and not afraid to speak her mind. Eva seemed okay too. Her auburn curls were chopped short in a face-framing, chaotic bob. She seemed to waste no time on things like formalities or ironing.

And it was clear that they both adored Phoebe, so that was worth high marks in Joey's book.

"Oh my God, Joey." Summer's voice was reaching orgasm capacity. "These cookies are the most incredible thing I've put in my mouth in the last…" She checked her watch. "Three hours."

"Oooh!" The rest of the women spread out between the kitchen and living spaces crooned.

"You guys and your Pierce brothers are killing me," Eva groaned as she sank down on the leather couch next to Phoebe.

"Yeah, seriously." Emma sighed from the kitchen where she cut a second sliver of Joey's death by chocolate cake. "I live in L.A., land of the hot guys, and they've got nothing on your Blue Moon men."

Summer and Gia looked appropriately smug. Joey settled for rolling her eyes.

"Don't give me that look." Summer pointed at Joey from her perch in one of the cozy armchairs. "You could have one if you wanted."

She was suddenly glad she had hidden the roses upstairs in her bedroom. "Can we please stop talking about penis and start talking about something, anything, else?" Joey grumbled.

Aurora looked up from her plate, cake smeared across her face. She giggled. "Penis!"

Gia sighed and smoothed her daughter's wild curls back from her face. "Well, at least you're teaching her the anatomically correct term."

"So, Summer," Phoebe called from her corner of the couch. "How's the magazine? Are you happy with the launch?"

Summer took her plate into the living room and flopped down on one of Joey's overstuffed armchairs. "I'm ecstatic," she said, biting into a crisp carrot. "If anyone had told me how successful the launch was going to be, I'd never have believed it. Mind blown. And don't even get me started on the attention that Gia's yoga piece is getting."

Gia waved away the compliment. "That was entirely Niko's photography. The man's a photography genius. Traffic to the site has been great, and so has the reaction to all of the content."

"Bottom line is, between Gia and I, the workload is massive, but we intersperse obsessive tasking with celebrations of our awesomeness. Especially when I got an email from my old boss, Katherine, at *Indulgence*."

"What did ol' Hot for Farmers want?" Joey laughed, dropping down in the chair across from Summer and tossing her leg over the arm. Katherine, an editor at Summer's old magazine, had taken Summer's article on Carter and the farm and turned it into a sex-god pictorial. It had been the kick Summer needed to quit her job, move in with Carter, and start her own online magazine. Meanwhile, the Pierces spent a solid month or two ignoring modeling offers from agencies.

Her friend tried to look casual. "Oh, not much. Just wanted to insincerely congratulate me on my pet project."

"B-word," Gia said definitively.

"And to do a little fishing to see if *Indulgence* could acquire Thrive," Summer added, spooning up a bit of the vegetable barley soup she had brought.

"What?" The question was shouted from all corners of the room.

Aurora covered her ears and giggled again. Summer grinned.

"Was she serious?" Phoebe asked.

"Serious enough to name a figure, one that would put these two through college," she said, patting her belly.

The room was unusually silent until Joey snickered. "Everyone's afraid to ask you what you decided." She grinned.

"And you're not?" Summer asked.

"Please. You gave her the professional equivalent of a—" She glanced at Aurora. "Eff off, and then I assume you immediately made a list targeting which of Katherine's contributors to go after for Thrive."

"You've learned a lot about my diabolical nature." Summer winked.

"So you said no?" Phoebe prompted.

"Were you tempted?" Eva wondered.

"Can I have more cake?" Aurora asked, tugging on Gia's sleeve.

The questions flew fast and loud. Joey sipped her very good margarita and watched. Hostessing wasn't so hard, she decided. Scrub a toilet, make some sugary treats, add alcohol, hide the conspicuous roses and candied bacon from Jax that arrived that afternoon, and viola, everyone entertains themselves.

"So, Joey," Eva began, dropping down on the ottoman next to Joey's chair. "What's it like running stables?"

"Exhausting and dirty. Why?"

Phoebe snorted. "Don't let her fool you, Eva. Joey was born to do what she does. She loves it."

"Did you always know you'd want to stay around here?" Eva asked.

It's home." She shrugged. And it was. Blue Moon Bend, Pierce Acres, the stables. It was where she belonged.

Eva smiled sweetly. "You don't like me asking all these questions, do you?"

"Not particularly."

Eva laughed. "I just like to know what makes people tick. You know, peel back the layers."

"My layers are fine where they are."

"Consider it research for a freelance assignment. I think it's fascinating, seeing women who aren't afraid to go out and follow their dreams. You know? Someone who believes in building exactly the kind of life they want and then going out and getting dirty and making it happen."

That's what she had done, wasn't it? She wanted a quiet life with her horses and her privacy, and that's exactly what she'd built. Fences and walls.

"I think it's brave for a woman to carve out an unconventional life," Eva continued.

Joey didn't feel brave. She felt safe. And that was a distinct difference.

"Does anyone know what the guys are up to tonight?" Gia asked, checking the clock on the mantel. Beckett's supposed to be picking up Rora five minutes ago."

Summer frowned. "They were awfully cagey about it. All I got from Carter was 'I'm helping Jax.'"

"Hmm," Phoebe said, her eyes darting to Joey. "Hmm," she said again.

"What?"

"Maybe it's a surprise for you?" Gia ventured. "Rumor has it two dozen roses were delivered here yesterday."

"You know, I did hear Phyllis at the post office talking about Joey's new meat of the month club," Phoebe mentioned.

Shit. Now she was going to have to share. And she hated sharing.

"Come on, Joey." Summer wiggled her eyebrows. "He

kissed the bejeezus out of you in the office. It's a miracle Gia and I didn't end up with second-degree burns from the sparks you two threw off."

"Why do I feel like I opened my door to a bunch of Anthony Berkowiczes?" Joey groaned.

She wilted under the weight of their expectant stares.

"No, we are not together. We can't even have a conversation without it turning into a fight."

"Sometimes a good fight just means there's strong feelings," Emma offered.

"Yeah, and sometimes a fight just means you don't like each other. Not all of us are so forgiving."

"Hey, I'm his mother," Phoebe interjected. "I'm legally required to forgive him. I think Joey has a right to make him squirm. If I weren't such a wonderful, enlightened, biologically obligated woman, I'd be holding a bit of a grudge too."

"Did Jax ever tell anyone why he left?" Gia asked.

Phoebe met Joey's gaze before shaking her head. "As far as I know, no. But he must have had a good reason. The night of the accident, he refused to leave your side. He wouldn't even let the nurses stitch him up." Phoebe cleared her throat. "Your father didn't, ah... agree with Jax's presence. John was trying to find a doctor, and your mother and I thought we were going to have to call security on them."

"What happened?" Joey asked despite herself.

"You woke up and told them to knock it off," Phoebe said with a wry smile. "You took your dad's hand and Jax's hand, and that was the end of it."

Joey's memories from that night were pretty foggy. But one thing was clear to her, something that night had made Jax decide to leave Blue Moon Bend. She wasn't sure if she believed as Phoebe did that there was a very good reason for it.

"On that note, let's change the subject to something that doesn't involve penises," Joey said, jumping up and heading for the blender. "For instance, how crazy is it that Summer 'I Plan Everything' doesn't want to know the babies' genders? How's the house building, Phoebe? And what's new at the studio, Gia? Tie anyone up in knots, yet?"

The conversation mercifully moved away from Jackson Pierce.

They topped off glasses and refilled plates while Phoebe told them that the floor plans had been finalized and building would begin in April. She was in the middle of explaining the bunkhouse to Emma and Eva when Joey's phone signaled a text from Jax.

Jax: Can you meet me on the porch?

Joey frowned at the screen and looked at her front door.

"What's wrong?" Gia asked.

Joey shook her head and got out of her chair. "Nothing, I'll be right back." She ducked out the door, closing it behind her. Jax was standing on the porch steps his breath a cloud in the soft glow of the porch light. He had one hand behind his back.

She crossed her arms to ward off the chill. "You're interrupting Girls Night, Ace."

He smiled, that slow, sexy, underwear-disintegrating smile. "I have something for you."

"I already got the bacon." The roses were a beautiful cliché, but the bacon? God that man knew her vices.

"Something else. Something you've wanted for a long time."

"Don't you dare take your pants off," she hissed. "There's a houseful of women staring at you!"

"Interesting and flattering that that's where your mind

goes, but I'm talking about this." He tugged on a green lead he had tucked behind his back. A wire-haired mutt scampered up the steps, stopping neatly at her feet. The dog was wriggling with excitement.

"This is Waffles," Jax said. "He's yours."

Waffles stared up at her with bi-colored eyes, his furry head cocked as if he were waiting for her to say something.

"You got me a dog?" Joey asked incredulously. "A dog named Waffles?" The dog's tail swished.

"As soon as I saw his name, I knew he was yours."

He remembered. Jax remembered. She had been nine when she asked for a dog for her birthday. When that day came and went without a four-legged best friend, Joey had started saving her allowance for a dog.

After months of saving, she sat down at the breakfast table, her mason jar stuffed full of allowance, and asked her father to take her to the rescue in town. That morning was the first time her father really let her down.

He'd refused. Told her he wasn't going to let her waste her money on some flea-bitten mutt. They didn't need a dog in the house, and they sure as hell weren't going to get one.

Jax had found her later that morning pouring her heart out to one of the ponies in his family's barn, and when he finally coaxed the story out of her, he announced that he'd share his dog with her. And he had. They'd spent hours together training the reluctant Pancake, a lazy lab content to spend his days swimming in the pond and sleeping on the porch.

She'd always meant to get herself a dog after college but had never gotten around to it.

"Hi, Waffles," she said, careful to keep any emotion out of her voice. Waffles's scraggly tail thumped on the porch boards, and he scooted an inch closer to her. Joey knelt down and stroked Waffles's head.

"I can't believe you got me a dog," she said again.

"The rescue said he's part cattle dog and part a bunch of other things. They think he'll do great here on the farm," Jax said, sitting down on the top step and scrubbing a hand over the ecstatic Waffles's belly. "You're killing me here, Jojo. Did I do good, or are you pissed?"

A ghost of a smile played over her lips. "You did good, Jax."

He blew out a cloud of breath, and she felt it on her face. They were close, leaning over the wriggling bag of fur. Their gazes met. Joey wet her lips, considering. Jax's hand grasped her wrist. He leaned in, and she let him, watching those gray eyes and perfect lips close in.

The doorknob jiggled behind them, and they broke apart. "But, Mama! Dere's a puppy out dere," Aurora screeched. "I hafta see the puppy!"

"Rain check?" Jax murmured.

"We'll see," Joey sighed. "What's that barking? Oh my God."

Beckett's SUV pulled up with dogs hanging out of every open window.

"You said you'd give me ten minutes," Jax growled.

"That was before Meatball puked," Beckett yelled. They all came pouring out, men and dogs from the SUV and women from the house, converging on the porch in a chaotic tornado of paws and questions and tangled leashes.

"What did you do?" Joey mouthed to Jax.

He pulled her and Waffles out of the fray and into the house, shutting and locking the door behind them.

"That circus outside wasn't part of the plan, but this was." He leaned in and brought his lips to hers.

6

_____

*J*ax kicked back in his chair and scrubbed his free hand through his hair while his agent cheerfully ran through her list of demands in his ear. The empty baggie of cookies Joey had given him taunted him.

"Hart wants a draft in his team's hands by the end of the month." Aisha Leigh coated every word in her honeyed Mississippi accent, a weapon she wielded on the unsuspecting at the negotiation table. Al, as she preferred to be called, was an infamous shark in Hollywood waters. She allowed herself two cigarettes a day and drove a vintage AC Cobra. Jax had been with her for five years and loved her as fiercely as he did his own mother.

"I got it, Al," he sighed in exasperation.

"I'm only reminding you, honey."

"Uh-huh. I know you've got your cut already spent," he teased.

"That beach house isn't gonna buy itself, sugar," she said breezily. "Speaking of real estate..."

Jax knew where Al was going with this.

"The house. Is there a problem with the tenants?"

"It's a prime piece of real estate, and you've been gone for more than six months. Don't you think you should make a decision?"

"I've made a decision. One that you ignored, if memory serves."

He could hear her roll those brown eyes from three thousand miles away.

"How was I supposed to know you were serious about moving back east? You call me in the middle of the night—"

"Ten," Jax corrected her.

Al ignored him and steamrolled on. "Blubbering about going home and true love."

"Have you ever thought about getting into acting? You've got a flair for the dramatic."

She gave an unladylike snort. "Please. I make more handling yahoos like you than I would on screen."

"Didn't I tell you to put my house on the market last June?" Jax said, knowing full well he had.

"And I told you to get a money manager to deal with these things. I'm your *agent*. I get you money. A money manager will help you keep it."

"And skim another ten percent off the top."

It was a conversation they'd run through a dozen times over the years, ever since Al had locked down his very first six-figure deal.

"*Anyway*," she continued. "Your tenants are interested in buying."

"Fine. Great."

Al sighed heavily in his ear. "Jackson, the responsible thing to do would be to get the place appraised, weigh your options, maybe list the property and see if we can get multiple offers."

"What are they offering?" Jax asked, cutting to the chase.

She named a figure that sounded more than fair.

"Consider it sold."

"You drive me crazy," she said fondly.

"Right back at ya, gorgeous. Now is there any other business you need to beat me over the head with, or can I go back to meeting my deadlines?"

"The premiere."

"Shit."

"It's in a couple of weeks, and the studio wants your sexy face there."

Jax rolled his shoulders. "Why?"

"Because you wrote the damn movie, and they're expecting it to be huge. Plus, you always look so pretty in your tux on the red carpet."

"Ah, shucks, Al. You're making me blush."

"I've seen you in action. I bet you haven't blushed since junior high. How many tickets do you want?"

Jax considered and a slow grin spread across his face. "Put me down for two."

"Hmm."

"What's that supposed to mean?"

"It means I can't wait to meet your date. Does she know she's already famous around here?"

"Very funny. See if you can schedule the closing on the house for the same weekend, okay?"

"Get a money manager," she grumbled, but Jax heard her keying notes into her computer.

"Why would I do that when I already have you?"

"Remind me to raise my fee," she said sweetly.

Jax hung up and stared at the screen of his laptop. He'd commandeered a corner table at the brewery to get some writing done this afternoon. But between interruptions from his staff and his agent, things weren't looking good for the story. It would be another late night... a very late night since it was his turn to babysit the brewery.

He and his brothers took turns being on hand to handle any crises that arose. And with a restaurant, there were a lot. From running out of pizza dough to a cook in need of stitches to the endless drama of the waitstaff, it was more work than any of them had anticipated.

He scrubbed his hand over his face. There was too much to do. Not enough time to do it all. He had a sense of impending doom. Something was going to give, and he was worried it would be something big.

It was one of the reasons he'd insisted on a meeting with his brothers today. They had to start thinking about the future.

Speak of the devils, Carter and Beckett slid into the chairs across from him, beers in hand. Carter handed a frosty glass to Jax while Beckett loosened his tie.

"You're supposed to be babysitting, not writing, Hollywood," Beckett teased.

Jax kicked his brother's chair half-heartedly.

"Yeah? Well you try working three full-time jobs and see how you do without multitasking."

Beckett snorted. "Woe is you. It's not easy being a full-time attorney and mayor. And you try keeping Gianna in line. Finding her keys, keeping track of her bills..."

Carter and Jax mimed a tiny violin duet.

"Assholes."

"Guys," Carter said, drawing their attention. "Twins." He mimed a mic drop and picked up his beer.

"Please. You can't use that excuse until they're actually here," Beckett argued. "There's no crying, no diapers, no late-night feedings."

"Are you kidding me? There's already crying and late-night feedings. Summer got matching onesies in the mail yesterday, and I found her sobbing over them and a bowl of cold spaghetti in the kitchen at midnight. She's the one who ordered them!"

Jax grinned.

"I'm worried she's going to drive herself insane between the hormones and the magazine," Carter continued.

"You're gonna have to drag her away from here," Jax said. "Get her to take a couple days off."

"A vacation?" Carter frowned.

"You guys didn't have a honeymoon." Beckett shrugged. "And you sure as hell won't be going anywhere once the kids are here."

"Sorry to interrupt, Jax." Cheryl, the bubbly weeknight bartender, approached the brothers. "But the bar drawer isn't coming out right."

Jax blew out his breath. "The lunch drawer or the dinner drawer?"

"Dinner," she said, shoving her heavy fringe of bangs off her forehead. "I counted it three times."

"I'll be back," he told his brothers.

After he counted the drawer three more times, confirmed that it was indeed twenty-five cents short, and threw in a quarter from his own pocket, he returned to the table where Carter was still considering the merits of a vacation. "Things are quiet enough on the farm. Maybe we could get away for a few days." Carter laughed. "How in the hell am I going to get Summer to agree? I have to use a pry bar on her to get her out of the office before eight every night."

Jax grinned, reaching for his beer. "Joey and Gia. Put them on her case and feed her something about trying out a guest editor now so she can tap them again during maternity leave."

"When the hell did you become the smart one?" Carter asked, impressed.

"One of us had to get the brains."

"I like it better when you two are fighting," Beckett grumbled.

"Then let's start looking at the brewery numbers, and we'll end up punching each other in the face over the price of French fries," Jax suggested.

Before he could bring up the document on his laptop, another distraction presented itself. "Hey, uh, Jax." The shaggy haired server named Deke shuffled up to the table. "There's some guy on the phone."

"Uh-huh," Jax said, waiting for more of an explanation. He ignored Beckett's smirk when Deke didn't provide one. "Does he want something?"

Deke shrugged. "Dunno."

Jax fixed him with a steely gaze that seemed to have no effect. "How about you ask him who he is and what he wants, and then we'll go from there?"

Deke shrugged again. "Cool," he said before shuffling off.

"Does he even know how to take an order?" Carter asked.

Jax rubbed his hands over his face and tried to remind himself he'd once been Deke's age. But he'd retained more brain cells.

"Let's get through these numbers before the kitchen burns down and all the kegs burst," he said swiveling the screen around to face his brothers.

"Hey, Jax?" Cheryl was back with the cordless from the host stand. "This guy says he's been on hold for ten minutes waiting to talk to you?"

Jax swore ripely and snagged the phone from her. Two more phone calls, an emergency restart of the POS, and a tripped breaker in the kitchen later, he was back at the table.

By the time he walked his brothers through the preliminary numbers, the tables were starting to fill up for the dinner crowd.

"So what you're saying is we could actually start seeing a profit eventually," Beckett said, pushing his empty glass around the table.

"I went over everything with Franklin, and he seems to think we're right where we need to be, if not a little ahead," Jax explained. "Which is all well and good, but I've got a suggestion that would push that profit back a ways."

"We're not burning the place down, Jax," Carter sighed.

"I'm talking about hiring a general manager, not arson."

That shut them up.

"It's something we were going to have to do eventually, and I don't know about you guys, but I can't deal with a hundred emergencies every shift. It's driving me insane. And I think it might make sense to hire someone experienced now before we fuck all this up."

His brothers shared a glance.

"We're already getting calls about events and catering," Carter admitted, running his hand through his hair.

Bottom Line Beckett was frowning. "I don't think there's anyone on staff who we could tap for that."

Jax shook his head in agreement. "We're gonna have to look outside."

"You sound like you have someone in mind," Carter said warily.

"I've got a long shot. A perfect long shot, but I need to do a little recon first."

"So we'll table the discussion for now," Beckett suggested.

"Fair enough," Carter agreed. "Now let me get us another round before the next item of business."

Jax watched his brother make his way to the bar, pausing

to wave or chat here and there. "You know what he wants to talk about?" he asked Beckett.

Beckett shrugged. "Got me. Maybe he wants to get another Clementine."

"Who knew lawyers were so funny?" Jax said, layering on the sarcasm.

"You sound like Gianna," Beckett said.

"How is the blushing bride?"

The grin that split his brother's face told Jax everything he needed to know.

"When are you gonna get yourself a blushing bride?" Beckett asked, poking him in the chest.

"When I figure out how to make Joey blush."

"Good luck with that," Beckett snorted.

Deke wandered up again, a tray of food in his hand. "Uh, hey, Jax. Do you know where table fourteen is?"

Jax took a measured breath and regretted it. Deke's last smoke break smelled more like pot than tobacco. He stood and clapped a hand on the boy's bony shoulder. "Listen, Deke. I don't think this is working out. I feel like this job just isn't playing to your strengths."

Deke's cell phone rang from the depths of his cargo shorts. "Can you hold this?" he asked, thrusting the tray into Jax's hands.

Beckett covered his laugh with a cough.

While Deke answered a call from someone who answered to "Hey, man," Jax hustled off to table fourteen to deliver the rapidly cooling food.

"Ladies," he said, pulling the first plate off the tray. "Who gets the sausage sandwich?"

Six hands flew up around the table, and then a riot of giggling erupted.

"I'll take that sausage off your hands, Jax." A breathy

blonde fluttered her eyelashes at him. Moon Beam Parker, with her waist-length, stick straight hair and pale blue eyes, wasn't one to shy away from the Pierce men. In fact, if memory served him, she'd been Beckett's first.

She took the plate from him, her mint green manicure dragging over his hand. He bobbled the plate, nearly sending the food to the floor. Moon Beam gave him a slow wink, and the rest of the table erupted again.

He could feel color rising to his face and danced out of Moon Beam's minty reach, seeking asylum behind her mother's chair. Mrs. Parker accepted the grilled Portobello salad from him and patted her platinum perm. "Imagine us getting the special treatment. Food delivered by the owner," she said, eyes roving Jax like he was an appetizer. Her gaze moved below his belt, and he could feel the sweat flowing freely now.

"Did you know Moon Beam's divorce is final now?" she purred, twirling a curl around her index finger.

"Congratulations," Jax said to the plate of spaghetti in his hand.

"Divorce is so lonely," Moon Beam sighed dramatically. "At the end of the day, it's just me all alone in my king-sized bed."

He all but dumped the other four plates on the table and ran to the bar. Cheryl eyed him up.

"What?" he demanded.

"Just checking for teeth marks." She grinned.

"I feel like a piece of meat." He shuddered.

"Those Parker women are like a Venus fly trap for men."

"Yeah, and they're trying to line me up as Moon Beam's third husband."

Cheryl filled a pint glass and shrugged. "Well, isn't some Moon Beam action better than no action at all?"

Jax glared at her. "No. No, it's not. Because I have a feeling she'd macramé me to her headboard and I'd never escape.

Now, I'll give you a hundred bucks if you take over that table of giggling vampires."

"Done. But why can't Deke resume service?" she asked, uncorking a bottle of Pinot Grigio.

"I'm in the middle of firing his ass."

"About friggin' time."

"Yeah, yeah. Now, go divvy up the rest of his tables, and don't let anyone with the last name Parker within twenty feet of me."

"Aye, aye, captain," Cheryl said, throwing a mock salute.

Jax returned to his table and collapsed in the chair.

Beckett shook his head and sighed. "It wasn't even two months ago that Mrs. Parker was trying to set me up with her daughter. Fickle, fickle women."

"I blame you," Jax groaned and drowned his sorrows in the beer in front of him. "So, what business involves buttering us up with another round?" he asked, changing the subject.

"Joey."

Carter had Jax's full attention with her name.

"Christ, you didn't have an aneurysm and are thinking about firing her?" Beckett asked.

Every muscle in Jax's body tensed for a fight.

Carter choked on his beer. "Jesus, no! Where did that come from?"

"I don't know! The way you said it made it sound really serious," Beckett said, tossing Carter a napkin. "You have beer in your beard."

"Can we get on with this?" Jax didn't like unfinished business attached to Joey's name.

"Yeah, Carter. You're making Hollywood nervous."

"I'm thinking we should make her a partner in the stables."

"No shit," Jax said succinctly. "I vote yes."

"Oh, come on. I prepared an argument and everything," Carter said with a mock pout.

"What's there to consider? There wouldn't be a riding program without her, the stables would be a pigsty—no offense to Dixie and Ham—and we wouldn't have ninety percent of the horses we do," Jax said, ticking off the points on his fingers.

Beckett's face remained impassive. "So why now? What brought this on?"

Carter tossed them each a stack of papers. "This is Joey's proposal for starting a breeding program here in a year or two."

Smart girl, Jax thought, flipping through the pages. "Why wouldn't we implement right away?" he asked.

"The upfront investment is pretty significant for an operation our size," Carter explained. A good stallion would cost—"

Beckett cut him off with a low whistle.

"I see you found the numbers."

"Holy shit," Beckett said.

"Yeah, those are conservative projections. The profits, even with cautious estimates, are worth talking about.

Jax and Beckett tore through their packets to the last page. Beckett squinted over the figures. And Jax frowned. "It looks like she's budgeting low for the stock."

"She's doing this with our numbers in mind. We don't have bottomless bank accounts to throw big money at newly retired racehorses. She's looking to start slowly and selectively so we don't go bankrupt."

"Hypothetically, if we doubled or tripled what we'd be willing to invest—"

"Then the profits would increase exponentially," Carter answered.

Jax grinned as a plan took shape. A plan that would give

Joey everything she ever wanted and more. The ultimate apology.

"Well, in the immortal words of Joey Greer, we'd be 'fucking stupid' not to move forward with this."

"Which brings us back to the partnership discussion," Carter reminded them.

"You already know my vote," Jax said, raising his glass.

They looked to Beckett who was still pouring over the figures.

"Well?" Carter kicked him under the table.

"If we can get this off the ground, it's going to mean a tidal wave of cash for the farm," Beckett said, frowning.

"And?" Jax asked, a hint of belligerence in his tone.

"And it would be a shame to keep all that money to ourselves," his brother said with a grin.

7

---

*J*oey kicked Romeo into a canter and enjoyed the bite of the wind against her cheeks. God, it was a beautiful day to ride, though it was cold enough to leave Waffles back at the stables. The January skies over Blue Moon were turquoise and cloudless. Being in perfect sync with well over a thousand pounds of thoroughbred muscle beneath her always amazed her. That two beings could be so connected without technology, without words. To her, that was the miracle.

She guided the horse in a sweeping turn along the fence line lest he think she was giving him the go ahead for the fence.

"Another time," she murmured to him. The bay's ears twitched an acknowledgement. She let him run for a few more minutes before slowing Romeo down to a walk. Joey took a deep breath of the razor-sharp winter air.

Gia had her yoga, and Joey had her solitary rides. Just her, a horse, and Mother Nature. This was her window of sanity in days otherwise packed with work and responsibility.

She had two lessons tonight and the paperwork she'd

been avoiding for days. But right now, she had this perfect, solitary window of peace. She loved it though. Every single second of it. She spent her time doing only the things that were important to her, except when Summer or Gia dragged her into something social. And even that she didn't mind much anymore. She had friends, she had her horses, and she had her work.

What more could she want? Joey automatically brushed aside the restlessness that arose without examining it.

Joey could feel Romeo's energy vibrating under her. He wanted to run, to play. And maybe she did too. "Okay, buddy. Let's have a little fun."

She kicked him into motion again and slid both boot-clad feet out of their stirrups. Keeping the reins in her hands, she gripped the saddle horn and brought one knee onto the saddle.

She extended her free leg back and up, toes pointing and stretching to the sky. Romeo maintained a rock steady canter while she balanced carefully, every muscle active, every breath deep.

She wasn't sure if she sensed him first or if Romeo did. But he was there all the same. Jax. He sat just on the edge of the tree line astride Cyrano, a dapple-gray quarter horse with an attitude.

She took a moment to hate the echo of awareness she had for a man she didn't know anymore.

Joey didn't have to see his face to know he was pissed.

And that pissed her off. She thought about turning and heading back to the stable, but Joey Greer never ran from a fight. Sometimes she galloped into them.

She pulled Romeo to a stop in front of Jax, careful to keep a safe distance between their mounts. Cyrano had the tendency to get a little mouthy.

"What the hell are you doing?" Jax said the words quietly, calmly. But there was a dangerous anger simmering beneath the surface.

"What does it look like I'm doing?" she asked evenly.

"Like you're trying to break your neck, riding like an idiot."

Far smaller sparks had ignited infernos between them. Joey took one of those deep, cleansing breaths that Gia was so fond of. The set of his jaw, the snap of fire in those sharp gray eyes. If he wanted a fight, then who was she to deny him.

"I know what I'm doing," she said coolly.

"Being incredibly irresponsible? What the hell kind of stunt was that?" Cyrano shifted nervously under him.

"One I've been working on for a while, along with several others. You've been gone a long time, Jax," she reminded. "I'm not a kid anymore."

"I can see that."

She swore the heat from his gaze penetrated her winter layers and licked flames over her skin.

"Then, using that stellar deductive reasoning of yours, you can probably figure out that a lot of things have changed around here in eight years, including my level of skill on the back of a horse." She said it flippantly in a way designed to goad him.

"I'm not questioning your goddamn skills, I'm questioning your sense. You flinging yourself around on the back of a horse without safety equipment or anyone to call 911 when you crack open your thick head is stupid."

Romeo had wandered close enough that Jax grabbed his bridle. He pulled her mount closer until their legs were brushing. "Would you let a student come out here by herself and mess around like that?"

"I was just having fun. I didn't realize that was illegal." She hated that he had a very small, practically insignificant point.

"I need you to be more careful. Do this shit in the indoor ring. With a helmet. And your trick saddle. And someone else around." He was waving his free hand around as if he was conducting a symphony of pissed-offness.

"Geez, *Mom*. Calm down." She rolled her eyes.

He grabbed her by the front of the jacket. "Don't." He said it quietly and with heat.

"Jesus, Jax. Knock it off," she said shoving at his hand.

"Promise me."

She could feel the muscle under her eye start to twitch. She hated conceding to anyone. Especially Jax. But he was more than stubborn enough to keep her out here until she agreed. It would take days for anyone to find their frozen bodies.

"Fine. I promise," she growled through gritted teeth.

"Good girl."

That pissed her off enough to take another dig. "Why do you even care anyway?"

He still had a good grip on her jacket. "You know why, Jojo." He yanked her closer until she had to brace herself against his thigh.

"Why?" she challenged. Why did she so desperately want to hear those words from him again? Would she start believing them if he kept saying them?

"Because I never stopped loving you. You're it for me."

And there it was, that jagged rush of elation followed by the slick dive of doubt. He left her, abandoned her in a hospital bed all those years ago. Whatever love meant to Jackson Pierce, it wasn't what it meant to her.

"Then where the hell have you been?" she snapped, trying to wrestle free from his grip. But without clocking him right in the face, he wasn't letting go. Joey growled in frustration.

"Forget it. Just forget it. I don't know how to ask you anymore than you know how to answer me."

A hint of a smile played over his lips. The dark stubble that covered his jaw gave him a dangerous look. "We never were very good at conversation. We communicated better in other ways."

She didn't fight him when he pulled her in to him. But the battle erupted when their lips met, each fighting to be the aggressor. It was a war that could leave them both as casualties.

Why did she want him? Why did she need his hands on her? Her heart would never forgive, so why did her body crave his touch? Could she be with him physically and still keep her heart safe? There was only one way to find out.

And it terrified her.

Joey steadied herself by bracing her hands on his hard thigh. His groan of approval had her fingers flexing into the denim. She let the warmth of his mouth flood her body with heat, testing, always testing how far she could go and still hold on to her heart.

She slid her hands an inch higher on his legs and was rewarded with a growl. Her tongue tangled with his, determined to take control. But his hand busied itself at the zipper of her jacket. It gave just enough for Jax to rip off his glove and shove his hand through the opening, palming her breast through the layers of thermal and flannel.

It was closer than they'd been in nearly a decade, and it wasn't close enough for either of them.

Romeo shifted nervously under her, and Joey pulled back, dragging her hands down his thighs as she went. His mount pawed the ground.

"We should move before Cyrano takes a chunk out of Romeo," she said through lips swollen from the kiss.

Jax was staring at her, his expression unreadable. There had been a time when she could read the thoughts that looped through his mind. But gone were the days she'd shared with the carefree boy, and now, in his place was a dangerous man.

He released her with what looked like reluctance, and Joey wheeled her mount around to give them all a little space.

"You need to come back to the barn," Jax told her.

She stared at him, daring him to give another order.

"Please?" he amended.

"I'm not going to have sex with you."

"Yet," he corrected. "You're not going to have sex with me *yet*. But there's a delivery that needs your signature."

"More flowers? More bacon? Not another dog. Waffles and I are just starting to enjoy our life together."

He grinned and for a second, the fun-loving boy she'd loved so much was evident in the face of the man before her.

"Even better."

"I don't think you can top Waffles."

"Guess you'll have to find out."

She arched a brow. "Race you back?"

8

*J*oey didn't wait for an answer. She kicked Romeo into a run and grinned when she heard the thunder of hooves behind her. Cyrano was fast. But Romeo was a sprinter. The wind stung her face as pine trees and fence posts whizzed by in a blur. With any luck, Colby and the rest of the stable help would think she was windburnt, not flushed from a scorching kiss.

She leaned low over the horse's neck and let him have his head.

They beat Jax by two full lengths, pulling up to a dignified walk on the slope behind the stable. Joey was still laughing when they came around the corner and she spotted the trailer in the drive.

A wisp of a man buried under a thick outer layer of Carhartts swaggered over to her. His red hair poked out in tufts under the thick wool cap, his cheeks pink from the air.

"You Joey Greer?" he asked, consulting a clipboard. She was a little disappointed that his accent was more Kentucky than Irish, taking away from his leprechaun-like appearance.

She dismounted and looped the reins over Romeo's head. "I might be. Depends on what you've got in the trailer.

The man's eyes sparkled. "Trust me. You're gonna want to be Joey Greer."

A shrill whinny erupted from the trailer followed by an impatient stamp.

Jax whistled and Carter and Colby ambled out of the barn.

Joey shot Jax a look. "Just what the hell did you do?"

He slid down off Cyrano's back and took Joey's reins. "Colby, you mind taking care of these two?"

Colby took the reins with a grin. "No problem. We made some room inside," he said with a wink.

"Why are we making room, and why the hell didn't someone consult me?" Joey snapped. These were *her* stables. This was *her* program. Horseflesh did not magically appear on the farm. She carefully researched, weighed options, and then negotiated the purchase with an iron spine and a meticulous plan.

No one was paying her any mind, and she was about to start yelling when the driver released the butterfly latches on the trailer ramp.

"Now, hold on here," she said following him. Without thinking, she helped him lower the ramp while she continued to argue. "There's been some kind of misunderstanding. I didn't buy a horse."

"Horses," Jax corrected behind her.

He and Carter were enjoying her irritation. Standing shoulder to shoulder, there was no mistaking the family resemblance, right down to their matching shit-eating grins. "You're both in a lot of trouble, so you might as well wipe those asshole smiles off your faces," she said, setting her jaw.

The southern-drawling leprechaun ignored the bickering and hustled into the back of the trailer.

"Mind your mouth!" The command came affectionately from Phoebe as she huffed and puffed her way across the drive. "Whew! I was worried I was going to miss this," she chirped, skimming a kiss on each son's cheek before doing the same to Joey.

"You're in on this mess too?" Joey felt ganged up on.

Phoebe shoved a red-mittened hand through Joey's arm. "Sweetie, I know you're not big on surprises, but trust me."

"This here is Calypso's Secret," the driver announced as a stunning mare picked her way daintily down the ramp.

"Calypso's Secret as in second place in last year's Breeder's Cup?"

"That's the one," the man bobbed his redhead as he walked. "She's retired now and looking forward to the good life."

"Oh, holy fuck," Joey muttered to herself.

The chestnut mare swung her head around and nuzzled at her pocket. Joey fished out a carrot from her stash and let the mare delicately nip it out of her gloved palm.

Jax approached to get a closer look.

"Jax?"

"Yeah?"

"What is Calypso's Secret doing in my yard?"

"I heard a rumor that you wanted to start a breeding program," he said, running a calloused hand down the mare's neck.

"You didn't."

"You said I owed you an apology."

"Jax." Joey's voice had the sharp bite of warning in it.

Damn right she wanted a breeding program. But she'd wanted it on her own terms. Terms that involved budgeting and starting with a broodmare less spectacular than Calypso. The horse in front of her—with the perfect white star on her nose and glossy coat—was levels above where she'd planned to start.

"If y'all want to move her out of the way, I'll get the big bastard out."

Joey shot Jax a murderous look. "Two horses? Two friggin' horses, Jax?"

He took Calypso's reins and passed them over to Carter. "You can't have a broodmare like this and a middle-of-the-road stallion."

"Y'all might want to move back. He's a handful," the driver warned.

Jax dragged her back a few steps. "What did you do?" Joey hissed at him.

The stamping and snorting escalated from the front stall in the trailer. Joey heard a well-placed kick strike the wall and wondered if there was anything left of the little driver.

But a moment later, she saw spectacular smoky black flank grudgingly emerge at the top of the ramp. A silky black tail swished in irritation.

He was huge. And pissed.

Sixteen hands at least and all lean muscle and attitude. He picked his way down the ramp with a delicacy that belied his twelve hundred pounds. The second all four feet were on the ground, he tried to rear up. The driver kept his head and his grip on the bridle, expertly wrangling the beast.

The stallion tossed his head and pawed at the ground.

"Yeah, yeah. You're a big deal. We know," he said, swatting at the horse's nose when he tried to take a bite out of his shoulder.

He certainly was a big bastard. A big, beautiful bastard. Joey was already in love.

But damn it. There was a budget. A plan. Maybe a decade

down the road they'd be able to invest in a horse like this. Not now. Not with Jax's bank account.

"Meet your stud. This is Apollo," Jax said, stepping in to take the lead from the driver. Testing, the horse started to rear, but Jax stood his ground and had the stallion chomping apple slices out of his hand in thirty seconds flat.

"Apollo, huh?" Joey said approaching the horse. Brown eyes followed her, and he tossed his head when she reached up to stroke his neck.

"As in 'Apologies,'" Jax said with a wink.

"I'm going to murder you, Ace," she told him succinctly.

Phoebe was too busy cooing over Calypso to hear Joey threaten her son's life.

It was cruel, taking over her dream, shoving it along. Seven figures of horseflesh stood before her and he called it an apology. That was a hell of an investment to make for an 'I'm sorry.'

She took the lead rope from Jax, let Apollo smell her. He stamped once and then nudged her with his nose, nibbling at the sleeve of her jacket.

God, he was spectacular.

She wouldn't accept. Couldn't accept. No matter how much she wanted them. And, oh, did she want them. But it was too much, too outrageous. And it put her in too vulnerable a position. She wasn't going to have Jax fund her dreams.

The horse nudged her again, this time in the pocket with carrots. She fished out a carrot and held it, palm flat. Apollo nosed her palm delicately. But rather than take the treat, he swung his head up aiming instead to take a chunk out of her shoulder. She blocked him easily.

"You are a bastard, aren't you?" she whispered to him.

His big, black head lifted as if in agreement before swooping in to take the carrot.

She shook her head. "Put them back on the trailer."

"Don't be stubborn," Jax warned.

"You think I'd actually accept a huge chunk of your bank account in the form of horseflesh?"

"If you don't, you're a stubborn idiot," he said mildly.

"Starting to piss me off."

"Back at ya, baby. Would you really turn these two away just to spite me?"

This wasn't the plan. She was going to start this on her own. From scratch. Small, selective. Build slowly to establish a reputation for quality. The program would be her baby.

And now Jax had his fingerprints all over it. She didn't need him or his flashy gifts. She felt her temper kick into a rolling boil.

"I'm not accepting them," she snapped.

Jax handed over Apollo's lead to Carter. "Get them bedded down," he told his brother. "I'll handle her."

"The hell you will!" Joey thought she caught a glimpse of Phoebe beaming at them like an idiot as Jax dragged her inside the stable and into her cramped office. He kicked the door closed behind him and crossed his arms, ready for the fight.

"Let's have it."

Happy to oblige, Joey launched into the argument. "You can't just come in here and run things," she said stalking back and forth keeping the shabby metal desk between them.

"Who says I'm trying to run things?"

But she was too wound up to converse. "You're either trying to manipulate me into sleeping with you, or you're trying to weasel control away from me."

"That's the stupidest thing I've ever heard you say, Joey. And I've known you since you were a kid." He was fired up now. "You forget that I know you. That means I know there is nothing under the sun that a man could buy you to make you feel obligated to fall into bed with him."

He had her there.

"So you bought them to run things and just generally drive me crazy?"

"They're in your name, Joey. You own them."

She slammed a hand down on her desk. "Bullshit. I didn't pay for them."

He shrugged. "It's your name on the bill of sale."

Joey yanked off her wool cap and threw it against the wall. *No. No. No. This wasn't how it was supposed to happen.*

"You were pissed because you thought they were mine. Now you're pissed because they're yours. Who was going to buy them in your plan?"

Carter. Well, the farm. The farm of which Jax was one-third owner.

She didn't answer him.

"This gives you more control, Joey. Take it."

She watched through the glass as Carter led Apollo to an empty stall. The stallion put up quite the fuss as he pranced past. Why wasn't anyone listening to her?

"I can't accept them," she said firmly.

"Why the hell not?"

Because her dreams of independence, of success, would be funded by the man who abandoned her. Her success would be his. Just another string binding them together.

"Because, Jax, normal businesswomen don't go around accepting gifts like this!" She shoved her hands into her hair just to give them something to do besides strangling him.

"Yes. They do. It's called an investment, and that's what I'm doing. I'm investing in you." He snagged her hand and dragged her out from behind the desk. "I believe in you. I believe in your plans. I believe in your ability to get shit done."

He pulled her closer even as she fought him.

"This gives you total control. You deserve it, and you'll see that as soon as you get this hissy fit out of your system."

"Hissy fit?" she gasped.

"I keep expecting you to bite me like Apollo. Two peas in a pod." Jax smirked.

She prodded him in the chest. "I don't want you to be tied up in my goals."

His smile faltered. "I know you don't, Jojo. And I'm hoping that someday you're going to let me get tied up with you in every way imaginable. But this isn't just about you. Ask yourself what these two are going to mean to the farm. We almost lost this place after Dad died."

Joey's eyes widened. She'd known there was trouble. Knew there was a rough patch after John's death, but she hadn't known how close it was.

"If you do what I know damn well you're capable of doing, you'll be putting the lean years behind us for good. You'll ensure the future of this farm for the next generation, maybe more. Carter and Summer's kids. Evan and Aurora. But we can only do this with you."

She ran her tongue around her teeth. He was going for the jugular. *Damn it! Was she going soft in the head? He was starting to make sense.*

"It's not just about you. Hell yes, I want to be tied to you in every way I can be, and I want to see every dream of yours come true, but I also want what's best for this place, for our family—because they're as much yours as they are mine—and it just so happens that this works out for everyone. But it doesn't work without you. I need you. We need you."

She could have pushed him one more time, but his voice had thickened with emotion. With love for this place, for family, for her.

Still she balked. He stepped in on her, crowding her against the desk.

"Uh-uh. No way!" She slapped a hand to his chest. "Do *not* kiss me right now."

His slow grin thawed her edges despite her resistance.

"Why not?"

"Because that's not how you close a business deal."

He framed her face with his big hands. "Are you closing this deal?"

Grudgingly, Joey shoved her hand between them and held it out. She waited until he let go of her face and took her hand in his.

"I'm paying you back. No matter how long it takes."

"Whatever," he said flippantly. "Can I kiss you now?"

"No! Maybe later... shut up."

Carter saved her from doing something stupid by poking his head in. "My turn?" he asked.

Jax squeezed her hand, his grip strong and firm. "She's all yours. For now."

As soon as he released her, Joey swiped her hand over the seat of her jeans to disrupt the tingles firing through her palm.

Jax slapped his brother on the shoulder and headed in the direction of the stable's new tenants.

"You got a minute?" Carter asked, sinking into the scarred metal chair in front of her desk.

Joey returned to the desk chair and flopped down. "This feels oddly official."

Carter propped his work boots up on the corner of the desk. "Better?"

Joey kicked back in her chair, her feet joined his on the battered top. "Much."

"I have a proposition for you," Carter began.

"I'm not sleeping with you either," Joey quipped.

Carter looked pained.

"Sorry, couldn't help it." Joey smirked and reached for the dredges of her cold coffee.

"Funny. We want to make you a partner."

The coffee lodged in her throat like a brick before shooting out of her facial orifices.

She was still gasping when Carter handed her a paper towel.

"What did you say?" Joey choked out, pressing the towel to her face.

Carter moved the coffee mug out of her reach. "We've decided to make you a partner in the stables."

"I'm... not sure you're speaking English. Or if I'm awake. Or having a stroke. This is a *family* farm, Carter."

"You're family. Always have been, always will be. Regardless of who you are or aren't sleeping with."

Joey slapped a hand to her forehead. This had Jax's fingerprints all over it.

"Before you say it, this was my idea," Carter said, reading her like a billboard.

She closed her mouth with a snap.

"I pitched it. My brothers were on board."

"Simple as that?" Joey asked.

Carter nodded. "Simple as that. You want it?"

She wanted it more than the box of candied bacon she'd squirreled away in the bottom desk drawer. Joey took a slow breath, let it out. "That depends. You swear on the lives of your twins that Jax didn't put you up to this? Because if you lie, you'll be punished with hellion children."

"It's me and Summer. We can only create hellion children," Carter cracked.

"Har har. Swear?"

"Swear. But Jax is obviously in favor of it. He told me it was 'about fucking time' and then went horse shopping."

Her father's words chose that moment to cycle through her head. *You'll never be anything to them...*

But she was. She was a solid, fucking investment, a friend. She was family. She had a bright future. Here, with the Pierces in her corner and she in theirs.

"Okay."

Carter grinned. In it she saw the likeness of John, of Jax. Men she had loved. She couldn't predict how this would go, but it was worth the risk.

"Now let's talk compensation."

9

That evening, Joey found herself on Gia and Beckett's wide front porch, clutching a bag of fresh applesauce muffins and Waffles's leash. She felt like an idiot.

But this was what you did with good news when you had friends. You shared it over baked goods and coffee.

Joey stabbed the doorbell with her finger and listened as little feet and paws pounded toward the front door. Giggles and barks met her when the door swung open.

Diesel, the floppy, fluffy puppy, tripped over his fat feet in his bid to sniff Waffles's butt. Aurora, looking like a five-year-old version of her mother, danced in place on the threshold.

"Hi, Waffles! Hi, Jo!" She was wearing orange and pink leggings and a teal hooded fleece with cookie crumbs embedded in it.

"Hey, Roar," Joey said in greeting. "Your mom around?"

"She's in da kitchen wiv Bucket. Dere puttin' a hole in da door."

Of course they were. In Joey's opinion, marriage made people do weird things. She sighed and stepped inside, bringing both dogs with her, and shrugging out of her fitted down jacket.

Diesel and Waffles continued to play, weaving in and out of her feet, while she shucked off her boots.

"Yeah? Well, maybe next time you should consult me before you go and add two members to our family." Gia's voice carried as she shoved open the kitchen door and marched down the hallway toward her. "Don't even think about it, Diesel!" She may have been dressed in cozy leggings with hearts all over them, but there was steel in her voice. Gia's command was delivered with a stern point of the finger at the puppy that had one of the boots Joey just discarded in his mouth.

The puppy dropped the boot and flopped over on his back, tail wagging. Gia rolled her eyes and rubbed the fat little belly. "You need to behave yourself," she said sternly. "Or I'll send you to Puppy Siberia." Diesel thumped his tail, immune to the threat.

"Hi," Gia said, finally shifting her focus to Joey. She gave her a hug before reaching down to scratch Waffles behind the ears. "See? This is what a good boy looks like," she crooned. "I bet you don't pee all over your mama's yoga clothes, do you?"

Joey wisely hid her grin and let Gia usher her into the parlor where a fire crackled cheerfully in the hearth. Here she could see the melding of Beckett's traditional tastes and Gia's eclectic style.

The room itself was an eyebrow raiser with its high ceilings and ornate woodwork. Thick carved moldings and wainscoting in a sedate navy were complimented by shimmering gold and silver accents that picked up the tones in the fleur de lis wallpaper.

Kitschy and antique finishes topped tables and filled

shelves. Two overstuffed tangerine floor pillows occupied the space between the fireplace and the low, square coffee table.

Candles flickered golden in a trio of cracked glass holders on the mantel already crowded by family photos. Gia and Beckett on their wedding day. The kids with Franklin and Phoebe at Christmas.

A bluesy song poured from a docking station tucked between leather-bound volumes and trashy romance paperbacks on the built-ins flanking the fireplace. Joey made a mental note to browse Gia's library to see if they could make any trades.

"Nice," Joey said, handing over the muffins.

"Thanks." Gia surveyed the room with pride. "This is my sanctuary. No kids, no pets, no Beckett, unless specifically invited." Aurora and Diesel chose that moment to scramble in. The little girl Supermanned onto a footstool while the puppy attacked the fringe on the cream-colored throw tossed over the arm of the sofa.

"Uh-uh," Gia said. "You take your furry friend here and go bother Beckett in the kitchen."

"But Mama!" Aurora's eyes were wide with the pain of rejection. "I want hot chocolate!"

"If you stop the whining this second and promise to take Diesel outside to do his business before your brother comes home, you can have hot chocolate."

"Yay!" Aurora jumped up, fueled by enthusiasm and the promise of liquid sugar.

"In the kitchen," Gia finished. She kept her expression stern while her daughter's shoulders slumped.

"Deal or no deal?" Gia asked.

Aurora sighed pitifully. "Deal," she pouted.

"Good. Now go take your four-legged monster to see Beckett."

"C'mon, Diesel," Aurora said, hefting the roly puppy in her little arms.

Waffles, sensing a possible eviction, curled up quietly next to the fire.

"Don't give the puppy any hot chocolate," Gia called after her.

"Awh."

Gia yanked the pocket doors closed. "You and I will be enjoying adult hot chocolate laced with booze," she announced.

"Are you sure tonight is a good time for you?" Joey asked skeptically.

"Yeah. Why?"

"Aurora said something about a hole in the door, and you seem a little insane."

"The hole is for the cat door so poor Tripod can escape to the basement when Diesel torments him too much. The insanity is just a side effect of raising children and being married." She grinned, looking much happier than her words suggested.

The doorbell rang. "That should be Summer," Gia said, sliding one of the doors open. "Or half of the town council. You never know, living in this house."

She reappeared moments later with a bundled-up Summer in tow. The pocket doors slid shut, and Joey wasn't certain, but she thought she heard the snick of a lock. Summer started shucking off layers starting with a purple knit cap and her buff-colored Uggs. She had a white fleecy sweater stretched tight across her rounded belly. The cheery scarf around her neck was next. "I'm so glad you guys called. I spent all day in the office, and then all of dinner I divided my time between arguing with Carter and ignoring two sets of beggy eyes."

"What are you two fighting about?" Joey asked.

"Oh, no!" Summer wagged a finger at her, and Joey wondered if the commanding finger was some kind of maternal trait. She'd have to ask her own mother. "I want to hear your news first," Summer said, easing herself down on one of the armchairs.

There was a thump from the rear set of doors.

"Hold that thought," Gia said. "Hot chocolate's here." She slid the doors open to reveal a tray-wielding Beckett. "There's my handsome butler."

He was still in his office attire. Neatly pressed gray pants and a light blue button down. The sleeves were rolled up to his elbows. "The two mugs on the right are the good ones," he said, dropping a kiss on Gia's cheek.

"Thank you, Jeeves," she said. "Have everything under control?"

"Rora and I are taking the demon hell spawn outside for a potty break, after which we are convening to the third floor for homework and video games. Evan should be home in the next five minutes or he's grounded."

"God, you're sexy when you know stuff," Gia sighed. She took her husband's face in her hands and gave him an R-rated kiss.

"Ladies," he said with a wink as he sauntered out of the room.

The second the pocket doors slid shut, Joey found both Summer and Gia staring at her.

"Well?" Summer prodded.

Suddenly awkward, Joey cleared her throat. She wasn't very comfortable talking about herself. It was easier to maintain a safe distance if she didn't go blabbing about herself all the time.

"I... uh..."

"Slept with Jax?" Gia offered.

Joey shook her head vehemently. "No!"

"Made out with Jax?" Summer tried.

"No, well yes. But no."

"Definitely coming back to that one," Summer said, fluffing her blonde hair.

"They made me a partner in the stables." Joey blurted it out and shoved part of a muffin in her mouth so she wouldn't have to say anything else right away.

"What?" Summer said, trying to heave herself out of the chair. Gia, unrestricted by the weight of pregnancy, flew at Joey, her arms outstretched.

"Oh my God! That's even more exciting than Jax!"

"It was the proposal, wasn't it?" Summer asking, finally gaining her feet.

Joey nodded and chewed.

"So how soon do you get to start the breeding program?" Gia asked, releasing her to dole out the mugs.

Joey swallowed hard. "I guess immediately, seeing as how Jax had a trailer full of perfect equine specimens delivered today."

"Jax bought horses?" Gia frowned.

Here Joey paused because it was here that trepidation warred with excitement. "He bought me two horses. As an investment."

"Ohhh." Summer and Gia got the implication immediately.

"I made a mistake, didn't I?" Joey flopped down on the floor pillow next to the sleeping Waffles. "Damn it. I knew it."

Gia placed a steaming cup and saucer on the coffee table in front of her.

"Why in the world would you think you made a mistake?" Summer asked, helping herself to a muffin.

"Because Jax," Gia answered, delivering Summer's hot chocolate.

"Why does yours smell better than mine?" Summer asked, sniffing the rim of her cup.

"Because whiskey and Irish cream." Gia grinned.

"That's going on the Things Summer Gets to Drink After Babies list. Now, back to this mistake nonsense."

"It's not nonsense," Joey argued. "Gia agrees with me."

"Uh-uh," Gia said, using her parent voice. "I *understand* that you're *concerned* with what Jax's role is in all of this. That doesn't mean I think you're right to doubt yourself. Because you're not."

"Why don't you walk us through the whole thing?" Summer suggested.

So she did, while stroking Waffles who had decided her lap was more comfortable than the pillow.

"Okay, so to summarize—can you tell I married an attorney?—Carter was so impressed with your proposal for a breeding program that he put it up for a vote to make you a partner. And Jax liked the plan so much that he invested in a pair of horses levels above where you hoped to start."

Joey nodded at Gia over the rim of her cup, the hot chocolate warming her from the inside out.

"I want props for not dropping any of the dozen 'looking a gift horse in the mouth' jokes I've thought of in the last five minutes," Summer told them.

"So what's really bothering you?" Gia asked, watching Joey intently. "I mean, really, this sounds like good business on all sides. Of course you should be a partner, and of course you should start with the best stock possible. So what's the real reason you're crumbling your muffin into little pieces?"

Joey looked down at her flannel now covered with muffin. She looked like she'd taken eating lessons from Aurora.

"I'm worried that he's serious." Joey said the words before she could tamp them down again. "I'd almost talked myself into having a nice little fling with Jax. The sparks are still there, and I'm not some wide-eyed eighteen-year-old kid anymore. I wouldn't break this time. I thought it was only a matter of time before he packed up and left again."

She paused and took another fortifying sip of hot chocolate. "But he's not packing. He's building a brewery and helping out around the stables and rescuing dogs and buying horses." Joey took a breath.

"You're worried Jax couldn't handle something casual," Summer said, her perfectly groomed eyebrows rocketing sky high.

"He told me he loves me."

"Of course he does," Gia smiled. "Anyone can see that."

"I don't want him to love me. I want things to be simple, uncomplicated. I can't seduce my business partner. I can't keep things casual with a man who thinks he loves me and wants to have some kind of future with me."

"Sure you can." Summer grinned. "It's called being honest. Jax is a big boy. And if there's a family resemblance down there, he's a very big boy."

Gia snickered.

"Sorry, pregnancy hormones. Where was I before the penis sidetrack?"

"Honesty," Gia supplied.

"Right. If you're honest with him about what you do want —like his hot body and impressive genitalia—and don't want a long-term relationship with said hot body, then it's up to him to deal with that."

"Huh," Joey said. "Are we just going to pretend that it's not weird having Summer giving advice about honesty in relationships?"

98

"Har har. Very funny. I'll have you know I'm a reformed dishonest relationship haver."

"Joey, what Summer here is trying to say between penis jokes is that you could have everything," Gia told her.

"Hmm."

10

Jax kicked back on the rickety desk chair and yanked his shirt over his nose.

"Christ, Meatball. What did you eat?"

The chubby beagle under his feet didn't bother pretending to be embarrassed about filling Jax's bedroom with a noxious cloud of dog farts.

"Your brother is disgusting," Jax told Valentina, who stretched her massive black and white Great Dane body across the double bed before flopping back onto her side. The dogs enjoyed keeping him company whenever Carter and Summer were out.

Jax glanced at the clock on his computer screen. It was after seven, and the January sun had set ages ago. He'd purposely kept his distance from Joey for the last two days. With the new horses and the partner news, she'd need time to process.

Otherwise she might be likely to take a swing at him.

So he was using his time wisely and trudging through a draft of the screenplay that he wondered if he'd ever finish.

He made a point never to get worked up about a project.

Never bothered worrying about failure. Jax had been through enough option periods on spec scripts to know projects fell through more often than not. In his young career, he'd been lucky enough to have a couple of notable projects make it to the big screen... and a dozen more rejected ones sitting in an archive file on his computer.

Most of his work was done on assignment by production companies, which meant his teenage obsession with shoot 'em up blockbusters was finally paying off. However, every once in a while, he snuck through a spec script. His very first green light had been on spec, and while it hadn't exploded at the box office, it had caught the eye of the right executives at the right time. He'd built his career carefully, choosing projects that he knew intuitively were the right ones. He'd even begun branching out into producing recently, something he planned to explore again with this project.

This script, another spec, was personal. He had some nerves tied up in this one. Not for the industry's reaction or the critics. He could give a damn about them. But this time the critics that mattered would be his family, his town. Joey.

Jax liked the process of writing screenplays. Liked the long, tedious hours of creation. The satisfaction of finishing a project crafted from your best effort. And he appreciated the practice of letting it go. Somehow, it reminded him of helping his father on the farm. The endless toiling. The gratifying last look through dirt and sweat at a freshly planted field. And the hope that the rains would come, the crops would grow, and the cycle would continue for another season, another generation.

He'd learned so much from John Pierce. Absorbed more than he had been aware of until his father was no longer walking the fields. Writers write what they know. However, every time Jax had tried to take an unbiased look at his father, he came up empty on the man's flaws.

In Jax's experience, everyone was deeply flawed. But his father had been a man above men. Quiet and calm, he dealt with the chaos of three boys with the patience of a saint. Finding words to be too complex to use to change minds and attitudes, he preferred to lead by example.

And by example, he'd shown his sons how to live. Treading lightly on the earth, moving easily with the natural rhythms of the world. Honoring where you came from while always sharing what you were lucky enough to have.

John Pierce was a hero to Jax. And his brothers had risen to the challenge as well. Carter went to war to defend the land he so loved. And when he came home, wounded and fractured, he let the land and the people help him rise again. Beckett learned and led. He had his father's patience and used it as mayor of Blue Moon. It was always family first with Beckett, and that family was never limited by blood.

As the youngest, Jax had always known the subtle pressure of a family tradition of goodness. His teachers remembered the older brothers' accomplishments and expected similar results from him. Pierce men were men to be counted on—protective partners, loyal friends, and trustworthy leaders. It wasn't until he was a teenager that he started to realize the enormity of the responsibility of being a Pierce.

At first it had irritated, then scraped, and by the time he was a senior facing his future, it had dug deep. That feeling of less than, of never quite measuring up. While Carter deployed with the Army and Beckett set his sights on law school, Jax delivered pizzas in his third-hand Camaro and helped his dad on the farm.

If he stayed in Blue Moon, he would always be measured

by his father, his brothers. There was no room to stand on his own two feet and be only himself.

If he was going to be someone, something, it would have to be beyond this cozy community where history and blood defined you to everyone. If he didn't leave, he'd always be known as the kid who replaced the principal's car with a hay wagon on the last day of school. Or the ninth grader caught ditching school to fish and drink pilfered beer with a leggy junior in daisy dukes and an El Camino.

Or the fuck-up who almost killed Joey Greer.

When he tallied up his sins, sometimes he wasn't sure he made the right call coming home.

His phone vibrated at his elbow, and he opened a text from Carter. A close-up of Clementine's demonic goat face filled his screen.

Carter: Your girlfriend misses you.

Jax's response was succinct.

Jax: Asshole.

But he grinned as he tossed his phone back on the desk. *Maybe it wasn't so bad to be home,* he thought. Being here to see his brothers settle into married life? Watching his mother shed the grief she'd carried since his father's death? It was good for the soul.

But waking up in the bed that he'd spent the majority of his life fantasizing about Joey Greer was an entirely different story.

It was time to stop dreaming. He wasn't going to think about what would happen if his plan failed. Just like with a script. He'd give it his all, do his best. And if Joey never forgave him... Well, that wasn't going to happen, so he wasn't going to waste any energy on that possibility.

The screen of his phone lit up again. He yanked out the ear buds and with them the 80s monster ballad that had cycled to the top of the playlist on his laptop.

"Nero's Pizza. You want anchovies on that?" he answered in the thickest Jersey accent he could muster.

"Very funny, favorite son of mine." His mother's voice carried a thread of easy affection that had the uncanny ability to untie his knots.

"I bet you say that to all your sons," he teased.

"Only the handsome ones."

Jax grinned and shook his head. "You're buttering me up for something."

"You're not only devastatingly handsome, you're also incredibly astute," Phoebe cooed, laying it on thick.

Staring out into the dark of a winter evening, Jax could imagine his mother in his mind's eye, pushing her glasses up her nose, an open book in her lap. "Uh-huh. How about you just come out and say what you have to say, and we'll save the compliments for later?"

"Okay, so it's two things. First thing is, can you change the oil in Franklin's SUV? The garage is all booked up, and I don't want him to forget about it again."

"Sure—"

"And since you're saying yes to things, would you mind being the guest of honor at the Blue Moon Movie Club tomorrow night?"

"Mom—"

"We're screening *Awake in the Night*, which my deeply talented and model-worthy son wrote," Phoebe plowed on. "So it would only be the best thing ever if you were our guest of honor so Frieda Blevins will stop gabbing about her niece taking a selfie with that damn vampire actor."

"Mom—"

"I mean seriously, it was a selfie in a bar. They weren't on a date, they weren't working on a movie together. She just stood in front of his table and made duck lips. Now, you actually write movies, and you won't have to do a thing. Just show up and smile. Maybe wave. Say you'll do it, please?"

Jax waited for a beat to make sure her word volcano was done erupting. The last thing he needed to add to his to-do list was a night out with his mother's friends so they could nitpick a movie—and potentially him—to death.

"Mother?"

"Jackson?"

"No."

"I refuse to accept that answer. And let me tell you why..."

Four minutes later, head on his desk, Jax caved.

"Okay. Fine. You gave birth to me and didn't murder me at any point during my childhood, despite provocation on my part," he said, reiterating her main points. "I'll go to your movie night."

"Really?" Phoebe sounded surprised. "I had more material prepared."

"You've been hanging out with Beckett too much," he told her.

"It's Evan. That kid can build a great argument when he wants something. Are you coming to his team's debate next week?"

"I didn't realize how demanding family was on time," Jax teased.

"Well, let me remind you how I basically lived out of our car for three years shuttling you and your brothers to swimming and lacrosse and—"

"For the love of God, Mom," Jax groaned. "How are the house plans coming?" he asked, desperate to change the subject.

"Oh! We finalized them with Calvin yesterday. I'll show them to you when you pick me up tomorrow."

"So we're driving together?"

"That way you have to show up and can't pull some fake 'farm emergency' situation," his mom explained cheerfully.

She knew him well.

"Fine, but I'll drive." Of all her many positive qualities, being a decent driver was not one of them. Hell, she wasn't even a passable driver. Growing up, he and his brothers had all experienced carsickness every time Phoebe Pierce took the wheel. Even on the seven-minute drive from the farm to the grocery store. Their vehicular-induced nausea had remained a mystery to Phoebe who insisted that they all just had sensitive inner ears.

"Great! Pick me up at 6:30. And you might want to prepare some material for the Q and A."

"What Q and A? Mom?" Jax asked, but his mother had already hung up.

He tossed his phone back on the desk. "Well, that sucked," he said to the dogs. Unimpressed, Meatball opened a blood-shot eye.

Jax ran a hand over his empty stomach. Maybe he'd head downstairs and start dinner for everyone since it looked like Carter and Summer were pulling a late night.

With the dogs on his heels, he padded downstairs barefoot with the intention to rummage through the fridge and cabinets. Grilled cheese sounded like a winner. Maybe he'd stick some bacon in his.

He flipped on the lights and made it two feet into the kitchen before the scene before him processed in his brain.

"Oh my God." Jax backpedaled and tripped over Valentina, landing on his ass in the doorway of the kitchen. His elbow made contact with the doorframe hard enough for him to see stars.

"Oh my God!" Summer shrieked, making a grab for a too-small dishtowel to cover body parts.

"Shit!" Carter, who was at least clothed on his upper half, muttered. He made a dive for Summer's discarded sweater and in the process tripped and went face first into the upper cabinet. He slid awkwardly to the floor. Meatball waddled around the island to investigate.

Summer hopped off the counter and cowered.

"We didn't know you were home," she said, still in shrieking volume.

"Jesus! I can't believe you guys are allowed to do that when you're that pregnant!" Jax said, rubbing his eyes to erase the image.

"The doctor said it was fine." Carter's muffled reply came from the floor.

"Are you okay, honey?" Summer leaned over to wriggle into her shirt and look at Carter's face. "Uh-oh. You're bleeding."

Jax pulled himself back to his feet.

"Oh, geez. You're bleeding too," Summer said, nodding at Jax's arm.

"Crap." He held up his bent elbow to survey the damage.

Summer dug through the pantry until she found the box of bandages they stashed there for emergencies.

"Okay, both of you come here. But no one look anyone else in the eye. Possibly ever again," she ordered.

Jax shuffled over to the island, and Carter dragged himself up to standing.

Jax didn't have the chance to look his brother in the eye. "At least put it back in your pants!"

Summer tossed Carter the dishtowel. His brother grinned. "Consider it payback for that time you and Mr. Mayor dragged your balls all over my couch."

"The couch that I fell asleep on last night?" Summer was back to shrieking.

"Put your dick back in your pants and slap a butterfly on your face before you bleed out," Jax smirked.

"We're gonna need to work out a system," Carter said as Summer taped up the cut on his cheek.

"Yeah, it's called doing it only in the bedroom with the door locked like I wanted to," Summer grumbled. "And same goes for you when you finally talk Joey into bed."

"Joey has her own house," Carter grumbled.

"Stop frowning," she ordered. "It makes you bleed more."

Jax slapped some gauze on his elbow. "You know what? How about I go out for dinner and you two can carry on with your depraved behavior in peace?"

Carter reached for the wallet on the island. He pulled out a twenty and tossed it to Jax. "Go buy yourself something greasy."

"That's my wallet, ass."

"That's my wife's rack you just saw, dick."

Summer turned an even deeper shade of scarlet and slapped the bandage in place on Carter's face. He winced.

"Point taken," Jax said, tearing the tape with his teeth. "I think I'll head into town and show off my battle wound. There'll probably be a lot of questions."

"You both suck," Summer groaned.

11

---

*J*oey's first day as partner was a busy one. Between feeding and turn out, she scheduled an end-of-the-day appointment with the large animal vet to check out Apollo and Calypso. She lent a hand with the mucking until Carter took over and then beat her head on her desk over lesson billing and paperwork for an hour before grabbing a thermos of soup and working her way through the stalls inspecting for damage that needed to be repaired.

She often thought of running the stables as playing house-mother to a bunch of teenagers. They each had their own personalities and bad habits—including kicking the shit out of the boards beneath their food bucket—and it was her job to keep them as safe and happy as possible.

She collected the lightweight horse blankets from the stall hooks and, after a quick hosing, tossed them in the industrial washer in the supply closet. She'd let Colby deal with the heavier blankets later. Waffles divided his time between following her around like a shadow and sleeping in the dog bed she'd put under the desk in the office earlier that week.

Joey took an early afternoon break to groom a couple of

the horses that wouldn't be used for lessons that night and scheduled a potential tack cleaning pizza party for the end of the month. It helped to have extra hands, and in the past, she'd learned that students and their parents had no problem with lending said hands in return for pizza and a ten percent discount on lesson sessions.

She was reviewing the spring show schedule when she spotted a big blue pickup pull up to the stables on the security feed.

Dr. Sammy Ames was as good with animals as her mother, the original and now retired Dr. Ames. Joey was thankful that, unlike her mother, Sammy also had a way with people. During a particularly scary colic case two years ago, Joey and Dr. Ames had nearly come to blows. Thankfully, Carter had stepped in with his cool head and a cooler six-pack, saving Joey from a potential arrest.

She met the vet at the door and waved her in.

"How's it going, Sammy?"

The woman yanked a red wool cap off her short honey blonde curls and tucked her gloves into the pockets of her down vest. "Not too bad, minus the wind chill. Were you aware that hell froze over, by the way? Other than that, it's been a nice quiet day of vaccinations and well checks."

"That's a good day."

"Sure is," she said, bending down to ruffle Waffles's ears and offer him a treat that she pulled out of her pocket. "We finally got the authority from Animal Control to cownap those emaciated jerseys over in Greenburg. Carter got any room for two hungry ladies?"

"I'll ask him and let you know." He would, Joey knew. Carter Pierce couldn't say no to an animal in need.

"I'd appreciate it," Sammy said. She let out a low whistle

when they got to Calypso's stall. "I feel like I'm meeting a unicorn who just won Miss Universe."

Joey grinned, and Calypso tossed her head in sassy agreement.

"She's gorgeous, and she knows it."

While Sammy slipped into the stall and started her exam, Joey fired off a text to Carter about the cows and told him to get in touch with Sammy.

"Well, you've got yourself the perfect mare here," Sammy said, finishing up in the stall. "I'm guessing you aren't going to see anything odd health-wise during her quarantine."

"That's what I was hoping you'd say. Ready to meet the beast?"

Sammy grinned and rubbed her palms together. "Oh, yeah. Bring him on!"

If she'd been impressed with Calypso, Sammy fell head over heels for Apollo the second he lunged his big head through the stall door.

Joey didn't bother cautioning Sammy to watch herself in the stall. The woman knew her way around bad-tempered livestock, and a seven-figure stallion was no different. She watched the exam with humor as Sammy had to outmaneuver Apollo every step of the way.

"Try that again and we're gonna have words," Sammy warned Apollo as he made a move to nip her back.

"He's a bit of an ass," Joey warned.

Sammy bent from the waist and slid her hand down the back of his front leg. "Come on, Sexy Ass. Gimmie your damn foot."

Apollo balked at first, but the vet out-stubborned him.

"There. That wasn't so bad, now was it?" Sammy asked, putting the foot back down and slapping the stallion on the shoulder.

Apollo gave a bad-tempered stamp in reply.

"I think I'm in love," Sammy sighed, running her hands through her curls. She looked like a fairy with her waif-like build and green eyes, not someone who wrestled stallions and birthed calves.

Joey stroked Apollo's velvet nose and gave him a peppermint treat for his only mildly offensive behavior. "Yeah, there's something we women love about an arrogant ass." Joey sighed. "Want a cup of coffee before you hit the road?"

Sammy glanced at her watch. "More than I want a foot rub. You got fresh?"

"It's January. We're making a pot every hour on the hour," Joey said, leading the way back to her office.

"Have you had Sexy Ass out for a ride, yet?" Sammy asked.

Joey shook her head and poured a steaming mug from the pot in the office. "On my list for today."

"I hear that list is getting longer now that you're partner," Sammy said, accepting the mug.

"How the hell did you hear that? It's been twenty-four hours."

"Please. It's Blue Moon. Colby's mom got her hair done at the Snip Shack with Elvira Eustace yesterday afternoon. Told everyone all about the new horses and job. If you hadn't called me this morning, I was already planning on coming out to check 'em out."

Crap. That meant she needed to call her parents now rather than in a few days or weeks like she'd been entertaining.

"If your breeding fees aren't too astronomical, I've got a pretty little mare at home ready for her first season this year." Sammy cocked her head to the side.

"We'll have to compare astronomicals sometime," Joey told her.

Over coffee, they nailed down the quarantine period for Apollo and Calypso before they could be introduced to the rest of the horses and settled on a deworming plan for spring.

When she waved Sammy off in the drive, Joey was already reaching for her phone, which was already ringing.

"Hi, Dad."

"So when were you going to decide to share the big news with your parents?" Forrest demanded gruffly.

Joey kicked the door and committed to a course of action.

"Who ruined my surprise? I'm going to kick their ass."

"I thought it was common knowledge and you just couldn't be bothered to share it with us. Your mother is very upset."

It seemed both parents could play each other as the martyr.

"No one was supposed to know until I told you two. I was going to have you come here and check out the new horses and then tell you. I can't believe someone ruined this! I wanted to be the one to tell you!" Well, that was mostly true. She bit her lip and waited to see which way her father would go.

"Now, Joey." Her dad's voice was placating. "You know you can't keep secrets in Blue Moon. Those people know what you had for breakfast before you even get out of bed."

"I just can't believe someone ruined my surprise. I was so excited to tell you." And more than a little nervous of his reaction.

"Well, tell me now," Forrest offered. "I can act surprised over the phone."

Joey smiled. As annoying as his bravado and protective-ness was, she knew that deep down all her father wanted was for her to be happy. And safe. And not dating Jax.

"Okay, but you have to sound surprised, or I'll still be mad."

"I'm ready." He cleared his throat. "So, what's new with you, Joey?"

"Well, Dad, I have some big news..."

The conversation went better than the cold call she'd anticipated making. Her father had pretended to be thrilled with the partner news and only asked her twice if she was certain it wasn't some slick move by Jax to worm his way back into her good graces. After her assurance that she'd earned the honor all on her own and his fatherly warning to watch herself around the Pierces, he passed the phone to her mother so they could coordinate a visit to the farm to meet the new horses.

By the time she hung up, she had a headache and overnight visitors on the books.

BY THE TIME her last lesson wrapped up at seven, the only thing Joey could think of was a medium rare burger with onion rings. She changed into mostly clean jeans that she found on the floor of her closet and a cozy flannel and pulled on fleece-lined snow boots that came to mid-calf to ward off the cold.

She gave Waffles an extra half scoop of food in his dish when he gave her the look of devastation at not being invited to dinner.

"Don't look at me like that. You don't want to go. You want to stay here and nap by the fire."

She could have sworn that his furry lower lip trembled.

"I'll turn the TV on for you, okay?" She grabbed the remote and flipped through the guide. "What do you want to watch? Cartoons? Sit coms?"

Waffles looked mildly interested in a Spanish soap opera, so she left it on and ducked out the front door.

Judging from Shorty's parking lot, everyone else in Blue Moon had decided they weren't cooking tonight either. She squeezed her truck into a space at the back of the lot and hustled through the cold to the front door.

She blamed her frostbitten eyeballs for the unfortunate fact that she claimed a barstool without recognizing her neighboring patron.

Jax.

"Well, well. You just made my night," he said with the trademark Pierce grin responsible for melting the underwear off an entire generation of women.

She debated about getting up and taking a seat on the other end of the bar, but Ed had already shoved a menu at her.

"Didn't know you had a date, Jax," Ed Avila, the bartender and owner of Shorty's, grinned.

"Not a date, Ed," Joey said with a glare.

"None of my business if you two want to have dinner together," Ed said. "Beer?"

"Yes to the beer."

"Put it on my tab," Jax said.

"Don't you start," Joey said, shifting her glare to him. "What happened to your elbow?"

Jax glanced down at his bloody sleeve and the makeshift gauze bandage. "I had a bad experience with a dark kitchen."

"Run backwards into the knife block, Ace?" Joey took a sip of the beer Ed delivered.

"Even worse. I walked in on Carter and Summer on the kitchen island."

"What were they—oh my God! That's disgusting. Are pregnant people even allowed to have sex?"

"That's exactly what I said. Apparently, it's no big deal."

Joey shuddered. "It's probably a big deal to the babies who are getting poked in the face by—"

"And now I'm never getting that image out of my head," Jax said, taking a healthy gulp of beer. "Let's talk about something else."

"How about heavy-duty sanitizers for kitchen surfaces?" Joey offered.

"How about horses?" Jax suggested.

Joey couldn't stop the grin on her face from spreading.

"You take him out yet?" Jax asked.

"Today. I didn't have a lot of time, but I put him through his paces in the ring. He's—"

"Perfect? Incredible? The most amazing specimen of horseflesh you've ever laid eyes on?"

She let Jax have his moment. After all, he was the reason she spent a satisfying hour of her afternoon battling it out with the stallion. "Apollo is pretty great," she admitted.

"Pretty great? That's the best you can do?" Jax scoffed.

"Shut up. He's freaking awesome. I'm surprised I haven't seen you sneak in there with a saddle yet."

"I wanted you to have the honors," Jax said, nudging her shoulder with his. "But now that you have, I'll be in tomorrow. Bright and early."

"Early?" she said skeptically.

"Well, not first feeding early." He winked.

"You haven't been much of a morning person since you came back," she observed.

"I'm on a deadline, and I write at night. But the clock will definitely say a.m. when I show my pretty face in your stables."

"I'll look for you at 11:59."

"You two love birds ready to order?" Ed interrupted.

"What'll it be, sweetheart?" Jax teased.

"I'm really tempted to take my business to Peace of Pizza right now," Joey threatened.

"Only playing, Joey. I know you could take me if you wanted to," Ed said.

"Keep that in mind when you're running your mouth."

"Yes, ma'am," Ed threw a salute. "What can I get you?"

She ordered her burger and onion rings and rolled her eyes when Jax ordered the same thing. "Seriously?"

"What? It sounded good."

"I've been craving a Shorty's burger and onion rings for the last seven hours. Change your order."

"Nope."

He was so good-natured in his response that Joey laughed.

"I've missed that sound," Jax said, suddenly all smoke and heat.

She shook her head. "How do you do that?"

"Do what?"

"Go from friendly and benign to all come hithery in half a second."

"Come hithery?" Jax grinned. "I forgot how much I like you."

"Oh, so it's *like* now," Joey said, feeling a chunk of hope and maybe the slightest hint of disappointment.

Jax lifted his glass to his lips, wicked thoughts evident in his eyes. "I never forgot that I love you. But it may have slipped my mind how much I like you."

Her stomach did a loop-de-loop.

"Here's a thought. How about we have a nice, *quiet* dinner together without either of us pushing an agenda?"

"A truce?"

"A truce."

"I'm willing to give it a shot," Jax said, raising his glass to her. "To truces."

She brought her pint to his. "To truces."

In the low light of the bar, he looked like a handsome devil sent here with the sole purpose of tempting her. He was comfortable. And not just in jeans that probably emphasized his spectacular ass and a bloodied thermal shirt that fit across his muscled chest and shoulders like a tailor had sewn it to his body. Jax was comfortable in his skin. Confident, strong, and completely sure that he'd wear her down.

Why did she find that so sexy?

He had his hand on the back of her barstool, his knee brushing hers. She hadn't realized that she was leaning in until she felt his breath on her face. He smelled like the outdoors and wood fires. His Arctic eyes were fixed on her face, and she was so close Joey swore she could hear his heartbeat.

She was weak with hunger. It was the only explanation besides her hormones revolting against her wasteland of a sex life. Either option was better than considering the possibility that she wanted Jackson Pierce as much as he wanted her.

"Hey, Jax. Hi, Joey." The spell was broken by the skinny man with glasses and neatly pressed khakis who climbed onto the stool on Jax's left.

Joey's hand clamped down on Jax's thigh. While Anthony Berkowicz looked about as harmless as a bucket of puppies, he was the son of Rainbow and Gordon Berkowicz and, as such, was second generation Beautification Committee, the nosiest, most meddling organization in town. He was also editor-in-chief of *The Monthly Moon*, Blue Moon's community newspaper or tabloid. The exposé he'd done on Summer and Carter before they were dating predicted they would have a half-dozen children after Summer gave up her career in the city and moved to Blue Moon.

Huh, Joey thought.

Well, he sure as hell wasn't getting any fodder on her, Joey decided.

"I'm going to the restroom, and he'd better be gone by the time I get back," she hissed at Jax.

"If you don't get your hand off my leg, we're going to have a bigger problem than Anthony Berkowicz," Jax whispered, looking pointedly at her hand. "A much bigger problem."

"Funny." Joey pulled her hand back faster than if she'd touched hot coals. "Nice to see you, Anthony," she called over her shoulder as she headed to the bathroom.

~

"How's the newspaper biz, Anthony?" Jax asked, willing the blood to return to his head.

Anthony's head bobbed. "Not bad. Not bad. How's the farm?"

"Good all around. What brings you out to Shorty's on this frigid night?"

"Just doing a little digging." Anthony slid his phone in front of Jax.

On the screen was a picture of him and Joey sitting side by side at the bar someone had posted to the Blue Moon Facebook group four minutes ago.

"Do you live upstairs or something? That's a faster response time than the fire department."

"I go where the stories take me," Anthony said.

Jax drummed his fingers on the bar, debating for a second. "Anthony, I'm going to lay this on the line. I'm after Joey. I intend to marry that girl, but if she gets a hint that the Beautification Committee is sniffing around us, she's going to head for the hills on principle. And if that happens and you're the reason behind it, I'm going to hunt you down and fill your apartment and your newspaper office with all kinds of shit. Pig, horse, goat, dog. I have access to an unlimited supply. Now, on the other hand, if you find yourself somehow useful to my cause, I'd be happy to give you an exclusive on whatever you deem fit after Joey marries me."

Anthony swallowed hard. "Uh-huh. I see."

"Can I get you something, Anthony?" Ed asked, dropping Jax and Joey's plates on the bar.

"Uh. Yeah. Can I get a diet?" He glanced at Jax. "To go, please."

Jax clapped him on the shoulder. "Glad we're on the same page."

The slim man paused, holding his soda. "Oh, yeah. Just so you know, you might want to have the same conversation with Ellery." He pointed in the direction of the ladies' room as a woman dressed for a death metal concert pushed through the door.

"Shit."

JOEY GRABBED a fistful of paper towels out of the dispenser in the ladies' room and dried her hands. She had faith that Jax could get rid of Anthony... if he wanted to. There was, of course, the possibility that he'd want Anthony to print a bunch of fake crap about them getting back together in hopes that it would convince her to give him a second chance.

And if he did that, Jax knew nothing about her, she realized.

The door swung open, and Ellery, Beckett's paralegal, strolled in, her chunky Frankenstein boots squeaking on the tile floor.

"Hey, Joey," she said cheerfully. "I'd ask what's new, but I already know. So I'll just say congratulations."

Freaking Blue Moon and its freaking big mouth. "Thanks." Joey grimaced. "And before you say it, no, I'm *not* on a date with Jax. I didn't even know he was coming here. So don't you get any nosey BC ideas."

Ellery leaned into the mirror to tug at her long spider leg lashes. Her hair was in braided pigtails, and she was wearing the reddest lipstick Joey had ever seen. "Got it!" she said triumphantly. She held a single lash on her fingertip. "God, that thing's been driving me nuts since I glued these on."

She dunked her hands under the faucet. "Anyway, what were you saying? Oh, yeah, you and Jax." She laughed.

Joey frowned. "What's so funny?"

"Oh, it's nothing personal. It's just the idea of you and Jax dating. I know you probably get all kinds of pressure about it since you used to be all hot and heavy way back in high school, but I'm with you. You and Jax would be a huge mistake. I think you're smart to keep your distance."

"You expect me to believe you and your prying little group aren't plotting right now to march me down the aisle with Jax?"

Ellery's eyes widened until Joey couldn't see her charcoal gray eye shadow. "Absolutely not. We take our matchmaking very seriously." She laid a hand on her heart, her black finger-nails glittering under the fluorescent lights. "And part of that is recognizing who does and doesn't have potential for a long-lasting, happy relationship."

"And you're saying that Jax and I don't have that potential?"

"Exactly. And it's not like I'm saying anything you haven't already said a hundred thousand times. You're just too differ-ent. Besides, who knows how long Jax will decide to stick around this time? You're being smart protecting yourself and just staying friends."

"Then why did Anthony show up here four seconds after I sat down next to Jax at the bar?"

Ellery shrugged her shoulders in her pink skull cardigan. "Maybe he just wanted a Diet Coke?" Her eyes lit up. "Trust me. The BC already had a conversation when Jax moved back. You two just aren't meant to be. Now, Jax and Moon Beam Parker? I wouldn't be surprised if we start seeing sparks from those two."

"Jax and Moon Beam?" Joey felt her right eyelid start to twitch and pressed the palm of her hand over it.

"Don't jinx it." Ellery grinned. "It's in the early stages. Just imagine how nice it'll be to have Jax chasing someone else and finally giving you your space."

"Yeah. Nice."

"Well, I gotta go see a man about a basket of cheese fries. See ya around," Ellery said cheerily as she strolled out the door.

"Nice," Joey said again as the door closed. She stared grimly at her reflection, not liking the feeling of doom that settled in her belly.

Back at the bar, her spirits lifted slightly when she noticed Jax no longer had a newspaperman for a neighbor.

"Is Anthony still alive, or do we need to dig a shallow grave?" Joey asked.

"He'll live to write another day," Jax promised, his gaze fixed to her face. "What's wrong?"

Joey shrugged. "Nothing. Just hungry," she said, reaching for the burger she no longer had any appetite for.

"I can still tell when you're lying, Jojo," Jax warned her.

She looked him in the eye and took a big bite. "Starving," she said through a mouthful of meat and cheese and ketchup.

Jax shook his head and turned his attention to his plate. His knee pressed against her leg, the contact sending a zing through her veins.

"Do you do that on purpose?" Joey asked, dropping her burger on the plate.

"Do what?"

Joey looked down pointedly at their legs.

Jax grinned. "What do you think?"

"I think you do it on purpose to annoy me."

Jax swiveled on his stool, pinning her knees between his legs. His hands rested on her thighs. "Or maybe it's because I can't stand to be so close to you and not touch you. Maybe when I'm touching you, everything feels better for just a second until the next breath when I need more."

Joey's breath was caught in her throat.

"Does that answer your question?" he asked, his grip strong on her legs.

Joey wet her lips. "What do you think of Moon Beam Parker?"

12

———

*J*ax had no idea what to wear to a movie club night, so he went for a step above farm wear with a clean pair of jeans, a white button down, and a lightweight forest green sweater. He couldn't find his loafers, wasn't even sure if they'd made the trip from L.A., so he went with the pair of suede lace-up boots he'd gotten from Willa, the owner of Blue Moon Boots.

He grabbed his dark wool coat out of the hall closet and yelled a goodbye to Carter and Summer in the kitchen.

"We're not having sex this time," his brother yelled back. "You're allowed to come back."

Jax made a show of stomping down the hall covering his eyes.

"I am entering the kitchen," he shouted.

Carter beaned him with a dinner roll, and Summer muttered something about never living things down as she loaded plates into the dishwasher. Valentina's ears were visible over the island as she helped with the clean up by licking the dishes before they went into the washer.

"Sorry, Summer," Jax said, without a hint of contrition.

She shot him a frown.

"Is that your mom look? Because it's pretty fierce."

She brightened. "Really? Good. Because if these two monsters are anything like you and your brothers, I'm going to need all the weapons I can get."

Carter stepped up behind her and wrapped his arms around her, his hands resting on her belly. "Honey, the twins aren't going to stand a chance against us."

"Please. Have you seen your brother look at Aurora? He's lucky she's a sweetheart because she could set the house on fire and steal a car and run over some old ladies, and he'd be putty in her little hands. What if we have two adorable little girls, and you're so busy being wrapped around their little evil fingers that I'm the one who has to be the bad guy?"

"You could have two boys who are idiots and decide they want to see how deep the hay has to be in order to survive a jump out of the loft in the barn," Jax suggested.

"Oh my God. I hadn't thought of that. What if we have two boys who run around trying to murder each other?" Summer asked, spinning around in Carter's arms.

"We'll make your parents move in with us. Five adults against two kids."

Summer nodded as if actually considering it. "Okay. That's a good option. Good thinking." She leaned into her husband's chest. "I love that you're a problem solver."

Carter met Jax's gaze over Summer's blonde hair, and he slowly shook his head. Jax grinned and winked.

He took his Nova just to be sure his mother wouldn't insist on driving and he wouldn't have to puke before they got to the theater. They'd yet to have their first big snowfall of the season, so his rear wheel drive was fine for the night, and the car's beefy heater pushed out tropically warm air.

He wondered if Joey was going to the movie night. She hadn't said anything about it at dinner last night.

It had felt like a date, he thought with a smile. It was clear that the heat between them wasn't all just anger anymore. He had never had the patience that his father had. He was his mother's son in that aspect. The fact that he'd been willing to chip away at Joey's resistance for six months proved that she mattered. More than anything else that he'd wanted in this lifetime. He just hoped he wouldn't still be chipping away in ten years. The woman had the resolve of a steel girder, unbending, never wielding. And he loved her for it.

He just needed to keep chipping away. And maybe pay Ellery a visit to find out what she said to put the shadows in Joey's eyes last night.

Jax got to Phoebe's townhouse a few minutes early and let himself in the front door. Mr. Snuffles peeked around a cardboard box near the front door. His corkscrew tail wiggled when he spotted Jax and he trotted over on his stumpy little legs. He made a grunt of approval when Jax bent to pick him up.

"I see the snot is clearing up nicely," Jax said to the dog.

Mr. Snuffles grunted a happy reply.

There were half-packed boxes everywhere. Phoebe and Franklin had been in the process of moving in together for months now while their search for a house was ongoing. Now that they were building a place on the farm, it would take another six months or so. At this stage, he couldn't tell if she was in the process of packing or unpacking and decided not to mention it in case she tried to enlist his help.

Jax had moved around enough in his time on the West Coast that he kept his personal belongings to a minimum. The house he'd bought furnished, and he'd sell it the same way. He had no attachment to anything in it. He had a small storage locker with clothes, personal items, and files that he'd have shipped home when he returned next month.

Maybe it was time to start looking for his own place to live, he considered. Carter and Summer deserved to have the house to themselves with the babies on the way. And he was going to need his own space at some point. A garage. An office. A king-sized bed. He'd have to think about it.

He heard a thumping noise upstairs.

"Mom? You ready to go?" he called up. Mr. Snuffles wiggled in his arms, so he set the dog down in the kitchen.

There was no answer from Phoebe, but there was another thump. She was probably in her closet. Jax took the stairs lightly two at a time. "Mom?"

Her bedroom door was ajar.

"Hey, Mom, are we going or—"

"You're early!"

"Oh my God." Jax turned to run out of the room and tripped over a box in the hallway. He almost went head first down the carpeted stairs but managed to catch himself on the railing only skidding down two stairs on his stomach.

"Jax, honey, are you okay?" his mom called.

"Don't come out here! Not until you put some clothes on."

"Sorry about that, Jax. Didn't realize it was so late." Franklin peeked out of the bedroom. His lack of wardrobe was blatantly evident.

"Oh my God. Oh my God. Oh my God." Jax chanted his way down the stairs, carefully clutching the banister. He had rug burn on his forehead and probably his knees. But it was his eyes that burned with the image that would take more than therapy and drugs to erase.

"I'll be in the car," he yelled over his shoulder from the kitchen. As his stomach pitched, he decided he'd better settle it with a little snack. He found some cheese and lunch meat in the refrigerator and grabbed a few slices of both. Jax tossed a slice of ham to Mr. Snuffles, who looked thoroughly confused, before hightailing it to his car to eat and pretend what happened hadn't happened and wonder if he was the only one in Blue Moon not having sex.

His mother hurried out of the house a few minutes later. Her cheeks were pinker than the fuchsia turtleneck she now wore.

Phoebe gave him a shameful look and a few moments of blessed silence when she got in the car and Jax headed toward downtown.

"Here," she said finally. "I brought you this. I know you eat when you get upset."

Jax glanced over at the beef stick his mother was brandishing. "Mom, that's the least appropriate snack you could have found in this situation."

"Jax, listen, what you saw is very natural," Phoebe began.

He gagged.

"Oh, honey, are you car sick? I can drive if you want me to."

TAKE TWO'S parking lot had more than two-dozen cars in it by the time they pulled in. "How many people are in your movie group?" Jax asked his mother, still not able to look her in the eye... or in her general direction.

"Oh, just a few. Forty-six, I think? And the members can bring guests if they want. Shelby won't be here because she's working nights at the hospital this month."

"I thought this was just a little thing," Jax said, feeling the panic rise. "You *said* this was just a little thing."

Phoebe patted his leg, and Jax bolted out his door. "I know where that hand's been, Mom!"

"Pull it together, Jackson, and put your big boy underpants on. Your mother has a vibrant, exciting sex life. Get used to it."

Jax bent from the waist and dry heaved. "I think I might die from this."

Phoebe slapped the beef stick against his chest. "Eat this, and stop thinking about... what you're thinking about."

Jax straightened and took a deep breath of the frigid Blue Moon air. He ripped the plastic off the beef stick and took a bite.

"Better?"

"Nothing a case of beer or amnesia won't cure," Jax said weakly.

"That's the spirit. Now get in there and let me show off my genius son."

"You'll understand if I don't look at you, right?"

"Of course, sweetie."

It was worse than he thought. Phoebe led him past the concession stand before he could order a full-moon sized bucket of popcorn to settle his stomach, and before he knew it, he was being dragged up on stage where a lone chair sat front and center.

"I'm not sitting on the stage, Mom," he hissed.

"It's only so everyone can see you," she said, ignoring his resistance and marching him up the stairs onto the stage. "Clayton, do you have the mic?"

"Right here, Phoebe." A man built like a retired linebacker lumbered toward Jax. His spectacular fro temporarily blocked the stage lights. Clayton's wife, Lavender, a tiny daisy of a woman, waved at Jax from the front row.

"Hey, Clayton," Jax greeted him and waved at the man's wife. Clayton and Lavender Fullmer were the owners of Take Two and the parents of Grayson Moon, one of Jax's lacrosse teammates.

"Hey, there Jax. Thanks for coming out tonight. The sooner Frieda Blevins gives up her niece's selfie story, the better," Clayton whispered.

"That's what I hear." Jax let Clayton hook the lavalier mic to the collar of his sweater. "How's Grayson doing these days?"

Clayton's face split into a wide grin. "Kid's a literal rocket scientist. Can you believe that?"

"No shit?" Jax asked.

"No shit," Clay shook his head with pride. "He works for one of those private companies on the West Coast that's building private spacecraft. He loves it. He's marrying a mountain-climbing ER doctor named Aimee this summer. I said to Lav the other day, 'How did someone we created turn out so good?'"

"And what did Lavender say?"

"Dumb luck."

Jax laughed. "I don't know about that. From my recollection, you two were pretty good at the whole parenting thing."

"We did okay. And so did yours judging by how you three turned out," Clayton said, handing Jax the body pack.

Jax hooked it on his belt in the back. "I wouldn't go that far. I've got a ways to go to catch up to Carter and Beckett."

Clayton clapped a meaty hand on his shoulder. "Son, your mom's busting with pride tonight, and half of Blue Moon showed up here for you. It's okay to bask a little."

Jax shrugged it off. He told stories for a living. When you measured that against rocket science or family law or organic farming, it seemed a silly, useless profession. And it made him feel foolish for being on stage in front of all these people to show off something that really didn't matter in the grand scheme of things.

Sometimes he wished he wasn't so compelled to tell these stories. Wished that the characters weren't alive and busy in his head. Maybe someday, after he told enough of their stories, they'd leave him alone, and he could find work he could be proud of.

Rainbow Berkowicz, in her boxy bank president suit, took the stage with Ernest Washington. Ernest, sporting his trademark bandana, threw Jax a peace sign. "That Nova still working out for you?"

Jax nodded and grinned. While Ernest was at heart a true VW aficionado, he usually had a classic project car squirreled away on his car lot somewhere. Jax had bought his '68 Nova from Ernest his first week back home when he and Summer had gone on a Blue Moon-style shopping spree.

"Cool," Ernest said, rolling on the balls of his feet.

"Ready to get started, Jax?" Rainbow asked.

Ready for what, exactly? "Sure," he said with a confidence he didn't feel.

Rainbow turned on the mic she held and addressed the crowd. "Excuse me. If I could have your attention please." The crowd slowly quieted, and Jax took his first good look around the theater.

It felt like a sea of faces the size of Beckett's wedding audience, but this time they were all looking at him. He picked out a few friendly faces here and there. Jules from the juice place was there with her husband, Rob. Gia, Evan, and Ellery were splitting a box of candy a few rows back from the front. His mother was cozied up between Fitz, who was sporting a pair of glasses that made him look like an academic burnout, and Elvira Eustace. Mrs. McCafferty from McCafferty's Farm Supply on the square was looking chipper in overalls and a purple turtleneck in the front row.

"Thank you all for coming tonight. As most of you know, we'll be viewing *Awake in the Night*, which was written by our very own Jackson Pierce."

The applause was overzealous and a little embarrassing in his opinion, but Jax waved politely. *It would all be over soon, wouldn't it?*

"Jax, would you like to give us a synopsis of the film and maybe take a few questions before we start?" Rainbow suggested.

"Uh, sure," Jax said, his amplified voice bounced around the theater. He stood up, more comfortable on the move than sitting under the scrutiny. "I wrote *Awake in the Night* on spec while I was working as a production assistant after moving to L.A. I think I was a little homesick for Blue Moon, which is why I wanted to write about a small town.

"It's about a woman who married her high school sweetheart right out of school, started a family, bought a house. And she just wakes up in the middle of the night one night and starts wondering if she made the right choice. Her whole life is routine. She works Monday through Friday in a job she doesn't care about. Wednesdays are laundry. Thursdays are groceries. Kids have swim team and soccer practice. She and her husband haven't had a conversation about anything but the school pickups or the lawn mower in weeks. And every night, she wakes up and lays there, regretting and wondering."

Jax paused. "Am I going to ruin this for anyone if I keep going?"

People in the audience were shaking their heads.

"Really? You've *all* seen this? Raise your hand if you've seen *Awake in the Night.*"

He froze as nearly every person in the audience raised their hands. "You've all watched it?" He watched the audience nod enthusiastically as one.

"We had a viewing party when it came out," Lavender called from the front row. "Even had a red carpet rolled out!"

It sounded vaguely familiar to him. His mother had probably mentioned it, probably hoped he'd come home for it. He hadn't, though. Jax had been too busy writing the next project, chasing the next paycheck. Hoping to come home when he was finally worthy.

"Wow. Well, thank you for watching. Anyway, I guess, for the four people who didn't raise their hands, the main character Jenny decides she's going to do something when she wakes up in the middle of the night instead of just lie there and think. So that night she goes up into the attic and digs out her old painting supplies, and she starts painting. Every night she paints these huge, abstract canvases. She'd painted in high school, the same crazy, vibrant scenes, but her art teacher told her no one would buy them, that she would never make it as an artist if she couldn't make art that the world understood. So she gave it up. She got married, trained to be a bookkeeper, and tried to be someone that the world understood. And now she lies awake every night and wonders why she feels so empty."

Jax took a few steps to the other side of the stage, uneasy with the audience's rapt attention.

"Soon, she's waking up with paint-splattered skin and a smile. She stops trying to be early for school drop off, stops worrying about her job, she even stops seeing her husband as a schmuck."

The audience chuckled.

"By painting, Jenny starts to see the beauty in her world, and she slowly comes back to life. And that's, well, that's basically it." Jax ran a nervous hand through his hair and wondered when he'd had his last haircut.

A slim hand rose slowly from the middle section of seats.

"Uh, yes? You in the red." The woman in her forties came to her feet and smiled shyly. She wore her hair cut short with a sweep of bangs that fell at an angle across her forehead. Her cheery tunic matched the glow of her cheeks.

Rainbow marched the microphone over to her, and the woman bobbled it before recovering. "Um, hello."

"Hi," Jax said with a smile. It was nice to know he wasn't the only nervous one in the theater.

"I'm Cynthia, and I'm not from Blue Moon, but when I heard you'd be here tonight, I was so excited to come. I wanted you to know that your movie changed my life."

Jax blinked.

Cynthia smiled even brighter. "I was Jenny. My husband and I dated in high school, and the week after we graduated college, we got married. Kids happened right away, and it wasn't long before I stopped thinking my life was about me. It was about everyone else but me. And I could feel little pieces of myself slipping away. There was no time to do the things I'd always loved to do, the things that made me feel alive. I was too busy working or coaching basketball or cooking dinner or buying eight thousand kid birthday presents."

She took a breath and looked at him dead in the eye. "And then I went to the movies with a couple of girlfriends on a Mom's Night. We saw *Awake,* and I woke up.

"I stopped on my way home and bought a bottle of champagne, and that night, after the kids went to bed, I dragged my husband out on the deck, and we drank the entire bottle and talked. Really talked."

Her smile blossomed across her face. "The next day, I quit my job and cashed out my 401k. I bought the campground my grandparents used to take me to when I was a little girl, and now I spend every day outside in nature. And I don't feel lost or sad or tired anymore. Because you wrote that story. Because I realized I didn't have to change everyone else in my life to make me happy. I just had to remember who I was."

There was a moment of complete silence when Jax felt like it was just him and Cynthia in the room. The connection was so strong. Then someone started clapping, and he couldn't hear anything but applause. But he did see Cynthia mouth the words "thank you," her eyes shining brightly with tears.

He did the only thing he could think of. He got off the stage and met her in the aisle. Her hug calmed his troubled mind. Her long, strong arms squeezed him gently.

"Thank you," she whispered again, in his ear.

He shook his head. "No. Thank you." She had no idea what it meant to him to hear those words, and he had no way to tell her.

Rainbow confiscated the microphone again. "Does anyone else have any questions for Jax before we show the film?"

Hands shot up around the theater, and Jax laughed. "Okay, we'll start over here."

THAT NIGHT, Jax lay in bed staring at his ceiling. His thoughts swirling in his head. There'd been questions and confessions after Cynthia's. Julia's husband Rob announced that after seeing *Awake,* he'd made a point to start talking to Julia about more than juice and babies. Mrs. Nordemann said the movie had inspired her to start writing and publishing erotic short stories.

And then there were the questions.

"Was Jenny based on Joey?"

He'd answered as vaguely as he could. Of course Jenny was Joey and that screenplay was him working through his feelings of leaving her. He'd started it with the intention of convincing himself that Joey would have been full of regret had she tied herself to him so young. But something had changed as Jenny had blossomed in his head. And the deeper he went, the more he realized that Jenny's problem wasn't her situation, it was her priorities.

He couldn't imagine Joey ever losing herself in a marriage or a job or parenthood. Joey was a woman who understood what was important to her. She was so much stronger than he realized when they were together. He'd nearly killed her and then abandoned her without a goodbye—which seemed to be the part that she wasn't willing to forgive—and Joey had picked herself up and built herself a life without him.

He thought about Cynthia's confession. A story he'd told had made a difference to someone. Made *the* difference. Something he created had resonated so deeply with a stranger that she'd changed her life because of it. That's what it was all about, wasn't it?

Mattering. Connecting. Resonating.

13

———

*J*ax spent the morning riding Calypso and then Apollo and generally getting in Joey's way. When he was completely satisfied in his investment of ridiculously perfect horses, Jax decided to pay a little visit to Ellery at Beckett's office and see what scheme she was up to.

"Hey, Jax! You here to see Beckett?" Ellery greeted him when he walked into his brother's law office. She had her dark hair pinned back in a tight bun at the base of her neck. Her choker necklace was made out of sterling silver links shaped like cats.

"I'm actually here to see you. Do you have a minute?"

"Sure! Can I get you something to drink?" she offered.

"I'll take some coffee if you have any made."

"Black, right?"

"Yeah, thanks."

Ellery bustled off to dig up a mug, and Jax shoved his hands in his pockets and wandered around the room. In many ways, it was the quintessential small-town law office. Hefty leather-bound books lined the built-in shelves, and impressive framed documents proclaimed Beckett a law school graduate, an attorney, and mayor.

But Jax could pick out small pieces of personality here and there. There was the crayon drawing Aurora had done when they'd moved from the guesthouse into the big house, as she called it. Stick-figure Beckett had a huge orange smile on his lopsided globe of a face and was holding stick hands with a lumpy stick Gia and a short, round stick Aurora. Presumably the purple blob on Gia's other side was Evan. Beckett had the drawing framed like it was a Manet. It hung on the wall next to his wedding announcement and a *Monthly Moon* clipping about Evan's debate team.

Ellery returned with a steaming mug.

"Here you go. What can I do for you?"

"I was just curious about something. Joey mentioned she talked to you at Shorty's the other night."

Ellery's smile widened to a grin, and she returned to sit behind her desk. "Did she now?"

"I'm a little curious about what you told her. She seemed a bit upset when she came back."

"Oh, sure. I told her you'd make a terrible couple and that we were working on matching you with Moon Beam."

Jax sank into her visitor's chair and pressed his fingers to his eyeballs, hoping to keep them in his head and not strangle Ellery's pretty little neck.

"Why in the holy hell would you tell her that? Are you trying to ruin my chances with her?"

Ellery steepled her fingertips. "Jax, Jax, Jax." She shook her head as if she was deeply disappointed with him. "First, let me make it very clear that I have no interest in you filling my house or your brother's office with fertilizer. Very creative threat, by the way. Anthony was shaking in his sneakers when I caught up with him outside."

"Thanks."

"Let's speak hypothetically, shall we?"

"By all means," Jax said, morosely sipping his coffee.

"Let's say that, hypothetically, I have a five-year-old daughter."

"Congratulations."

"Thank you. Now let's say she's incredibly stubborn. Like brick wall stubborn."

"Uh-huh."

"She wants what she wants, and nothing you can say can change her mind because everything has to be her idea. She wants chocolate for lunch, but you want her to eat broccoli."

"Okay."

"Even though broccoli is clearly good for her and is definitely the right choice, do you think shoving broccoli in her face and telling her it's good for her is going to make her want to eat broccoli?"

"Um. No?"

Ellery broke into a broad smile. "Exactly. She's going to throw up roadblocks left and right when it comes to broccoli. But what happens if you tell Miss Stubborn that she absolutely can't have broccoli. Ever."

A slow grin spread across Jax's face. "Then maybe she decides she can't live without broccoli."

"Exactly," Ellery said proudly.

"That's a pretty high-risk strategy, even for the Beautification Committee. How'd you come up with that?"

Ellery reached into her desk drawer and pulled out a textbook. She held it up.

"*The Psychology of Love*," Jax read.

"We're taking online courses to help us become more efficient at matchmaking."

"So the BC does want us together?" Jax clarified.

"Duh, Jax." Ellery rolled her cat-lined eyes. "There've never been two people more destined to be together than you and Joey. So don't screw it up this time or I swear to God we really will make you Moon Beam's third husband," she said, pointing a sharp fingernail at him.

"You're a diabolical woman, Ellery."

"Yep. You want to see Beckett now since you're here?"

Jax looked pained for a moment. "Can you do me a huge favor and please make sure he's wearing pants before I go in?"

"Pants?"

"Trust me. I've had some bad experiences lately."

BECKETT WAS INDEED WEARING pants and frowning fiercely at his monitor when Jax walked in his office.

"What's with the face? Gia breaking your spirit?"

Beckett's expression transformed at the mention of his wife's name. Geez, his brothers had turned into grinning idiots over their women. But Jax couldn't blame them. If he had Joey to go home to every night, he'd have the same stupid smile on his face as Beckett did right now.

His brother swiveled away from the screen and kicked back in his chair. "No, just a custody agreement that's headed toward battle."

"That sucks."

Beckett nodded. "Yeah, it's the kids that pay the price. Anyway, what brings you by?"

"I was interrogating Ellery on why she told Joey we'd be making a huge mistake by getting back together."

Beckett's eyebrows winged up. "Ellery? Beautification Committee Ellery with the cunning and the strategy?"

"The same. Apparently she's even more cunning than we

thought. She's reverse psychologizing Joey by telling her she can't have me. The BC is hoping she'll give them the middle finger and run to my arms."

Beckett nodded in approval. "Damn. They did their homework this time."

"Literally. They're taking psychology classes."

Beckett laughed. "You realize you're the first Pierce to embrace what they do."

"Anything that gets me back in Joey's good graces." Jax shrugged. "Besides, it seems to have worked out just fine for you and Carter."

Beckett straightened his tie and grinned.

"Will you please wipe that afternoon delight grin off your face?"

"I don't know what you're talking about," Beckett said, his smile edging toward shit-eating.

"Everyone in this town is getting laid but me." Jax lamented, putting his face in his hands.

"I highly doubt that."

"I walked in on Carter and Summer getting it on in the kitchen on the freaking island. And then last night...Well, I don't even want to talk about last night."

"What? Were they doing it in the living room?"

Jax shook his head. "Worse. So much worse. It wasn't them." His stomach pitched a little. "It was Mom and Frank—"

"Nope! Nope!" Beckett covered his ears. "If you try to finish that sentence, I will murder you and feed you to Diesel," he yelled.

"I went to Mom's place to pick her up, and she wasn't downstairs," Jax continued, oblivious to his brother's threats.

Beckett jumped out of his seat, hands clutching his ears. "I can't hear you! I'm not listening!"

"I thought she was in the closet. But she wasn't. She was on the bed."

Beckett tripped over his trashcan and gagged.

"They were..." Jax gulped, caught in the endless loop of horror in his head. "Naked. And her leg was like—"

The blow from Beckett's fist to his face surprised him more than stunned him. Jax shook his head.

"Wow. Thanks, man," he said, rubbing his jaw.

Beckett laid a hand on his shoulder. "Anytime. Listen, we're both just going to forget everything you just said. Forget it. Bury it. Lock it up and never let it out."

Jax nodded. "Okay. Yeah. That sounds good."

Beckett stabbed a button on his phone. "Ellery? Can you bring two scotches in here?"

"Regular pour or Buchanan pour?"

Beckett glanced at Jax before answering. "Buchanan pour, definitely."

"Are they still showing up here for 'counseling'?" Jax asked. The Buchanans were the couple who held the longest record for being on the marital rocks in Blue Moon history. They'd been on the verge of divorce since marrying twenty-two years ago. The couple came to Beckett every six months or so to work on a new divorce agreement that usually ended in a reconciliation for them and a two-day migraine for Beckett.

"They were here last week and couldn't decide who should get the kayaks, so they decided to stay together until next fall after kayaking season is over."

Ellery bustled in with a tray. She set it down on the desk and distributed the glasses. "I also brought you cookies since you're both emotional eaters."

"Thanks, Ellery," Jax said, shoving an oatmeal raisin in his mouth.

"Thank you." Beckett nodded, reaching for the scotch like it was a life preserver and he was on the *Titanic*.

Ellery flashed them a smile and shut the doors behind her.

"So..." Jax said, finally reaching for the scotch.

"I don't know what to talk about besides the horrifying elephant you brought into the room," Beckett admitted.

"How about this? I'm thinking about getting my own place."

"You'd be smart to do that before the twins arrive. Otherwise you'll end up getting penciled in on the night feeding shifts."

"I was thinking more along the lines of making room in the house for Summer's parents who are probably going to want to visit for a while. But you make an excellent point."

"Our guest house is open if you're interested," Beckett offered. He had a two-bedroom guest house in his backyard that recently became vacant after he married the last tenant.

"I'd rather be closer to the farm, if possible, but I may have a potential tenant for you if you're interested in renting it out again," Jax told his brother.

"It would have to be the perfect tenant," Beckett said, sipping his scotch. "I don't want to have any weirdos in the backyard with the kids and Gia here."

"Ever think that this is a town full of weirdos?"

"Yeah, but we're the harmless kind of weirdos. We're charming in our weirdness."

"I'll let you know about the tenant if it works out. I don't think you'll have any complaints."

Beckett nodded and studied his glass. "So... Carter and Summer in the kitchen? Are they even allowed to be doing that?"

∽

AFTER SOME CONVERSATION that didn't involve their mother's sex life, Beckett had to prepare for a conference call, and Jax decided that while he was there, he'd pay a visit to Gia. There was something he'd been meaning to bring up to her, and now seemed like as good a time as any.

He headed through the door in Beckett's office that connected with the rambling Victorian's main living room. Beckett said Gia would be between yoga classes and probably working on the studio financials that he'd reminded her about for the third time that morning.

Jax found her in the parlor on the other side of the house. His sister-in-law wasn't working on bookkeeping. She was curled up on the sofa with the puppy snoring in a ball against her and Tripod, the three-legged cat, napping on her shoulder.

The click from his phone's camera as he captured the cozy scene woke her.

"Crap," she muttered sleepily.

Diesel wiggled a little closer and rolled over, exposing his round belly.

"Busted."

"Don't you dare tell your brother that I love these fur monsters," she warned him, slowly working her way into a seated position. Tripod clung to her shoulder until the last possible second before jumping to the floor and looking annoyed. "Or that I was napping instead of working on those stupid financials. That's what we have an accountant for."

Jax laughed. "You have couch face," he said pointing to her cheek that had the imprint of nap and pillow.

"Ugh!" Gia got up and scrubbed at her face. "I usually don't sneak naps this long."

"But you had an exerting lunch break," Jax supplied.

She shot him a dark look. "Your brother has a big mouth."

"No. He just has a satisfied look on his face. Like all the time."

Gia fought her smile. "Well, when you and Joey finally get over history, you can disgust us with your sex life."

That thought cheered him considerably. "I like your optimism."

"It's one of my finer qualities," she agreed. "Do you want anything to eat or drink? I always need a post-nap snack."

"I just had scotch and cookies with Beckett."

"Scotch and cookies?"

"I upset him with a gruesome story about Mom's sex life."

"Oh boy. I guess it'll be lasagna tonight for comfort food. Also, go Phoebe and Dad!"

Jax shook his head. *Women processed things in very different ways than men*, he decided.

"How about we split a PB and J?" Gia offered.

"Perfect," he said, following her through the dining room back to the kitchen. At home here as he was at Carter's, Jax pulled the bread and peanut butter—organic, of course—out of the pantry.

Gia danced around the kitchen barefoot, collecting plates and jelly. She was dressed in yoga pants and a long-sleeved tunic t-shirt. Her explosion of red curls was tamed into a knot on the top of her head. It was her trademark winter outfit. In the summer, she'd trade it in for stretchy shorts and flowy tanks. It still cracked him up that Beckett had fallen for a hippie yoga instructor rather than one of the slick, upmarket women he'd always dated.

"You look like you've got something on your mind," she said, her wide green eyes searching his face.

"A couple of things. Tell me about Emma."

"Emma? Why? You aren't giving up on Joey, are you?" Gia gasped.

"Not in this lifetime." Jax gave a little half smile. "How happy is your sister in L.A.?"

Gia frowned, considering. "You know, I wouldn't say happy. I'd say comfortable."

"Think she'd be interested in making a change?"

"Like what—Oh my God! The brewery!" Gia grabbed his arms in a surprisingly strong grip for someone so petite. "Have Emma move here and manage it! You're a freaking genius!"

Jax laughed. "It would give me a lot more time to chase Joey if I wasn't babysitting that place all the time. She'd help us grow it, guide us into catering and weddings. Plus, you'd have a sister and Franklin would have another daughter in town."

"I could make out with your face right now," Gia announced.

Jax held up his hands and laughed. "Whoa there. There's a code. No making out with another brother's woman."

He saw a flicker in her eyes. "What?" he asked. "Are you disappointed you can't make out with my face?"

The flicker was gone as quickly as it had come. "That must be it," she said lightly before scooping an obscene amount of jelly on the bread.

"Anyway, keep it quiet about your sister. I'd like to talk to her before I get Carter and Beckett excited about the possibility."

"My lips are sealed," Gia said, sliding half a sandwich toward him. "But, if you can make this happen, my dad and I will be really, really grateful."

"Grateful enough to make me a lasagna?"

"Every month for the rest of your life."

14

Jax filled a pint glass of the thick, black stout with one hand while searching frantically for a second clean glass with his other.

The bar of the brewery was hopping, and the tables were already filling up with the dinner crowd. He would have been pleased had it not been for the fact that his bartender called in sick and one of the cooks was a no-show. And then, due to an issue with the supply company, they'd had to eighty-six the wings and pulled pork.

Everyone on staff was pulling double duty.

Jax was manning the bar and trying to help at the host stand. The servers were taking turns expoing food between waiting tables. He'd left a panicked voicemail for his mother but drew the line at calling either of his brothers. They'd each taken a turn this week playing manager on duty. Plus, he didn't want to hear their taunts about 'poor baby Hollywood' who can't handle the dinner shift.

If the orderly Beckett were here, he'd try to organize the chaos instead of moving with it. Diners would wait for an hour for their appetizers. And Carter would do his best until he had enough, and then he'd sneak out for some peace and quiet.

Nope. Tonight it was up to him. Keeping the staff on task, keeping the customers happy. Oh, yeah, and this was the night he was supposed to finish up the draft of the script that had been hanging in limbo for eight months. Now that the studio had locked in a new hotshot director, it was suddenly imperative that he finish the script.

Two more customers sat down at the bar, and Jax wanted to just pour himself a shot and join them. Instead, he tossed them menus and grabbed the phone that had been ringing incessantly for the last hour.

"Yeah? What? I mean, John Pierce Brews," Jax answered.

"Jax? You sound like you're running a marathon," his mother chirped.

"Mom, I will go to every fucking Movie Club meeting from now on if you can get in here and help. I'm drowning."

"Be there in fifteen." Phoebe hung up without another word, and Jax sent up a prayer of thanks for family. She might take special enjoyment in torturing him, but when backs were to the wall, Phoebe Pierce would ride into battle for her boys.

Sunny, a waitress barely old enough to buy her own beer, hustled around the corner and flung a burger and fries at him.

"Order up for Pete."

Jax stared down at the plate. "No onions. It's supposed to have no onions," Jax yelled over the noise.

Sunny slapped the ticket on the bar. "Your fingers were on the wrong keys in the POS. Says MP PMOMD."

"Fuck," Jax muttered. He spun around and dumped the plate in front of Pete McDougall, the flannel-wearing proprietor of Karma Kustard. "Two choices, Pete. You can pick off the onions, or I can."

Pete wisely chose to see to the chore himself.

"You've earned yourself a free beer," Jax told him.

Pete whooped and sank his teeth into his newly onion-less burger.

Jax tossed a dozen glasses in the rotating washer and hustled to the far end of the bar. Of course everyone down there needed another round. At least they were entertaining themselves.

He found a stash of clean glasses behind the bar and started pouring drafts. Jax was thankful that in a brewery, the clientele was more likely to order beers than mixed drinks. He could handle a rum and coke or vodka rocks but was dreading the day some smart ass asked for a cosmo. His cell phone buzzed next to the register. It was a call from Al. She'd called three times in the last two days. He knew he was making her more nervous by not answering, but it wasn't really an option now.

He felt a zap of electricity shoot up his spine. An awareness of presence.

Joey.

He turned around and spotted her sliding onto a stool at the corner of the bar. She looked entirely too good. Her hair was loose, framing her delicate oval face in chestnut waves. There was color on her high cheekbones, probably flushed from the winter wind.

Thick lashes accented eyes the color of cognac. She wore a simple ribbed sweater with a v-neck deep enough to be interesting.

But he didn't have time for interesting. Not with Fred and Phil waving him down for another round and the bar printer spitting out a continuous stream of drink orders from the servers. He was also pretty sure he smelled smoke, which meant someone's entrée was going to be a while longer. Or the whole place was going up in flames.

"I don't have time to go a few rounds with you right now," he snapped at Joey.

He dove for the taps as the printer spat out another order. The tape now reached down to the floor.

"You look a little understaffed," Joey observed.

"You think?" He didn't have time to deal with her smart-ass observations from her smart-ass, sexy-as-hell mouth. "'Cause this feels like a walk in the damn park to me."

"Jax, we got a problem," Sunny said, rushing up to the bar, bringing a stronger waft of smoke with her. His cell phone rang again.

"Oh for fuck's sake! How do you make a Sex on the Beach?" he muttered staring at the six-foot tape of drink orders.

Joey slid off her stool and slipped behind the bar. Jax caught a whiff of her shampoo as she brushed past him.

"What the hell are you doing?" he snapped.

"Showing you how it's done. What's your login for the POS?" she asked, jerking a thumb toward the register's touch screen.

"Hey, Joey, can we get a round down here?" Bruce Oakleigh called, waving an empty wine glass.

"Who comes to a brewery and orders wine?" Joey muttered to Jax.

"Bruce does."

"Keep your pants on, Bruce, and I'll throw in a dish of maraschino cherries," Joey said good-naturedly. Login?" She arched an expectant eyebrow at Jax.

Fine. The night was destined to be a disaster anyway. What did it matter if the kitchen caught fire and people were walking out on tabs? No one would ever come back to John Pierce Brews after tonight.

He scrawled his login code on a napkin and abandoned

the bar and Joey to follow Sunny into the kitchen where his first order of business was putting out a fire on the grill.

"It says well done, Julio, not meteoric."

The cook flashed a gold tooth at Jax. "I aim to please."

Lila, one of the dining room servers, ducked her head under the heat lamps. "Jax, we need an expo to get us back on track," she said, waving at the window overflowing with food. "Then I need some discounts for some disgruntleds."

"Anyone walk out yet?"

"Staff or customers?" she asked, loading up a tray of meat-loaf and burgers.

"Both. Either," Jax said morosely.

"Still got everyone, but some complimentary desserts and table touching will go a long way."

"The cream ale ready yet?" Julio asked.

"Kegged and ready to go. We're releasing it next weekend."

"You could do a free preview tonight. Send out samplers to the tables," he suggested.

"You're a genius, Julio."

"That's what they tell me," the cook said, turning back to the grill, his dark hair tied back in a stumpy ponytail.

"I'll hook up the cream and tell Joey," Lila volunteered. "And if you're in the mood to give things away, a round of drinks and a big, fat thank you might go far with the staff tonight."

"Consider it done," Jax said.

Lila winked at Julio and danced out of the kitchen, tray laden with steaming hot entrees.

Jax worked furiously, traying up food, hopping on the line to help Julio and Nan on the grill and fryers. He became an expert in building side salads and dropping fries. He kept an ear out for sounds of unrest from the bar, but the chaos in the kitchen kept his full attention.

He was covered in sweat and nursing a deep fryer burn when Joey poked her head around the corner.

"Need a shit load of clean glasses and a new keg of lager. And Al said if you don't get a draft to her by Sunday, she's going to fly out here and slap you upside the head," she announced before disappearing again.

Jax blinked. Joey didn't look panicked or pissed off, and she'd had time to answer his phone, which meant things must have quieted down out front.

He hurried down the back stairs to the key room. The cooler felt like heaven to his overheated body. His comfortable Henley had seemed like the logical choice on a ball-freezing January night. But between the heat lamps, the grill, and the ten miles he must have sprinted so far tonight, he was wishing for gym shorts and a t-shirt.

Jax unhooked the kicked keg and tapped a fresh one. He reminded himself to take a look at the sales numbers tonight. After the chaos, of course.

What had he been thinking opening a brewery? he wondered. Those visions of sampling beers and arguing with his brothers at the bar seemed like a naïve fantasy compared to the reality of actually running a bar and restaurant.

Jax skirted the expo line and grabbed a tray of clean glasses before swinging back around to the front of the house. Maybe if things had slowed down enough out front, he could talk Joey into grabbing a bite with him. He wanted to know how things were going at the stables with the new additions and partnership.

It was another naïve fantasy. Jax bobbled the tray when he was greeted with the mob scene. Joey had ditched her sexy little sweater and had stripped down to a slinky black tank. She'd pulled those dark brown waves back into a high ponytail. Pulling pints and laughing, she looked like every man's fantasy.

It was three-deep at the bar. Jax set the tray down hard enough to have the glasses tremble, but no one noticed him.

"Okay, on three," Joey yelled over the noise.

The bar counted down with her as she ticked off the numbers on her fingers overhead.

"Three, two, one—"

Everyone made grabs for the shallow bowls Joey had spaced out at intervals on the bar.

Jax peeked in the bowl closest to him. Maraschino cherries.

"Cherry stem tying contest," Wilson Abramovich announced at his elbow. Wilson, Blue Moon's jeweler and loyal Beautification Committee member, was grinning at his wife Penny as she contorted her face in a valiant effort to win.

"Don't get too creative there, Phil," Joey yelled to one-half of the newlywed couple as she poured two drafts simultaneously. "I don't wanna have to give you the Heimlich." The bar roared with laughter.

Joey reached for the tape the printer spat out, and Jax watched her catch Lila's eye from the service bar. She made a slicing hand over her neck. Cutting someone off apparently.

Joey glanced in Jax's direction. "Care to try your *tongue*, boss?"

"Ohhh," the crowd cheered at the challenge.

Jax leaned in close enough that he could tell Joey wanted to back up.

"You already know the things I can do with my tongue, Jojo."

Another woman would have blushed or slapped him, but not Joey. She took it as a challenge.

She held out the bowl of cherries to him. "Race ya."

As if he could say no to the laughter in those eyes or that cocky-as-hell grin. No, he'd always been in over his head when it came to Joey Greer.

Wordlessly, he plucked a cherry out of the bowl and, with his gaze never leaving Joey's face, popped it into his mouth. One bite and the sweet juice tickled his taste buds. But there was something even sweeter he wanted to taste.

Her.

As if reading his mind, Joey leisurely fished a cherry out of the bowl.

"You'd better hurry up, Joey," Mrs. Penskee from the animal rescue warned from the middle of the bar.

"I'm giving him a handicap since he can't keep up," she said with a wink, inciting another round of "Ooohs."

Joey brought the cherry to her lips, parting them just enough that Jax and every other man in the bar leaned forward in anticipation. Jax briefly forgot what he was doing with the cherry stem and nearly choked on it.

She knew exactly what she was doing, but that did nothing to slow the southern migration of his blood.

Holding the stem, Joey popped the cherry into her mouth, and Jax felt his cock turn to stone.

She gave him a feline grin. "Get ready."

If he were any readier, he'd drag her down to the beer-soaked floor and tear off her clothes.

Joey popped the stem into her mouth, reminding Jax that his tongue had its own business besides panting after her. He'd just bent the stem in a V when Joey hooted triumphantly. One end of the stem poked through her lips.

"No freaking way," Jax challenged.

"Bet me," she said, the tip of the stem moving hypnotically between her full, pink lips.

"A hundred bucks," he heard himself say, knowing he'd already lost.

"Deal."

"C'mon and show us," Jax said, gesturing at the crowd.

Someone started a drumroll and others joined in.

"Come see for yourself." It was a taunt, and he took advantage of it. Jax closed the gap between them, but rather than using his fingers to pluck the stem from her lips, he used something more fun.

His open mouth settled on her full, ripe lips for just a second. Long enough for the crowd to erupt and his dick to get impossibly harder.

His teeth scraped her lips as they closed over the stem and drew it out of her mouth, a perfect knot intact.

He didn't hear the hoots and hollers of his neighbors and friends. Didn't see the cell phones recording the moment or the looks of interest that passed between customers.

All he saw was the fire in Joey's eyes. Unpredictable, that fire was. He stayed close so she couldn't swing hard with her fist should she decide to react that way.

But she didn't hit him. She held out her hand, palm up. Cocky as a quarterback after a game-winning touchdown.

"I believe you owe me a hundred bucks."

He owed her more than that. Jax took the cherry stem out of his mouth and fished out his wallet. He made a show of counting out the bills to the delight of the crowd.

He dropped the money into her waiting hand and watched her count it. Satisfied, she held up the cash. "Next round's on Jax," she called, sauntering away to applause. God, she was something. The girl of his dreams, the source of his torment. She was everything he wanted in this lifetime.

"Ooh! A cherry stem tying contest? Let me try."

His mother's voice had the effect on his fantasies of the arm of a record player yanked off vinyl.

"Geez, Mom. When did you get here?"

Phoebe wore a chunky knit poncho the color of persimmons over dark, slim jeans. She winked at him. "I've been here about an hour. I took over hosting duties, and you're paying me in wine," she said wiggling an empty wine glass and heading toward Joey.

Franklin bustled in from the dining room a tub full of dirty dishes in his hands and a cheerful grin on his face. "Good crowd tonight, Jax," he said as he headed into the kitchen.

"Where do you want us, Hollywood?"

Beckett slapped him on his shoulder. Carter was behind him, directing Summer to a table of Gia's yoga students with strict instructions to sit her ass down and relax. Gia was answering the phone at the host stand while Evan and Aurora wiped down menus.

"Hi, Jazz!" Aurora waved cheerfully.

"What are you guys doing here?" Jax asked.

"We're here for dinner," Carter grinned.

"You might be waiting until breakfast to get it."

Carter tossed an arm over his shoulders. "Just look at this place."

They did. Dozens of Mooners spending their Friday night in a place they built, enjoying themselves with beers they brewed. Lila dashed past a notebook full of new orders, and Joey called out a greeting to customers coming through the door behind them. Phoebe, wine glass refilled, was turning over tables like it was her super power.

He felt a little tickle in his throat. This was home and heart. People he'd known his whole life showing up just to support his family. And his family showing up without needing to be asked to lend a hand, break a sweat, and make sure that someone's dream came true.

In this moment, he loved them all, fiercely.

This is where he was supposed to be.

"Maybe this wasn't the shittiest idea in the world," Beckett said, pride evident on his face.

"This might actually work," Jax agreed.

"I'll table touch," Beckett volunteered.

"I'll expo," Carter decided.

"I'll bar back," Jax said with a slow grin. And the three went their separate ways to make it all work.

15

___

It was an hour before his brothers and their families could eat and another half an hour after that before Phoebe dragged him out of the kitchen and threw a bowl of chili in front of him.

"Take a break. Eat," she ordered.

Wearily, Jax sank down on the chair. A beer appeared at his elbow, dropped off by a smiling Sunny. "Making bank tonight." She winked, patting her tip stash through the apron pocket.

Phoebe took the seat across from him and smiled expectantly.

Jax picked up the soup spoon and dug in. "What?"

"What the hell are you doing, Jax?"

The bite of chili lodged in his throat, and he coughed until he could breathe again. "I'm trying to eat chili, Mom."

"You know what I mean. Don't play dumb with me."

"You're going to have to be more specific."

"How about I tell you what I see with my all-seeing mother's eyes, and then you tell me what's really going on?" Phoebe suggested. "I see you pushing yourself to exhaustion between the farm, this place, and your writing. Not to mention chasing that lovely young woman behind the bar. You're putting down roots, but you're digging them so fast and deep you're running yourself ragged. So I ask myself 'what are you trying to prove and to who?'" She frowned. "Whom? Damn it."

Jax twirled his glass on the table.

"Did Dad ever feel like he wasn't good enough?"

Phoebe blinked and then laughed. "Every damn day."

"Be serious now," Jax sighed.

"I am being serious. Your father always wondered if he was doing the best he could as a farmer, a father, heck, even a husband some days."

Jax shook his head. "That's ridiculous. He was the best at everything."

"Kiddo, that's part of being an adult. Holding up a mirror to yourself and seeing those glorious flaws."

"Dad didn't have flaws."

Phoebe shot him a look. "I think you meant to say 'my stunningly beautiful genius of a mother doesn't have flaws.'"

Jax cracked a grin. "That's definitely what I meant to say. Even though you are a deeply, beautifully flawed human being."

"Takes one to know one." She stuck her tongue out at him, her nose scrunching behind her glasses, and he loved her just a little bit more because of it.

"Very mature, Mother."

She laughed and took his hand.

"I just want to be as good as Dad," he admitted quietly. "I don't want to be a screw-up anymore."

"Sweetie, you've never been a screw-up. Mule-headed, sure. Too adventurous for your own good, absolutely. But your father and I never, ever looked at you like a screw-up."

"Come on, Mom. What about after the accident?"

"Which accident? The one where Carter backed your grandfather's truck through the garage door? Or the time Beckett's car ended up buried in Carson's cornfield because he tried to spin a donut in the snow to impress Moon Beam Parker?"

"*The* accident, Mom. The Joey's-in-the-hospital-unconscious accident."

"It was a deer, you idiot." Phoebe squeezed his hand. "Don't carry that around with you because one of God's creatures decided to a cross a road that you happened to be using. And don't try to turn that into some kind of martyrdom where you don't deserve to be happy until you've accomplished this or made up for that."

Jax stirred the chili.

Phoebe laid a hand on his arm. "If we waited to go for something until we feel worthy, no one would ever do anything."

"But if I can make a go of this place—"

"If you can, you can. If you can't, you'll do something else. That's what life is all about. Living. Trying. Loving."

His gaze darted to Joey behind the bar, working the taps and the crowd like a pro.

"You're good enough as is. And I don't care if someone ever told you different," Phoebe said stubbornly.

Jax eyed up his mother. *She couldn't know, could she? After all these years, could she have known the reason he left?*

"You're good enough just by being born. So stop trying to prove yourself by working yourself into exhaustion trying to be eight different people and work twenty hours a day. Do what you want to do, not what you think you have to do."

"Do you think Dad would be proud of me now?"

His mother looked legitimately shocked. "What in blue Heaven would ever make you think he wasn't?"

"I write words on a screen. What's so great about that? Dad fed people and rescued animals. He raised a family. He was always there whenever anyone needed him. I ran away."

"Being sent away is different than running away."

She did know. Son of a bitch. All these years, he thought it was a secret between him and his father. "I still had the choice, and I made it."

Phoebe's smile was a little sad. "Oh, kiddo, you're a lot more like him than you know." She pulled a large yellow envelope out of a purse big enough to hold groceries and slid it across the table to him.

"What's this?"

"Something of your father's that I found while I was packing and organizing. It's yours now." She pushed her chair back from the table and stood. "You take a little break, and I'm going to go find my handsome fiancé and talk him into splitting a piece of that Irish cream cheesecake with me." She dropped a kiss on his head. "Don't ever let anyone make you feel less than, and that includes yourself," she ordered, before heading off in search of Franklin.

Jax stared at the worn and battered envelope. A red string closure kept its secrets secure.

He carefully unwound the string and pulled out a thick stack of papers.

Jax held his breath, paging through the top of the stack. Dozens of short stories written by his father. A man he'd never seen turn on the family computer, much less sit down to type something out.

There were stories about the farm, his brothers, his mother. One in particular caught his eye.

A Mid-Summer Night's Splash
   By John Pierce

July in Blue Moon Bend means painting the landscape with humidity thick as a wet blanket. The sun cracks the earth, sending shimmers of mirages dancing along the horizon. It means the kids are already a month into summer vacation and singing a chorus of "I'm boreds" and "Do I have tos?" To the farmer, it means we spend the month holding our collective breath for rain, in the right amounts and the right times.

It was a hard July. We were slipping past the "It would be nice to have a good rain" conversations into desperate times. Another week without a good, soaking rain, and we'd all start to lose crops.

I'd spent the day in the fields with varying degrees of participation from the boys as we coaxed, cajoled, and then threatened the irrigation into working order. The days were all long, sweltering, and edging toward hopeless.

All the work of the spring could be dried up and murdered at the whim of Mother Nature. One storm can change the entire growing season. Now, I'm not a worrier by design. I've found if you've done your job as well as you can, when it's time to hand over your work to the next person, the next stage, there's no room for worrying about the outcome.

But this afternoon, my back against the oak overlooking the trickle that used to be a creek, I felt the tiniest parade of What Ifs arise.

What if the rain never came? What if we lost all the crops? What if the farm failed?

Who would I be if not a farmer?

The buzz of the locusts and the waterfall of sweat between my shoulder blades brought me back, and I shook it off. I returned to the fields like a soldier marching into battle. No time for worry. There was only room for work.

The boys had disappeared under the pretense of a drink break, but it wasn't long before I heard the shrieks and threats and the unmistakable sound of a garden hose wielded as a weapon.

For a moment, the thing I wanted most in the world was to join in their water war. But the work was calling. The responsibility of an uncertain future needed to be fed my best effort.

I worked late, taking a sandwich in the barn for dinner while I greased the sprayer for the next day. Phoebe had put the boys to work weeding in the garden for an hour before letting them scatter to their summer night childhoods. Freedom of the best kind.

I was pretending to read in bed after midnight while cursing myself for telling Phoebe air conditioning in the house could wait until next summer when I heard the suspicious sound of silence. It was followed by the more suspicious sound of bedroom doors shutting quietly and footsteps avoiding the squeaky floorboards.

I waited until I heard the front door open before getting up.

Through the open, breezeless window I spied my sons, congratulating themselves on a stealthy exit. They moved as a haphazard pack, jogging and stopping, hurrying and meandering.

I knew where they were going. The only place that three boys with six years between them would agree upon on a steamy July night.

I could have hollered, sent them back to bed. Probably should have. It's what my father would have done. But I didn't. I wanted the break as much as they did. A break from the heat and responsibility. A break from adulthood.

I wandered down after them, fighting the battle between parent and human being. I wanted to stop them, teach them how to sneak out of the house effectively. Jax especially who considers a stomp near silence. What would I feel in a few years when he's sneaking out to meet his Joey, I wondered.

Considering this, and Phoebe's reaction to a father teaching his impressionable sons how to sneak out, I decided it was a lesson that could wait a few years.

I found the three of them in the pond, splashing and laughing like the loons. They didn't even know I was there until I raced *down the dock and jumped over their heads. Beckett told me later that the water level in the pond lost a foot from that cannonball.*

We won that night. Defeating the stifling night swelter with brisk, black pond water under a full moon. It didn't matter that we'd track mud all the way back and through the house or that Phoebe would murder all of us when she found out that we'd helped ourselves to two boxes of cereal on the porch afterwards.

What did matter is we took a moment, a slice of a day, and did with it exactly as we wished. A lesson I could never iterate in a father's lecture but one so essential to the way a man lives. Find your slice and live it.

I'll carry that memory with me, take it out to examine it in the years to come, and remember that one perfect night when the crickets sang and the boys laughed. And the rains finally came as we sat together on the midnight porch.

Jax felt his throat tighten at the memories that leapt off the page. It was as if his father had just pulled up a chair next to him to recount that night. The tone and flow of the words, Jax could hear his father's voice rolling over each syllable. His easy, unhurried speech so familiar to Jax's ear even after all these years. A little on the soft-spoken side, always with half a smile.

John Pierce the writer.

Jax had never known that they shared a similar passion for storytelling. His dad was clearly a natural, and Jax felt a rush of pride. A connection he hadn't realized was suddenly there, bonding them together through time. He held in his hands an actual, tangible piece of his father.

Jax reverently tucked the stories back into the envelope. He held the envelope in his hands and for just a moment imagined his hands as his father's, strong and callused with a purpose. A destiny.

He glanced up, around the barn that his father had begun to restore before his death, and spotted his brothers kicked back at a table with their wives and the kids taking their slice of time together. They all deserved to know this piece of the man they'd loved. He'd share this with them soon. But for now, he'd keep it to himself. And he'd take his slice too.

JAX BIDED his time through the rest of the late dinner crowd, keeping an eye on the front of the house. And when he saw Joey duck into the supply closet, he made his move.

She had a bottle of Chardonnay in one hand and a fistful of towels in the other. And she brandished them like weapons when she realized he had her trapped.

"Out of the way, boss. I've got some thirsty ladies out there."

"Cards on the table, Jojo," Jax said, crossing his arms to keep from grabbing her.

Joey Greer didn't scare easily, but if she knew the dark fantasies that were running through his mind, she'd probably break his nose with that left hook of hers.

She watched him like a doe scenting danger. Only danger never made Joey more cautious. "You've lost every hand of poker that we've played. Pick a better metaphor."

"I want my hands on you, Joey. I haven't thought about anything but how good it would feel to touch you, to taste you, in eight years." He moved a step closer, and Joey brandished the wine bottle.

"Every dream I've ever had has been you. And that counts the years I was gone. But I'm back, and I'm tired of being patient. It's going to be now or never."

"We're sure as hell not having sex in a supply closet, Jax."

"Tonight. Your house, your bed."

She was quiet for a minute, studying him. "Phoebe Pierce didn't raise her boys to pressure girls into bed," she reminded him.

Jax shook his head. "I am asking you to do us a favor and get out of your own damn way. I came back for you, and I don't want to spend another night staring up at the ceiling wishing you were next to me like I have every night since I was fourteen.

"I love you, Joey, and if you don't want to make room for me, tell me tonight, and I'll leave you alone."

"You mean you'll leave," she corrected.

Jax shook his head. "I'm sticking. This," he circled his finger, "the brewery, the stables, the farm. They're roots. I'm staying put whether or not you come to your senses. But if you tell me this last time to leave you alone. I will. For good.

Joey started to roll her eyes.

"Don't." Jax shook his head. "I'm serious, Jojo. If you don't want to give things a go, then you've got to cut me loose. Either way, tonight we stop playing games."

She watched him, calculating, and he wished he could read her thoughts. He reached for the wine and towels.

"Thanks for the help tonight," he told her. "You saved all our asses. Your shift's over. Leave your door unlocked if you want company tonight. If not, I'll see you around."

He opened the closet door and stepped out.

"I'm keeping the tips," she called after him.

Jax felt the corners of his mouth lift.

16

eave your door unlocked.

Her damn door was always unlocked, and now she was going to have to purposely lock it to keep him out. Joey fumed as she took the shortcut through the pasture. The moon in the crisp night sky guided her home with nearly three hundred dollars in tips tucked in her pocket.

She let herself in the backdoor to the happy yips from Waffles as he wove in and out of her legs.

Joey crouched down to give his wiry fur a good ruffle. Just a few days with a dog and it seemed like she'd had him her entire life. She knew she'd never get tired of the celebration every time she came home.

"Buddy, it wasn't even three hours," she laughed as he danced onto his hind legs to lick her face. "Okay, how about you keep your feet on the floor, and I'll get you a t-r-e-a-t?"

Waffles trotted after her into the kitchen and happily accepted the breath-freshening cookie Joey retrieved from the jar on the counter. She wrinkled her nose. The treats tasted like mint-flavored tuna. She knew because she'd sampled one. And one had been enough. She'd ordered a large pack of homemade pet treats from Vern and Sylvia, farmer's market regulars who had a pet stand. Organic chicken treats would undoubtedly taste better than mint tuna.

As Waffles snarfed down his treat, Joey stared pensively at the front door. She was going to lock it. She knew better than to give into temptation when it came to Jackson Pierce.

Obviously there were still sparks between them. There probably always would be. She had to admit, the flirting, the teasing, it had been fun once she realized that she had the power. She wasn't that skinny, pie-eyed kid anymore.

He'd hurt her once. Left her feeling weak, vulnerable. But things were different. She was different. She was the kind of strong that came from learning not to depend on anyone else. Never tying her dreams and goals to someone. Hell yes, she was strong. But was she strong enough to pursue a fling with Jax? Strong enough to enjoy that heady, physical rush without going under, without losing herself?

Joey strode over to the front door. The thick mahogany kept the cold out and would just as easily keep out the man who'd once been so careless with her heart. Just one twist of the lock, and things would be settled between them forever.

He'd made sure she knew it was her call. She was in control.

She stared at the deadbolt and then through the glass side-light into the night.

Her call.

HOURS LATER, Jax pulled up to Joey's house, his fingers pausing on the ignition, debating. There were a handful of lights on in the first-floor windows. Was that a good sign, or did she just want to be awake to witness his devastation?

What was he going to do if he climbed those steps and found the door locked? God, to spend the rest of his life seeing the girl of his dreams every day. Watching her fall in love with some other guy who hadn't broken her heart like an asshole. They'd probably have six kids, just to rub it in. He'd take up drinking and be Drunk Uncle Jax.

If that door was locked, everything—all of it since he'd left home—would be for nothing. God, he was afraid of the no.

Why did he have to push her? Why couldn't he have given her just a little more time? He berated himself as he trudged up the porch steps like a prisoner facing his execution.

Jax closed his eyes and took a deep, slow breath.

It couldn't be locked. He'd known that Joey Greer was his future since he was fourteen years old, probably longer. "Now or never," he muttered.

It turned easily in his grip, and he spent a few more seconds contemplating whether she'd just locked the deadbolt to give him a false sense of hope before crushing him like a cockroach.

Fuck it, he decided. He pushed and stared dumbly down at Waffles who was now pawing at his legs.

"She left it open?"

Waffles wriggled in happiness as if he understood the significance of the unlocked door.

"Hey, buddy," Jax said, scruffing up the dog's fur. "Where's your mom?" She wasn't downstairs, he noted, though there was a fire in the hearth. Maybe she left the door open to an empty house as a slap in the face. He hadn't considered that possibility.

The dog's tail thumped against the floor, and he looked up adoringly at Jax with one blue eye and one brown.

"You like it here, bud? You like your mom?"

Waffles's tail swished against the hardwood.

"Yeah, I do too. Let's see if she's around." Jax took a cursory glance up the stairs, but the second floor was dark. However, the outside lights were on in the back. With the dog trailing him, Jax made his way through the living room to the French doors off the kitchen.

He could hear music faintly through the glass.

What the hell was she doing outside at night in the dead of winter? Was this some kind of trap?

He opened the door and, signaling Waffles to stay put, stepped outside. And into a fantasy.

His breath frozen in his throat. The music, low and bluesy, pulsed through outdoor speakers. Joey, her hair piled on top of her head, reclined in a cloud of steam that hovered above the claw foot tub she soaked in. She was bathed in a soft golden glow from the outdoor lights.

Under her spell, Jax moved in closer.

Joey turned her head against the lip of the tub. "Hi," she said.

"The door was open." Jax said stupidly.

Smooth move, idiot, he chastised himself.

"Was it now?" she asked with a ghost of a smile on her full, naked lips.

"Did you forget to lock it?" Still not believing it was true, Jax held his breath. All his mental preparations had dealt with a locked door.

She turned toward him, arms draped over the edge of the tub.

"There's one thing I need you to be clear on," she said, ignoring his question.

"What's that?" Jax asked.

"I'm not looking for a relationship, and I'm not interested in picking up where we left off."

"What do you want?" His voice sounded like sandpaper.

She answered him without words. Bracing her hands on the tub, she rose. Water streamed off her naked body, and steam rose from her skin.

She'd been a fantasy in high school, all long limbs and soft, subtle curves. But now? Now, she was a goddess.

She was spectacular. Lithe muscle, smooth curves, her skin glowed in the moonlight. Every inch of her was perfection. Jax went instantly hard.

Aching with the need to touch her, he moved forward until he stood before her.

"Joey."

"Hand me the towel, will you?" She said it lightly, still keeping that almost imperceptible distance between them.

His hand shook as he held out the white terrycloth, breath caught when their fingers brushed. It was then that he knew he wouldn't survive this. Her fire would incinerate him, and he didn't care. Jax was willing to sacrifice himself. Every time he kissed her, he lost a piece of his soul. What did the rest of those pieces amount to?

She wrapped the towel around her, and he saw the first apprehension in those warm brown eyes. But it was gone just as quickly as it had come. And then she put her hands on his shoulders.

He watched himself, as if from a great distance, lift her out of the tub.

She shivered against him from the cold, from the heat. And then her mouth was on his. And there was no more winter night, only that scorching flame.

Jax slid his hands under the towel, palms skimming her perfect ass. He gripped and lifted, pulling her up. Her legs wrapped around his waist, hands dove into his hair. Their mouths fused in fire.

Blindly, he carried her to the door, reveling in the feel of her wrapped around him. Her lips crushed hungrily against his. He dove into the kiss, the fire. And when she opened for him, when her tongue stroked his, he felt another piece of his soul loosen and break free.

She could have it. She could have it all. Every broken piece of him. And once she had them all, she could put him back together or scatter them to the wind. It didn't matter. All that did matter was that he gave her everything.

She groaned against him. "Door, Jax," she murmured.

"Sorry," he whispered, peeling her off the frosty glass and shoving the door open. Something crashed to the floor, pieces splintering.

Waffles danced out of their path as they reeled past. Jax paused by the table, debating bedroom or fire. Proximity won.

He carried her over to the stone hearth, his shin smarting as it smacked into the coffee table. He kicked the table out of the way, and something else fell to the floor.

In the fire's warm glow, Joey unwound her legs from his waist, and he reluctantly let her slide down. When she took a step back, Jax snagged her wrist. He couldn't stand to not touch her.

"Stay, please." If she went too far, the spell would be broken.

Watching him, she gave the towel she wore one swift tug, sending it to the floor. She stood before him, naked and proud.

Jax dropped to his knees and rested his forehead against her taut stomach. She was a queen, a witch, and he was her devoted servant. He breathed her in. Joey wasted no time with perfumes or scented lotions. Her own scent was spellbinding, all smoke and fire and earth. There was no one like her in the world.

She nudged his chin up so he would look at her. "Something's not right with this picture," she said softly.

Jax looked down. Joey was luminescent in the firelight as it played over bare curves and valleys. Yet he was fully dressed and still wearing a winter coat.

He shrugged out of the coat, yanked his shirt over his head and leaned in to trail kisses over her abdomen, climbing the curve of her hip. He dragged his teeth over her flesh, cautioning himself to be careful even as the wild within him demanded to be loosed.

Joey shivered, and he ran his tongue over the crop of goose bumps that appeared on her skin.

"God, I love every inch of you," he murmured, lips skimming over the inside of her hip bone and lower to the v of her thighs. Her legs quivered, and Jax smiled against the smooth skin. He was getting to her. There were cracks appearing in her cool defense.

Jax trailed his fingers down the backs of her thighs and heard her sigh. He wanted to make her do that again and again. His hands continued their quest, skirting her hips to stroke her thighs, his thumbs moved to rest just below her very center.

Neither of them breathed, but even without oxygen, his heart knocked against his chest in an incessant pounding. A razor-sharp anticipation.

He stroked the pad of one thumb over her slit, a feather-light touch. Her breath was a gasp, and Joey's fingers curled into his shoulders.

"Wait," she whispered.

Reacting to the tremble in her voice, Jax froze. He dropped his hands. "We can stop. It's okay." He would probably literally die if they did, was fairly certain his heart would just stop if she asked him to stop now.

"No," she said, with a breathless laugh. "I mean you need to catch up." She knelt down and set her hands to work on his belt. The moment her fingers skimmed his bare stomach, Jax felt his cock strain against the confines of his jeans. She seemed to know exactly what she was doing to him. Killing him slowly with excruciating anticipation.

Needing to touch her, Jax put his hands on her slim hips and rested his forehead on hers. Joey stared into him and as one hand worked his zipper down, her other moved to cup his hard-on through the jeans.

His eyes slammed closed, hips flexed into her hand. God, he was going to lose it, and he still had his damn pants on. She'd given him a chance, and he was seconds away from humiliating himself. No other woman had ever made him feel so... powerless... so hungry.

"Jojo, you're killing me here." He whispered it over her lips until she kissed him. But it didn't stop her busy hands. She shoved his jeans down his thighs along with his underwear. His dick sprang free, arcing heavily toward her.

Her breath was coming in pants now, which did nothing to alleviate the tightness in his balls.

"Wait." It was his turn to beg for a moment. "If you touch me now, it's not going to be sweet and slow. It's going to be fast and mean."

"I'm not a sweet and slow kinda girl, Jax," she whispered, her tongue darting out to trace his lower lip. She reached for him, and he stopped her.

"I need you to be sure," he said, squeezing her wrist a little too hard. "Be sure about all of this."

"Haven't I made myself clear?" Joey gripped his aching shaft in one hand and cupped his balls with the other. "I guess I need to learn to communicate better."

"Fuck."

Jax took her to the ground with no finesse and more than a little violence. He covered her with his body, reveling in the feel of her under him. His cock was nestled between her legs, her breasts crushed against his chest.

He held her chin in place and ravaged her mouth as he felt the wet heat from her core tease the head of his cock.

He broke free from her lips and sent his mouth cruising lower where his hot breath taunted a hard nipple until it budded. He leaned in and took the sensitive peak into his mouth.

Joey groaned and arched against him. He lathed the nub with his tongue before starting to suck. She gasped, but he wanted more. He wanted her begging.

He brought a hand to the juncture of her thighs, and as his tongue flicked at her breast, he slid a finger into her heat. It was more than a gasp. It was something close to a scream.

Out of the corner of his eye, he saw Waffles curl up in the corner of the room facing away from them. *Nice, a dog with privacy settings.*

He returned his attention to Joey's other breast, giving it the same treatment. A rough lap of the tongue before closing over it to suckle deeply.

"Jax," she gasped as he entered her with another finger.

The taste of her alone was enough to drive a man mad, but his name on her lips was hypnotic.

"I can't come yet!" She wriggled backward out of his arms.

"Yes, you can, baby," he said with a wicked smile. She scooted back on the rug, but his fingers closed over her ankle, pulling her back. He leaned down between her open thighs and placed a hard kiss between her legs. Her thighs tried to close on him, but he was faster. And so was his mouth. His tongue blazed a trail to the swollen nub and back to her wet center. He felt her arching into him, desperate to be closer.

His fingers sank into her wet flesh.

"Jax!" It wasn't begging. It was a warning that had him

stroking her slick folds faster. He took no prisoners in this pleasure war game. He didn't slow when he felt her start to quicken around him. When those beautiful muscles closed on his fingers. He licked and stroked and teased her through every tremor of her release until she lay like water beneath him.

"Told ya," he teased.

The slap she delivered to his face had no real heat to it. Just enough sting to make him forget about the control he'd so carefully conserved. Taking advantage of her weakened state, he gripped her hips and yanked her down so he was looming over her. Jax anchored her hands over her head in the plush rug. The crown of his cock stroked against her folds, stopping just shy of the entrance to Heaven. "One more time, Jojo. Be sure."

Eyes closed, she brought her knees up higher, letting them fall open.

He shook her once, and she opened her eyes. "Are you sure?" He was already sweating with the effort to hold back. The sensation of her wet lips around the head of his shaft had him seeing spots dance in his vision.

"Yes," she moaned.

"Do you want me to put on a condom?"

"Do you have one?" she asked.

Shit. "Not with me." He gritted his teeth with the effort of denying his baser instincts to drive into her, consequences be damned.

"But you'd go get one if I told you to?"

His cock twitched against her, and she wiggled under him. "Of course."

She grinned. "I'm on birth control."

"So we're good?"

She fought against his grip on her hands. "I swear to God I'm going to kick your ass for this build-up. Yes, we're good!"

There was probably more to her rant, but the words never made it past her lips because Jax thrust into her, hard and deep. Completely sheathed in her, he stopped and held.

Home. He was finally, finally home.

Belatedly, something between a scream and a moan ripped through Joey. He wanted to give her a chance to get used to the invasion, to being filled. She was so tight he could feel every ripple of her muscles as she trembled beneath him. He flexed his hips into her, and she gasped.

"Jesus, did you come again?"

"Don't judge," she gasped.

This is where he needed to be. With less finesse than he liked, he pulled out almost all the way before driving into her again. He was coated in her juices, their sweat mingling as slick skin slid over slick skin.

Her hips pumped, trying to control the pace. She wanted the ferocity of speed, he wanted to make it last. Or at least try to.

She moaned again in his ear as he filled her. Lost in her, Jax made the mistake of loosening his grip on her wrists. Joey took advantage. She shoved and rolled. Jax lolled to the side. Someone's leg kicked into an end table, tipping it over.

Victory lit Joey's eyes as she gained the top. She began to move, slowly at first, teasingly. She was glorious, a warrior queen riding into battle.

As she slid down his shaft, inch by glorious inch, Jax felt his eyes begin to close. But he forced them open, not wanting to miss a second of this magic. Joey leaned forward bracing her hands on his shoulders and began to ride. Their gazes locked, and he saw the wonder, the desire, and that little shadow of fear in her.

She quickened the pace again, riding for her life. Rising up, she yanked the tie out of her hair, sending it tumbling down in thick, dark waves. She spread her arms wide, let her head drop back.

It was too much for him. Too much beauty, too much power. Jax reared up and claimed her breast with his mouth. He felt the storm building in them both and wasn't sure if either of them would come out alive.

She was already tightening around his shaft. He could feel the muscles dance along his hard length. His vision grayed as he found the very edge of his release. Just one. More. Thrust.

She slammed down on him, and he unleashed his orgasm into her depths. "Joey." Only her name on his lips. She was coming with him, a riot of sensation. He held her tight, his face pressed to her breast, content to pour himself into her while she shattered around him.

"Yes, Jax. Yes," she chanted until everything but his name was incoherent.

17

———

Her body felt loose and limp. Like honey, gold and thick. Sated, finally, after years of longing. Her world had been rocked. Her soul shaken. Her body teased and used until it exploded beyond its boundaries. Yet, even after her soul-wrecking release, she wanted more of him.

Their years apart had only intensified their physical connection. She'd have to be careful there. Getting swept away in his arms would be so easy... and so dangerous.

She felt raw and exposed and craved the safety of a healthy distance. Which, she reminded herself as his still hard cock twitched inside her, might prove to be as difficult as it was ironic.

Shit. She was draped over him like a saddle blanket. Her face was pressed against his neck where she could feel his pulse rate slowly returning to normal. She was not a cuddler. And most importantly, she wasn't a cuddler with Jax. She didn't need him getting the wrong idea. They were just having fun. Fun that felt like the earth had moved and started spinning backward on its axis.

The feel of his strong, rough hands stroking her back was like heaven.

She mustered every ounce of self-control and rolled off him.

His hand snaked out to grab her wrist. "Where are you going?"

She glanced down at him, his sleepy, sated eyes, hair just long enough to curl a little was disheveled from her hands. Her heart stumbled, and Joey knew she was on dangerous ground.

"Drink?" she asked.

He looked at her, into her, with those storm cloud eyes. She could feel him silently probing her defenses. But she wasn't going to let him in.

"Sure," he said quietly, still studying her.

She steeled herself against the disappointment she heard in his tone.

Keep it light, she reminded herself. Incredible, mutually satisfying sex with a gorgeous man was nothing to feel guilty about. She'd been clear about where they stood. She was in charge.

Naked, she tiptoed around the shards of lamp that hadn't survived their tryst. She escaped to the sideboard by the dining table where she kept a bottle of bourbon. She poured three fingers each into two glasses and took her time wandering back to the fire.

Waffles had picked his way through the debris—a broom and dustpan weren't going to cut it—and was flopped on his back offering his belly to Jax for scratches.

She handed Jax a glass and, against her better judgment, snagged his shirt. She pulled it over her head and settled on the floor against the couch, just out of his reach.

Jax raised up on an elbow and studied her.

Whether it was from the bite of bourbon, the warmth of the fire, or the heat from his gaze, Joey felt immune to the winter's chill. He was staring at her, and she let him, meeting his gaze with a calm that she didn't feel inside. His eyes were darker here in the firelight. He had two days' worth of stubble that gave him that devilish, dangerous look.

Muscled and lean—just looking at him made her mouth water. He'd filled out more since they'd been together last. His shoulders and chest were broader, but he still hadn't lost the enviable abs that had the entire female population of their senior class drooling over him at the pool.

Oh, the things he could do with that body.

"You're staring." He said it with a quiet smirk.

"Can you blame me?" She rolled her eyes.

"What are you doing all the way over there?"

Joey wriggled her bare toes in the rug. "I'm having a drink with a friend," she said innocently.

She saw the flare in his eyes and wasn't sure if it was anger or a challenge.

"Is that what we are?"

"We wouldn't have done what we just did if we weren't friendly," she said mildly.

He moved, quick as a snake, and Joey found herself pinned between a naked, hard Jax and the couch. She sat against his thighs with no place to go, no escape to be made.

Waffles scrambled off to the corner and lay down.

"I know what you're doing, Jojo," Jax said, his lips nipping at hers.

It was a purely biological response that had her opening for him, melting under him.

"What am I doing?" she murmured. Her lips moving over the sandpaper of his stubble.

"Staying in control." He whispered his way down her neck. "Setting boundaries."

He shifted forward, and Joey felt his erection full and hard against her. He was inhuman. It was the only explanation.

"It won't work, you know."

"Why not?" she shivered.

"Because I want more, Joey. I'm not settling for a friendly roll in the hay. I want it all."

Using his hand, he guided the head of his shaft between her thighs. She tried to smother the gasp that tore past her lips at the intimate contact.

"I told you what I wanted," she said, a touch of panic in her tone.

"And I appreciate your honesty. Now I'm returning the favor." He flexed his hips, and the tip of his cock breeched her entrance.

Joey's breath was coming in short gasps. A need so fierce it threatened to choke her clawed its way up her throat.

"I came back for you, Jojo. I wasted too many years. I'm not wasting any more. I'm yours, and I'm not going to stop until you're mine."

"I don't want that, any of that," Joey whispered.

"I know, baby," Jax said, resting his forehead on hers. His breath was ragged. "But you deserve everything, and I'm not letting you settle."

He shifted again. Another agonizing inch.

"Jax!" Joey's voice broke, but she was too far gone to care.

"I'll stop if you want me to, Jojo. Just tell me."

She couldn't catch her breath, couldn't find any words for what she wanted. The only thing that made sense to her was taking him in, filling her need.

"Tell me, Joey," Jax gritted out.

She felt tears prick her eyes and closed her lids to hold them prisoner. "Don't stop, Jax. Please don't stop."

He surged into her on a groan. "I love you, Jojo."

Full, so full. It was enough to turn off her doubts, to give herself over to the moment. There was nothing that mattered more than those gray eyes looking into her as he filled her.

She moaned, trying to block out his words, but he chanted them over and over again. "I love you. I love you." Every thrust.

Why? Why did she want this so badly? Why was she setting aside eight years of hurt and anger?

"You were made for me."

"Shut up, Jax," she groaned, her fingers digging into his biceps.

"Come for me, baby. I need to feel you come again." His hand snaked down between her legs to stroke her where all the nerves in her body seemed to meet.

It was too much. She was too vulnerable. She could get hurt like this. Joey wanted the safety and security of being in control. She struggled against him. Jax was too close. She just needed to catch her breath and...

And it was too late. The wall of pleasure that had been building within her cracked.

She whimpered his name.

"Just let go, baby. I've got you." His voice was strained from effort.

She did what he asked and gave herself over to him. The wall broke and tumbled down, and as she came, she felt Jax tense as he found his own release. He groaned in her ear, a primitive growl, and she felt him let loose inside her.

"I love you." He whispered it again, over and over as they trembled together.

Joey pretended that the single tear that blazed a trail down her cheek never escaped.

~

A COLD, wet nose pressed into his hip, startling Jax from his reverie. "I think Waffles wants something," he murmured against the soft skin of Joey's throat.

Joey responded with a sleepy "Mmm."

The nose returned, and Jax reluctantly pulled himself out of and away from Joey.

Her eyes were still closed, and she didn't even put up a fight when he leaned back in to place a hard kiss on her mouth.

"C'mon, buddy," Jax said to the dog. Waffles padded along with him to the back door. Jax let him out and rummaged around the kitchen for treats. He found them in a jar with a paw print and discovered a chocolate chip treat for himself in the neighboring cookie jar.

"Are you foraging?" Joey called lazily from the couch.

"I'm carb-loading," he said through a mouthful of cookie.

Jax let the now chipper Waffles back inside and handed over the treat. The dog's butt hit the floor, and his wiry tail swished a happy beat on the hardwood. Waffles looked at him adoringly.

"Don't over treat him." Joey's order was softened by her yawn. "Too many and he gets a stomach ache."

Jax grinned and ruffled Waffles fur. "You made out pretty good, didn't you, boy?"

Was it possible to be jealous of a dog? Joey had made a good life for herself here. The job that suited her, the cabin that exactly reflected her tastes, the small circle of friends that she tolerated.

The only thing missing, as far as he could see, was him.

And come hell or high water, he'd find a place in her life.

As if pulled by gravity, he returned to Joey's side. She'd stretched out on the floor, still wearing his shirt, and Jax hoped he never got it back.

Her eyes were closed, but the corners of those sweet lips were curved up. She was the picture of satisfaction. He'd never get tired of seeing her like this or in any of her other configurations.

Joey as the quiet, steadfast friend, or the fiery fighter, the confident queen on horseback. There were pieces of Joey Greer in every female lead he wrote. His fascination with her was endless. Even now, watching the flicker of firelight over her flawless features, he felt the urge to write. Inspiration from his unwitting muse.

"Come on, Jojo. Let's get you to bed." He leaned down to tickle her ribs.

"Mmm," she grumbled. "Bed's so far."

"I'll carry you."

Warily, one of Joey's eyes flickered open. "Not happening," she said. She slowly worked her way into a seated position where she surveyed the damage to the living room. The broken lamp, the coffee table shoved into the chair, its contents strewn onto the rug.

"Looks like a war zone in here," she said.

"Waffles did it." Jax winked and offered a hand, pulling her to her feet.

"If he did that, he's also ate four of those cookies when they were cooling on the rack."

"Doggy kindergarten is in his future," Jax predicted.

Oblivious to the blatant lies being told about him, the dog sat at the foot of the stairs.

"He's ready for bed," Jax observed.

"That makes two of us," Joey yawned. "You staying?"

She hadn't meant to ask him. He could tell by the pure panic lighting her eyes. He hid his grin. She'd fight it, fight him, but in the end, he would win.

"I'm staying," he said, guiding her to the stairs. "Do you have a computer I could borrow? I'm feeling a little writer's inspiration."

"It's after two," Joey reminded him, her hips swaying mesmerizingly in front of him as she trudged up the stairs.

"You're the one who talked to Al tonight. She's serious as a heart attack when she says she'll show up here."

He followed Joey through a doorway into the master bedroom to end all master bedrooms. A wrought iron king-sized bed dominated one wall facing a two-way fireplace. The far wall had a built-in window seat that looked out over the dark of her backyard.

Waffles hopped up on the bed, curling into a tight ball on the hand-stitched quilt. The dog let out a satisfied sigh.

"Lucky guy," Jax murmured stroking his head.

"I'd say you got lucky too," Joey said, a dark eyebrow arching wickedly.

"I'd have to agree."

He was already leaning into her when she slapped a hand to his bare chest. "If we go for another round, it'll be dawn, and I won't be able to walk let alone ride a horse. You have writing to do. I have sleeping to do."

She picked up the laptop on her nightstand and handed it over. "Charger's downstairs on the island."

"This isn't over." It was a statement of fact.

"I guess we'll see," Joey said, as she sauntered off into the bathroom.

The sway of her hips, the way the hem of his shirt coasted

along her thighs—Jax almost followed her. He actually took a step after her before snapping out of it. He had a story to tell.

Reluctantly, he went back downstairs. He took a few minutes to clean up the damage their lovemaking had caused. He owed her a lamp, and the coffee table had a deep gouge in it. Next time, they'd keep it to the bed. Less property damage that way. He found a broken picture frame next to the back door. He turned it over in his hands and found himself staring into the smiling face of Joey's father, his arm looped over Joey's shoulder. She was decked out in her college riding team uniform and clutched a fistful of blue ribbons.

Behind the pride, the easy smile, Jax could see the fierce protectiveness Forrest Greer wore like a coat when it came to his daughters. He was all too familiar with how far Joey's father would go to keep Joey safe. It was something that would have to be addressed sooner rather than later.

Jax cleaned up the glass and grabbed a bottle of water from the fridge before settling on Joey's couch and booting up the laptop.

JOEY BLINDLY GROPED for the source of her torment, only to smack her phone and send it tumbling to the floor where the alarm continued to sound undaunted.

Through the slit of one eye, she could see the sun just beginning to crest the tree line. She was generally a morning person, and an early start with the horses usually bought her a pocket of time in the afternoon with the bulk of the days' work behind her.

But this morning, bed tempted her with a siren's song. She felt warm and happy under the covers. They seemed heavier today, as if they were holding her captive. The soft snore in her ear had her bolting out of bed looking for a weapon.

Jax, his arms suddenly empty, frowned.

Jackson Pierce was in her bed asleep.

He fidgeted, reaching for her in his sleep. Joey shoved a pillow into his arms and—after one last look at his shirtless, sleepy self—tiptoed into the bathroom. She usually didn't bother showering until after she was finished in the stables, but after last night's mind-blowing rolls in the hay that were all coming back to her now, she felt like she deserved some hot water action.

She shut the door quietly behind her and studied herself in the mirror over the vanity. She didn't look like a guilt-ridden, regretful woman. She looked satisfied. Damn satisfied.

So Jax loved her, okay. He knew she wasn't interested in a relationship, that she wasn't a Summer or a Gia. She had chosen her path. Her goals were laid out. And if the occasional sex fest with Jax fit in here or there, she'd be an idiot not to enjoy them.

Conscience cleared, she nodded at her reflection. She had this. Piece of cake.

HOURS LATER, a bleary-eyed Jax made his way downstairs with Waffles padding along behind him. He'd crawled into bed with Joey after six and, after dragging her against his side, slept like the dead.

He'd finished it, finally. The draft of the screenplay had been sent on its merry way to Al, who had responded immediately in the inhuman West Coast time difference. He had his suspicions that the woman never slept. She was always, always there when he needed her no matter what the day or time.

Like his mother. Not that he'd be dumb enough to voice that comparison aloud to Al who hadn't celebrated a birthday since she turned forty.

Her email had been succinct.

Reading it. I'll be in touch.

He was nervous about the script. Even fictionalized, it was still deeply personal. It was his story. Their story. And until he'd taken in a Lakers game with a studio exec and blurted out the story over too many beers, he hadn't thought of it as anything but his history.

And until last night, he wasn't sure how he wanted the story to end.

The draft was rough and needed a few weeks of polishing, but he knew in his gut it was a guaranteed green light. What he didn't know was how Joey would react to it.

Jax stumbled into the kitchen and spotted the note taped to the coffee maker.

Push this button.

He did as instructed and was rewarded with the smell of brewing coffee. The woman was a goddess. There was another note on the island next to a plate of cookies.

Breakfast of champions. I have rug burn on my ass.

It was as close to a love note as Joey Greer would ever write. Jax folded the note neatly and tucked it into his wallet.

The perfect souvenir of their first night back together.

18

---

*J*ax found her in the stables standing in the doorway of the feed room arguing with the feed rep.

"I understand your dilemma, Chuck. And yet I still don't care," Joey said, crossing her arms over her chest. "We're not eating a ten percent increase just because you say transportation costs have gone up."

They bickered back and forth until she spotted Jax leaning against Lolly's stall, watching and grinning. She promptly lost her train of thought as every thrust, every orgasm, from the night before ran through her brain in vivid detail.

One look at his sexy smirk and heated gray gaze and she knew he was thinking the same thing. Her resolve to stay cool was already wavering, and Jax hadn't even said a word to her yet. All he was doing was standing there looking gorgeous and smoldery, and she was turning into a puddle.

"So we're agreed on five then?" Chuck clarified. "We'll split the difference?"

"Huh? Sure. Five," Joey said, ignoring the look of blatant relief on the man's face.

"I'll just go call my supervisor and get that approved." Chuck practically skipped out of the stables.

"Yeah, you do that," Joey said.

"You could have got him at three," Jax told her.

"I was going for two when I got distracted."

He gave her a sexy, crooked grin. "Hi," he said softly.

"Hi, yourself. Did you sleep well?" Joey asked.

"Great. At least until a certain beautiful cowgirl snuck out of bed this morning."

"Horses need fed. Every day." She shrugged. "It's not a hobby for me." For some reason, she was itching for a fight. Or maybe she was looking for a different release of energy.

Jax's fingers snaked into the waistband of her breeches, pulling her against him.

Stay cool. Don't think about all those orgasms, Joey ordered herself.

"Didn't Carter tell you to hire more help?" Jax asked, already knowing the answer.

"I'm in charge no matter how many hands we have. It's my responsibility to make sure things get done and get done right." She felt defensive and off kilter.

"I find your work ethic very sexy," Jax told her.

"That's because you have the libido of an entire high school lacrosse team," Joey shot back. "Speaking of work ethics, you were up late."

"Finished the draft and sent it off to the powers that be," he told her, his fingers tightening on her pants.

"Must have been quite the inspiration that struck last night," Joey teased, running her hands up his chest and completely ignoring her decision to maintain a little emotional, if not physical, distance from Jax.

"I could go for another round of inspiration," he murmured, lowering his lips to hers.

The kiss went from playful to possessive in the span of a breath. Any thought of not getting swept away disappeared from her mind as her lips parted, welcoming him in.

His fingers dug into her hips, and he pushed her back against the wall.

"God, I want you so much." Jax mouthed the words against her lips. "Why do you do this to me?"

"I'm not doing anything," she growled, nipping at his lower lip.

"Don't even tell me that's nothing," he groaned.

"Hey, Joey? Do you know where—"

Joey shoved Jax back a step and leaned against Lolly's stall door in what she hoped was a casual position.

Colby came around the corner carrying a broken feed scoop. "Oh, hey, Jax. I didn't know you were..." he trailed off, looking back and forth between them.

"You were looking for me?" Joey asked a little too sharply, ruining the nonchalance she was going for.

Lolly chose that moment to stick her gray spotted head out of the stall and nibble at Joey's hair.

Joey jumped out of her skin and into Jax's arms. Lolly tossed her head, enjoying the game.

"Everyone okay?" Colby asked, concern weighed on his tone.

"We had sex." Joey blurted out the words. "Jax and I. Last night. Had sex."

Colby and Jax's faces wore twin expressions of shock.

"Jesus, Jojo." Jax covered his eyes with his hand.

"Um. Okay then. Congratulations?" Colby looked more embarrassed than Jax.

"Yeah. Thanks. Okay, now we can all get back to work." She nodded.

"Do you know where the other feed scoop is?" Colby asked

holding up the mangled scoop. "Apollo got bored and decided to eat this one."

"Feed room, second shelf on the left," she said, jerking a thumb toward the open door behind them.

Colby nodded. "Okay then. I'll just go get it."

Jax was intently studying the toes of his work boots. Joey cleared her throat. "So... that happened," she drawled.

He looked up, a grin on his face. "I thought it would take me months to talk you into going public."

"I didn't go public. I told Colby, who walked in on us mauling each other in the middle of the aisle. Besides, look what happened to Carter and Beckett when they tried to be all sneaky about their relationships."

"So we're in a relationship," Jax said, stepping in closer, a hunter scenting prey.

"No. We're having sex," Joey corrected, backing up a step.

Lolly took the opportunity to go for her hair again. "Jesus, Lolly!" Joey shoved a peppermint treat at the horse.

"Are we having sex with other people?" Jax asked.

"No!" The word flew out a little more forcefully than she'd intended. "We're not having sex with other people," she corrected more calmly.

"Then we're in a monogamous..." He took a step toward her. "Committed. Relationship."

Joey shook her head back and forth so hard she felt her teeth rattle. "No. Uh-uh. We are casually enjoying each other's..." She waved her hand in front of Jax's crotch. "Bodies."

"We're dating."

"Absolutely not. Why do we need a label, anyway?"

"Because if we don't say what it is we're doing, someone else is going to label it for us, and you don't want the Beautification Committee renting a wedding venue for us, do you?"

The damn Beautification Committee and their damn plan to match Jax with Moon Beam. A shiver of nausea slithered around Joey's stomach. Whatever black magic they weaved, they always got their couple. Maybe she didn't want to be in a serious relationship with Jax, but that didn't mean she wanted to see him in one with someone else. Certainly not with a Moon Beam Parker-type whose sticky sweetness attracted men like flies to a fly strip, sapping them of their free will and spending money. Once sated, she got bored quickly and moved on to her next victim.

The Beautification Committee be damned. She was saving Jax from a Moon Beam future.

"We are seeing each other." She slapped a hand on his chest when he took a joyful step forward, hands slipping around her waist. "Casually."

"I can live with that," Jax said, nibbling his way down her throat. "For now."

She growled low in her throat. "God, you drive me nuts."

"Right back atcha, baby," he said. "I need you."

"Tack room?" Joey suggested, suddenly desperate for more than just stolen kisses.

He half-dragged, half-shoved her across the aisle to the door of the tack room.

"Wait," Joey said, putting her hands on his shoulders. "What about Chuck?"

"He'll wait," Jax said, impatiently pushing her through the open door.

"Shit! What about my parents?"

Jax actually spun around to look behind him. "Are they here?" he hissed, reaching down to adjust what looked like an uncomfortable bulge in his jeans. "Why didn't you say something?"

"No! They're not here. But if we're casually seeing each other, I have to tell them or face the consequences."

"What kind of consequences are we talking here?" Jax reached for her again, but she slapped his hands away.

She shook her head. "Who knows? This could be worse than the Silent Treatment Thanksgiving of '93 or the baby christening when Mom's cousin Drew showed up an hour late because of a flat tire. He was shunned from family events for a year."

"Shunning doesn't sound so bad."

"It was bad enough that they heard from someone else about the partnership. I can't let Blue Moon do the dirty work again."

"They need to know, Joey. No matter how badly it goes, you need to tell them."

"Just checking, but should we compare notes on why we both think telling my parents would be horrible?" Joey asked. She knew what her reasons were but wasn't clear on Jax's fears.

"I think it's best if we leave that one lie," Jax advised. "Rule Number Two in our relationship: neither can speak ill of the other's family."

"That seems fair. We each can still speak ill of our own family, right?"

"Yeah. Definitely a requirement."

"Is not sleeping with other people while we're sleeping with each other Rule Number One?"

Jax nodded, the heat returning to his gaze.

"Wipe that look off your face until after I call my mother," Joey warned him. She began backing away from him down the aisle toward her office. "Just hold that thought. And if you get a chance, go find Colby and feed his phone to Clementine before he can post on Facebook that we had sex."

"Oh, geez. You guys had sex?" Carter said from behind her.

"Jesus! Did everyone around here start taking ninja classes?" Joey slapped a hand over her thudding heart. "You can handle this one." She pointed at Jax and hustled into the office for her cell phone before she blabbed to anyone else that she was having sex again.

"Is everything okay, Joey?" Her mother's voice was laced with panic on the other end of the phone.

"Everything's fine, Mom," Joey said, biting back a sigh. Her parents' tendency to overreact over anything out of the norm was a constant stressor for the entire family.

"You don't usually call in the middle of the day."

"Yeah, well, I had some more news I wanted to share with you."

"Oh my God, wait until I sit down."

"Mom, it's not sit-down news."

"I just don't want to faint if you say 'cancer' or 'unplanned pregnancy' or something like that," April said, her voice a wispy note of anxiety now.

"I'm seeing Jax. Casually." She emphasized the last word and hoped it would break through her mother's fear fog.

"And you're pregnant."

"No. I'm not."

"You're not sick? Or hurt? There wasn't a fire?"

"Oh, for God's sake, Mom. I slept with Jax last night. I'm probably going to do it again." *Hopefully today. In the tack room.*

There was silence on her mother's end as April processed the news.

"Well, your father isn't going to be pleased, but I'm really not surprised."

"You're not?" It was Joey who was surprised.

"Sweetie, I'm not an idiot."

"Okay. Sooo, how do you feel about it?" Joey would have rather bitten off her own arm than ask the question, but it was always better to know where one stood when facing a battle.

Her mother sighed. "I've been expecting this call since Jax moved back last year. I've had a lot of time to process in anticipation. You held out a lot longer than I would have."

She was still holding out. Sort of.

"That's it? That's all you have to say?" Joey was wary of things that were too easy.

"Your father blames Jax for your accident."

"Yeah, that came through pretty loud and clear over the years, Mom."

"I never blamed him for it."

"But?"

"But what I do blame him for is abandoning my daughter when she was in the hospital and needed him."

"I blame him for that too," Joey confessed.

"Maybe he had a good reason, or maybe he was just a scared young man. But either way, you needed him there, and he wasn't. So I'm just asking you to be careful."

"I will, Mom. I promise."

"Good. So, what do we do about your father?"

Joey's toes curled inside her boots. "I was thinking maybe you could tell him for me?" Her voice had gone up an entire octave.

"You're lucky he's not on Facebook." April sighed. "I'll see what I can do. He's usually in a good mood on Tuesdays. It's dollar draft night at the fire company."

"He got me a dog, Mom."

"Oh, boy."

"Yeah."

"Well, be careful." It was her mother's blanket cautionary demand that covered everything from crossing the street to not slipping in the shower. But this time, Joey knew it meant something more specific.

"I will. Thanks, Mom. And thanks for telling Dad for me. You're the best."

"I am pretty great, aren't I? Say hey to Jax for me."

"Will do. Thanks, Mom. I mean it."

With that done, there were two more women who needed to know under penalty of murder.

Joey decided a text would do.

Joey: Had sex with Jax last night.

She debated adding a smiley face but decided that would be too weird. There. Summer and Gia were now in the know. Short of posting a post-coital selfie in the Blue Moon Facebook group, she'd done what needed to be done to share the news, control the spin, and hopefully shove Moon Beam Parker onto some other unsuspecting soul with a dick and a wallet.

"Now, I don't want you to take this the wrong way, but—"

Jax cut Carter off and tossed a bale of straw onto the third tier in the barn. "You don't want my relationship with Joey to mess things up around here."

"Yeah." His brother nodded and hefted a bale onto clean pallets to start a new row. "Don't get me wrong. I'm happy for you."

"I can tell," Jax said sarcastically.

"Don't be a dick. It's been so long coming, I think I kind of thought it wouldn't happen."

"Don't underestimate the Pierce charm." Jax reached for another bale. "Joey did."

"Total rookie mistake." Carter shook his head. "So where do you see this going?"

"Are you seriously giving me the talk?" Jax wasn't sure if he should be amused or offended.

"It's like a spin on the talk. A weird spin," Carter told him. "You know I've known Joey her entire life, and I love her like a sister, so if you fuck with her again, I'm going to feed you to Clementine. But you *are* my brother, and I love you. And I think you're hoping for marriage and kids and stuff here, so if she ruins that and sends you packing, I'm going to have to at least force her to babysit the twins every week so Summer and I can have more sex in the kitchen."

"You're very creative with your choice of punishments."

"I started a list for the twins so I don't have to think of anything on the fly when they steal Summer's car or set the drapes on fire."

Jax grimaced. "I forgot about that. Mom wouldn't let us watch TV for a month after that bit of arson."

"Yeah, and she made us reenact all of her favorite episodes of *The Golden Girls*."

"You made a really great Blanche," Jax recalled. "Mom was insane."

"I hope I'm half as insane as she and Dad were raising us. Then at least one kid will turn out okay."

Jax thumped Carter on the shoulder. "Don't forget. You've got Summer, and she's way more organized and diabolical than Mom and Dad ever were."

Carter smiled. "Remember all of those bologna sandwich

dinners because no one could ever remember who was supposed to cook?"

"Your kids will have memories just as good," Jax predicted. "Except it will be like disgusting soy tofu sandwiches on organic bread with vegan cheese."

"Are *Golden Girls* reruns still on?" Carter wondered wistfully.

"I don't know, but did I tell you I walked in on Mom pulling a Blanche this week?"

19

While Jax and Carter finished stacking the straw bales, Joey placed a call to a friend of a friend who happened to be director of a racing stable in New Jersey to see about scheduling a facility visit. Waffles snoozed under her desk.

She was just wrapping up when Gia and Summer's excited faces plastered against the glass of her office door.

"That works for me, Sheri. I'll put it on the calendar and email you closer to the date," she said before ending the call.

Joey debated sitting there and pretending she was still on the phone until the girls got bored and went away. But no one would believe that she would willingly stay on the phone for longer than five minutes at a time.

With a sigh, she hung up.

They burst through the door in a bubble of energy.

Summer flopped down in a chair while Gia made a beeline for the coffee.

"Okay, tell us everything," Summer demanded.

"Well, the feed price went up ten percent, but I was able to talk Chuck down to five—"

"Look who has a sense of humor when she gets laid," Gia teased.

"Don't you two have a magazine to run or something?"

"All business is officially on hold until you spill," Summer said, tilting her head.

"Yeah, we could keep you in here for days, so you might as well start talking," Gia said airily.

"Jax and I had sex. What more is there to say about it?"

"It must have been really disappointing. Otherwise, she'd want to share at least an orgasm count," Gia speculated.

"I think you're right. It was probably awful, and they're never going to do it again," Summer agreed.

"So did his genitalia shrink since high school, or did you just forget how Tab A fits into Slot B?" Gia asked.

"There's something incredibly wrong with you two," Joey said, shaking her head. "It wasn't awful. It was great. Really great. So great it hurts to sit on a horse today."

Gia squealed.

"I'm just going to start holding up fingers, and you tell me when to stop when I hit the correct number of orgasms," Summer told Joey.

"Okay, so what does this all mean? Are you together? Was it just a one-time thing?" Gia demanded.

Joey was momentarily grateful that Jax had forced her to put a label on it. "It means we are casually seeing each other. Keyword *casually,* so don't either of you get any bridal magazine ideas."

Gia clapped her hands together. "I'm so happy for you two! It's like Christmas all over again."

"Yeah, if Santa doled out orgasms," Summer cracked. "Which, by the way, did you forget we're playing how many O faces?" She wiggled her fingers.

Joey kicked back in her chair. "I didn't forget. You just didn't hit the magic number yet."

They whistled their approval.

"Those Pierces know how to deliver," Summer said proudly. "So how do you feel?"

Sore. Happy. Satisfied. Scared shitless. Guilty. The list went on and on. "Fine."

Gia rolled her eyes. "Fine? That's the answer Evan gives me when I ask him about his day at school and he got detention for a food fight and an incomplete because Diesel ate his Civil War diorama."

"Oddly specific," Joey commented. She looked through the dusty glass to make sure Jax wasn't lurking. "Is it normal to feel a little conflicted? Maybe a lot conflicted?" She let her breath out in a whoosh.

Gia and Summer exchanged a glance and remained eerily quiet.

"I'm just... confused? I guess?" Joey frowned. "I told him in no uncertain terms that I'm not looking for a relationship. I even made sure to tell him before we had sex."

"Uh-huh," Summer said.

"And so then we have sex, with the knowledge that I have no intention of pursuing a future with him."

"And then?" Gia asked.

"And then after—and maybe a little bit during—sex he tells me he loves me."

"Oh, boy. That's sneaky," Gia said with approval.

Summer grinned and shifted in her seat. "Okay, I seriously have to pee so I'm going to make this quick. It sounds like you both were clear with your intentions, and now it's just a battle of the wills to see who wins."

"You make it sound like we're going to war."

Gia snickered. "You're going to the mattresses!"

"Oh, because now we're in the mafia, obviously." Joey rolled her eyes.

"On that note, pee break." Summer pushed herself out of the chair.

Joey waited until Summer left the office. "She looks tired."

"She's working too much," Gia agreed. "Did Carter say anything to you?"

"About convincing her to take a honeybaby?"

"I think you mean a babymoon," Gia corrected.

"Yeah, that."

"What's the likelihood of her letting us pry her away from her computer, shove her in a car, and send her away from work for a long weekend?"

"A hundred million to one. Lucky for her, I've got the one," Joey said smugly.

"Really? I'm intrigued." Gia leaned forward.

"Care to make a wager?"

Gia pursed her lips. "I'm game. What do you have in mind?"

"If I win, you make sure to tell everyone who listens that Jax and I are just casually seeing each other."

"And if I win?"

"I'll watch the kids for a night while you and Beckett do whatever married Pierces do, which, from what I hear about Summer and Carter, is have sex on the kitchen island."

"Beckett shared that little tidbit with me. Did you hear about Jax walking in on Phoebe and my dad?"

They were still laughing when Summer shuffled back into the room. "Kids better be worth it. I'm starting to worry that my bladder will never recover and my feet won't unswell to a pre-pregnancy shoe size."

"They are," Gia said over the rim of her coffee mug. "Mostly. Like sixty percent of the time."

"Oh goodie. A majority."

"I'm actually glad you stopped by, even if it was to stick your nose in my business," Joey began, shooting Gia a look. "What's going on with Carter?"

"What do you mean?" Summer looked immediately concerned.

"I noticed he's looking a little... I don't know, run down lately?" Joey said.

"I thought so, too, the last time he stopped by the house," Gia said, catching the drift. "Is he under the weather?" she asked Summer.

Summer frowned and shook her head. "No. He's as healthy as a California vegan."

"Maybe he's just working too much," Joey said.

"He's probably just got a lot on his mind what with the farm and the brewery and the twins," Gia mused.

"I've been getting work emails from him in the middle of the night," Joey improvised.

"The other week he mentioned something about going away for the weekend," Summer confessed. "But I told him it wasn't a good time with the magazine and everything." She chewed on her lip.

"You're probably right," Gia said. "You've got a lot on your plate, and you probably wouldn't even be able to relax."

"Well, I do need to vet a substitute editor for when I'm on maternity leave," Summer sighed.

"Like a short-term dry run. That's not a horrible idea." Joey tried to keep the gloat out of her voice. "And maybe you could use the vacation to confess to Carter that you already know the sex of the babies."

Summer stuck her tongue out at Joey. "Funny. It's very important to Carter that we're surprised. So we are going to be surprised. This is my way of proving how much I love him."

"By doing something completely against your nature?" Joey asked.

"Exactly." Summer nodded.

Joey rolled her eyes. Love made normally smart people do very stupid things. At least by casually seeing Jax, she'd be able to keep her wits about her.

Summer was busy rolling with the idea of a weekend away. "I suppose it could work. I could afford to take a few days off. If we work ahead with the editorial calendar and have the content scheduled out."

"I don't think it would be a problem." Gia nodded.

Joey slapped her palm on the top of her desk. "You should surprise him!"

"What?"

"Yeah! Plan the trip, book it, and then tell him about it. Jax and I can cover the farm. He won't have an excuse not to go."

"Yeah," Summer nodded. "Yeah! I can do this. I can surprise my husband with a getaway and use the time to work out the kinks with a new editor. I'm gonna do it!" She pulled out her phone and started swiping furiously through screens. "Now, where should we go?"

Joey shot Gia her cockiest grin. Behind Summer's chair, Gia bowed in unworthiness.

It was early afternoon before Jax was able to catch back up with Joey. She had a self-satisfied smile on her face as she loosened the girth on Tucker's saddle.

"I like seeing you smile," he told her, stepping in with the dual purpose to help and to be closer to her.

Joey snorted. "You like seeing a lot more than my smile."

"You speak the truth." Jax pulled the saddle and blanket

off the big bay and placed it on the bench that Waffles was wriggling under to investigate one of the barn cats. He sent the dog into a spiral of delight with a good belly scratch.

"What could possibly put you in such a good mood today?" he asked with a devilish grin.

"Keep your happy wand in your pants, Ace. I just orchestrated some high-level mental espionage that I'm feeling really good about."

"Care to elaborate?"

Joey unclipped Tucker's lead from the eyehook on the wall. "I may have convinced Summer to take a long weekend trip with Carter. I also may have made it her idea."

Jax took the lead rope from her. "You're so sexy when you're manipulative."

Joey tossed her braid over her shoulder and followed along as Jax led Tucker back to his stall, her hands shoved into the pockets of her down vest. "I am, aren't I?"

"How did it go with your parents?" he asked.

Joey shrugged. "Mom wasn't surprised. And she's going to be the one to break it to Dad. So it was better than I expected."

With Tucker happily munching on a scoop of grain in his stall, Jax hung the lead on a hook outside the stall and secured the door. "Did you have lunch yet?"

"Not yet." Her voice was suddenly husky, and it went straight to his groin. "Where are Carter and Colby?"

"Over at the barn."

"So we have the place to ourselves? Interesting." Joey said, sidling a little closer. She ran a finger down his flannel-covered chest.

It was one finger touching shirt, and it was enough to have Jax grabbing her and attacking her mouth. He walked them backwards until the wood of the wall bit into her back.

"Let's go to your house," he muttered, his mouth continuing its assault.

"Too far," Joey breathed. Her fingers threaded through his hair and fisted.

"Tack room?"

"Tack room."

Joey shoved the door closed behind them, and Jax immediately pounced, shoving her against the wall. A tangle of bridles came crashing down on her. She fought her way away from the wall and backed Jax up against the sink cabinet. He shoved her winter vest off her shoulders and sent his long, nimble fingers dancing under her sweater.

"God, you are so sexy when you're dressed for work."

"You have the weirdest fetishes," Joey teased, sliding her hand lower to cup him through his jeans. She felt him hard and throbbing against her palm. "Wow, you really do like breeches and boots."

"I like anything you're wearing, anything that I can take off." He pulled her against him and shifted his hips to grind into her.

Their tongues and breath tangled, and Joey hooked one leg over his hip. The friction was magic, and she wanted more of it. Jax picked her up and spun her around so she sat on the edge of the counter.

He pulled her legs high on his waist, grinding his hard-on against the exact spot that Joey needed the pressure. She unbuttoned his flannel and dipped her hands inside, stroking hard muscle, hot flesh.

She felt dizzy with need. Arousal pooled between her thighs, begging him for more. He slid her sweater up revealing a serviceable sports bra. And when he flicked his thumbs over the nipples straining beneath the fabric, Joey thought she was going to come right then and there.

Until she heard her name being called from the other side of the door.

"Chuck," she gasped.

"My name's Jax."

"No, Chuck!" she hissed, pushing against Jax's chest.

"Fine. You can call me Chuck."

This time when Chuck called her name, Jax heard it too. "Oh, that Chuck."

"Dammit!" Joey jumped off the counter and tried to straighten her sweater. "Do I look like I was just about to have sex?"

"Oh, yeah," Jax said with an appreciative grin.

"Stop it!"

"Stop what?"

"Stop looking at me that way or I'm sending you out there."

Jax looked down pointedly at his raging erection. "Yeah, 'cause that would be good business."

Joey made herself as presentable as she could before reaching for the doorknob. She paused and glanced back at Jax. His hair was messed up, his shirt was unbuttoned, and he had a cocky grin fixed on his face.

"Rain check?"

Joey grinned despite herself. "Yeah."

20

_____

$\mathcal{I}$t was a small, inconvenient twist of fate that had Carter and Summer booking a long weekend at Niagara Falls the same frigid week that Beckett and Gia headed to Belize on their honeymoon.

The inconvenience lay in the weather forecast. It also happened to be the same timeframe that the meteorologists started making noise about the first blizzard of the year.

Carter had immediately balked about leaving. He didn't want to dump blizzard management and cleanup on Jax and Joey, but Jax knew his brother was also painfully aware that it was imperative to pry Summer away from her magazine for a few days for a pre-twin invasion break. The morning of the storm, Jax, Joey, and Colby had staged an intervention and practically packed the couple's bags themselves while promising to call if they couldn't handle things on their own.

Beckett and Gia had also half-heartedly volunteered to reschedule their honeymoon to be on hand for the incoming snowpocalypse, but their offer was brushed aside. Phoebe and Franklin would be taking Mr. Snuffles and staying at Beckett's with the kids and pets to keep their routine as close to normal as possible.

It was amusing—and a little insulting—to Jax that Carter was worried he couldn't handle the farm for a few days without him. It wasn't anything he hadn't dealt with a hundred times before while growing up here.

He'd always loved snowstorms, even if they meant extra work. Except for a few trips to Tahoe, he hadn't seen snow since his move. Despite the extra responsibility a heavy snow-fall incurred, he still felt like a little kid staring out the class-room window waiting for the first flakes.

Jax—keeping the latest forecast numbers for the storm to himself—tossed Carter and Summer's bags in the truck himself and waved them off from the front porch with Valentina and Meatball at his side. Colby ambled out of the barn after Carter's truck disappeared down the drive.

"We are screwed if this storm is as bad as they're calling for tonight," he said, shoving his hands in the pockets of his jacket and grinning.

"Yep," Jax agreed. "Guess we'd better make a plan?"

"Let's go see Joey," Colby said.

"We'll take the Jeep. It's too cold to walk."

Carter had thoughtfully attached the plow to the front of his Jeep, putting Jax and his team a little ahead in their bliz-zard countdown preparations. When the dogs followed them to the garage, Jax shrugged and let them clamor into the back. Well, Valentina's long legs clambered. Meatball sat on the ground and barked until Colby picked him up and shoved him in next to his sister.

They pulled up in front of the stables where Jax spotted Joey in the paddock on a pretty little quarter horse. Meatball gave a little woof and squeezed through the door as soon as Jax opened it.

Joey swung down off the horse's back and headed their way.

"Geez! I thought you were Carter coming to say he changed his mind about leaving." Joey sighed in relief, her breath coming out in a cloud.

"Nope. We just waved them off with lies that the snow wouldn't be that bad and that we've got everything under control," Jax assured her, watching as Valentina loped over to sniff Waffles's ass. Meatball barreled over and the three dogs took off around the stables.

"If they come back covered in horse shit, you're in charge of bath time," Joey warned him.

He threw a salute. "Aye, aye."

She cracked a smile and that was all the invitation he needed to drop a fast kiss on her mouth before she could pull back. They'd spent a few more very satisfying nights together at her house since last week, but Joey still refused to be as affectionate in public as she was when they were alone.

Colby looked away, whistling.

Joey shot Jax a disapproving look, which had absolutely no effect on him. She was going to get used to being his girl one way or another. And Jax knew from experience that Joey responded well to trial by fire.

"You two realize that we're fucked this entire weekend, right? The latest forecast says thirty-two inches starting after midnight tonight," she said, leading the horse toward the barn.

"I heard thirty-five and starting at ten," Colby said as they followed her into the stables.

"Go grab some coffee, and I'll be back in a minute," Joey said, leading the horse into the stables ahead of them.

Jax led the way to the office and got busy pouring coffees.

Colby made himself at home in one of the rickety visitors' chairs.

"So I started a list," Joey said, bustling into the room and flopping down in the chair behind her desk.

"Let's have it," Jax said, handing her a mug.

"Snow removal is going to be the priority, obviously. But since we have some advance warning, I want to get all the horses lunged and exercised since they won't be seeing the pastures anytime soon."

"We're going to need some help with that," Colby predicted.

"I think I'll call in some favors with the students. If I can get four or five of them in here before lunch, we should be in good shape."

"Problem solved. What's next?" Jax asked, comfortable letting her take the lead.

"You and Carter already stocked the straw for bedding, so we're good there. But we need to double check the furnace in the stable and the barn, and I think it would be a good idea to add some extra insulation to the pipes to make sure nothing freezes. I don't want to be hauling water to the horses from the house."

"I'll see what we've got left over from last winter, and then I can make a run into town for supplies," Jax volunteered.

"Great. I've got a shopping list, too, if you're going into town."

"No problem. So snow removal—I'm thinking we should keep the Jeep over here to dig out here and at the brewery. We should be able to clear at the farmhouse with one or two of the ATVs. Colby and I can hook up the plows to them today."

"How about the generators?" Joey asked.

"Gas tanks were filled last week for the brewery. I'll check yours and the farmhouse while we still have some daylight,"

Jax told her. "We've got a portable one in the garage we can roll out for emergencies."

"If we work our asses off today, we just might earn ourselves a nice little vacation," Colby said.

"I wouldn't say no to a little R and R," Jax said, giving Joey a wink.

~

BEFORE THE FIRST FLAKES FELL, Jax gave Joey a hand turning out the horses. Six students showed up to help lunge and ride in an effort to get everyone's energy out while they still could. If the forecast was even close to accurate, it would be days before the horses saw the pasture again.

While Joey saddled up one of the spunkier mounts, Jax, Colby, and Waffles made sure the furnaces in the barn and stables were up to the challenge of a winter storm of epic proportions.

In the barn, he gave the pigs, Dixie and Hamlet, some extra bedding and threw a ball in their box stall for entertainment purposes. Dixie's curly tail wiggled with pleasure when he gave her a quick pat. One stall down, Clementine, the evil goat monster, was safely secured. But that didn't stop her from charging the gate when she saw Jax.

Her demonic little hooves scrambled at the wood and her ears twitched. Clementine's creepy yellow eyes glowed under the barn's fluorescent lights.

"Clearly not enjoying your captivity, are you?" Jax asked smugly. "You're not so tough when you're behind bars, are you?" He took a step closer.

He wasn't sure if it was possible, but it looked like the goat narrowed her eyes at him. Pressing his luck, Jax waved his left hand at her, and when the goat followed the movement with her satanic gaze, he swooped in with his right and patted her on the head.

It wasn't anything his brothers hadn't done before. Joey and the girls regularly gave the four-legged beast ear scratches. Hell, Evan and Aurora could hug her around the neck. But one pat on the head from Jax, and the goat lost her shit. She sprang at the door, hooves clamoring. Something close to a scream erupted from her goat throat.

Jax jumped back in case the enraged goat managed to levitate over the door.

Waffles, fearless defender that he was, jumped at the door and barked three short yips.

Clementine stared down the furry bodyguard, and Jax could almost hear her calculating the odds that she could take Waffles in a fight. After a tense few seconds, Clementine must have decided the odds were not in her favor, and she slowly retreated, sliding down the inside of the door and sauntering over to her feed bucket.

"You're getting an entire plate of bacon tonight," Jax told the dog. Waffles blinked at him in understanding. The dog returned to Jax's side, tail wagging happily. They wandered down to another large box stall where Carter's latest charity cases were happily munching on hay. The two neglected Jersey cows that Dr. Ames had guilted his brother into taking in were already putting weight back on.

"You ladies have everything you need?" he asked, glancing at their bedding and feed and water buckets.

One of them swung her wet nose in his direction and lowed.

"I'll take that as a yes. I'll bring you some bread as a special snowed-in treat tomorrow."

The Jersey's glossy brown eyes remained interested in him, and she approached the gate. She stuck her nose between the slats and sniffed at Waffles. Accommodating as always, Waffles tolerated the sniffing.

Jax moved on to double-check that the flashlights at the barn entrance had working batteries and then loaded the gas cans and Waffles into the Jeep and fired off a text to Joey before heading into town.

Jax: Taking Waffles with me to town.

Joey responded immediately and Jax chuckled.

Joey: Sure. Leave me the horse-sized one and the walking fart cloud. What does Carter feed this thing?

Jax: How about I pick you up something special at the liquor store to make it up to you?

Joey: I will accept your apology with nothing less than a good bottle of tequila.

Jax: See you in an hour with apology tequila.

Ninety minutes later, he considered just opening the bottle of tequila and drinking it while he stood in the checkout line. If the grocery store had been a nightmare—with a fistfight almost breaking out over the last bottle of kombucha—the liquor store was the third circle of hell.

Everyone in town was stocking up in anticipation of the storm. The line snaked around the register and up and down the last three aisles of the store. Bill Fitzsimmons was currently holding up the line trying to decide which pineapple-flavored vodka was superior. He'd been having a heated discussion with Mildred, the clerk, for the last ten minutes and the townsfolk were ready to revolt.

Jax caught Taneisha Duval's eye. Blue Moon's long-distance running star rolled her eyes at him. "I will pay for your tequila if you get him the hell out of here," she said, jerking her chin in Fitz's direction.

"Deal." Jax handed over the bottle and stormed the front of the line. "Is there a problem here, Fitz?" he asked.

Fitz looked over his reading glasses at Jax. "Oh good. Weigh in here, would you, Jax? I was leaning toward the Highland Pineapple but saw this one was on sale. Now Mildred tells me—"

Jax yanked the bottles out of Fitz's hands and placed them on the counter with a little more force than necessary. "You should do a taste test. At home. My treat." Jax fished his credit card out of his wallet and handed it over.

"Well, that's very generous of you," Fitz said. "But I still need to pick out my mini liquors. I always like to treat myself to a little something special. Now, let's see..." He leaned in to examine the register's display of little plastic bottles.

The line behind him groaned, and Jax swore under his breath.

"And now it's snowing," someone called from the back of the line.

"We're gonna get snowed in here, and there's no TV."

The grumbling got louder.

Desperate times called for desperate measures. Jax swept the entire mini display off the shelf and dumped it into a plastic bag. "Now you don't have to choose."

Fitz looked like he'd just hit the lottery. "Well, if you insist—"

Mildred swiped Jax's credit card so fast he thought he saw

sparks. The crowd cheered as Fitz staggered out of the store under the weight of his haul. He waved cheerfully.

"My hero," Taneisha called from the middle of the line.

～

JOEY RODE APOLLO HARD, setting a grueling pace around the upper meadow trying to burn off the energy that she knew would turn stubborn sassy mounts into destructive dicks when locked up for a few days. She was thankful the indoor riding ring would give them some room to exercise in the coming days.

The air was thick with the onset of snow.

She thundered back into the yard at the stables, Apollo's sides steaming from a good run. The flakes were already coating the grass and drive. She'd lived through enough New York winters to know that this storm was going to be the doozy that was predicted.

But they were as prepared as they were going to get. Animals secure, food supply stocked, and every precaution for a deep freeze and a mountainous dig out had been taken.

She dismounted and, flipping the reins over Apollo's head, led him toward the stable. Joey was almost looking forward to the storm. A cozy night in with man and dogs, fire and food.

The Jeep eased up the lane, windshield wipers flying to clear the fat flakes from the glass. Waffles stood with his front paws on the dashboard playing four-legged navigator. She caught Jax's smoldering look at her through the driver's side window.

It would seem she wasn't the only one planning for an interesting evening.

She detacked Apollo and returned him to his stall before heading up to the house. The Jeep was parked out front and foot, and paw prints led up the steps onto the front porch. She grabbed the last few bags out of the back and followed the trail.

She found him unloading groceries in the kitchen in a cozy scene. Jax, with snow in his hair, was putting vegetables in the refrigerator while Waffles inhaled the remains of his breakfast.

It felt... good, comfortable.

And that worried her. Was she already getting too attached? Or was she just appreciating the fine male form taking care of a domestic task? She'd probably feel the same way if she found Jax folding laundry, which was a task that she didn't bother wasting time on.

She tabled her concern for the moment and dumped her bags on the island.

"Colby took the dogs back to the farmhouse for now," she told him. "They got tired running around the stables."

"I'll check in on them when I head back out."

"How was town?"

"I forgot how stupid snow makes everyone," Jax said, filling a glass with water from the tap and downing it.

"Fistfights over bread and milk?"

"No, but there was almost a civil war over pineapple vodka."

"Yay! You got the tequila," Joey said, picking up the bottle. "I should have warned you that the liquor store before a snow storm is busier than Mrs. McCafferty's mouth."

"Actually, you can thank Taneisha for the tequila. It's a long story that involves Fitz, so don't ask. But I did get you these." He pulled out a bag of salt and vinegar chips.

"Gimmie!"

Jax handed them over and watched her rip into the bag with enthusiasm. "Oh my God. I haven't had these in forever."

Joey peered into the bag and frowned. "Why can't they put more chips and less air in the bags?"

"Because then you'd just have a big pile of chip dust."

"I'll eat all of these before dinner." She sighed mournfully.

"Then it's a good thing I got you a second bag and hid it already."

"You sure know the way to a girl's..." Joey shut herself up before she said anything stupid. She shoved another handful of chips into her face for added measure.

"So have you thought of the living arrangements for the storm?" Jax asked.

"You're staying here, right?" Joey mumbled through a mouthful of salt and vinegar. "I mean, it just makes sense logistics wise. That way we can tag team snow removal in the morning."

"I'd have two extra dogs with me," he reminded her.

Joey shrugged. "That's what the guest room is for."

"Okay then. I'm going to finish up some things on the farm, and I'll swing by the house and get the dog beds and food."

"Bring pants with an elastic waistband," Joey said. "You'll need them after dinner. I'm planning a blizzard feast."

"Beds, food, and a pair of Summer's maternity pants. Got it," Jax said, leaning against the island.

Joey smirked at the thought. She grabbed a fistful of his shirt and pulled him toward her placing a smacking kiss on his mouth.

"That better be an appetizer of what's to come," he said, moving in for another kiss.

She let him take the lead, deepening the kiss on a sigh. The kiss chased away the chill of the storm and brought Joey's blood up to a simmer. It was just their lips that touched, but she could feel the effects throughout her entire body. Like an engine revving, ready to throw caution to the wind.

He pulled back with a growl and ran his thumb over her lower lip. "I need to get back out there and finish up a few things before dark. Hold that thought?"

Breathless, Joey settled for a wide-eyed nod as an acceptable response.

He reached down to adjust himself. "I need to buy roomier jeans if we're gonna keep this up," he muttered.

Joey bit her kiss-swollen lip and watched him toss a chip in Waffles's bowl before striding out the front door.

"Get it together, Greer. You're not eighteen anymore," she mumbled to herself and set about unpacking the rest of the groceries.

As the snow fell faster outside her windows, Joey worked her way around the house, making sure she was domestically prepared for a good snow in. The generator was good to go, her propane tanks full, and the fridge stocked. There was a snow shovel at the front and back doors and a pair of snow-shoes on the back porch. Pet-friendly salt for the steps and walkways was in a heavy bucket topped with a scoop.

She hustled upstairs and put fresh sheets on the bed and pulled some extra blankets out of the linen closet. She spread out an old picnic blanket, one she'd stolen from her parents years ago, over the bed in the guest room to minimize the dog hair her overnight guests were sure to leave behind.

With Jax taking care of the last check-in for the horses, Joey jumped in the shower before changing into plaid pajama pants and a tank top. She pulled her hair back into an unruly ponytail as she took the stairs back to the first floor.

The kitchen was the place outside the stables that she felt most at home. Recipes made sense to her. She put the right ingredients in the right amounts together, followed the directions, and she was rewarded with exactly what she set out to make. It was the predictability that she found appealing. The predictability and deliciousness.

She'd baked because her mother and grandmother had baked. Her father was always a willing guinea pig and sampled every recipe from her triumphant Boston Cream cupcakes to her failed first attempt at flan. Jax and his teenage appetite had become her second biggest fan. She sometimes wondered if it wasn't her baking that lured him to her in the first place. Maybe he couldn't stand the thought of Bannon Bullock having her cookies to himself?

In college, baking had bled into cooking by necessity. Nowadays, in her well-stocked kitchen, Joey could whip up just about anything. Tonight, it was her favorite chili, a hearty recipe she reserved for the dead of winter and snowstorms. She diced onions and peppers with the efficiency of a network food show star, and while they sautéed, she unwrapped the cubed chuck and gathered her spices.

She took a minute to sync up a playlist from her laptop and shifted her cooking rhythm to match Chris Stapleton's smoky vocals.

Waffles came to investigate when Joey put the chuck in the pan, his nose sniffing with heightened interest.

"Nice try, buddy. You can settle for some tasty chicken and rice stuff."

Waffles looked disappointed. She was amazed at how quickly she'd gotten used to sharing her life with a dog. Granted, Waffles was probably an anomaly. Gia was full of stories of Diesel the puppy doing his best to destroy their house, and Carter and Summer had their hands full with the medicated Meatball.

But Waffles was the dog that always came when called and sat by the back door when he had to go outside. He'd taken to life on the farm as if he'd been born there, befriending horses and barn cats and entertaining her riding students before class. And at night, he curled into a tight ball at her feet as if he was grateful for it all. But Joey was the grateful one. Whatever happened between her and Jax, Joey knew she'd always owe him for Waffles.

She helped herself to a bottle of porter from the fridge and opened it with the bottle opener mounted on the wall next to her back door. The beer was thick and flavorful. Perfect for drinking and seasoning. She poured a half-cup into the chili and stirred. The smells were making her mouth water, and she realized she'd forgotten to grab lunch. Fueled by coffee and a need to set things in order before white, flakey chaos fell from the sky, she'd blown right past any thoughts of food.

With the chili nicely taking shape in the big pot on the range, Joey turned her attention to starting the cornbread in a cast iron skillet.

The flakes were falling fat and fast outside her cozy home. She kept an eye out the window as day turned to dusk and the snow continued to accumulate. She caught a glimpse of headlights coming up the drive and pushed the second garage door opener button signaling Jax to pull into the bay she'd emptied for him that afternoon. It would save them both time if they didn't have to dig the Jeep out from under three feet of snow.

Waffles gave a welcoming woof when Jax bustled through the front door a minute later. Valentina and Meatball were attached to leashes looped over his wrist.

Valentina headed straight for the couch while Meatball tried to scramble up the stairs, resulting in a tangle of dogs, leashes, and man. Jax extricated himself and unsnapped the leashes.

"They're not too wet. Just from the snow between here and

the garage," he said apologetically as damp footprints splattered over Joey's clean floors.

"Don't worry about it. The floors will be a mess tomorrow anyway. Consider this the pregame," she said.

Meatball hurtled up the stairs with Waffles on his heels. Valentina couldn't be bothered to be interested in her new surroundings. She ambled over to the fireplace and flopped down on a floor cushion.

"I'm gonna grab their stuff. Be back in a second."

"Do you need help?" she offered.

"If I can get those beasts in here myself, I think I can handle anything."

Meatball howled on the second floor.

Joey narrowed her eyes. "You're not going to just get in the Jeep and drive back to an empty house leaving me with this motley crew, are you?"

"The thought had occurred to me, but I'd be awfully lonely in that bed by myself." He winked.

When he returned, he was loaded down with a duffle bag, two bags of dog food, and two dog beds.

"Are you moving in?"

"Eventually. We'll probably have to add on. I'm thinking a nice, big sunroom off the back with another bedroom and office upstairs. But we'll talk about that later."

"You're insane." Joey shook her head.

Jax dumped his haul on the floor and yanked off his boots. He set them in the tray next to the door to contain the drips. Snowflakes as big as nickels clung to his head and shoulders. He shrugged out of his coat and hung it on the hook next to Joey's.

"It smells like Heaven in here," he said, coming into the kitchen to investigate.

He dropped a kiss on her cheek as he peered over her

shoulder at the stove. "Chili? And what's this? If you tell me that's cheesy cornbread, I'm going to marry you."

"Then no, it's definitely not cheesy cornbread. It's boiled Brussels sprouts."

"Liar. I'm totally marrying you." Jax turned her around and put his hands on her hips. "Hi," he said softly, before bringing his lips to hers.

It was a soft, warm kiss. The kind that melted Joey's insides like chocolate over a low flame. Decadent, delicious.

"Hi, yourself," she said when he pulled back.

"You taste like beer and beautiful," he told her.

"What does beautiful taste like?" she asked, arching an eyebrow at the line.

"You."

"Oh, boy. The snow brought me Mr. Smooth," she teased.

"Do I have time for a shower before dinner?" he asked.

"Sure, help yourself," she said, giving him a one-shoulder shrug before turning back to the stove.

"Care to join me?"

"I already had my shower. Why don't you take a beer up there to keep you company while I finish dinner?"

"Have I told you that I love you?"

"Get out of my kitchen," she ordered, rolling her eyes.

Jax grinned and helped himself to a beer from the fridge. She pointed at the bottle opener on the wall before he could ask.

"I'm serious about that marriage thing," he said, taking a swig from the bottle.

"I'm serious about the you getting out of my way thing," she said lightly.

He pressed a quick kiss to her neck. "I guess we'll see which one of us gets our way."

Jax tossed the dog beds into Joey's spare room and took the beer with him into the shower.

Usually only a summer ritual, the shower beer seemed appropriate enough for tonight. His body was sore from the physical demands of the day while his mind revved from the sense of urgency he'd worked under.

He cranked the hot water and let it pelt his aching shoulders and neck. Joey's shower was a marvel, neutral stone tile walls with jets aplenty. There was room enough for two, possibly more in the walk-in. He felt like he was standing under a tropical waterfall as the water steamed and sluiced its way down his skin.

He was never leaving. He would stand under this water until his body dissolved and flowed down the drain.

He helped himself to a swig of beer and then began to peruse Joey's bath accessories. He'd been in bathrooms of women with thousands of dollars of bath products, shelves crammed full of bottles that claimed they would tighten, soften, soothe, or protect.

Not Joey. No, Joey's bathroom had a bottle of two-in-one shampoo and conditioner, a loofa, and a bottle of generic body wash. He sniffed it, making sure it wasn't some froufrou, cloying floral scent before dumping some onto the loofa.

He could deal with smelling like "cool morning cucumber."

He stayed under the showerhead until his body forgot about the cold of the day and his beer was empty. Twisting off the water, he stepped out of the shower and grabbed one of the two neatly folded towels on the vanity and dried off. He strolled naked into the bedroom where he found Meatball snoring on his duffle bag.

"Sorry, bud. You're gonna have to move your ass. I need pants for dinner." He pushed and prodded Meatball until the beagle reluctantly got off the bag and wandered off grumbling.

He pulled on a pair of flannel pants and an old t-shirt, dug out his laptop and charger, and followed his nose back downstairs.

Joey was ladling the steamy chili into a pair of hand-thrown bowls he recognized from Purely Pottery in town. She glanced up at him and proceeded to dribble chili onto the counter.

Jax knew when a woman was interested in him. He'd seen the look in others' eyes, but it had never been as gratifying or as punch-in-the-gut exciting as when it was Joey looking at him like she was right now.

It hit him fast and bright, how much he loved her. How much he'd always loved her. Being with her in this homey scene sharpened the keen desire he had to make *this* their everyday.

"You're staring," she said in her husky voice.

"Same goes."

Her mouth curved up the slightest bit and she went back to ladling chili.

Drawn to her—and the kitchen scents—Jax followed his heart and stomach into the kitchen so he could crowd her.

She topped each bowl with a dollop of sour cream and cut thick slices of cornbread to float on top.

"Drinks?"

Joey nodded toward the fridge. "How does dinner on the couch sound?"

"Almost as good as what we did on the couch the other night," he quipped, holding up two beers. "Did the dogs eat?"

"I fed them all while you were in the shower. That's some detailed list of instructions Summer left."

Jax laughed. His brother and sister-in-law had left a long, step-by-step thesis detailing the dogs' daily routines and medications and the timing thereof. "Yeah, we have to give Meatball his thyroid meds tonight."

"Already done. I think he'll eat anything that's wrapped in cheese," Joey said, leading the way into the living room.

He followed her to the couch where he stepped in to coax Valentina off it so he and Joey could claim it for their dining pleasure.

Valentina looked devastated for half a second before climbing onto an armchair and attempting to curl up on the seat.

Jax and Joey settled side-by-side on the leather couch, both propping their bare feet on the coffee table.

"She does realize she's one hundred and twenty pounds of hugeness, right?" Joey asked, eyeing the dog.

"She's a delicate one-hundred-and-twenty-pound Great Dane flower," Jax said. All coherent thoughts immediately left his brain with the first bite of chili. "Sweet Jesus, woman. This is the best chili I've ever had in my life."

Joey laughed and blew on her spoon. "I'm surprised you didn't scald the taste buds off your tongue. Didn't your mother teach you not to inhale hot food?"

"Caution must be thrown to the wind when something that tastes like this is in front of me."

"I feel you reaching for a euphemism here," Joey told him.

"You know me well."

Joey frowned over her bowl. "Actually, no I don't."

"Jojo, you've known me since kindergarten."

"I knew you until senior year. After that, you're a mystery," she countered.

He wished more than anything that she could just forget. Forgive and forget without an explanation. Because that explanation, that why, would result in someone being cut out of her life forever, and Jax was no longer sure it would be just him. He couldn't tell her. He couldn't take that risk, not yet.

"What do you want to know?"

She arched an eyebrow at him. He knew she wanted the *why*.

"Besides that. Ask me anything, and I'll tell you."

"Anything? I like the sound of that."

His stomach unclenched when she shifted her focus to lighter things.

"How many women did you sleep with after me?"

Jax choked on a piece of cornbread and guzzled down some beer to unblock his throat. "Jesus, Joey."

She threw her head back against the cushion of the couch and laughed. "Your face was priceless. Do *not* answer that, by the way. I don't want any numbers, just like you probably don't want mine."

Jax was back to queasy at the thought. And, of course, now he could think of nothing else but the guys who'd... Was he having an aneurysm?

"What was your house in L.A. like?" Joey's question ripped him out of a waking nightmare imagining Joey screaming someone else's name in the throes of passion. *"Oh, Lester. Yes, Lester." Where the hell did Lester come from?*

"Sorry, what?"

"What was your house like?"

"My house? Uh. I don't know. Hollywood-ish I guess. Everything out there that hasn't been bulldozed and rebuilt by incredibly rich, fickle people hasn't seen a facelift since the seventies."

"Unlike the incredibly rich, fickle people," Joey quipped.

Jax grinned. "Exactly. My place was built by some semi-famous architect in the late sixties. Huge windows with a hilltop view, sunken living room. The front yard was a cliff face. I bought it furnished with this very artsy, very uncomfortable furniture."

"So is that the new Jackson Pierce? Artsy, uncomfortable, rich, and fickle?"

Jax shook his head. "That was a waypoint. I bought it mainly as an investment, which will have done quite nicely if the closing happens next month."

"You're going back?" Joey asked.

She'd kept her voice neutral, but Jax saw the way the spoon paused halfway to her mouth.

"Actually, that's something I wanted to talk to you about," he began, his tone serious.

She set her bowl down with a hard clank on the coffee table. "You're moving back to L.A.?"

Jax was about to point out that she was shouting, but he didn't have to as three dog heads all lifted from various positions of slumber to investigate.

"What about the brewery and the breeding program?" she demanded.

"You do care." He grinned, depositing his bowl next to hers. "You like me!"

"What the hell are you talking about?"

"You should see your face."

"I'm about to punch a hole in yours," she said, anger shimmering off her. Waffles stretched lazily and wandered over to sit at her feet.

"I'm not moving back. I'm flying back for a weekend to settle on the house and to go to a lame premiere."

"And then you're coming back to Blue Moon?"

Jax nodded and grabbed her hand. "I want you to come with me."

She still looked pissed. "What the hell would I do in California?"

"Me, for one. And you could put on a long, sexy dress and go to a party with me. Not to mention visiting any of the several racing stables and riding academies in the state. Plus, there's Disneyland, the Getty Center if you're into art, hiking in the canyons..."

She was staring at him like he was a lunatic.

"It's sunny there. And warm."

"Tell me more about this strange place that isn't under nearly a foot of snow already," Joey demanded, her lips twitching.

Relieved, he told her about some of his favorite things to see and do.

She shook her head. "It's just so crazy to me. None of this sounds like the Jax that left all those years ago. You have a *tailor*."

"Lots of people have tailors."

"I bet you own a tux, don't you? Normal people just rent them, you know. But I bet you had your fancy tailor make you a fancy tux."

Two actually, but he wasn't about to admit to that.

"I'm still the same guy you loved in high school, Joey." And maybe that was the problem. "Look, just say yes. Come with me. We'll go out, have a great time, laugh about how weird Hollywood is, and then we'll come home."

She was considering it. He could tell. "I don't know if I can get away from the farm," she said slowly.

"Joey."

She looked at him, cocking her head to the side.

"What do you think all this is?" he asked, circling a finger in the air. "We're babysitting the farm during a Mach seven blizzard while Carter, Summer, Beckett, and Gia gallivant around and have sex. We have a free pass."

She bit her lip in a way that he found so sexy, Jax had to stop himself from leaning over and dragging her to the ground.

"A free pass, huh?"

He nodded.

"And we'd only be gone a couple of days?"

"Three. Four tops."

She bit again. "Okay, let's go to L.A."

"Seriously?"

She shrugged. "Sure, why not?"

She didn't even see the hug tackle coming.

21

—————

*J*oey wasn't sure how they made it up the stairs, but she did know there was a trail of clothing marking the path and a pile of disappointed dogs on the other side of the bedroom door that Jax had kicked closed. He backed her up against the bed, and her fingers flew to the fly of his pants.

"Wait," he whispered against her lips.

But she wasn't interested in waiting. She tugged his drawstring free and shoved her hand inside, wrapping her fingers around his straining shaft. His groan of surrender brought flutters of excitement to her stomach. She loved the power she had over his body.

His hands slid up to cup her already bare breasts, and she lost her breath.

"God, yes," he murmured, his lips moving over her hair and forehead. She shoved his pants down his legs until he was completely naked, bared to her.

"You ever think about becoming a model?" she teased breathlessly.

He tossed her down on the bed on her back. "Funny." His

fingers dipped into the waistband of her underwear, and with a swift pull, they slid down her thighs. "Mmm."

Jax's approval drove her even closer to crazy. His long fingers skimmed over the curve of her hips and around to the backs of her thighs. He knelt between her legs, her heat seeking the fulfillment only he could offer her.

When he leaned over her, Joey let her knees fall open, welcoming him to her. He adjusted his hard-on so the smooth crown coasted over her slick folds. She gasped when the hot, smooth head teased her.

She could see his pulse in his neck as he leaned closer, his mouth nibbling at her lower lip. She bridged her hips, welcoming another teasing thrust over her growing wetness. He moved his hands to her shoulders, and she accepted his weight as he changed the angle and skimmed his mouth down to take a nipple between his lips.

His tongue darted out and stroked the straining tip until it budded in his mouth. He closed over it and began to suck. Joey's hips reflexively shot off the mattress just as his cock parted her folds and slicked over her sensitive nub.

"Jax!" The contact at her breast and between her legs was enough to shove her into a fast, edgy orgasm.

"My God. I love how you respond to me," Jax groaned. He switched to her other breast and replaced his erection with his fingers. He slid two of them inside her to catch the last tremors of her release.

Everything he did to her felt even better than the last touch, the last stroke. With his fingers inside her, Joey felt her orgasm spiral on and on. She lay rag-doll limp on the bed basking in the pleasure. But when his mouth released her breast and coasted lower, she found her bones again.

"Uh-uh. It's my turn," she said, shoving him over and onto his side with her leg.

She reversed their position, pushing him down on his back and kneeling between his thighs. She lightly kissed and bit her way up the inside of his thigh toward her target and delighted at the tensing of his muscles.

He let her play, but she could tell from his tense muscles that he wouldn't let it go on too long. She lowered her lips to the base of his shaft and pressed a soft kiss there on the hot, smooth skin stretched tight with desire.

His breath came out in a whoosh when she let her tongue dart out between her lips, forging a trail from base to crown.

Jax muttered something unintelligible and violent. Joey responded by taking him into her mouth with no preamble.

She could have sworn that he levitated right off the bed. His hands fisted on the comforter under them. Joey felt strength and restraint coiled in his body, muscles and energy begging for release. Still, he let her play and taste and stroke.

She gripped the base of his shaft and, on the next slide of her mouth, used her hand to stroke. Over and over again, her lips parted to take him to the back of her throat.

Having Jax helpless beneath her was thrilling. It made her feel powerful, strong, alive. Having him at her mercy was intoxicating.

He was fighting the pleasure so hard, she wasn't surprised when he sat bolt upright and yanked her up his body. They rolled, tangled in bedding and each other, the urgency coursing through both of them like a drum beat. She needed him inside her more than she needed oxygen.

Their mouths met in a desperate collision of heat and need. Joey's foot caught on one of the nightstands, and she heard the heavy thump of something tumbling to the floor. She shoved Jax toward the middle of the bed to save other poor defenseless home décor from a similar fate.

They met in the center of the bed on their knees where Jax

used her ponytail to gain leverage, tugging her head back. He trailed greedy kisses down her neck, teeth scraping skin. Her nails raked over Jax's strong shoulders.

"I can't wait anymore," she whispered to him.

Jax spun her around to face the headboard, and she sensed danger. He pressed against her back, hot skin, sinewy muscle holding her in place. "Are you okay like this?" he asked, brushing his lips gently against the nape of her neck.

Joey shivered and nodded. She was okay with whatever as long as the pace was fast and furious. As long as he was inside her and she was no longer aching.

"Sure?"

"Jax, stop stalling!"

She heard his husky laugh behind her, and then his hands were closing her fingers around the iron bars of her headboard. "You're gonna need to hang on." His voice was gravelly and strained in her ear. Every nerve in her body was on high alert so that even his breath against her earlobe had her shaking with anticipation.

God, yes.

He forced her legs a little wider with his knee, and she barely managed to stifle a gasp when she felt him against her. The smooth head of his cock probed with the lightest pressure against her primed center. His hands closed over hers again, and in one sure thrust, he was sheathed inside her.

Joey did moan now. This was what she wanted, this feeling of fullness that chased all other thoughts out of her head. There was room for nothing but pleasure and the craving for more.

He was moving now, an achingly slow rhythm that had her head falling back against his shoulder.

"You're everything to me." He gritted the words out against

her throat, sliding into her until every inch of him was buried in her heat.

She taunted him with her hips, swiveling them and pressing back against him. She wanted him fast and a little rough. Not whispering sweet nothings in her ear, sweet nothings that shot straight to her bruised heart.

His hands abandoned hers for her breasts, cupping them in his calloused palms. The speed she was so desperate for came now. A fast thrill raced through her as she felt Jax's control slip just a little more.

She bent at the waist, her head dipping between her outstretched arms and hips driving back against him as he thrust harder. The snow outside her windows was forgotten as the heat rose degree by scorching degree.

Exhilaration and anticipation spiked in her. This was what she'd silently mourned deep in her soul all those years. This need tangled with an intimacy so raw she couldn't tell whether they were two or one. She'd never had this with another man, had feared she would never find it again.

And what exactly did that mean that she had found it again with Jax? But the thought tumbled out of her head when he skimmed a palm over her stomach and then lower to stroke her.

His thrusts were becoming wilder, more erratic. Her fingers cramped on the thin bars that she gripped like lifelines. Sounds of desire—the slap of flesh to flesh, the short gasps of breath—filled the room.

"I need you to come, Joey," he ordered.

"Come with me." She selfishly wanted to feel it again, that second when two people couldn't be any closer. She wanted her release to drag him with her, to share the fall and spiral down, down, down together.

The pads of his fingers worked her sensitive nub,

swamping her system with a pleasure there was no defense against.

"Jax." His name was a gasp, a prayer.

"I'm with you. I'm with you."

And he was. As she felt the first tremors of her release, Jax gave a triumphant shout behind her. He poured himself into her matching tremor for tremor as she dissolved around him. Joey didn't see snowflakes. She saw fireworks. Bright and bold in the night as she surrendered everything.

"Jax?"

"Huh?"

"Are you alive?"

Jax took an inventory of his body. It was still there, sprawled over Joey's bed and part of Joey. His heart still beat. His breath still moved. But he couldn't seem to find the will to move.

"I think so."

"Good." Joey's voice was muffled by the pillow her face was in. "Am I alive?"

"More or less." He mustered the energy and rolled over, pulling her with him so she could breathe.

"So that's what it feels like," she said, stretching lazily.

"That's what what feels like?"

"The earth moving." She gave him a sleepy smile.

Jax laughed. "Angels singing."

"Fireworks. There were definitely fireworks."

"Fireworks in a blizzard. I like that we can do that." Jax sighed, wishing she would roll again and nestle into him.

But Joey liked space for her long limbs.

"You know what would make this even better?" Joey asked wistfully.

"What's that?"

"Another bowl of chili."

Downstairs, they found their bowls licked clean under the coffee table. Waffles wouldn't meet Joey's gaze, and Valentina looked guilty. Meatball was still licking his chops by the fire.

"I'll get clean bowls," Jax volunteered.

Joey went to the back door and opened it. "We're up to a foot already," she said, gauging the depth of the snow. The dogs roused themselves to trot through the door for an impromptu potty break. Jax watched as Joey tugged on a pair of snow boots and stomped her way to the edge of the deck to watch the dogs tear around the backyard.

He ladled chili into both bowls and popped them in the microwave.

"Jax, come see," Joey called from the deck.

Every time Jax thought he couldn't love her more, he fell just a little bit further. This was no different. She stood bathed in the spotlight mounted on the back of the house. Fat flakes floated down to land in hair the color of chestnuts. The dogs raced a zigzag pattern in the yard in front of her, barking and yipping, sending clouds of snow up to mingle with the falling flakes.

Behind him, the warmth of fire and home. He'd never wanted anything more than this. This was where he belonged. Her world was his, and he needed her to understand that, to believe that. But now was not the time for declarations or ultimatums. Joey didn't respond to either of those. He would find a way to make her see that he belonged here with her.

Joey laughed as Meatball took a turn too tight and tumbled, sending snow in all directions. She looked back at Jax, her hair tousled from his hands, her color high. Her legs bare between the hem of his shirt that she'd pulled on and the tops of her boots.

"I think we're going to need some towels for these idiots," she said jerking a thumb at the dog action behind her.

"I'll grab some as soon as I do this," Jax said, crossing the deck to her. One hand wound around the back of her neck. The other gripped her hip. Her lips parted as if she was going to ask a question, but he silenced her with his mouth.

He kissed her under the porch light, under the sky of snow. He moved both hands to cup her jaw, gentling the pressure. He poured his love for her into the kiss so there could be no doubt in her mind. Flakes fell silently, landing in their hair and on their shoulders, and still he kissed her, claiming her mouth in a gentle prison of breath and taste.

When he felt her knees buckle, he steadied her and broke contact with her mouth.

She laughed nervously. "What the hell was that?" Her voice was a whisper.

Jax grinned and tapped her nose with his finger. "I'll go get some towels. Come inside before you get frostbite on that perfect ass of yours."

When she only nodded, he felt he'd won a victory of sorts.

He went back inside and found some rough looking towels in the bottom of her linen closet.

"Are you ready for us?" Joey called from the backdoor when Jax came down the stairs.

They let one dog in at a time and scrubbed them down with towels until they were dry enough to turn loose on the house. Meatball repeatedly licked Joey in the face while she tried to dry his paws.

"He really grows on you, doesn't he?" she asked as the beagle scampered off to check his food dish.

"Even his farts have a certain charm about them," Jax admitted.

"Well I wouldn't go that far."

They reconvened to the couch with loose muscles and second supper. Jax put his feet up on the coffee table, and Joey tucked hers into his lap.

They ate in companionable silence, ignoring three pairs of brown beggy eyes. And when the dishes were done and the leftovers tucked away, they returned to the couch, Jax with his laptop and papers and Joey with her romance novel.

His phone signaled from the coffee table. He glanced at the screen and snorted.

"What?" Joey asked, stretching lazily.

"Carter wants to know how many inches we have here. They've got six inches in the hotel parking lot."

"Tell him that's what we have here. Otherwise he's going to text us both incessantly."

"Lie to my brother?" Jax gasped in feigned horror.

Joey eyed him over her book.

"You're right. Good call. Lying to my brother," he said, as he fired off a quick text.

She looked restlessly out the back window at the falling snow.

"What's wrong?" Jax asked.

She shrugged her slim shoulders. "I just wish I could do one more check on the horses, but I really don't feel like wading through a foot of snow between here and the stables."

"Then allow me to direct your attention here..." Jax said, swiveling his laptop around to face her with a flourish. He opened a browser window and keyed in a URL and then handed the computer over to her.

"What's this? Hey, that's Lolly and Romeo!" Joey said,

sitting up and peering at the screen in delight. "How did you do that?"

"I set up a couple of Wi-Fi-enabled cameras around the stable and the barn. This way we can keep an eye on everything from the safety and warmth of your couch."

"You're a freaking genius."

"Trust me. It was purely selfish. I knew you'd be dragging me up there in the dead of night, and I thought this would be easier and warmer."

"Look! You got the cows and Clementine in the barn."

Clementine's yellow eyes glowed on camera as she stared eerily at the camera.

"Does she ever blink?" Jax asked. "I mean seriously, even on camera she looks like a demon."

"Leave poor Clementine alone," Joey teased.

"Poor Clementine? Did I tell you how she tried to attack me through the door of her stall today? Waffles had to rescue me."

"Poor baby," Joey crooned.

"That goat has it in for me," Jax muttered.

"Did you see how much weight those Jerseys have put on this week? Dr. Ames is going to be thrilled when she sees them next week."

"If we dig out by then," Jax teased.

"I wouldn't say no to being snowed in for a few days. It's nice to not have so many people around all the time." Joey sighed.

"My pretty little introvert."

"I thought I was just grumpy."

"Maybe a little of that too," he said, tugging her ponytail.

Satisfied that her animals were safe and cozy despite the active blizzard, Joey turned her attention back to her hardback, and Jax took out the folder of his father's essays. With limited free time recently, he'd only read a handful of the stories so far, but tonight seemed like the perfect time to catch up.

Code Word: Livestock Auction by John Pierce

The title caught his eye as Jax fondly remembered that every summer for years, he and his brothers would be shipped off to Aunt Rose and Uncle Melvin's home in the Pocono Mountains of Pennsylvania for a long weekend when their parents traveled to the Tri-State Livestock Auction. When they were younger, they clambered to go along with their parents. When they were older, they clambered to be left home by themselves. But the answer was always no.

Every year, like clockwork, his parents packed up and off they went, sale papers and stock stats in hand. His parents never told them much about the auction, and they never seemed to buy anything, but they had always come home happier and more relaxed than when they left. He was curious what kind of experience his father would have that made him want to document the memory.

Even a man so firmly planted in the earth as a family farmer can experience the wistful beckon of wanderlust. It is particularly poignant when everyone around you prepares for beach vacations or lake getaways while you protect your harvest from Mother Nature morning 'til night.

For Phoebe it was often worse. Managing our books and house, lending me a hand a dozen times a day, all while running herd on one, two, and then three boys meant just about every hour of every day was spoken for.

It happened by accident, our desire to do right by the land, by the boys, by each other, that we forgot about what we might need.

One particularly steamy July night, I came home to chaos.

Carter, in his five-year-old glory, had attempted to glue Beckett's head to the table—thankfully he had gone with Elmer's and not any of the heavy-duty adhesives I had, until that point, left in plain sight throughout the barn and garage. The dog had rolled in something that smelled like a garbage dump full of dead bodies and apparently had eaten a good portion of it because he threw it up in front of the stove where Phoebe was making dinner.

It had been a long day for me, as well, sweating and bleeding over equipment too old to see it through one more season and fields that were hell bent on being destroyed by drought and those goddamn spider mites.

I walked into the house and saw the woman I love, the woman my heart beats for, one second away from a justified meltdown. I saw her take a breath, a shallow shaky one, pull it all back in, order the boys upstairs to the bath and the dog outside so she could clean up the mess for no other reason than to be prepared for the next disaster. Our suitcase was by the front door, packed and ready for the Tristate Livestock Auction the next day, and dinner was burning on the stovetop.

I did what I'd learned to do living with a fiery, mule-headed woman who would stubbornly stay the course despite the rocks ahead. I walked into the kitchen, turned off the stove, and poured Phoebe the biggest glass—this time a mason jar—of wine I could find. Then I turned my attention to cleaning up whatever carcass Pancake had retched up.

After a few healthy sips, Phoebe went upstairs to check on the boys, and I started to think. When was the last time we'd had a vacation, just the two of us? The livestock auction certainly didn't count, and every other road trip or winter vacation happened with three boys in tow.

Maybe it was time for a change?

The next morning, we packed up the car and drove the kids to

Phoebe's sister and brother-in-law's place in the Poconos. And then instead of driving to the auction, I took my wife to the Jersey Shore. Her face lit up when I pulled up in front of the shabby bed and breakfast I'd desperately booked the night before. And it made me feel equal parts hero and fool, wishing I had done this years ago.

We spent the next three days lazing on the beach, eating in restaurants that would have horrified our PB and J kids, and pretending we had all the time in the world to do the things we wanted.

We never went back to the auction. Every year after that, the Livestock Auction was code for freedom. It became a tradition that I booked the trip and surprised Phoebe with the destination. We counted down the days to our next adventure together, not as parents or farmers or even adults. But as partners in crime. And crime it became.

This year, with an iffy harvest on the horizon, we stayed close to home to explore the Finger Lakes. The summer was hotter than ever, and despite the ice-cold air conditioning in our hotel room and the crystal blue waters of its pool, something crazy took hold of us.

Maybe it was the oysters we shared at dinner. Maybe it was the heady feeling of freedom on our first night away from home. Whatever it was, we found ourselves jumping off a dock on Cayuga Lake at midnight. Naked.

It was as if, between the moonlight and the lake waters, all sense of responsibility and propriety was washed away. We were two souls, enjoying the romance of the moment unhindered by societal and familial roles. Splashing, playing, teasing.

I'd learned long ago that actions spoke louder than words with my Phoebe. A man could say "I love you" 'til he was blue in the face, but send her out on the porch with fresh lemonade while I do the dishes or surprise her with a ridiculous and completely sappy bouquet of flowers picked in the fields, and she heard me loud and clear.

This particular night the only thing we heard loud and clear was "Come out of the water, now," as spoken by the annoyed state trooper over the loudspeaker of her car.

In our midnight fun, we'd somehow missed her arrival. She stood on the dock, sweating in full uniform, between the discarded piles of our clothes. A consummate professional, the officer was. We couldn't tell if she was surprised that she was rousting two forty-year-olds from the cool lake waters.

She handed us our clothes without a hint of a smile, and while I tried to shimmy my way into my underwear, Phoebe babbled on about escaping our three children and our lives at home.

The trooper nodded silently, taking notes in her notebook. She took our licenses back to the patrol car, and we dressed quickly, vacillating between laughter and embarrassment. Would our first arrest be for public nudity? In Blue Moon Bend it was a perfectly respectable thing to be arrested for. The community had hosted a clothing-optional Summer Solstice party until the late seventies.

The trooper returned, licenses in hand. She turned them over to us, and we waited for the punishment to be meted out.

"I have two kids under the age of two at home," she said.

And with that, she turned and got back in her car and drove off. No ticket, no citation, no order to appear in front of a judge.

Phoebe and I laughed ourselves silly the whole way back to the hotel where we had to perform a soggy walk of shame past the front desk. It was worth it, every single second, to share that with my wife.

Even now, years later, I can say the words "Cayuga Lake" to Phoebe, and we'll both be transported back to that night, that taste of freedom, that brush with the law. The excitement of a single spontaneous moment.

It's made us better partners and better parents. As we can

easily remember the lure of the moment, the siren song of adventure, and the sting of reprimand. Now, when the boys get caught doing something so stupid you have to wonder if they've had a head trauma, I remember Cayuga Lake and the Livestock Auction, and I know what it's like to want to jump head first into freedom.

Jax cleared his throat, trying to dislodge the emotion that clogged it. He'd never be able to put into words what it meant to him to have access to his father like this. Unfiltered by a father-son relationship, just his true words on paper painting a picture of his parents that he'd never had before.

"Everything okay?" Joey asked over her open book.

He looked at her and smiled. Everything was great. And maybe he'd take a page out of his father's book and surprise Joey with something besides whispered words of love tomorrow.

But first, he'd text his mother.

Jax: Cayuga Lake.

Her response was succinct.

Phoebe: Smart ass.

22

---

*D*ig out began promptly at six the next morning despite the fact that the snow was still briskly falling. Twenty-eight inches of white, fluffy flakes coated the pre-dawn world of Blue Moon.

Joey's priority—after having Jax dig out a dog-friendly potty break area in the yard—was to clear a path with the Jeep to the stables so she could start the morning feeding.

Colby texted to say he and his little brother were on their way to the farm on snowmobiles. They'd start the dig out there with the ATVs. Jax would split his time between the two sites, and they'd all meet back at Joey's for breakfast at ten.

She climbed into the freezing cold passenger seat of Carter's Jeep and hit the button on the garage door opener. The door rolled up to reveal a monstrous drift blocking their path.

"Ready?" Jax asked with a grin.

Joey gripped the handle on the dash. "Oh, yeah. Punch it."

The Jeep lurched forward, sending plumes of snow over the hood as they charged out of the garage.

Joey hooted her approval while Jax expertly plowed a path down the hill toward the stables.

They pulled up to the front of the barn and eyed the five-foot drift that glistened in the headlights in front of the door. "Next time we're putting up a snow fence," Joey grumbled. She grabbed the shovel out of the backseat. "I'll start on the drift," she told Jax.

"I'll clear in front of the building and come help with feeding," he told her.

"Enjoy your nice warm vehicle." Joey sighed and slipped out the passenger door. She'd dressed in layers, knowing how quickly shoveling got her temperature up. Plus, the furnace in the barn would keep the temperature close to fifty degrees, so she'd be able to shuck the heavy Carhartt jacket in no time.

She tackled the drift efficiently, working to clear the snow away from the door and mounding it to prevent more drifts. Her body felt primed and ready for a challenge. Last night's sexual acrobatics and the deepest sleep she could remember in recent history left her feeling energetic, almost cheerful.

Just as dawn began to break behind her, the shovel finally met the base of the door, and she scooped the last foot out of the way.

The barn door swung open, and with the flip of a light switch, Joey was relieved to see the normalcy inside. The furnace had survived the night, which meant the pipes shouldn't be frozen and her morning had just gotten a whole lot easier.

A couple of barn cats meandered out of their hidey-holes to greet her. She refilled their food dishes and checked their water before moving down the aisle to greet her horses.

Everyone was awake and ready for breakfast. She stopped in the office to shed her jacket and start the coffee. Water buckets were first. Joey started at the back of the stables and worked her way forward, emptying the heated buckets, cleaning them, and refilling them with warm water. Each bucket hung flat against the stall wall near a recessed outlet. The power kept the water at a warm enough temperature to prevent freezing, enticing the horses to drink.

Jax came in, stomping snow off his boots and sending the barn cats scurrying for cover. He sniffed the air and went straight for the coffee in the office. He reappeared and handed her his mug. She took a deep pull, wrinkling her nose at the sugarless brew.

"I'll start haying at the back while you finish the water," he said, taking his mug back.

"Sounds good." Joey nodded and watched him saunter toward the feed room. His jeans were worn and hung low on his hips. There were holes in the knee and one in the ass that offered a glimpse of dark purple underwear. One of the sleeves of his blue- and white-checked flannel jacket was torn, and the gray Henley beneath it was cut tight over his chest. Two days of stubble at his jaw and bed-tousled hair given to curl at the ends gave him the look of a sleepy-eyed fallen angel.

What she wouldn't give to get him back in her bed right now.

She shook herself and rolled her eyes at her schoolgirl fantasies. They had work to do. Livestock didn't wait patiently for her to roll out of bed and skip down the aisle with feed. There was a schedule to be followed, order to be upheld. And maybe later she could sink her hands into Jax's lightly curling hair and do all those unspeakable things she wanted to do.

She made quick work of the rest of the water buckets and took over the haying duties from Jax. With a parting kiss and another coffee refill, he headed out to blaze a trail between stables and farm.

Joey opened her music app on the computer in the office and piped soothing classical songs into the barn. The horses responded well to classical—and country—and she hoped to keep them mellow for as long as possible while confined to their stalls. The next two hours passed quickly while she mucked and hit the feed bins with a second breakfast of grain.

She swept the stable alley clean of straw and nodded her satisfaction at a job well done. Usually Colby and another part-time helper handled the morning feeding, and she'd forgotten how productive she felt with thirty mounts all happily fed and stalls cleaned.

It was time to head back to the house to check in on the dogs and get a breakfast of champions started. Her stomach growled in agreement. She closed up the stable door and hustled through the three inches of new snowfall back to the house.

Peering through the window, Joey found all three dogs curled up on the couch happily snoozing the morning away. The turning of the handle brought them all to the door barking and shedding and skittering for purchase.

"Okay, okay. Everybody outside before you get too excited and pee." She looked sternly at Meatball. Waffles, understanding everything she said, scampered to the back door. She ushered them out and went into the kitchen to start breakfast. Bacon and cheddar waffles with a side of sausage links was what a morning like this called for. And coffee. Gallons of coffee.

She enjoyed it, the meal preparation for more than just herself. Cooking for others had always held a secret kind of pleasure for her. And just because this was a mid-morning break from hard labor didn't mean she shouldn't fuss a little.

JAX DROVE Colby and his younger brother Brody up to Joey's house, stopping at the skinny shovel-cleared path to the front door. Three semi-frozen men looking for a hot meal and a reason to take off their boots poured out of the Jeep and up the porch steps.

He opened the front door to twelve dancing feet as the dogs swarmed them.

Joey waved a greeting with a spatula from the kitchen. "Grab some coffee, guys. Breakfast'll be ready in a minute."

They shucked off snowy layers and hung them on the drying rack Joey had thoughtfully set up inside the door.

"How's the farm?" Joey asked from the stove.

"Under an avalanche, but I think we got a good bit cleared," Colby answered, making a beeline for the coffee.

"Creamer's in the fridge if you want any," Jax said, remembering the bottle Joey had him buy yesterday.

He made a move to drop a kiss on Joey's cheek, and she dodged him. He bit back a sigh at her shyness. An audience shouldn't matter, and the fact that she was still acting like this was a casual fling was going to start pissing him off.

He took in the spread she'd laid out on the island. A stack of piping hot waffles with—dear Lord, was that bacon?—sat next to the tray that she was dumping perfectly browned sausage links onto. A jar of homemade strawberry jam was open next to the toaster and a loaf of bread. Creamy grits topped with cheese and hot sauce warmed on the stove.

This was love. This was how Joey showed her heart. Baking and cooking. Feeding the ones she cared about. For years, she'd squirreled away little bags of cookies for him. Every dessert she'd ever brought to family get-togethers, it was all her heart she was serving up. He wondered if she knew it. If she realized that with every waffle, every sausage link, every perfect cup of coffee, she was saying "I love you."

His father's words ran through his head. *I'd learned long ago that actions spoke louder than words...*

Maybe it was time for him to find a better way to tell her he loved her.

Brody poured himself a glass of orange juice from the pitcher and pulled out a barstool to sit. His straw-colored hair stuck up at all angles after swiping off the orange knit cap.

"This looks awesome, Jo," he told her.

"Thanks, Bro." She winked.

The tops of his hormonal, teenaged ears pinked up.

Jax rolled his eyes at Colby. He remembered what it was like to be eighteen and knew the thoughts that were rolling around in there, especially where Joey Greer was concerned.

His phone vibrated in the back pocket of his jeans. It was a text from Carter with screenshots of Blue Moon's Facebook group, all snowy scenes from downtown.

Carter: Your pants are on fire.

Jax smirked. He fired back a response.

Jax: That's the only thing keeping my balls from freezing while I dig your farm out from under eight feet of snow.

Carter's reply came quickly.

Carter: Not sure whether to say fuck you or thank you.

Jax laughed and passed his phone to Joey so she could read the texts while he loaded up a plate of heavenly breakfast. He'd show her in kind. And, in doing so, would give a nod to his father's insights on how to love a stubborn woman.

~

WITH THE BULK of the snow cleared from the essential access points of the farm by early afternoon, Jax sent Colby and Brody home and set about cleaning up the fresh snowfall. Carter had texted him so many times that Jax finally left his phone in the Jeep and enjoyed the blissful solitude.

The snow was finally starting to taper off, and with it the work. With breakfast far behind them, lunch was sounding like a better and better idea. And it would be the perfect opportunity to drag Joey away from work to surprise her with a little slice of fun.

What would be more romantic than a blizzard picnic?

He surveyed the barn, looking for the ideal spot. He settled on the small storage room off the main door. It had a handful of small windows that looked out on the snow, and it was far enough away from Clementine's stall that she wouldn't ruin the moment.

In the farmhouse, he pulled the quilt off his bed and gathered some floor pillows from the great room. He tweaked the set up on the barn floor, angling the quilt this way and that for effect until he was satisfied. Then it was back to the house to forage for a lunch that didn't look thrown together.

It wasn't easy in a household of vegetarians. But Jax raided his own lunchmeat stash and built a pair of sandwiches that would make a deli proud. He wrapped up dill pickles and stole two of the single serve bags of chips that Summer rationed for herself. Dessert was difficult. There was no ice cream in the freezer, and if he wanted baked goods, he'd have to sneak into Joey's cookie jar. Finally, he spotted

Oreos in the back of the pantry and filled a sandwich bag with them.

He dug out a bottle of champagne that Carter had tucked away after Beckett and Gia's wedding in the wine cooler. Jax grabbed two champagne flutes and threw everything into a cardboard box he found upstairs and headed back across the yard to the barn. The mound of snow next to the door made a convenient champagne ice bucket, so he screwed the bottle into the drift up to its neck and left the glasses sitting on the window's ledge.

Back inside, he unloaded his haul and neatly laid sandwiches on plates and accessorized with chips, pickles, and Oreos.

He folded the paper towels he'd brought as napkins and tucked them under each plate. The whole scene looked cozy and romantic. *Even Joey wouldn't be able to resist*, he thought with a satisfied nod.

He took the Jeep over to the stables and found Joey picking the hooves of a freshly groomed pony on the crossties in the stable aisle. Jax loved watching her when she worked. Every move was competent, efficient. No energy was wasted. She moved with a precision and a purpose that made horses and people fall in line to keep up. It was obvious that her heart was here too.

She never skimped on the care of her horses, never let anyone else give a sub-par effort there either. It was one of the reasons her riding lesson program had grown so quickly. She had a way of impressing the importance of care and discipline while still preserving the wonder of what it felt like to ride and be in tune with a mount.

"Good boy, Roscoe," she said, patting the pony's neck. "Everything healed up nicely."

"Thrush?" Jax asked.

Surprised by his presence, Joey glanced up. "Nope. A sole bruise. But everything looks good now."

"Good. Are you hungry?"

Joey frowned. "What time is it?"

"Almost three. I thought we could break for a late lunch."

"Sounds good. I've got chili leftovers at the house," she offered.

He shook his head. "I took the liberty of arranging lunch for us."

Joey raised her eyebrows. "Well, aren't you thoughtful? Let me put Roscoe here back in his stall, and I'll be ready. Where are we eating?"

"I thought we'd do a little farm to table in the barn."

"That sounds... odd."

Jax grinned at his practical girl.

They bumped along the snowy drive from stables to farm, pausing briefly to note that the plows hadn't yet come through on the road.

"We could be snowed in for days," Joey said, sliding out of the passenger seat.

Jax led the way to the barn door. "I wouldn't mind."

"The only downside is Carter and Summer can't come back and pick up the slack. Summer already texted me four times asking me to go into her office just to check this and check that."

"She's probably driven the guest editor insane by now, and that's why she's coming to you," Jax predicted, he pulled the bottle of champagne out of the snow.

"The thought had crossed my mind. Just exactly what kind of lunch are we having here?" Joey asked suspiciously.

"A blizzard picnic," he said, twisting the cork until it popped free.

He plucked the flutes off the windowsill and filled them with the festive liquid.

"To blizzards," he toasted.

"To blizzards," Joey echoed, raising the glass to her lips.

Jax pulled the door open and stepped aside motioning her inside.

"I know we're not eating with Clementine," Joey joked. "Are we in with the pigs?"

"We have our own space today," he said, gesturing toward the storage room.

Joey stuck her head in the door. "Oh shit," she said.

"What's wrong? Don't you like sandwiches?"

Joey turned around and put a hand on his chest to stop him from going through the doorway.

"Don't freak out, okay?"

"Why would I freak out—" He heard the demonic bleat of a goat. But it wasn't coming from Clementine's stall. It was coming from his picnic.

He stormed through the door and took in the scene. "What the hell?"

Clementine stood on the quilt devouring the second sandwich. She'd also eaten a hole in one of the cushions, shredded the cardboard box he'd used to cart everything outside, and crapped on his damn quilt.

"I'm going to murder her," Jax growled. Joey made a grab for him, and he made a grab for the goat, but Clementine saw him coming and danced to the side.

Jax and Joey ended up in a tangle of limbs on the floor.

"You are the worst farm animal in the history of farm animals," Jax yelled, trying to extricate himself from Joey's arms.

Clementine swooped back around and grabbed an Oreo off one of the plates.

"Those are my cookies!"

Joey was laughing so hard she still hadn't stood back up.

"It's not funny. This was supposed to be sweet and romantic," he grumbled, making another grab for the goat.

That only made her laugh harder until she snorted. "Don't be mad, Jax," Joey giggled.

Clementine bleated in glee.

"I'm going to find a goat rescue that specializes in asshole goats, and that's where you're going," he told Clementine. She feinted left, and when he sprang in that direction, Clementine turned to the right and ran out the door into the main barn.

Jax tripped over a bale of hay and landed face first on his ruined picnic.

"Please stop. Please," Joey gasped. "If you move or say one more thing, I'm going to pee my pants." She took a deep breath and tried to calm the laughter. "Oh my God. Oh my God. I am never going to forget this as long as I live."

Well, it looked like he had his own Cayuga Lake now. At least the cops weren't involved.

JOEY FELT guilty enough for laughing hysterically all over Jax's disastrous attempt at lunch that she decided to make up for it. She roasted a chicken and made mashed potatoes and gravy for dinner that night. All of which she served wearing her cozy white robe tied tight.

For dessert, she took off her robe and gave Jax an eyeful of sexy, sheer bralette and shorts. It was completely impractical as far as underwear was concerned. The set had come free with an order of the sturdy sports bras she preferred for work, and she hadn't had a use for it, until tonight.

It seemed to do the job, though, as Jax cheered up considerably and stopped threatening to deport Clementine to Siberia. And after a spectacular round of orgasms for them both, they ate slices of second dessert, chocolate cake with peanut butter icing, in bed.

The dogs exhausted themselves playing outside for an hour and fell asleep in a clump at their feet. Meatball, his little Beagle face resting on Valentina's back, was snoring. Joey turned on the bedroom TV to a sitcom and snuggled deeper into the pillows. She stuffed her bare toes under Jax's leg for warmth.

Jax pulled out his laptop and divided his time between frowning at his screen while typing furiously and sending sidelong glances at her.

"What are you working on?" Joey asked.

"Answering brewery emails—we're closed tomorrow, by the way—and working on some script polishing."

"Is this the one you turned in to Scary Al?"

He grinned. "I'll have to tell her you said that. She'll love it. And yes, it's the same script."

"What's it about?"

He paused just long enough for her to know what came out of his mouth next wasn't the entire truth, and it made her curious.

"It's, uh, a love story."

"Don't you usually write the shoot 'em up, blow 'em to bits stuff?" she asked, even more curious now.

"Every once in a while, I like to dabble."

"Huh," Joey said. She rolled over to face him. "So what's the process like?"

"For a screenplay?"

"Yeah."

"Well, either you get an assignment from a studio saying 'write this' or you have an idea of your own and write it on spec to sell to a studio. Once a studio picks it up, they try to get their ducks in a row to actually develop the project. That's when a whole bunch of people get involved and I send Al in to handle it all for me. She hammers out a purchase price that she's happy with and twists some arms to get it, and then I get to work with the studio's team to handle rewrites."

"Do you have any say in what happens to it after a studio buys your stuff?"

"Not everyone does, but Al always makes sure I'm involved and have a voice. I started doing some producing a year or two ago and that helps keep my vision intact."

Joey grinned. "You have vision."

"Shut up."

Joey's phone dinged on the nightstand next to her. She rolled over to look at the screen and laughed.

"I think your Mom needs a break from babysitting."

She held up her phone so Jax could see Phoebe's text.

Phoebe: If the roads are clear, I'm coming to your house tomorrow, drinking a bottle of wine, and napping.

Jax laughed. "She raised me and my brothers. How hard can Evan and Aurora be?"

Joey texted her back.

Joey: Kids driving you nuts?

Phoebe: I raised three boys. And right now I'm thanking the universe that it wasn't three girls.

Joey: Bring them by tomorrow. I could use Evan's help in the stables. We'll put Jax on Aurora duty.

Phoebe: Thank you, thank you, thank you! You're my favorite out of all my children.

Joey read the text and made a hmm noise.

"What's that noise mean?" Jax asked.

"Your mom just said I'm one of her kids, which makes what we just did in this bed illegal and gross."

23

Joey waved as Franklin's red SUV coasted to a stop in front of the stables. Phoebe sprang out of the passenger seat before the kids piled out of the back.

"We brought you children and an extra dog," she said as Diesel tumbled out of the backseat and into the snow. "I owe you big time," she added in a whisper.

The fat gray puppy yipped excitedly when he saw Waffles and the two dogs took off running up the drive toward the house.

"Okay, I owe Waffles too. Tripod and Mr. Snuffles are enjoying a quiet, peaceful house without Cutie Destructo there." Phoebe leaned in to give Joey a hug. "Now where's that handsome son of mine?"

"He's inside finishing up the mucking and stealing all of my coffee," Joey said, jerking her thumb behind her.

"Hey, Joey," Evan said, stuffing his gloved hands into the pockets of his winter coat.

"How's it going, Ev? I could use a hand exercising some of the horses if you don't mind."

"Sure," he said, beaming. He leaned in a little closer to her and lowered his voice. "We should probably take Aurora with us. I think she's driving Phoebe and Grampa nuts."

Joey riffed the bill of his cap. "Good call, kid. Hey, Aurora, feel like riding Princess this morning?"

"Yay!" Aurora in her pink snowsuit clapped her mittened hands together. "I get to ride Princess!"

Jax ambled out of the barn with Valentina on his heels. "Hey, Mom," he said, giving Phoebe a peck on the cheek. He gave Franklin and Evan hearty handshakes and then swept Aurora up into the air and spun her around until she squealed in delight.

"Jazz, I'm gonna ride Princess today!" the little girl announced.

"Well, I guess we'd better get her saddled up then," Jax said, tickling her. "How were the roads?" he asked Franklin.

"Plows have one lane cleared between here and town. They should be able to open up the second lane sometime this afternoon."

"How's the rest of town look?"

"Oh, you know Blue Moon," Phoebe said waving her hand. "Everyone's been out and about with snow shoes and cross-country skis since yesterday morning. They all want to know if the brewery will be open tomorrow."

"I have a call in to Calvin to see if his brother-in-law can bring his plow truck in to do the parking lot today," Jax said, setting Aurora down on the ground. "So what are you two doing while we give the horses some exercise?"

Phoebe looked pleadingly at Joey.

"Why don't you two head over to the farm and make sure the house is still standing since no one's been staying there," Joey suggested.

Phoebe's pleading look immediately changed to one of keen interest. "Oh, so Jax has been staying...?"

"Here, *Mother*," Jax said pointedly.

"Well, isn't that nice?" Phoebe's grin was so big it looked like it might split her face wide open. "Isn't that nice, dear?" she said again to Franklin.

"If you say it's nice, then it's very nice," Franklin agreed. "If it's okay with you guys, we can make lunch at the farmhouse."

"What's for lunch?" Joey asked, perking up.

"Chicken parmesan and breadsticks," Franklin said.

Joey whooped.

"What time do you want us there?" Jax asked, scratching Valentina's head.

"How about around noon?" Phoebe suggested.

"We'll be there exactly at noon. So be ready and presentable," Jax said.

"Very funny, *son*."

"Do we have to get dressed up?" Evan asked with concern.

"No, but everyone is required to wear pants," Joey explained, enjoying Phoebe and Franklin's discomfort.

"I like pants," Aurora announced cheerfully.

BETWEEN JOEY, Jax, and Evan, they were able to lunge or ride ten of the more energetic mounts and run herd on Aurora. The girl never stopped. Joey made a note to herself to ask Gia if the kid walked and talked in her sleep.

Evan, on the other hand, turned out to be a huge help. He had all the makings of a good, solid horseman. His face had remained serious when she'd mentioned as much to him, but his ears turned pink with pride.

After the last pony was groomed and the aisle swept clean,

they rounded up the dogs and started for the farmhouse. With two adults, two kids, and four dogs, it was easier to just walk. So they meandered down the plowed trail toward Carter's house. It was a peaceful walk with Aurora chattering on about school and Princess and Grampa and Phoebe letting her stay up late.

Jax fell back from their group, and Joey's instincts were a split second too late. The snowball caught her in the shoulder just as she dodged to the left.

"We're under fire!" she yelled to the kids. Evan responded immediately, scooping a fistful of snow and hurling it at Aurora.

"Hey!" Aurora yelled. She dug her mittened hands into the snow and scooped it like a shovel at Diesel who tried to eat the snow shower.

"We're turning on each other," Joey yelled. "We need to band together against the enemy!" She pointed at Jax who was building a snowball arsenal while they fought amongst themselves.

Her snowball hit Jax squarely in the chest. The battle raged fast and furious with snowballs flying in all directions. Aurora hit Joey in the side of the face with a tiny clump of snow while Evan outflanked Jax and hit him in the ass with a perfect shot.

They held their ground as long as they could, but Jax's superiority in snowball production and delivery soon became clear.

"Fall back, troops," Joey called and started to run toward the farmhouse. Aurora scampered in front of Joey, and she picked the little girl up and tossed her into a snow bank.

"Run, Evan! He'll go after the weakest one first," Joey yelled over her shoulder. Evan laughed hysterically at his little sister trying to wiggle out of the snowdrift.

"Time out! I'm stuck!" Aurora giggled.

Jax pulled the little girl out by her feet and dumped a handful of snow on her head.

The dogs, energized by the heat of battle, raced ahead. Joey tripped over Diesel when he made an unexpected cut in front of her, and Jax was on her before she could regain her feet.

He flipped her over and straddled her hips. "Who wants a face full of snow?"

"Joey does!" Evan snickered.

"I think Evan's right. Joey looks like she wants a snow sandwich," Jax agreed.

Joey wiggled hoping to dislodge him, and when she realized she wasn't getting out of a snow pie to the face, she braced for the blow.

Jax none-too-gently shoved two handfuls of snow into her face. Joey shrieked and brought her snow-filled hands up to smack Jax on both sides of the face. In a move so slick it looked like it had been planned, Evan jumped on Jax's back and shoveled half a ton of snow down his collar.

Jax screamed like a girl. Aurora, not wanting to miss out on the fun, ran over and threw herself into the pile.

"Well fought, troops," Joey said, spitting snow out of her mouth. "Well fought."

They arrived at the farmhouse tired, cold, and still laughing. Phoebe took one look at them and banned them to the porch until she could gather towels and the changes of clothes she'd brought for the kids. Jax and Joey ended up in Summer and Carter's sweats, and all their wet clothes went straight into the dryer.

"How was your nap?" Joey teased Phoebe.

She smiled smugly. "We slept for almost two hours on the

couches. It was so quiet, so peaceful," Phoebe sighed. "Bless you for that."

"I'm thinking you owe me some compensation," Joey decided.

Phoebe's gaze narrowed, calculating. "What's it going to cost me?"

"Your recipe for your raspberry cream cheese coffee cake."

Phoebe gasped in mock horror. "Never! I'll take that recipe to my grave."

"That can be arranged," Joey told her. "I can just pump the little one full of espresso right before you go home. Summer showed me how to make it."

"You're diabolical," Phoebe said, bringing the back of her hand to her forehead. "Cruel, cruel world, making me give away my award-winning recipe."

"One recipe and the kid gets zero caffeine," Joey reiterated.

"Fine," Phoebe grumbled. "I'll email it to you."

"Oh, no. I fell for that once before. You sent me some random Pinterest recipe after I went with you to Frieda Blevins sex toy party which, I might add, you said was a kitchen party. I want to see your handwritten recipe card."

"I don't know whether to be proud of you or disappointed in you twisting an old lady's arm like this," Phoebe said, patting Joey's hand. "I suppose it's time to pass on my recipe to a new generation of scheming women."

"And no scribbling a new one down and making it look old, either. I'm not falling for that again."

"Fine," Phoebe grumbled. "You know, a glass of wine would probably make me feel slightly less terrible about breaking my promise to Great-Aunt Felicia."

"I will get you a glass so you can drown your shame."

Joey poured Phoebe a glass of wine and watched out of the corner of her eye as Jax held a conversation with Evan about the plot points of a movie they'd both seen while juggling Aurora from knee to knee and answering her thousand "but why" questions. He looked like a natural, completely relaxed and engaged. She wondered if he wanted kids and remembered when Summer had come to her to ask if she knew whether Carter wanted a family.

At the time, Summer thought she couldn't have kids. Thought it would be a deal-breaker for Carter and had ended up leaving him to go back to the city. And now there were twins on the way.

Joey had never really thought about the future in those terms. She'd always had plans and goals for the stables. But she'd never really considered whether she wanted a family. She didn't like that watching Jax hang out with his niece and nephew had her contemplating such topics.

She poured herself a glass of wine and went to stick her nose in Franklin's chicken parm.

They ate family style around Carter and Summer's dining room table, the dogs waiting patiently for scraps to fall. They passed dishes back and forth, taking turns cutting up food for Aurora and shoveling seconds and, in Jax's case, thirds onto their plates. Joey snapped a picture of the table and texted it to Summer and Gia so they could see that the house was still standing and the dogs and children were not suffering from malnutrition.

"So, Jax," Phoebe began. "You and Joey are..." she shot a furtive glance at Evan and Aurora. "Planting a garden together?"

"Uh, what?" Jax frowned.

"You know," Phoebe stared at him pointedly. "That garden you started a long time ago? You've decided to replant?"

Jax looked at Joey in confusion. "Are you planting a

garden? Why don't you just plant stuff in the big garden out back?"

Joey rolled her eyes. "Phoebe's talking about a different garden. The garden we had when we were seniors in high school."

"We didn't have a garden—"

Phoebe cleared her throat and tilted her head in Evan and Aurora's direction. Evan was watching them with interest while Aurora was driving a breadstick through marinara as if it were a speedboat.

Joey kicked Jax under the table.

"I wouldn't say we're interested in growing a full-blown garden at this point," she said to Phoebe. "We're just experimenting with a few... uh, raised beds at this point."

"Raised beds?" Phoebe asked.

Jax finally caught on. "Oh, *gardening*. Right... Actually, I think planting a big garden is the way to go. I mean we both like..." He glanced at the kids. "Watermelons, and watermelons require a lot of space. So why not start a garden?"

"I don't like watermelons," Joey said pointedly. "And I don't like the responsibilities that come with maintaining a big garden. I thought we'd agreed to just enjoy our small, low-maintenance raised beds."

"I thought I made it clear that I'm in this gardening thing for the long haul. I think we should plant a whole damn orchard." Jax's voice raised to a low roar.

"What do you hope to grow in your raised beds?" Phoebe broke in.

"I don't really know," Joey said in exasperation. "Something small and easy to take care of. Something that we can rip out if we don't like how it grows."

"Like radishes?" Franklin offered.

"Sure." Joey shrugged. "Radishes. If I don't like how they

look or if they try to take over everything, I can just rip 'em out."

Phoebe and Jax were frowning now. Franklin cleared his throat.

"Gardening, on whatever scale, seems to agree with you both," he commented. "And you work well together."

"Working well together and enjoying gardening doesn't necessarily make a good... harvest," Joey said, biting into a breadstick.

"There aren't any guarantees," Franklin agreed.

"A garden is just like anything else," Jax said. "You get what you put into it. So if you half-ass your gardening efforts and don't weed and don't use the right fertilizer, you're guaranteeing yourself a crappy crop."

"Well, maybe I'm not looking for a whole harvest. Maybe I just want some damn cherry tomatoes."

"You can grow cherry tomatoes in a pot on your deck. Just go out and pick one up and bring it home with you."

"If you're insinuating that I am not picky about the produce that comes home with me, then you are dead wrong!" Joey said, tossing her breadstick on her plate. "I've been poisoned before by produce that I thought was good for me. You can't expect me to just commit to a garden when I've had food poisoning."

Jax crumpled his napkin and threw it down on the table. He looked like he wanted to yell for a second before the urge dissipated. "You're right," he said. "You're right to be cautious about what produce you allow in your garden. Maybe by the end of the growing season, you'll be willing to trust that this produce is good for you."

Joey wasn't about to agree to that one. It would be cruel to give hope where she wasn't sure there was any.

"I uh... Franklin?" Phoebe cleared her throat and looked at Franklin for help.

"I think what Phoebe means is we didn't mean to pry into your gardening habits. We only wanted you both to know that we think it's great that you're gardening together at whatever scale you're comfortable. Whether you're potting plants or growing an acre of potatoes, you both seem happy."

Joey stared at her plate and felt guilty. Things weren't as settled as she hoped they were.

"So you guys are dating, huh?" Evan said, reaching for another helping.

"You got all that from gardening?" Joey asked.

"Girls make everything so much more difficult than they need to be." Evan sighed.

"Amen to that brother," Jax mumbled.

"It sounds like you have experience in matters of the heart," Franklin prompted his grandson.

Evan shrugged. "Girls are okay. But some of them just drive you nuts. Take Oceana for example."

Joey smirked into her water glass. Oceana was in Evan's grade at school. The girl had an IQ bigger than most forty-year-olds and the face of a future heartbreaker. She lived on a sheep farm on the other side of town, and her hobbies included meditation and the manufacturing of soy candles.

"What about Oceana?" Jax, the proud uncle, was all ears.

"Well, we're kind of seeing each other, and I noticed she'd moved some things into my locker, which was fine with me. But when I said that she could move all her stuff into my locker, she got all weird and moved all her stuff out."

"Maybe she needed space and she wants you to leave her alone," Joey suggested a little more defensively than she meant to.

"Maybe she just thinks she needs space, and what she

really needs is a good push in the right direction," Jax suggested stubbornly.

"Maybe Evan has a better solution," Phoebe suggested.

Evan shrugged. "I did what any normal human being would do. I laid out all the benefits to sharing a locker like we would be able to see each other more between classes, and I explained to her that that's the direction I'd like to see us move in, and if she's not ready for such a commitment, I'd understand, and we could still be friends. She's not the only Oceana in the sea, and if we weren't meant to be, we weren't meant to be."

"So what did she do?" Jax asked with rapt attention.

Evan grinned and twirled spaghetti noodles on his fork. "Let's just say it's a lot harder to find my math book now."

24

———

"*R*elax, Jojo," Jax said, covering her hand on the seat's armrest with his own.

The plane leveled off its ascent as they headed west. Away from the farm and the horses. Away from her house and her dog.

L.A. was not her idea of a vacation—sign her up for a booze fest on a tropical beach—but she had to admit, she was curious about seeing the lure of the place Jax had called home for so many years.

"Are you sure Carter can handle everything?"

"You already know the answer to that."

"What if Waffles misses me and won't eat?"

"Then you can video chat with him and make him eat."

Joey knew she was being ridiculous but couldn't seem to help it. It had been a long time since she'd been so far away from the stables and the farm. And the last time, a family beach vacation with her parents and sister, she hadn't been in charge of a dog, thirty horses, and a calendar full of lessons.

She stretched her long legs forward, appreciating the legroom that first class provided, and wondered what that extra twelve inches cost. When she'd asked, Jax told her not to worry about it. The studio paid for travel to premieres, which was good news for her that she didn't have to dip into her nest egg and scrunch herself into coach between Jax and some guy who smelled like an ashtray and snored.

She smiled to herself. "It's like we're finally taking that trip we talked about that night in the car," she told him.

Jax flinched and rubbed her hand silently.

"What's wrong? Are you nervous about flying?" Joey asked.

Jax shook his head. "I just don't like thinking about that night."

"I don't remember much about the... after," she confessed. "What do you remember?"

What happened to make him leave the hospital, pack a bag, and leave her? What happened in those hours that changed the course of both their lives?

"Jojo, I really don't want to talk about it."

She bit her tongue and let it drop. Maybe not knowing was better somehow? *Probably not.*

Jax sighed heavily next to her. "After the crash, it was so quiet. It smelled like engine coolant—you know, that maple syrup smell? I couldn't see much. I'd hit my head on the steering wheel, and there was blood in my eyes." His voice tightened at the memories.

Joey squeezed his hand.

"I looked over at you, touched you. There was so much blood, and you weren't moving. You were slumped forward over the seatbelt. *I thought you were gone.*" He whispered the words.

"I'm not exactly sure what happened next. I think there was a car behind us that saw the whole thing. The guy pulled me out of the car, but we couldn't get your door open. You still weren't moving." He shook his head.

"I got back in the car with you. There were lights, sirens coming, and then I could see where the blood was coming from." He took her right hand, rolled her arm over and traced the thin scar that zigged and zagged its way from wrist to elbow.

"The guy who stopped was a nurse, and as soon as he said 'artery,' my heart stopped. I took off my shirt and wrapped it around your arm, put pressure on it, and the next thing I know is the EMTs are there, saying they got you. But I couldn't let go."

Joey turned her arm over, pulled his hand into her lap. She felt guilty that her need to know hurt him by remembering. She wished she could take the memories from him. Wished that she could change the events of the past for them both. But that wasn't possible, and the only way out of those memories was through them.

She didn't want him to hurt anymore, so she changed the subject.

"So what kind of a dress am I going to have to wear tomorrow?"

EVERYTHING ABOUT L.A. WAS EXCESSIVE. From the glossy black Uber with tinted windows that picked them up at the airport to the hotel suite that was bigger than the first floor of her house. "This shower could hold twelve people." Joey's voice echoed off the bathroom walls and fixtures that gleamed gold in the late afternoon sun. "Even the walls are marble."

Jax leaned against the doorframe and watched her lean in to examine the goose-necked tub faucet. "This is insane. Do you know how many horses I could buy with what it cost to outfit this bathroom?"

She pushed past him and walked into the suite's bedroom. "This can't be a king-size. This is like NBA-player-size," she said, flopping down on the cloud-like mattress. "I can roll one, two, three, four, five, six times before I get to the other edge," she said as she demonstrated. Jax let her flop over on her back in the center of the bed before launching himself at her.

"Do all screenwriters get digs like this?" Joey asked as Jax settled himself between her legs, resting his weight on his hands.

"Ones who win side bets with a producer do. Do you want to have dinner here or go out?"

"Do we have to wear clothes if we have dinner here?" Joey asked dipping her fingers into the scooped neckline of her shirt.

"Mmm," Jax nuzzled into her neck. "Clothing is entirely optional. I'll call room service."

They dined in their suite, enjoying wine, white sea bass, and a steak so tender Joey barely needed to chew it. The sun set low over the hill, casting a rosy glow through the wall of glass. Slow rock from the state-of-the-art stereo played softly in the background.

Joey could still see the shadows of memories in those gray eyes. She'd put them there with her questions on the plane. She reached across the table and wrapped her fingers around his wrist. "Jax."

He lifted his gaze from the wine glass he'd been staring into pensively.

"I'm going to whip out my Blue Moon hippie logic here. Did you ever think that maybe the accident was supposed to happen?" Joey asked.

"Like destiny?"

She nodded. "And destiny isn't a mistake."

"So I was meant to leave?"

"Jax, we're going to the premiere of a movie you wrote. One of the movies you wrote. Don't think for a second that would have happened without the accident. Sure, maybe we would have gone on our road trip, but we would have come back. I would have made you come back. I had our future already mapped out, and L.A. and movies and orgy showers were not part of the plan."

"I could have said no."

Joey grinned. "Please. Eighteen-year-old Jax couldn't say no to me. He was too hampered by respect and wanting desperately to make sure I got everything I wanted."

"Sounds like twenty-seven-year-old Jax too." He smiled wryly.

"Maybe it does."

"But you need to consider something else with that Blue Moon hippie logic. If I was meant to leave, then I was also meant to come back."

It was Joey's turn to study her wine. "Maybe you were."

"And if I was meant to come back, then maybe we're meant to be."

She took a long swallow of wine and stared hard at the last sliver of sun as it disappeared behind the far-off hill. "Maybe we are."

She said it softly, but the way his gaze sharpened, the way his muscles tightened under her hand, she knew he heard her. Knew he heard the significance.

"You're different now," she said quietly. "But so am I. We're both stronger, sharper. We challenge the hell out of each other, but you get me. You honestly get me. And I keep waiting and watching, looking for that sign of 'he's going to bolt again' or 'he's going to break my heart again.' And dammit, Jax, I'm so tired of waiting and watching."

The intensity of his gaze burned through her. She was

under a spotlight, and he was the one watching and waiting now.

"What exactly are you saying, Joey?"

She could feel the tension coursing through him like a current. He wanted the words, and for the first time, she wanted to say them.

"I'm saying that..." God, she just couldn't get them out. Eight years of walls and hurt. She took a slow deep breath. "I'm saying... I have to go to the bathroom."

She stood up and ran full speed into the cavern of marble. Slamming the door, she pulled out her cell phone and started typing frantically.

Joey: HELP! I'm trying to tell Jax how I feel, and the words won't come out. So I locked myself in the bathroom.

Summer responded immediately.

Summer: Okay. Don't panic! First thing's first. Look in the mirror.

Joey: I am not giving myself a pep talk in the mirror.

Summer: No, dumbass, you're checking your makeup. If you're making a declaration of love that's eight thousand years in the making, you're doing it looking good.

Joey rolled her eyes and then did as Summer told her. She swiped a finger under each eye, ran a brush through her hair, and checked her teeth for dinner.

Joey: Okay. Reflection doesn't look nearly as freaked out as I feel.

Gia chimed in a second later.

Gia: Oh, holy moly! This is so exciting!! Quick question. What exactly are your feelings for Jax?

Joey: I want to tell him that I'm willing to give us another chance.

A series of smiley face emojis exploded on her screen.

Joey: Not helping.

Gia: Sorry! Also you're going to have to get out there soon because Beckett just asked me why I was jumping on the couch, and I told him. So he's totally going to text Jax.

Summer: Ditto. Minus the jumping.

"Shit," Joey muttered. She tossed her phone and her unhelpful friends onto the bathroom counter and stormed through the door before she could lose her nerve... and before big mouths Beckett and Carter could get to Jax first.

"Put your phone down," she said when she spotted him by the window, phone in hand.

"Okaaaaay." Jax put the phone down on the table as if it were a gun and she the cops.

Joey stopped inches in front of him.

"I'm saying let's plant a damn garden."

She was in his arms before the words were completely out. "This is all I've wanted for so long, and all I can think is to ask if you're sure. Are you sure, Jojo? Are you really sure?"

She wet her lips and nodded. "As sure as I can be."

He brought his lips to hers, his fingers gently holding her steady. It was a slow burn, and Joey felt the locks inside that had been sealed so long ago start to give.

"I'm scared." She hadn't realized she'd said the words out loud until Jax pulled back a millimeter.

"I am too," he whispered over her mouth. "Terrified, actually."

"But we're still going to do this, right?"

"Jojo, all the best things are scary. And you're the scariest."

"That's weirdly sweet," she said, moving in to feel his heat against her. To get closer to him and make everything else disappear. Her fingers dug into his shirt, desperate to cling. "Did you know everything is always better when you're touching me?"

He had no words, but the fire in his eyes told her he felt the same. His hands were moving down her arms, up her back, stroking her and keeping her close. A sensual prison that she had no desire to escape.

"Show me what it's like, Jax."

"What what's like, Jojo?"

"Show me what it's like to be loved."

Emotion keen and bright lit his cool gray eyes. His hands gentled and returned to trace her jaw. "You're the reason my heart beats." He whispered the words against her lips, sweetly softly.

She shivered, and Jax drew her closer. When his lips pressed hers, she felt a slow burn spread through her body like the glow of a sunrise. New beginnings all had a shine like this, bright and warm.

He sampled her slowly as if he had all the time in the world to explore her. Joey's breath came in hitches. "I can't breathe," she whispered.

Jax released her mouth and brought his forehead to hers. His thumbs made lazy circles on the hollows of her cheeks. They swayed from side to side to the music they'd both forgotten.

"Better?" he asked, his voice a rasp.

She nodded.

He lowered to her again, gently tasting. He turned her slowly so her back was to the cool glass of the window. There, with the city behind her, he lifted the hem of her t-shirt and slid his hands under it. His palms skimmed up, and her arms rose of their own accord. Free of her shirt, Joey brought her hands to Jax's broad, shoulders as he sunk to his knees.

He rained kisses across her chest and down her belly, and when his fingers dipped into the waistband of her jeans, her head fell back against the glass, hitting it with a thump. He worked her jeans down her legs, letting his fingertips skim the outside of her bare legs as the denim bunched at her ankles. He guided one foot at a time out of her jeans and threw them aside before working his way back up.

His busy mouth spent a few extra seconds sampling the flesh around her simple black briefs before pressing against the exact spot that thrummed a hard beat.

Her words were gone, her voice missing. All she could do was sigh with pleasure as she felt his tongue brush flesh through cotton. Too soon, he rose higher, pausing again to nibble his way over the curves of both breasts, his tongue teasing the edge of the black lace that separated him from her.

When his hands skimmed around her back, Joey bit her lip. With a deft flick, he released her bra closure. "Slide the straps down your arms," he ordered, and she complied without hesitation.

Her hands shook as she knocked the straps off both shoulders, letting them fall to her elbows. When she dropped her hands, the bra tumbled to the floor, and his callused palms were there waiting to catch her breasts.

His thumbs brushed her nipples, once, twice, inciting.

Another gasp tore from her lips. "Jax." His name rose unbidden from a throat tight with emotion.

"Mine," he said, claiming the pert tip of one breast with his mouth. Joey's fingers dug into his shoulders. A current of lust ignited in her veins at the intimate touch. He was worshipping her body with the unhurried patience of the truly reverent.

His tongue lathed her nipple until her knees buckled. He caught her, strong hands gripping the curve of her hips. He pressed against her, bracing her against the window, and then moved his attention to her other breast.

As he licked and tasted, Joey felt the ache between her legs expand in intensity until it consumed her. When she felt his fingers skim the waistband of her underwear, her pulse ratcheted up another notch. There was nothing in the world that she needed more in that moment than to be filled by him.

As if reading her thoughts, Jax hooked two fingers in the front of her briefs. He dragged them down her legs, leaving her bared to him, body and soul. And then his mouth was on her where she craved him most. She widened her stance for him, and he took advantage of the new angle, spreading her slick folds with one hand while bracing her against the glass with his other.

When his tongue skimmed over her pulsing core, Joey's hips ground against him, desperate for more, deeper, faster, harder. She buried her fingers in his hair, gripping the dark waves in a tight hold.

He was brushing and stroking with the rough texture of his tongue, and when he slid two fingers home, stretching up inside her, she knew that a release unlike any other was eminent. Leisurely, he lapped at her electrified nub until she anticipated each lick with the thrust of her hips.

His fingers flexed in her, brushing that sweet spot, and she was lost as the ground disappeared from her feet and she hurtled into space. The orgasm robbed her of all senses, leaving her only with the shock of harsh pleasure ripping through her from her core and spiraling outward.

She began to slide down the glass inch by inch as the vibrations quaked through her. Jax waited until the last of her release dissolved before picking her up and carrying her to the bed.

"What was that?" Joey murmured into the crook of his neck.

His answer gutted her. "That was love," he whispered.

Jax placed her on the bed as if she was the finest china.

"Come be with me," she pleaded.

He brought her knuckles to his lips, brushed over them gently. "We have all night."

"You have all your clothes on," she reminded him.

He smiled so tenderly that Joey felt her heart clench in her chest.

"I can fix that," he promised. He stood by the side of the bed and, without breaking their eye contact, pulled his shirt over his head. He tossed it carelessly behind him, and Joey's eyes hungrily took in the perfect build he revealed. Broad shoulders, a chest built for shows of strength, muscles tapering into chiseled abs and narrow hips. God, he was magnificent.

Reading her gaze, Jax took his time sliding his jeans down thumbs brushing the indents inside his hipbones, the exact spot that Joey wanted to bite. He wore boxer briefs in a sedate navy. They were stretched impossibly tight over his straining erection. It was amazing what just touching her did to him without any provocation.

His thumbs hooked into the waistband of his underwear, and Joey felt her mouth go dry. She'd seen him naked, felt him inside her, yet every time the anticipation nearly killed her. Tonight, it might actually do just that.

Her breath came out in a whoosh when he pushed the barrier down his legs. His impressive hard-on sprung free, and Joey wet her lips. "Can I touch you?"

Wordlessly, he moved closer to the bed, and Joey reached out, fingers grazing his thick shaft. She saw the clench in his jaw and knew that he had a firm grip on his control. Joey wrapped her fingers around him and stroked, watching in fascination as a single bead of moisture appeared at the crown.

Jax's hand flashed out and grabbed her wrist. "Tonight is about you, Joey."

He climbed onto the bed, the mattress dipping slightly under his weight as he crawled over her. Joey shivered as he lowered himself on to her, flesh to flesh. His weight on her was an anchor, keeping her still and safe. He rested on his forearms, his fingers toying with her hair, thumbs stroking the side of her face.

She opened her legs and sighed as he settled between her thighs. The crown of his cock nestled into her heat with the promise of unspeakable pleasure.

"I can feel your heart pounding," he said, nibbling a path along her jawline, the scrape of his teeth heightening her senses.

Joey lifted her hips straining toward him, needing him to fill her, wanting to feel that powerful surge as he entered her to lay his claim. Beads of sweat clung to their bodies as the anticipation built.

"I belong to you, Joey," he said, raining kisses soft as butterflies' wings on her face. "I always have. You know that don't you?"

She nodded, eyes tightly closed to hold back tears. She

had always known it. She had always had his heart, and he had hers. From childhood games to teenage angst to the grief of a lost love, her love, her body, her soul all belonged to one man.

"Say the words, Joey." His voice was low and rough.

She took a short breath, her toes curling against his legs as she begged him with her body to take her, to make her whole.

"I belong to you," she whispered. A single hot tear worked its way free and slid down her temple into her hair.

"Now tell me you love me. I need to hear the words."

Joey felt like her heart was being squeezed. Emotions from terror to elation raced through her body. Her mind had given up its hold on the situation a long time ago. It was just her heart and her gut.

Jax pressed his hips into her and the broad, smooth tip of his erection was encircled by her wet entrance. "Say it."

"I love you, Jax. I love you. I love you." She chanted the words until, with a single powerful thrust, he was inside her. Filling her, loving her, branding her.

A cry rose from her throat. She didn't know what it meant that the words she'd guarded for so long had been ripped free. She only knew that he was with her, as close as two people could be. Bonded by a need so great it could destroy them if they weren't careful.

She opened her eyes to look at him to see what her words had done to him. His eyes were squeezed shut, his jaw set. Steeped in pleasure and purpose, he began to move in her. And when his lashes fluttered up, when those cool gray eyes looked into the depths of her soul, she knew. She knew what it was like to be loved, to be worshipped.

Tears fell unbound as he slid out slowly, achingly, before he glided back in filling her to the hilt. He set the pace, a slow and steady climb up into the stars.

She could already feel the quickening inside her. The flutter signaling her release, her surrender to his body. Her heart had already surrendered.

"I love you," she whispered, the words unbidden this time, and stroked her hands up his back. Saw his eyes go glassy, saw his throat work against the strain of emotion.

Joey was vulnerable and open, stripped bare for him. Never before had she been this raw. Never before had she welcomed the exposure of being completely real and free.

His thumb brushed her trembling lower lip before his fingers dove into her hair. "My beautiful Joey." He sent her over the edge with another measured thrust, and as the pleasure of the moment clawed its way out of her throat in a scream, she felt him stiffen, heard him groan on his own release. They moved together, her release draining his, until there was nothing left but them and the stars in the night sky behind them.

25

_____

"Wake up, baby. It's time to get up." Jax's voice sounded like it was coming from a hundred miles away rather than the pillow next to her head.

"You've got to be kidding me." She opened one eye suspiciously. "We don't have to be there until six tonight, right?"

"Yeah, but we have to get you a dress. Besides, it's like ten o'clock eastern time."

"I'm on vacation. Vacation means not getting up until at least eleven," she said, her voice muffled by pillow. "A good boyfriend would know that."

"You can sleep as late as you want tomorrow, and your boyfriend will murder anyone who tries to drag you out of bed early."

Eyes closed, Joey let the corners of her lips curl up. *Boyfriend. Last night hadn't been just a beautiful, terrifying dream after all.*

"Come on, let's try out the twelve-person shower together." He dragged her out from under the tangle of sheets and pillows and guided her into the bathroom.

"You know what this marble mausoleum doesn't have?" she grumbled. "A damn coffeemaker."

"I'll get you coffee after the shower," Jax promised, twisting the faucets to release a steamy stream of water from both showerheads. "Come on. You'll feel better when you're awake."

"Still don't see why we have to start getting ready so early," Joey muttered. But she ducked her head under the gentle flow from the rain showerhead.

"You can use these, too, if you want," Jax said, demonstrating how to turn on the wall of jets.

"Maybe this isn't so bad," Joey admitted grudgingly as the pulsing water hit her full force. And when Jax came up behind her, wet and hard, she decided it might have actually been worth getting out of bed for.

After some sudsy fun, Joey contemplated crawling back into bed to bask in the post-lovemaking bliss until Jax tossed a pair of jeans at her and a t-shirt.

"Where are we going?" she asked, digging through her bag for a bra.

"We're going to get you coffee and a dress."

Joey grudgingly dried her hair and pulled on clothes and flip-flops. Jax marched her through the lobby and out the glass front of the hotel. It was another sunny Southern California day with temperatures in the high fifties and not a foot of snow to be seen anywhere. They started down the block on a quest for coffee that Joey felt strongly should have been readily available in their room.

"How far do you Californians travel for coffee?" she muttered, letting Jax pull her along.

"As far as we have to. In this case, half a block," he said pointing at the café and juice bar sign in front of them.

"I'm not drinking any of that juice crap," Joey warned him.

"Strictly caffeine for us, Jojo," Jax told her, holding the glass door open for her.

She stepped inside the bright space. It reminded her of OJs by Julia in Blue Moon with its décor, but this place was overflowing with people. Some were in workout gear, others in suits, a few wearing jeans that cost more than her mortgage. One woman had a tiny dog in her very large purse. The only things all the customers had in common was the fact that they all wore their sunglasses indoors and they were all on their cell phones.

"This place is weird," Joey whispered to Jax.

"Yeah, but the coffee is good." He winked and ran his hand down her back.

"I feel like we should put our sunglasses back on and call each other."

Jax rubbed the tension out of her shoulders. "Just pretend you're observing a new horse for any odd behaviors in quarantine."

"Oh, I'm observing the hell out of some odd behaviors," she said, nodding at the woman in front of them dropping f-bombs on a conference call.

The baristas were completely unfazed by the weirdness of it all. They called out orders like mochachino non-fat whip and hemp milk green goodness over the dull roar of everyone else's preoccupation.

By the time they got to the front of the line, Joey wasn't sure if the staff was even speaking English anymore.

"Welcome to Zia's. What may I serve you today?" the wan, six-foot-tall blonde with nose ring asked.

"Uh, coffee? With sugar?" Joey tried.

"We have a Sulawesi, a Tanzania Peaberry, a Guatemalan reserve, a Costa Rica Helsar—"

"Oh my God. Just a regular coffee with sugar."

"For your choice of sweetener, we have demarara, Stevia, natural sugar cane..."

Joey looked at Jax in panic.

"We'll have two café cubanos to go, please," he said, swiping his credit card.

Joey looked at him in horror as he escorted her toward the pick-up counter. "What the hell is a café cubano? And did you really just pay thirteen dollars for two cups of coffee?"

"Relax. It's all part of the experience."

"Is this what homesickness feels like?" she wondered out loud.

Jax laughed, and his eyes crinkled in that way that made Joey's stomach feel warm and slippery. "God, I love you. I'm so glad I brought you out here. I can't wait to see you at the premiere tonight."

"Oh. My. God," a breathy baby angel voice floated about the din of the coffee shop. "Jackson Pierce! When did you get back in town?"

Joey turned toward the sound of the nebulous voice and almost poked her eyes out on a pair of breasts the size of prize-winning watermelons. The breasts looked vaguely familiar.

They and their owner, a curvy, perfectly made-up woman with silver blonde hair and wide brown eyes, were now hugging Jax. She gave him a smacking kiss on the cheek leaving behind a crimson stain.

Joey would have stepped in with a nice right hook, but the look of pure fear on Jax's face was enough to make her temporarily holster her temper.

"Didi," was all Jax managed to say. He was gaping like a fish looking back and forth between Joey and Didi. She had to give him credit. At least he was looking the woman in the eyes and not the rack. And that's when it clicked. During one of her backslides into looking Jax up online, she'd come across a picture of Jax with Boobs Magee on his arm at some red carpet thing.

"Didi," Jax began again. "This is Joey. Joey, this is Didi."

Joey held out a hand to the woman and was immediately engulfed in a very soft, squishy hug. She wondered if it was possible that boobs that big could be real.

"Ah, okay. You're a hugger." Joey patted her awkwardly on the shoulder.

Didi giggled. "Guilty! We're all huggers back home."

Judging from the twang, home was somewhere in the heart of Texas.

"Joey's my girlfriend," Jax said, still working through the shellshock.

"We're seeing each other, sort of," Joey corrected reflexively. Jax glared at her, and Joey stuck her tongue out at him.

"What a coincidence! Jax and I dated a while back," Didi said, looking inordinately pleased.

"Oh, you did, did you?" Joey shot a pointed look at Jax who looked like he was praying the bamboo floor would open up and transport him anywhere but here.

"We sure did. That was what a year or two ago?" Didi said, tapping a neatly manicured fingertip to her chin. "Wait a minute. Are you *the* Joey?"

Joey wasn't sure if she was *the* Joey. She also didn't think it was possible for Jax to be more uncomfortable.

"This is so exciting!" Didi chirped. "You're the reason Jax and I broke up. I always knew you two would end up together."

"I'm... sorry?" Joey looked back and forth between Jax and Didi wondering what alternate universe she'd stepped into. *Oh, right. L.A.*

"One night we had too much sake, and Jax here just spilled his guts—figuratively—about this girl he left at home. And just the way he talked about you, I just knew you were his one and only. So I broke up with him, and now here we are!"

"And here we are," Joey echoed.

"Oh, my goodness! I almost forgot. Congratulations on your guild nomination. You must be over the moon," Didi gushed.

Jax's color rose, and Joey listened raptly. A window to the L.A. world that Jax lived had just opened for Joey.

"Nominated for what?" she asked.

"Modest to a fault, this one," Didi said shaking her head. "Jax was nominated for best original screen play."

"It's not a big deal," Jax said, shrugging uncomfortably.

"It sounds like a big deal," Joey corrected.

"Oh, it is. There are writers who've been doing this for decades and never see a nomination. Jax is one of the youngest nominees in guild history."

"Is it one of those big awards ceremonies?" Joey wondered.

"It's strictly for writers, so the ceremony's more low-key than the Oscars or the Emmys. But it's still a very big deal," Didi said. "So what brings y'all to town?"

"Two café cubanos," the barista called from the counter.

Jax like a man who had just been offered a reprieve. "Oh, what a shame. That's our order. I should—"

"Oh, no." Joey shook her head at him. "I'll go grab them. You two catch up." She snickered the whole way up to the counter where she picked up two recycled paper cups filled with a creamy-looking liquid. She snagged lids and snazzy cardboard sleeves and made her way back to Jax and Didi.

Didi punctuated every word with a facial expression and a matching hand gesture. The woman had to be an actress.

"Oh my gosh, Jax was just telling me you're in town for the premiere. How exciting is that?"

"Very?" Joey guessed. "Are you going?"

"I'll be the very sparkly date of a certain handsome actor. We're just friends, but we're working on a project together," she said proudly. "So who are you wearing?"

"Huh?"

"I sound like one of those entertainment hosts on the red carpet. I mean who's the designer who did your dress?" Didi giggled, and somewhere Joey imagined a unicorn just got its wings.

"I don't have a dress yet. We're going shopping now."

Didi gasped. "Jax! No dress yet! Do you not know how things work around here?"

"Relax. I'm taking her to Brigid's place."

"Who's Brigid?" Joey asked. *And had Jax dated her too*, she wondered.

Didi clapped her hands together. "Perfect! Maybe you're not such a putz. Brigid is a costume designer who is planning to launch her own label. She's amazing!"

"So who are you wearing?" Joey asked.

"Dior," Didi sighed, clasping her hands together.

"Uh, awesome. Dior is... great."

"Now what about hair and makeup?"

Shit. "I guess I'm doing my own?" Joey looked at Jax who shrugged.

"Yeah, I'm sure that will be fine," he said encouragingly.

Didi looked at him as if he'd suddenly squatted down in the middle of the café and started quacking like a duck. "No, it will not be fine. Don't worry, Joey. I'll take care of everything," Didi announced, whipping out her cell phone. "Where are you staying?"

"The Cyprus," Joey said. Jax stepped on her foot.

"Perfect, that's even closer to the theatre than my place. I'll bring hair and makeup to you, and we can get ready together. What's your number?"

~

"WHAT JUST HAPPENED BACK THERE? Did I imagine the whole thing? Am I in a coma?" Joey asked, blindly reaching for Jax's hand.

"I'm not really sure what just happened. How many apologies do I owe you for this?" He steered her down the block and called for an Uber on his phone. "Drink your coffee. You'll feel better with some caffeine in you."

Joey took a hesitant sip and then looked at the cup. "Hey, this is kind of really good."

"I had a feeling you'd like it."

"So back to Didi—"

Jax cringed. He felt like a jerk. If it had been one of Joey's exes, he'd probably have punched the guy out the second he swooped in to kiss her hello. "I'll call her and tell her there's been a change of plans. I'll get us out of this somehow. I'm so sorry."

"I think an apology would only be necessary if Didi was a grade A bitch. She actually seems pretty nice."

"She is. She's just a lot of work."

"Speaking of work—"

Jax shook his head and put his sunglasses back on. "Do not ask me that question. We aren't discussing the anatomy of former significant others."

"They're significant all right. But are they real? Like seriously. I have to know."

He shoved her into the backseat of a baby blue Prius. "Drink your coffee and be quiet."

"Is that any way to talk to your girlfriend?" Joey demanded.

His girlfriend. It really had happened. Joey Greer agreed to be his girl, and he wasn't going to stop there. He intended to make her his wife.

He pulled her into him, still not believing that she was his. "That may not be the best way to treat my girlfriend, but this is." He lowered his mouth to hers, and desire sparked the second her lips parted for him. He teased her, gently at first, but found himself wrapped up in the taste of her. He wanted to breathe her in, to be as close as possible to her. He wanted to memorize every inch of her body and then spend his life worshipping it.

He finally gathered his wits about him and pulled back. "Behave yourself," he teased her.

"I believe you are the one who stuck his tongue down my throat," she shot back, snuggling into his side.

"Point taken." His lips brushed her temple as she watched the traffic and buildings flash by her window. "So what do you think of L.A. so far?"

She turned her head and gave him that heart-breaking smartass smile. "It doesn't suck too much."

He pinched her in the side, and she laughed. It was beautiful to see her so free, so relaxed. The woman could roll with just about anything. And that was good because tonight he was going to tell her about the screenplay before anyone else could drop that particular bombshell on her.

The car pulled up in front of a Spanish-style duplex, and they got out. "I was expecting a store," Joey said, skeptically studying the broad expanse of white garage door. "Am I just pawing through some stranger's closet?"

It was Jax's turn to grin. "Something like that," he said and rang the bell next to the bland brown front door.

∾

THE DOOR BURST OPEN, and they were greeted by a little yappy dog and a woman with dyed pewter hair that matched the stud in her nose. She wore violet contact lenses and scarred motorcycle boots under seriously distressed jeans decorated with safety pins.

"Jax!" She threw her lean arms around his neck and gave him a smacking kiss on the mouth.

Before Joey had the chance to decide whether she wanted to knock Brigid's block off, the woman turned and grabbed Joey's hand. "It's cool. I'm a lesbian," she said with a quick grin. "You must be Joey. I'm Brigid. Damn, Jax. You weren't kidding. She is gorgeous."

Joey shot a bemused look at him, and Jax smiled innocently.

"Come on in," Brigid said, stooping to pick up the tan ball of fluff that had yet to stop barking. She waved them into a narrow ceramic tiled hallway and opened the first door on the right.

Brigid had converted her garage into a design studio. Fabrics in every shade of the rainbow and textures sumptuous enough to wrap up in cascaded from tables, racks, and shelves. Three rolling racks held dresses in varying stages of completion on the far wall. Two counter height tables held matching industrial-looking sewing machines. There were colorful displays of threads, dishes of sparkle, and a three-way mirror in front of a curtained off corner.

"Welcome to my lair," Brigid said, setting the little dog down on the floor and bowing with a flourish.

"Wow," Joey said. It looked to Joey as if a rainbow and a craft store had an orgy.

"Okay, so I have a head's up on what the trend for tonight is. A lot of black and white—as if we haven't done that to death—so I pulled two pieces that I think would make a statement without pushing you too far outside your comfort zone," she chattered on.

"Uh, you're looking at my comfort zone," Joey said raising her arms and looking down at her long-sleeved t-shirt and jeans.

Brigid eyed her up and down. "Sequins are definitely out," she said to Jax. "But I think I have the absolutely perfect thing. Come with me."

She gave Joey no room to disagree and herded her toward the curtained corner. Joey nervously clutched her coffee and flopped down on a padded ottoman behind the gray drapes.

"I'll be right back," Brigid announced and disappeared.

She reappeared in seconds with a garment bag slung over her arm. "Okay, this is my number one pick, and if you hate it, you're going to crush my artistic spirit, and I'll hate you forever."

"Don't hate the dress. Got it." Joey nodded.

Brigid hung the bag from a hook and unzipped it, revealing layers of dusky rose tulle.

"Uhh…"

"Don't freak out yet. In fact, don't even look until I get it on you. Strip," Brigid ordered.

Not usually one to take off her clothes in front of a stranger, Joey decided when in L.A. she might as well do as the Angelinos do. She peeled her t-shirt and jeans off and tossed them on the ottoman.

"Okay, just step in," Brigid said, pooling the dress on the rug.

Joey did as she was told and let Brigid stuff her into the dress. The top was an ivory tank in some kind of silky material with just the slightest shimmer to it. The skirt was a fantasy of rosy tulle layers that fell from a cinched waist.

"How's that for comfortable?" Brigid asked, eyeing the fit.

Joey's hands traveled down over the full skirt and discovered pockets sewn into soft jersey lining under the tulle.

"Pockets? Awesome," Joey said.

"Yep. You can stash your phone in there and some lip gloss and be good to go. How does it feel?"

Joey swayed her hips from side to side, letting the tulle bell out. She moved to the ottoman and sat. Nothing embarrassing popped out, and she didn't feel like she was being strangled by anything.

"It feels pretty good," Joey said suspiciously, waiting for something to poke her or the material to rip in two.

"Let's see how it looks." Brigid led the way out of the dressing area and pushed Joey in front of the three-way mirror.

She looked... good. Great, actually. Joey turned from one side to the other.

"Oh, yeah." Brigid nodded. "How tall are you?"

"Five-nine?"

"Perfect. I don't even have to hem the length. I can take it in here and here," she said gesturing to the waist. "And the straps need to be shortened just a hair, but other than that, it's perfect. What do you think, Jax?"

Joey looked at him in the reflection and was pleasantly surprised to see a dumbfounded expression on his face.

"You okay?" Joey asked him.

Jax snapped back and walked over. "You look... just wow." He told her to spin with a circle of his finger.

Joey obliged with a sassy pirouette, enjoying the feel of the full skirt as the tulle billowed out.

Brigid was grinning. "I freaking rock."

"You sure do," Jax said, still not taking his eyes off Joey.

"You'll wear your hair down like it is now," Brigid instructed. "Maybe add some loose curls. Keep it kind of fanciful. Really dewy makeup. Yeah, you're going to be the hit of the red carpet."

While Brigid chattered on, Joey's gaze stayed locked on Jax. There was something new flaming to life in those cool gray eyes, and though she couldn't read it, its significance was palpable. He looked at her, into her, his expression both dark and loving.

"So what do you think?" Brigid asked.

"Perfection," Jax answered.

"And who am I wearing?" Joey asked, running her palms over the tulle.

"Brigid Winston. Don't you forget it," she said through a mouthful of pins as she tucked and tweaked the shape of the dress.

The dress was like nothing she'd ever worn before. She stuck with jeans whenever possible, and on the rare occasion that dressing up was required, she had two dresses in her closet. A black sheath and a navy wrap. Both serviceable and classic. She'd never have an occasion to wear this romantic dream of a dress again, but, oh, she wanted it.

"How much?" Joey asked.

"It's already paid for," Jax cut in.

Joey whirled, her skirt swirling with her. "Oh, no. First the bacon and then the dog and the horses. You're not getting the dress too."

"Bacon? Nice," Brigid said approvingly. "And you can quit arguing because the dress is on me."

"The hell it is," Jax and Joey said in unison.

"Look, I need to get this business off the ground so I can stop fixing on-set wardrobe malfunctions for models-slash-actresses who lie about their measurements. And if you wear this dress on that carpet tonight, people are going to notice. And if you blubber about how deeply talented and exclusive this no-name designer is, I'll have five publicists knocking on my door tomorrow morning."

Joey shared a look with Jax.

"So you're not paying for it, but you will gush," Brigid instructed her.

"I can gush," Joey nodded at her reflection.

Jax was circling her, taking her in from all angles. "You look incredible," he said finally.

"Thanks," Joey and Brigid said in unison.

26

With her dress securely stowed in the garment bag and a tasty lunch in her stomach, Joey was almost cheerful about the prospect of attending the premiere. She waltzed into their hotel room ahead of Jax and tossed her sunglasses on the marble topped entryway table.

Jax hauled her dress and a few other bags from their impromptu shopping spree inside and tossed everything over a chair. He reached for her, pulling her in.

"You know, we have some time before you have to start getting ready," he hinted.

"Is that so?" Joey said, twining her arms around his neck. "I think I have a few ideas of how we could pass the time."

Her mouth was a breath away from his when the knock sounded on the door.

"Yoo hoo!"

"Oh my God. I forgot about Didi," Joey whispered.

"Just keep quiet, and maybe she'll go away," Jax suggested.

"Nice try." Joey extricated herself from his arms and opened the door.

Didi, in all her platinum blonde glory, sashayed inside

followed by a parade of people carrying boxes, bags, and what looked like colorful tackle boxes.

Didi whistled as she peeked around the room over her sunglasses. "Not bad, Jax. Not bad. Now which way to the bathroom?"

Jax pointed the way, and Didi clamped a hand on Joey's wrist and tugged her along. "We'd better get started! You don't even have your nails done yet."

Joey looked over her shoulder and mouthed "help me" to Jax. But he just grinned and wandered toward the suite's bar. "I'll bring you ladies a drink," he called.

In a matter of seconds, Joey found herself seated on a tufted ottoman in front of the mirror while some guy named Solomon in a muscle shirt sprayed stuff in her hair and Sylvia with the pink highlights furiously filed her nails. Didi chattered on as rock-star thin Becca started smearing colors on her face in a pattern that looked like war paint.

"Are you excited for tonight?" Didi asked.

"I am. I've never seen one of Jax's movies before."

Didi gasped, and the hair and makeup team froze. "Never ever?"

Joey shook her head. "I don't have time to watch a lot of movies, and I kind of hated him for a few years."

"Well, that makes sense. He's really good. Like really good. There's talent there under all those sexy smoldering looks."

Joey felt weird talking about Jax with a woman who'd also shared his bed.

Didi must have picked up on the awkward vibe. "Sorry! I mean that in the most respectful way possible. We dated very briefly, and it was never anything close to serious. Now, you two? Well that looks like a very different story."

"I guess," Joey said, watching as Sylvia pulled out a bottle of lavender polish and started slicking it on her newly shaped nails.

"Puh-lease," Didi snickered, puckering up for another layer of paint on her high cheekbones. "I think Jax has been pining over you since forever. In fact, after meeting you, I can see bits and pieces of you that he's used in his leading ladies."

Now that was enough to make a girl feel strange. Just what qualities of hers had he lent his characters? Hard-headedness? A mean, unforgiving streak?

Joey decided when she got back, she was going to have a Jackson Pierce Moviethon all by herself so she could pick apart the leads and see the parts of her that he decided to share with the world.

That squishy feeling was back in her stomach, so Joey changed the subject asking about Didi's date.

Two hours later, Joey had been plucked, painted, and curled into a higher standard of beauty. She leaned forward in the mirror, turning her head this way and that, trying to identify with the reflection. The old Joey Greer was still there but more polished, she decided.

Didi leaned in next to her and snapped a selfie in the mirror. "Damn, we look good."

"You look like a bombshell," Joey told her.

Didi had poured herself into a white sequined gown that put her most noticeable assets on display. Her short blonde hair was done up Marilyn Monroe style. Red nails and lips pushed the needle into Old Hollywood glam.

She flashed a million-dollar smile at Joey. "Okay, now we have just enough time to practice standing."

"I know how to stand," Joey told her.

"No, you know how to hold yourself upright. I'm going to show you how to pose on the red carpet."

She moved to the far end of the bathroom and paused, one

hand on her hip, one foot kicked out. "Now, Jax is a writer, so you aren't going to have to do the whole big press line. But you'll still be getting your picture taken, and when you do, this is *the* way to stand."

Didi moved toward Joey with the prance and attitude of a thoroughbred. "See, if you give your feet a little kick with every step, you move the skirt of your dress out of the way, and you won't be as likely to trip."

Joey hadn't thought about falling. She hadn't thought to worry about walking. She decided she wasn't going to let go of Jax's arm. If she went down, she was going to take him down with her.

"So it's like a kick stomp?" Joey asked.

"Exactly. You give it a try."

Joey mechanically kick-stomped her way across the marble, glad she'd chosen sparkly flat sandals rather than those icicle thin stilettos at the store.

Didi watched her intently. "I think you need to loosen up your hips more. You look like you're marching into battle."

Joey gave a little shimmy to warm up her hip flexors and tried again.

Didi nodded her approval. "Okay, now when you stop, I want you to think boobs out, tailbone in, hand on hip, and foot point." She demonstrated and instantly looked half her size.

Joey frowned. "Boobs. Butt. Hand... and what?"

"Foot."

"Okay, foot. I feel completely unnatural."

"Then you're doing it right." Didi smiled. "Do the walk again, and then plant in this pose."

Joey tried it a half dozen times before Didi was satisfied. "You're going to look like a natural when they shove those cameras in your face."

"Uh, yay?"

A knock sounded at the door. "Five-minute warning, ladies," Jax said through the door.

"Yikes! I'd better call my car," Didi said. "I'm going to go out first, and you wait a minute so you can make your entrance."

"My mom isn't on the other side of that door with a camera, is she?" Joey asked.

"Trust me, the entrance is the most memorable part."

Didi slipped through the door, and Joey could hear her chit-chatting with Jax and the rest of the crew. She took one last look at herself in the mirror. She looked pretty freaking great. The makeup was all soft hues that played up her features without making her look like a drag queen or a reality TV star. And the dress. Oh, the dress.

She felt beautiful, maybe even a little stunning.

Joey counted to ten and took a few deep breaths before opening the bathroom door. Jax had his back to her, but she could tell the second he sensed her presence. That tingle of awareness at the back of his neck. He turned to her, a glass of scotch in his hands. The smile slid right off his face as his mouth fell open. He set the glass down on the edge of the table with a snap, almost missing it completely.

In his crisp suit, he looked every bit the leading man. He'd gone with a skinny tie instead of a bowtie, and he left his jacket unbuttoned. He looked debonair and dashing with that hint of rebel just beneath the slick surface.

"Wow," she said.

Jax moved to her, his hands reaching for her, and she took them. They stood at arm's length studying each other for a moment until Joey heard the click of a camera phone. Didi grinned at them from across the room. "Don't worry, I'm texting it to y'all."

Joey turned her attention back to the still speechless Jax.

"So what do you think?" Joey asked him, nerves fluttering in her belly.

"I think you look like a goddess," he said, bringing the knuckles of her hand to his lips. "I'm still not sure I deserve you."

Joey gave an unladylike snort. "Maybe you should stop trying to deserve me and just start enjoying me."

"Maybe I should," he agreed, reeling her in.

"Oh, no you don't!" Didi cried rushing over. She put her hands between them. "Don't you dare mess up her hair and makeup. She looks absolutely perfect, and if you put your big ol' paws on her, she's going to get to the premiere looking like a wilted flower."

Jax's eyes glinted, a hunter reluctant to give up his prey.

"Okay, posse, let's head out," Didi announced to her entourage. "Joey, you look stunning. Don't let him wreck you until after the red carpet. Got it?"

Joey threw a mock salute. "Got it." She surprised herself by wrapping Didi in a hug. "Thank you for everything, Didi."

"Awh, aren't you a sweetie. This one's a keeper, Jax," Didi announced as she made her way to the door with her team. "I'll see you at the theater!"

Joey said her thanks and goodbyes to the rest of the crew, and then they were alone.

"You know, we could just skip this whole thing," Jax began.

"No freaking way, Ace. I think the world deserves to see me in this dress."

"But I'm the one who gets to take you out of it," he told her.

~

WHEN THEY SETTLED into the backseat of the car Al sent for them, Jax pulled Joey against him. She looked like a vision, one that he would never get out of his mind. When he saw her standing there in front of him in the hotel, all he could think of was how much he wanted this woman to be his wife. He could see her, standing in a meadow wearing that dress and saying the vows he'd longed to hear. How much longer would he have to wait before she was ready for that?

"Jax?"

"Hmm?"

"Didi said something that I was curious about."

"You didn't ask her about her boobs, did you?"

"No, but I saw her change. They're totally real. She's a freak of nature."

He smiled, brushing his lips against her hair. "What did she say?"

"She said that you put pieces of me into your characters. Is it true?"

"It is. You've always been a muse to me."

"What pieces did you use? I mean, are the women... hard or mean or—"

He laughed but weighed his words. "Is that what you think I see in you?"

"I'm not exactly the warm and fuzzy type."

She was curled around him in the backseat of a limo. Where she got the idea that anyone would think her cold confounded him.

"I picked the brightest, shiniest parts of you, of which there are many. Your loyalty, your confidence, your uncanny ability to keep your cool when things are crazy."

"And people like characters like that?"

He nodded. "People relate to characters like that. You're real. And those pieces of you make my characters real."

She still didn't look thrilled. "I guess maybe I'll watch some of your movies and then decide whether your portrayal is accurate."

"That's very fair of you. Have I told you how absolutely beautiful you are tonight?"

"Nice dodge, but we're not done chatting yet," she said. "Didi made it sound like people here know of me. Why is that?"

Well, he wasn't going to get a better lead-in than that, and if he didn't tell her now, he was a pathetic coward. "I've told our story before, and it seemed to resonate with some people. In fact, that screenplay I turned in a few weeks ago? That's us. That's our story."

Joey pulled back and sat up. "What do you mean 'our story'?"

"All of it. Starting from when we were kids and moving on through high school and after."

He could see the thoughts and questions rise and waited for her to pick one to start with.

"How does it end?" she asked.

He could hear the concern, the distrust, and he wanted to make it all go away. Jax cupped her face in his hands. "How do you want it to end?"

The car eased to the curb in front of the theater. The tinted glass divider slid down. "We're here, sir," the driver announced.

"Thanks, we're about ready," Jax told him. He didn't like leaving the car and walking into the evening with this hanging over their heads.

"Joey?"

She shook her head. "Let's talk about that later. Let's get through this first before we wade into a history of us and what you deemed fit for the big screen."

He dropped his hands and squeezed one of hers. "I understand that you're not happy about it, but I'm really grateful that you're here. We'll talk about this later, I promise. Are you ready for this?" he asked.

She was peering out the window and frowning.

"That is a lot of people out there. Why are they all screaming?"

"Because they all want a piece of you... or at least the stars."

"Well, that's sad and creepy. And it makes me happy that we're just the little people here."

"Me too, Jojo. Me too."

Aisha Leigh scooped them up just as they stepped off the end of the red carpet. Joey looked shell-shocked. For the date of a writer, she'd gotten a bit more attention than either of them expected.

"Well, well. Look who didn't blow off the premiere," Al said, leaning in and giving Jax a peck on the cheek. Her rust-colored cocktail dress perfectly complimented her rich skin and dark, glossy hair.

"Beautiful as always, Al."

His agent slid her neatly manicured hands down her hips. "Well, I've got to do something with all that money you make me, sugar. And you must be Joey," she said, stretching her arms out.

Joey offered her hand and shook firmly. "I think we spoke on the phone when Jax was avoiding you."

Al smiled in appreciation. "We certainly did, and now I know who to call next time I need this one to get things done."

"That may have been a freak occurrence," Joey warned. "So is there a bar around here?"

"You poor thing," Al said, looping her arm through Joey's. "Let's get you liquored up so you can forget about that red-carpet experience."

Al looked over her shoulder at Jax as they walked inside. Her perfectly sculpted eyebrows raised in approval. "Nice work," she mouthed to him.

∾

JAX SIPPED his beer and scanned the crowd while two studio execs talked around him about yet another project. Joey had been confiscated by half a dozen people at varying points in the evening. Al had introduced her to half of the executives at the party. And judging from their reactions to her, he knew it was a calculated move on Al's part to boost the interest in his script. Didi had rescued Joey after the screening when she and Jax were cornered by a producer and two screen-writers.

He kept catching glimpses of Joey through the crowd but hadn't been able to get to her for the last forty-five minutes. Finally, the crowds shifted, and he spotted her, back to him facing a circle of enthusiastic men. He recognized a handful of actors in the mix and figured now was probably an excellent time to excuse himself from his conversation.

"Gentlemen, if you'll excuse me, there's a beautiful woman who needs rescued."

He crossed the room and tapped her on one alabaster shoulder. She twirled around, and her face lit up when she spotted him.

"Jax!"

Her face wasn't the only thing lit. Joey was clearly enjoying a very pleasant buzz, and her crowd of admirers was enjoying her enjoying it.

Joey Greer didn't need rescued. She needed corralled.

He slid his arm around her waist and pulled her into him placing a very satisfying kiss squarely on her mouth. "Hello, beautiful."

"Hi, Ace. We were just talking about you."

Jax raised an eyebrow. "You were, were you?"

"We all thought the movie was great," Joey gushed.

"Good. Great. Come with me," he said, leading her away.

Joey waved over her shoulder at her new friends and let Jax drag her off.

"Someone's been hitting the champagne a little hard," he teased her, pulling her into a secluded corner.

"I'm celebrating," she told him with a goofy smile.

"And what exactly are you celebrating?"

"My brilliant boyfriend, of course," she said, wrapping her arms around his neck.

"Okay, there's something more than champagne going on in there," he said, brushing a loose curl over her shoulder.

"What are you doing in Blue Moon?" she asked, toying with the ends of his hair.

"Chasing you."

"Why would you give all this up? Everyone knows you here. Everyone freaking loves you here. They all want a piece of you. Also, there's no snow."

He laughed then. "Well, the weather is certainly a plus to west coast living, but there's no Joey here. Believe me, I looked. Everyone knows me at home. I'm liked there too, and I think I'm pretty good at brewing beer."

"You'll give up all of this so you can brew beer and sleep in my bed?"

"It's a nice bed. And I'm still going to write, and maybe I'll still do some producing on occasion. But my heart belongs with you."

"That is a very sweet, romantic thing to say."

"I'm a sweet, romantic guy," Jax agreed. "So what do you think of your first Hollywood premiere?"

She leaned in close as if to whisper, but her voice was still loud. "Well, I like Al. She loves you in like a family way. Like if anyone here tried to screw you out of something, I could see her showing up at their house with a chainsaw and a smile."

Jax nodded. It was a very accurate assessment of his Al. "How about the rest of the evening?"

"This is like an alternate universe. Why is everything a question out here, and why is the traffic so bad? Did I tell you I met a model named, get this, *Kale*. She was a six-foot-tall Indian woman named Kale. *Kale*, Jax."

He laughed and pulled her closer. "What do you say we get out of here and get some food in you?"

"Can we have burgers?" Her brown eyes looked at him with the hope and anticipation of a puppy.

He took her for burgers and fries, which they enjoyed in an orange vinyl booth under fluorescent lights still wearing their evening finery. They dissected the film together, and Joey gave him the colorful highlights of all the people she met, including Kale.

She showed him the picture Didi had taken of them in the hotel suite.

"Wait, this is in Blue Moon's Facebook group," Jax said, peering at her phone's screen.

"Oh, yeah. I figured we might as well control the spin on this," she said with a dainty shrug.

Jax grinned. Someone was getting more and more comfortable with the idea of being his girl again.

"Listen," Joey said, gesturing with a fistful of fries. She was mostly sober now, but the red meat and soda kept her from reverting too far into her shell. "I've been thinking about something."

He prayed it wasn't the screenplay. If only she knew how conflicted he was to share their story. On one hand, it deserved to be told. On the other, there were things long buried that perhaps should stay that way for the good of many. He'd been compelled to write it and with the ending he'd had in mind for them all along. Now, whether reality would mirror the big screen remained to be seen. He couldn't begin to anticipate Joey's reaction beyond the initial pissed off phase. How many relationships would the truth damage?

He needed more time. Needed to find the right way to tell her why he left all those years ago. And why it would all be okay.

"That awards ceremony for the guild thing," she continued, taking a bite of fry.

"What about it?" Selfish relief coursed through him. He didn't have to ruin tonight with a run at the truth.

"I think you should take your mom."

"My mom? Really?"

Joey gave an exaggerated roll of her eyes. "Jax, you would be her hero. A fancy dress, a weekend away. Famous people."

"It would definitely shut up Frieda Blevins about her niece's selfie," Jax mused.

"Or you could do everyone a favor and take Frieda so she has something else to talk about besides duck face."

"I like that you look out for my mom," Jax said, trapping her feet between his under the table. "She told me what you did while everyone was at my dad's funeral."

Joey became very interested in her burger and didn't respond.

"You've always been there for my family, even when I wasn't."

Joey swallowed hard. "Don't be an idiot. You were there when they needed you, and you're there now. I mean not *now* now because obviously we're in L.A. So if something horrible happens while we're gone, it's totally your fault for not being there. But other than right now."

"God you're cute when you drink."

"You're cute like all the time," Joey said through another bite of burger. "I really love you."

His heart stuttered in his chest. Someday he hoped to have the words to tell Joey just what it meant to him to hear her say it.

"You realize you've only said those words when I'm inside you or you're drunk, right?"

Joey shrugged. "Eh, baby steps. I'm going to read your screenplay, by the way."

27

_I_t was good to be home. Especially when home came with a woman who officially loved him, an adoring dog, and a brewery that—mercifully—hadn't burned down while they were gone. The closing on his L.A. house had gone without a hitch, and Joey had agreed to wait for a fresh draft of the script to read, buying him a little extra time.

In the meantime, Joey and the girls had enjoyed following the mentions of Joey's dress on social media after the event. And Brigid was feeling the after effects of the free viral advertising with publicists literally knocking on her door.

Life was looking good enough to Jax that he paid a visit to Wilson Abramovich, Blue Moon's jeweler and the only discreet member of the Beautification Committee. After swearing the man to secrecy and squirreling away the velvet jewelry box in his dresser at Carter's, Jax turned his attention to finding the right moment to start pressing Joey on the future he'd waited his whole life for.

Jax spent every night with Joey, and she quietly made space for him in drawers, in the closet, and shelves in the bathroom. He found he could write better in her house, tucked away in the spare room, than anywhere else. For Valentine's Day, he'd kept it low-key and bought her every movie he'd ever written. She made him his favorite dinner for Valentine's Day, pot roast and mashed potatoes, and together they watched movies into the late night.

In this exact moment, life was perfect.

Even when they were arguing, as they were now over pasture groups, it felt good. It felt right. It felt like home.

"You can't put Cyrano out there with Tucker and Romeo. It's a meltdown waiting to happen," Joey said, moving away from Cyrano and poking Jax in the shoulder.

Jax took advantage of her proximity and dipped his fingers into the neck of her thermal shirt and tugged her into him.

"I'm not making out with you, Ace. I'm arguing with you."

Jax was undeterred. He boxed her in against Lolly's stall and let his mouth take what it wanted. She pretended to put up a fuss, but in seconds, Joey was opening for him, surrendering. It got him straight in the chest every time she gave up her desire for control and gave in to her desire for him.

He wouldn't do her wrong this time. He promised himself he'd spend the rest of his life making all her dreams come true.

She threaded her fingers through his hair, swiping the gray wool cap off his head.

"Get your hands off her!"

Jax turned, putting himself between Joey and the threat. Forrest Greer, larger than life, stormed down the stable aisle toward them, a freight train without brakes.

"Uh, hi, Dad." Joey said, guiltily jumping away from Jax. "I thought you weren't coming until next weekend."

Jax hauled Joey back into his side.

Joey's mother, April, hurried in behind her husband.

"Uh, Mom?" Joey's voice was a squeak.

April stood at the end of the aisle, nervously twisting her hands. "It didn't go as well as I hoped, sweetie."

Forrest slapped a crumpled newspaper against the wall in front of Joey. It was *The Monthly Moon*. And there above the fold was a picture of Joey and Jax in their movie premiere finery.

"So you're back with this one, are you?" Forrest demanded, his tone fanning the flames that sprang to life inside Jax. This wasn't going to happen again. He wouldn't let it.

Jax tucked Joey behind his back and stood toe-to-toe with the man who had changed the course of his future with one threat.

"I'm going to ask you to lower your voice," Jax said calmly.

"I'll speak when and how I want, especially when it comes to *my* daughter."

"*Your* daughter is an adult, and what makes you think that showing up at her work and causing a scene is the best way to approach her?"

Forrest went a deeper shade of red.

"I told you to stay away from her."

"And I did. For eight years. I'm back. I've earned my way back."

"You've earned nothing."

Cyrano's nerves got the best of him, and he tried to rear up in the crossties.

"Enough!" Joey's voice cut through the fog of battle that had settled between them. "I want all three of you to walk out that front door right now."

"I'm your father. You can't throw us out," Forrest began.

"You're scaring my horses. Go outside, don't say a damn word, and wait for me to put Cyrano back in his stall," Joey said, her jaw set like granite. "All of you. Now!"

Jax led the way, stalking out the front door while April

dragged Forrest with her and murmured her apologies. Anger kept him warm against the bracing breeze.

Jax waited until Forrest and April walked past him and took his position just outside the door. No one was getting to Joey without going through him first, not even her own father.

"Just what the hell do you think you're doing with my daughter?" Forrest spat out, pacing three steps out and back. Forrest Greer was built like a brawler. Anger snapped off him like electricity through downed wires.

"I plan to marry her." Jax's announcement was emphasized by a puff of breath that nearly made the words visible.

"The hell you will," he growled. "You're not good enough for her. You never were. I meant it then, and it still stands now."

"No argument here. No one is good enough for her," Jax agreed. He kept his hands at his sides in case push came to shove. "But I make her happy. If she chooses me, you have to find a way to deal with it."

"You almost killed her. You think I'm going to stand by and let it happen again?"

"It was an accident. You know I would never hurt her on purpose."

April wrung her hands. "Forrest, you need to let this go."

"I made you leave once. I can make you do it again."

"What the hell did you do?" Joey's voice snapped out. She was standing in the doorway of the stable.

"I made sure he never had the opportunity to hurt you again!"

Forrest may not have sensed the fact that he was pouring gasoline on a bonfire, but Jax sure did. He took a step toward Joey, but she held up her hand, stopping him in his tracks. He didn't want her to hear it this way. Wished she didn't have to hear it at all.

"You were laying there in a hospital bed that he put you in." Forrest pointed accusingly at Jax. "You wouldn't have left him. You would have forgiven him like a lovesick teenager. I couldn't lose you. He had to go."

"Is there a problem here?" Carter and Beckett strolled around the side of the stables coming from the direction of the brewery. His brothers looked wary... and ready for a fight. They came to a stop on either side of him, closing ranks.

"This is a family matter," Forrest told them.

"Joey is family," the Pierce brothers said as one.

"What did you do?" Joey asked again, her voice deceptively calm.

"I did what any good father would do. I told him if he didn't leave town that night, I would file a lawsuit. I'd take their farm." Forrest nodded as if daring anyone to argue with him.

"And what about Joey?" Jax prompted. It was time to get it all out in the open. Ripping off the bandage and prodding at a wound that had never properly healed.

Forrest didn't look so sure of his stance now. "I'd send you away and forbid you from attending Centenary."

Jax saw Joey take the words like a well-placed blow. She curled in on herself for a second before her spine snapped her back. "You had no right. You threatened to sue the Pierces, take everything they've worked for, unless they gave up one of their sons because a deer ran out in front of a car that I was riding in? What in the ever-living hell is wrong with you?" The calm was gone, and in its place was the storm.

"It wasn't an accident. It was his fault." Forrest was pointing his meaty finger again at Jax, and Jax was half tempted to break it.

"I can't believe you. You *knew* that I loved him, and you chased him away. You threatened his family—a family that has been nothing but kind and generous to me from day one. You knew what Centenary meant to me, and you threatened that. How could you do that?" Joey's hands were in her hair.

"You always were more loyal to that family than your own," Forrest spat out. "Even now."

Oh shit. Jax almost felt sorry for Forrest. The man was waving a red flag in front of a charging bull. No one questioned Joey Greer's loyalty and lived to tell the tale.

"You do not get to choose who I share my life with. You do not get to threaten a family because I got hurt. You do not get to make threats about me toward someone who loved me. You do not get to make decisions for me and expect me to go along with them."

"You were better off without him! I did you a favor that you weren't strong enough to do yourself."

April slapped her hand on Forrest's arm. "Forrest!" she said sharply.

"I am not weak. I am not stupid. And I am *not* disloyal," Joey said, her voice shaking with rage. "What I am is your daughter, and that does not give you the right to do what you did. It was my life then, and it's my life now. And right now, you are unwelcome in it."

"You don't mean that," Forrest said, waving her words away. "You were better off without him. He already had one foot out the door. John knew it wasn't worth trying to convince him to stay."

"John knew?" Joey whirled on Jax now. "Your dad was involved?"

Jax felt his brothers stiffen beside him. "He was part of the conversation," he said quietly. And just like that, the three men Joey had loved the most fell from grace. Jax could see the betrayal she felt written plainly on her face.

"You're just upset," Forrest said. "Once you calm down, you'll see why he had to go."

"Oh, I'm upset all right. I'm freaking furious. You don't call the shots in my life anymore. And you," she said, turning to face Jax. "You left without a word. You could have come to me, could have told me what was happening. I could have fixed it. But you didn't. You just left. You used it as your excuse, and you got out. Turned your back on all of us and just left." Joey's voice broke and with it, Jax's heart.

But she reeled it in, took a steadying breath.

"You two took it upon yourselves to make decisions for me, and I tell you now, that will never happen again. As far as I'm concerned, you both can go to hell. Now get away from my stables and don't come back."

Jax made a move toward her, and Joey shut him down with an ice-cold look. Carter lay a hand on his shoulder.

She wrenched open the stable door and stormed inside.

April shot Forrest and Jax a stern look and skirted around Beckett to follow Joey inside. But Jax beat her to the door. "April, I just need a minute with her."

April crossed her slim arms over her chest. Her dark hair and eyes had been handed down to both daughters. But where Joey was a warrior, April was a peacemaker.

"Fine. But I'm going to be on the other side of this door, and if I hear anything I don't like, I'm coming after you with a pitchfork."

"Understood and well-deserved," Jax said.

He charged through the door, momentum carrying him to where she leaned against the window of her office. Joey swiped an arm over her face.

"Baby."

"Don't say anything to me. I can't even look at you."

Jax went against his better judgment and wrapped her up

in his arms, forcing her head against his shoulder. Her shoulders shook with silent sobs, and Jax felt like the lowest human being on the planet.

"I'm so sorry, Jojo. I'm so, so sorry."

She pushed away from him, shoved him back a step. "You made me think there was something wrong with me. That you left me because I wasn't enough. I didn't deserve to spend my life thinking that, feeling that. You owed me more than disappearing in the middle of the night when I needed you most."

"I'm so sorry, Joey," he said again. "I was scared. I thought my dad could lose everything because of me. I thought your dad would ruin your dreams. I screwed up, and you and my family were paying the price."

"He wouldn't have done it. I would have talked to him, and he wouldn't have done anything. No lawsuit, no sending me away. But you didn't even give me the chance. You decided everyone was better off without you, and you abandoned us all."

"Joey, it was the worst fucking night of my life. You almost died, and I thought I'd destroyed everything my family had spent years building."

"It was the worst night of my life too. When the men that I believed in, men that I loved, decided I was too weak to make my own decisions. I've never been weak. But I may have been stupid."

"You're not stupid."

"I let you back in without knowing the truth. It never occurred to me that my father pulled any strings to get you out of my life. And I never had a clue that your dad knew and kept your secrets. So maybe I'm stupid."

"You've never been stupid a day in your life."

"I need you to do something for me," Joey said, crossing her arms.

"Anything. Name it, Jojo."

"I need you to leave me alone."

He was already shaking his head. "No. Absolutely not."

"I can't face you or him right now," she said, jerking her chin toward the door that separated them from her father.

He grabbed her arms. "Joey, I love you. You are my life. I'm not walking away again. Not even if you ask me to."

"I need time."

"Jojo, I can't do that."

"You have to," she said, shrugging out of his grasp. "This time, I'm the one walking away."

She didn't go far, but when she shut the office door behind her, he felt her shutting the doors of her heart.

He reached for the doorknob.

"I wouldn't do that if I were you." April unzipped her baby blue parka.

"She needs to listen to me."

"Jax, sweetheart. She's not going to hear anything you say right now."

"I love her, April. I'm not leaving her again."

"I know you're not. But you're not going to get through to her right now. Any convincing you try to do is going to come across as you trying to make decisions for her again."

Jax kicked at the wall, frustration and fear curdling in his blood.

"I'm not going to lose her again."

"Let me talk to her."

"If she needs to fight it out, I will. I'll fight for her. Hell, I'll fight her for her." Panic licked at him. *What if she couldn't forgive him?*

"Just give her a little space right now, okay? We'll work this out. And then I'm going to murder my husband."

"My money's on you," Jax said.

"And mine's on you."

"I suppose you were in on this too?" Joey snapped at her mother even as she poured April a cup of coffee.

April accepted the mug and leaned against the desk. "Your father never said a word to me. And for that he will pay."

Her long denim-clad legs tucked into waterproof boots in a cheery purple. She wore her hair to her shoulders and rarely bothered with makeup. She'd spent her adulthood raising her daughters and working part-time as a bookkeeper for a car dealership. At home, April ruled with a martyr's manipulation. Joey had no doubt her mother could make her dad's life miserable.

"How could he have done that? Why does he hate Jax so much?"

"Joey, your father thought he'd lost you that night. Can you imagine what that was like for him? For me? When we knew you were going to be okay, his only thought was to protect you from anything like that ever happening again."

"So you smothered the crap out of me, and he threatened to take Pierce Acres away from John."

"I'm not saying he did the right thing. In fact, I'm saying he did the stupidest thing he could have. But he did it because he didn't want to lose you."

"Well, guess what? He lost me anyway." Joey stared morosely into her coffee.

"It doesn't need to be this way," April prodded. "You and Jax seem so happy together. Why can't you go back to that?"

"Because."

"He's worked so hard to win back your trust."

"There's one thing that he should have done from the

beginning: Not leave. He should have stormed into my room and told me what Dad said to him. Barring that, when he came home, he should have fucking told me why he left. But he didn't. He tried to distract me with presents and sex instead of telling me the truth."

"You're right. They both should have been honest with you long before now."

That shut Joey up. She sank down in the chair behind the desk. "So what do I do?"

"Do you want to be with Jax?"

"I honestly don't know. It was one betrayal that I had to live through twice. Maybe that means something."

"Maybe it does, maybe it doesn't. So what does your gut tell you?"

"My gut's confused," Joey admitted. It was. She felt twisted up and hung out to dry. For the second time in less than a decade, her life had been turned upside down by the same man.

"What does your head say?"

"Kick their asses and leave them both hanging for a while."

Her mother smiled at her and sipped her coffee. "I think that's a fair decision."

THE MINUTE FORREST and April drove off, his brothers dragged Jax up to the brewery and cornered him outside the keg room.

"That's why you left? Because your girlfriend's dad scared you off with a lawsuit?" Carter said from his perch on an empty keg, his finger and thumb pinching the bridge of his nose.

Jax nodded.

"Jesus. I thought you just felt guilty over the accident and couldn't face Joey again," Beckett said, adding his two cents.

Jax paced a tight line from door to cooler. "How can the same damn thing fuck everything up twice?" He shoved his hands through his hair.

"When you're not honest about shit, shit comes back to bite you in the ass," Carter preached.

"Thank you, Mr. Philosophical."

"We could have fixed this." Beckett shook his head.

"That seems to be everyone's opinion."

"Why didn't you come to us?" Carter demanded.

"You weren't home," Jax shot back. "You were in the Army. Beckett was busy with his internship. And Dad was involved."

Carter and Beckett shared a look.

"I don't understand why Dad would have just let you leave," Beckett said.

"The three of us were in the hall. Forrest had dragged me out of Joey's room. He told us that he was going to give us a choice. Either I left town immediately or he was going to sue us for everything we had. The farm, the house, everything. And that he'd send Joey away, refuse to pay for Centenary so she'd have to go somewhere else away from me."

"And Dad was fine with giving you up to potentially avoid a bogus lawsuit brought by a guy who wasn't thinking straight?" Beckett the lawyer was itching for a fight.

Jax shook his head and resumed pacing. "It wasn't like that. Dad took some convincing, but Forrest was dead serious. I'd almost killed his daughter, and the only way he could think to protect her was to get me out of the picture."

"So you left," Carter said quietly.

"So I left. I was scared shitless. I was eighteen and just watched the most important person in my life almost die in front of me. And it was my fault. How was I supposed to live with that? And if Dad had lost the farm because of me? Family loyalty shouldn't be expected to go that far."

"A, it wasn't your fault, dumbass. And B, how did no one ever tell Joey?" Beckett wanted to know.

Jax shook his head. "It was part of the deal with her dad that I not contact her again. She thought I was just an ass who got scared and left town."

"Well, if she can forgive you for that, hopefully she'll be willing to cut you a break for the real reason." Carter sighed. "I also hope you're done with the whole 'I almost killed her' bullshit."

"I'm getting there," Jax answered. He was. Slowly. It had been an accident, one with dire consequences. But an accident all the same.

"Good. I'm glad you're getting less stupid in your old age," Beckett said.

Jax could always count on his brothers for a well-timed put down to cheer him up.

"I don't have a good feeling about this. She's not going to get over this, and it won't be just me that she cuts out this time. It'll be her father too," Jax told them.

His brothers nodded.

Jax stopped pacing and leaned against the wall. "I got her a ring."

"Shit," Carter sympathized.

He looked around him. His brothers' faces were dark and broody as they shared his pain. Their connection had deepened since he'd come home. Equals. Partners. He wasn't just the youngest Pierce anymore. He'd built something here. This very brewery existed because he came home for a new beginning. In the last few months, he'd laid the groundwork for a new life, the life he'd always wanted. This was not going to be all for nothing. He'd fix this.

"So what are you going to do? You're sure as hell not going to quit now," Beckett said, trying to rally the troops.

"I'm gonna fix this," Jax said, lacing his fingers behind his head.

"How?"

"I have no fucking idea."

28

———

*J*ax put in a full day on the farm and a full night in the brewery. He didn't know whether to be grateful to or pissed off at Carter and Beckett for taking advantage of his current predicament by burying him in work. It kept him physically preoccupied, but his mind and his heart never wavered from Joey.

He trudged in the front door well after midnight and was greeted by Meatball's soft "woof." The dog's white-tipped tail thumped a lazy rhythm against the floor.

"What are you still doing up, buddy?" Jax whispered, shucking off his coat and stuffing it in the closet.

The beagle slowly worked his way up to his feet and wandered over for scratches. "Come on. Let's have a snack," Jax said, leading the way back to the kitchen. He pulled his laptop out of his bag and set it on the island before peeking into the fridge. He grimaced at the disgusting tofu scramble leftovers that Carter and Summer had for dinner. *Vegetarians*, he thought with distaste.

He settled on a mixing bowl of cereal and shared some— minus the milk—with Meatball in his food dish. Jax settled on a barstool and reached into his bag for his charger, but his fingers brushed an envelope instead. He pulled out the folder that held the stack of his father's short stories.

It seemed every time he read one of his father's essays, some nugget of truth resonated with him. And he could really use his father's words of wisdom now more than ever. Unwinding the red string, Jax slid the stack of stories out. He'd been slowly shuffling the essays he read to the bottom of the pile.

He paged through until his father's still familiar handwriting scrawled across the paper caught his eye.

There was no title, only the opening line...

Today was the hardest day I've ever endured as a father.

Jax knew without a doubt what day his father was talking about, and guilt simmered in his gut. He and his dad had never spoke of what happened that day, and there was part of Jax that didn't want to expose himself to his father's take and pain on the accident.

But there was a louder part, the writer in him, who needed to know. Needed to peel back the layers to look at the whys. So he read on. It wasn't a carefully crafted story like the rest of his father's writings. This was a stream of consciousness, a purging.

Today was the hardest day I've ever endured as a father. A typical day was followed by a typical evening. Phoebe and I were washing up the dishes after a late dinner. Beckett was out with the girl-of-the-month, as we'd come to call his dates, and Jax was due back from his date with Joey any minute.

And then the phone rang.

Phoebe answered it with her cheerful "Hello, Pierces."

And I saw the color leave her face in an instant.

I didn't know which son it was. But I knew it was one of them. No other news delivered could make my wife's heart stop like that.

Was it Carter in Afghanistan? His first deployment was a source of pride and terror. He'd been gone long enough that I'd stopped being afraid of the telephone ringing. But it all came back now.

"It's Jax," Phoebe said, her face white as the clean sheets she'd just put on his bed that afternoon.

The phone tumbled from her grip, and I took it. Who? What? Where? I peppered the police on the other end with rapid-fire questions.

Alive. Jax was alive. That's all they would say, and they were even cagier on Joey's condition. Yes, she was in the car. Yes, she was going to the hospital with Jax. But that's all they could say.

We grabbed keys and were out the door in a heartbeat. Silence reigned in the car, but we'd known each other too long to not hear the unasked questions that echoed in the other's head.

How badly were they hurt?

How had it happened?

What could we have done to prevent it?

What if... What if the one thing neither of us could bring ourselves to think happened? What if we lost him? What if we lost her?

At the hospital, Phoebe jumped out while I parked. The visitors lot felt like it was miles away. And that long walk under lonely streetlights and that full summer moon was an out-of-body experience.

In front of me, the glow of the Emergency Room sign. The answers I sought were through those glass doors. But I wasn't sure I was ready for those answers. Wasn't sure I could live with those answers if our son had been taken from us.

It's funny the things you think of in moments like that. A whirl of chaos, a windmill of every nightmare imaginable, shows itself. I saw a funeral, a wedding, scars, and blood. I thought about Jax when he was seven and I taught him to drive the tractor. His mechanical aptitude had quickly surpassed either of his brothers'. His love of all things with engines. That car that he was so proud of, the one that the cops told me was now wrapped around a tree just past Diller's pond.

I thought of the way he looked at Joey during their prom pictures. It had made me drag him outside for just a minute to remind him of the merits of being safe. He'd rolled his eyes at me then. "I know Dad. We've got big plans together. I'm not going to screw that up with some accidental pregnancy."

I'd never put much stock in high school sweethearts. Until Jax and Joey. There was something about them that seemed older than time. Joey had been a part of the family since she and Jax met in kindergarten. And when they stopped tiptoeing around what everyone else already saw and started dating, I'd sent up a silent prayer that it wasn't a huge mistake.

Because by that time, Joey was already the daughter of my heart. A serious little girl, she'd grown into a driven young woman. She would lend a hand whether it was in the fields or at the kitchen sink without anyone ever asking her to. She knew what she wanted—horses—and how she was going to get there before most others her age had their driver's license.

Her seriousness focused Jax, who would rather party with the lacrosse team than work on a history paper. The semester they started dating, his GPA went up, and he made the honor roll for the first time ever. And in return, he gave her the fun and silliness that she'd always seemed to be on the outside of looking in. He carved out a place of belonging for her.

They balanced each other, and I hoped that it could stay that way without anyone getting hurt. Only now someone had.

I walked into those hospital doors not knowing if I'd lost family and future.

Phoebe is a woman you want on your side in a crisis. She was waiting for me by the desk. Joey's parents, April and Forrest, came in behind me and, before anyone said a word, Phoebe was dragging us back through a set of doors marked Do Not Enter. She'd found them, she said. Her face was grim, and I knew the news wasn't good.

She marched us through the chaotic maze of a busy emergency room. Past families facing the worst night of their lives. Past relieved parents who were just told good news. Past exhausted nurses who were long over the end of their shift.

"They're in there," she said, stopping at a curtained-off corner.

Forrest pushed past us and yanked open the curtain. When I saw Jax standing on his own two feet, I went weak in the knees. When he turned to face us, and I saw the blood...

There is nothing like being a parent. A piece of you is walking around the earth maybe with your eyes and your wife's smile. And that piece of you has to grow up and build his or her own life, feel the pain of that life, and find the joy in that life. When you see that piece of you hurt and scared, it is a horrible, helpless feeling. Because you just want to fix it, swoop in and take over and solve the problems and protect them from this hurt.

But you can't. Because they aren't just a piece of you. They are a human being learning how to survive and thrive in this world. And if you clean up every mess and bandage every scrape and shield them from every hurt, you take that self-reliance away from them. And that is what turns children into good men and women.

Jax was holding gauze on his forehead with one hand while gripping Joey's hand in the other. His t-shirt was missing, and I had a sick feeling it had to do with the blood that was drying on his chest and torso. Blood that wasn't his.

Joey's eyes were closed. Her face whiter than the sheet under her head. Her right arm was being worked on by two women in scrubs. A bag of blood hung from her IV pole.

"My little girl." Forrest stared down brokenly at his daughter.

April was crying silent tears at the foot of her bed, and Phoebe, my rock, had her arm around her as if to keep her from dissolving.

"I'm sorry Dad," Jax said, not daring to take his eyes off of Joey's face.

"It's not your fault. Everything is going to be okay."

"She hasn't woken up yet," he said. His thumb stroked hers over and over again, silently willing her to wake up.

Forrest pressed too close to the doctor and nurse and was ordered back.

"She's my daughter. I've more of a right to be here than him," he said, pointing at my son. Jax gave no reaction to the words.

The doctor, a woman in her early thirties, placed the last suture in Joey's arm before turning around on her stool to face him.

"I understand that you're upset, but now is not the time." Her voice was calm and cool, and I could see why she was in emergency medicine. The voice of reason in a world of chaos.

"Is she going to be okay?" April's whisper of a voice asked the one question we all needed the answer to.

"Are you her mother?" the doctor asked, stripping off her gloves and tossing them in a bin on the floor.

"Yes."

"Joey's lost a lot of blood. But Jax here did a good job with a makeshift tourniquet at the accident. Without it, I don't know if she would have made it. She's going to have a couple of transfusions, and I think once she has that blood in her she's going to wake up. Recovery will take a while, but she will recover."

I saw Forrest working hard to swallow some of the emotion that must have been choking him. Felt the wave of hope and relief that crashed over all of us at the news. All of us, except Jax. There was no sign that he was even hearing our conversation, his attention never wavering from Joey as if he was willing her to wake up.

"Graduation is in five days..." April trailed off.

"I wouldn't be surprised if she's out of here and walking across that stage," the doctor said, laying a cool hand on April's shoulder.

"She'll... she'll wake up then?" Forrest asked, still staring at his daughter's ghost white face.

The doctor turned back to him. "She will."

Forrest bent from the waist to catch his breath with a relief so strong it nearly swept him off his feet. In that moment, we shared something that could never be put into words. We'd come within millimeters of losing something irreplaceable, and the knowledge that everything could go back to normal was like a summer rain after weeks of drought. Being faced with the thing you didn't have any control over and then rewarded with normal? It was a humbling experience. Unfortunately not for all.

With Joey stitched up, the doctor finally convinced Jax to let her take a look at his forehead. He sat in a chair, never releasing Joey's hand while the doctor made quick work of the cuts on his head and hands.

With the good news, Forrest channeled his energy into attack mode.

I can't remember all that was said, in the heat of the moment, but voices—including mine—were raised, and Forrest was one second away from demanding that security remove Jax from Joey's bedside.

April was in tears again, and Phoebe was spitting fire.

It was that moment that Joey decided to return to this world. She opened her eyes with a flutter and told everyone to keep it down. She held Jax's hand in one of her own and her father's in the other. And once again helplessness was redirected into relief.

It was the middle of the night before Jax was officially released and Joey was admitted. We stayed on to see her moved to a room, and something happened in those hours between heartbreak and hope that changed the course of our family.

I was returning with hot, stale vending machine coffee for all when I saw Forrest and Jax having a heated discussion in the doorway of an empty waiting room. I walked in on the word "lawsuit."

He laid it out for us. If Jax didn't leave Blue Moon, Forrest would file a lawsuit against us. And to make sure his daughter stayed away from Jax, he wouldn't pay for her to go to Centenary with him. Anything to keep them apart.

I thought it was just the hurt and scared talking. But Jax saw something else. He saw Joey's dreams dashed. He saw a drawn-out legal battle for his family. He saw only one way out.

I tried to talk him out of it. We would figure it out, I told him. Leaving everything he'd worked for, everyone he loved was an unfair punishment for something that wasn't his fault. But Jax was adamant. I saw that it was his moment, his choice, and he was doing what he thought was best for the people he loved.

In that moment, I saw my son clearly standing on his own two feet taking—too much—responsibility for his life. If I stepped in, discounted his feelings, and tried to protect him by sweeping up the mess, it could do even more damage. If Forrest did sue, if he won, how responsible would Jax feel then for the outcome? How would Jax and Joey survive with their families so bitterly divided? He'd already thought of these things and weighed them unaccept-able. He'd rather face the unknown of starting over on his own than taking his family into a battle that he didn't want us to fight.

I was proud and devastated. The profound concern for others beyond his eighteen-year-old self was a side his mother and I had only caught glimpses of. But now, stripped and raw, he was ready to take this burden on himself for the good of us all.

I didn't tell Phoebe, and that I know I'll come to regret. When *we drove home, the air was heavy with unspoken words. Phoebe gave Jax a long hug and told him she loved him before she went upstairs to bed. Jax went upstairs to pack. I waited for him in the kitchen second-, third-, and fourth-guessing myself.*

I wanted to tell him not to go. That I didn't want him to go. I had been prepared for the separation of college in the fall, not the sudden and life-altering separation that was about to happen tonight. But then a quiet voice whispered deep inside. Jax could get out. Unburdened from any expectation and responsibility, Jax could build a life of freedom.

Over the years, I had faced nights where I wondered quietly what would be different if I hadn't started this farm? If I wasn't carrying the weight and burden of this place? What would my life look like had I just driven south or west? Would it be easier? Better? Brighter?

I never pondered these thoughts too long. I was married to this land. I had a wife to love and a family to provide for, to enjoy, to watch grow as if they too were crops to be harvested. I loved it. But it is hard. Harder than I ever could have imagined. Balancing, juggling, hoping, influencing, sweating, challenging Mother Nature to a duel year after year.

But Jax could start over. He wouldn't be the Jackson Pierce whose story and family everyone knows. Whose eighteen years were well documented and expectations pinned on him from birth. He wouldn't be the other half of a couple, at least not yet. It was one of the dangers of love so young. Being half of a couple often comes before being a whole person.

Maybe it was selfish of me to let him go. To let him do what I never had the guts to do. To drive him to that bus station, wrap him in a hug so tight I thought we were almost the same person. I tucked what he and his brothers had affectionately dubbed the "oh shit fund" money into his hand. And when he tried to give it back, I told him that if he was starting over, he was doing it with an investment from me. Because I believed in him. And I did.

I sit here in the dark of the kitchen waiting for Phoebe to wake up and read the note Jax left her. I don't know if she'll forgive me, and I'm not sure how much of my role I can confess to her and still live to see noon. My heart hurts for me, for them, for Joey, and for Jax. But it's also soaring for him because I know that this is just the beginning for him and he will be back. And I'll be all the prouder for it.

THE PIECES of that night that Jax hadn't known he'd lost came rushing back as he rested his head in his hands. The relief on his parents' faces when they pulled back the curtain and it wasn't him in the bed. The overwhelming feelings that swamped him when Joey's beautiful brown eyes opened, disoriented and hurt but *alive*. And that sick slide into guilt, knowing he'd put her in that bed, knowing he'd put his family in danger of losing it all.

To read his father's take on it all was a painful and beautiful kind of therapy. His dad had never blamed him like Jax had feared he had. He'd been proud. Since that night there had been a nagging question in the back of his mind about why his father had let him go. And now he knew. And knowing meant healing.

A plan began to form in Jax's mind and with it, hope in his heart. He scanned a copy of his father's story with his phone and sent it to the printer upstairs. He fired off a middle-of-the-night email to Ellery. Then he opened his screenplay and got to work.

29

———

*J*oey was in a bad mood, and throwing herself into her work didn't seem to help. At home, Waffles was happy to curl up with her on the couch and in her lonely bed, but at work when she had to deal with the incompetence of everyone, the dog decided he was better off following Carter around than sticking with her.

She'd ripped the bottom drawer out of the filing cabinet in her office when it failed to glide open smoothly. While fixing a loose board on the indoor ring's mounting block, she'd given her thumb a good smack with a hammer and then rained down four-letter words until the horses were nervous.

High-strung Calypso had chosen that day to give her a swift kick when she wasn't looking, and now she had a goddamn hoof print on her thigh.

When Colby had the audacity to ask her what "crawled up her butt and died," she put the fear of the Almighty in him with a look frosty enough to freeze boiling water and a few colorful choice words about his genitalia and parentage.

It was at that point that Carter told her that she was taking the night off from lessons so she didn't "drop kick any paying students" and open them up to a lawsuit.

She didn't think that lawsuit jokes were remotely funny. Carter, on the other hand, found it hilarious.

Just what the hell was she supposed to do with an evening to herself? An evening alone.

She'd effectively shut down every attempt by Summer and Gia to talk it out or commiserate or whatever else girls wanted to do when their feelings were hurt by idiots with penises.

The sense of betrayal she felt toward her father and Jax was so overwhelming she worried that it would swamp her. The nights since the day the truth had been revealed held little sleep and still so many questions. The main question being: What in the hell was wrong with them?

But there were no easy answers, just disappointment. And hurt. Some rage. And a rawness that just kept getting rawer. What made it worse was the radio silence on Jax's end. She'd become so used to his relentless onslaught of sneaky, manipulative affection that his absence was noticeable.

She'd tucked his toothbrush in a drawer just so she didn't have to stare at it every night and every morning. The small pile of dirty laundry he left in the corner of her room that Waffles had used as a bed? She shoved it under the guest room bed because she certainly wasn't going to wash it for him and coolly return it. That's what adults did. She preferred to fantasize about setting it on fire in his driveway.

Of course it was time for another Meat of the Month delivery. And she couldn't even bring herself to open the teriyaki Kobe beef jerky. Of course, she couldn't just throw it out either. So that went to the back of her pantry until such a time that she could enjoy it hate-free.

Joey felt like her life had spiraled completely out of control in that one moment, standing in front of the stables she'd practically built and between the two men she'd loved. What in the hell was she supposed to do now? There was no way she was just going to sit here and stew all night long.

She looked at the clock on the mantel. Desperate times called for desperate measures.

The lights were on in Gia's yoga studio, and the windows were steamy from the last class, hot power yoga. Joey wasn't desperate enough to suffer through one of those. But restorative yoga? She could handle that.

She darted past Gia who was deep in conversation with Maizie, the server at Peace of Pizza, and Rob, co-founder of OJ's by Julia.

Relieved that there was no bikini-bottom-clad Fitz, Joey unrolled a mat in the back row and pretended to stare at her phone to discourage anyone from trying to talk to her. It worked until Donovan Cardona flopped down on a mat next to her.

Blue Moon's most popular sheriff to date, he was also brazenly single, and Joey had a feeling he'd avoided the efforts of the Beautification Committee long enough. Once they had hooked Jax and Moon Beam up, they'd probably have Donovan marching down the aisle before Memorial Day.

And now she was back to pissed off.

"Hey, haven't seen much of you lately," Donovan said, stretching his legs straight and reaching desperately for his toes.

"I've been busy," Joey grumbled.

"So I hear."

"What do you hear? That I've been busy being betrayed by Jax and my father?"

"Uh. No?" Donovan peaked at her with concerned blue eyes under a muscular bicep. "I was talking about the whole partnership thing. I figured you've been busy with the breeding program and all that. I didn't know anything about any betrayal."

Joey felt like a jerk. "I'm sorry. I'm just…"

"Hungry?"

She shook her head.

"Bloated?"

"No!"

"Murderous?"

"Maybe a little."

"Cantankerous?"

That brought the corners of her lips up a little bit. Cardona was a funny guy. In the years between Jax's disappearance and reappearance, Joey had been invited to the poker table more than once, and she'd enjoyed kicking the sheriff's ass when she had the opportunity. He was a decent poker player with a smile like a Ken doll and a master's in organizational leadership. Why couldn't she have fallen for a guy like him?

Why did her heart have to belong to Jackson "Love 'Em and Crush 'Em Like Bugs" Pierce?

"You're a funny guy, Cardona."

"Thanks, but looks aren't everything. My mama always told me I'd grow into my nose."

"A real riot. How is it the B.C. hasn't lined you up with some cute candle-making hippie by now?"

"I've threatened to arrest every single one of them on disturbing the peace charges if they try it."

"Nice try. This is Blue Moon. Disturbing the peace arrest records go on resumes here."

"Every time I get trapped in a conversation with one of the B.C. members, I fake an emergency and run away like an Olympic sprinter." He glanced down at his phone.

Joey looked around her. Everyone in the studio with the

exception of her was staring intently at their phones, typing away with their thumbs.

"This is what's wrong with society," Joey grumbled.

"What's that?" Donovan asked, shoving his phone in his gym bag.

"Look at everyone texting and Facebooking and whatever else they do on a phone."

Donovan looked guilty. "They're probably just turning their phones off for class. So are you going this weekend?"

"What's this weekend?" Joey asked, still distracted by the thoughts of phones taking over the world.

"The Sit-In. It's Saturday."

"God, no. I have too much work to do." And zero desire to surround herself by an entire town who probably now knew her shame. Besides, Jax would be there. You didn't live in Blue Moon and miss this event.

Nope. She'd stay at home with Waffles and work. With Apollo's stud fee finally decided on, she could start reaching out to potential clients for spring.

"That's a shame," Donovan said. "I hear it's going to be even better than last year."

"Last year the popcorn stand caught fire in the gym. The school smelled like burnt popcorn until summer."

"Nowhere to go but up!" Donovan shrugged.

JOEY, feeling marginally less murderous after yoga, headed home. The heater in her pickup pumped out warm air in an endless battle against the upstate New York winter. She'd avoided Gia's well-meaning invitation to go get a drink and talk about the surprise baby shower they were planning for Summer, which was code for "drag information out of you in the name of friendship and then offer completely useless platitudes like 'forgive and forget.'"

Nope. Joey was going to go home, curl up with her dog, and stare at the TV until it was time for bed, at which point she would go upstairs and stare at her bedroom ceiling and try not to think of all the amazing orgasms she'd recently enjoyed in said bed. Yeah, life was just really freaking grand right now.

When she got home the first thing that tipped her off to a break-in was the fact that Waffles was enjoying a massive chew bone the size of a cattle leg. The second thing that tipped her off was the note on the microwave that said "Open Me."

Inside was a Shorty's to-go box with a burger and onion rings. This was clearly the work of Jax.

She really needed to start locking her doors.

The next note was on the counter and directed her to look at her coffee table. She was tempted to ignore it and just go upstairs and wash away her troubles in the shower. She could just throw the burger in the garbage and warm up whatever the hell leftovers she had in her fridge.

Or she could just eat the burger. No one would have to know. It would be a shame to waste a perfectly good, still warm Shorty's burger.

She took the takeout box over to her couch, furtively glancing out front and back windows to make sure no one was witnessing her dinner surrender. Satisfied that it was just her and Waffles, Joey flopped down on the couch.

On the coffee table in front of her was a fat envelope topped with a bottle of bourbon and a ridiculous coffee mug plastered with horses and hearts.

There was another note rolled up in the mug.

Joey,

I saw this horse mug, and it made me think of you, especially since the last horse mug I gave you shattered against the wall when you threw it at me. Consider this a replacement. The booze is to accompany what's in the envelope and your burger. Please don't throw out your burger to spite me. That would be sacrilege.

I've been wracking my brain trying to come up with the right way to tell you how sorry I am that I've hurt you again and remind you of how much I love you. But I realized that until you know everything about that night and after, there's no chance of that ever happening. So here it is. My screenplay. Our story.

I'll be in touch.

Love always,

Your Jax

Joey put down the note and slouched as low as she could on the cushion. All the answers to the questions she'd been asking for nearly a decade were neatly packaged before her. And yet she hesitated.

What if the answers she got weren't forgivable?

Waffles gave up on his bone and hopped up on the couch next to her, his bi-colored eyes watching her pitifully hoping for a bite of burger.

Her indecisiveness lasted exactly two seconds longer when she reached for the burger and the folder.

"Screw it. Right, Waffles?"

Waffles' tail thumped on the couch as he looked at her adoringly.

ONE HUNDRED AND ten pages and two fingers of bourbon later, Joey swiped at perhaps the hundredth tear as it sluiced its way down her cheek.

Her guts had been ripped out and shoved back in upside

down. He'd given her the answers she'd needed in a way that was wholly Jax. Gutted, she was nowhere nearer to a solution than she had been before she came home that night. But at least she had her answers.

She hadn't expected to learn so much about the course of their relationship. How long he'd loved her. How long he'd noticed her and yet talked himself out of making a move on the girl his brothers thought of as a sister, the girl his parents thought of as a daughter. Instead, he kept her at arm's length until he couldn't be without her for one more day. To see the longing that she'd so acutely felt growing up mirrored in his words was indescribable.

And what he saw in her? What he poured into her character? Strength, beauty, single-minded determination. In those pages, she saw herself as Jax saw her.

It clutched at her heart to read about the accident from his point of view, the guilt and the fear, of feeling responsible for nearly destroying the one thing you valued above all else. It hadn't been an easy decision to live with, she learned. Jax hadn't just walked away without a backward glance. He'd never stopped thinking of her, stalking her online with news alerts and social media, loving her. Did that help? Knowing that they'd needlessly wasted eight years because of a decision she still didn't agree with?

She felt raw and open, like a fresh wound. Knowing for certain now that he had loved her as deeply and expansively as she did him loosened something around her heart. Something that had constricted years ago. Another wall, another lock.

But what did that mean for the end of their story?

Instead of the final pages of his screenplay, he'd included a photocopy of his father's account of the evening. A story from three sides that still added up to men who thought they knew better than she did.

It was galling. It was heartbreaking. And somehow, through Jax's own typed words, she could begin to comprehend the why. It was hard to see past her own anger, but the words of two Pierce men had slowly blazed a trail through the hurt.

She wasn't sure if she was ready to feel anything other than anger toward Jax. Except for a strong desire to find out how his screenplay ended. That she could admit to being curious about.

Joey picked up John's essay again, stared at the handwriting of a man long lost to this world. He'd seen something deep and enduring in her relationship with Jax. A foundation and a prison. Had she ever thought of their relationship as a prison? Had Jax?

She'd been so certain then that their futures had been twined together. That Jax was a given in her life. And then when he was gone, her foundation cracked, and she rebuilt it slowly, independently, determined to never again build a life around someone else. She did what she wanted. She went after her dreams with dogged determination, and she built this life and these walls that would keep her safe.

Yet, once again, she'd let Jax in. And, once again, she'd been rocked. That had to mean something. There wouldn't be so much hurt if they were supposed to be, would there?

There was one person she could ask.

She picked up her phone and dialed.

∽

MR. SNUFFLES WAS PAWING at the door of Phoebe's townhouse until Franklin opened it. The little dog sniffed Joey's boot, sneezed, and ran back into the kitchen.

At least nothing green and slimy had flown out of his nose.

"Sorry for bothering you guys so late," Joey told Franklin as he took her coat.

Franklin, dressed in flannel pajamas and slippers, tut-tutted. "You're always welcome, Joey."

The ever-present moving boxes had been neatly stacked along the wall behind the dining table. Phoebe and Franklin's quest to move in together seemed like it was taking longer than a college education. But Calvin was ready to break ground on their new home in a sunny pasture back on the farm. And soon Franklin would be watching TV or whipping up a gourmet Italian meal in those pajamas in their brand-new house. Probably with grandkids and granddogs underfoot.

Phoebe, in fleecy pajama bottoms decorated with pink flamingos, bustled out of the kitchen and wrapped Joey in a hug. "It's good to see you, sweetie."

"I'll start the tea," Franklin said, winking at Phoebe and dropping a kiss on her cheek.

Phoebe blushed prettily.

"Oh, crap. I'm not interrupting anything, am I?" Joey asked, embarrassed that she might be crashing a pajama party.

"No, dear. We finished anything worth interrupting before you called." Phoebe winked.

Joey smirked. Love knew no age, that was for sure.

"Come on in and make yourself comfortable," Phoebe said, leading the way into her living room. "You sounded upset on the phone."

Joey sank down on the couch. "I was. Am. I'm sure you heard by now about... everything."

Phoebe nodded. "I heard Jax and your father had a bit of a run-in the other day."

"Did you know Jax is writing a screenplay about me?"

Phoebe's eyes widened behind her glasses. "I had no idea! Oh, I bet it's wonderful!"

Joey rolled her eyes. "Yeah, let's put the maternal pride on hold for a second. He started it before he came back and has it sold to a studio already. It's our whole story. From kindergarten on up to present."

"He let you read it."

Joey nodded. "Most of it. He kept the ending. But he did include John's write-up of the accident."

"Smart boy," Phoebe said proudly.

Joey shot her a look.

"Sorry." Phoebe grinned. "But you have to admit that's a pretty creative apology. Giving you the other two sides to what happened the night of the accident."

"Yeah, yeah. Creative. Whatever. How did you forgive John for letting him go and not telling you?"

Now it was Phoebe's turn to roll her eyes. "Oh, Joey. That situation taught me more about love and forgiveness than any other I've ever been in. I was heartbroken that Jax left, and I was so angry at John for letting him."

Phoebe shook her head at the memories. "I felt betrayed by them both for quite some time."

"How did you get unbetrayed?"

"I had to trust that John felt that the decision was the right one. Now that's completely different from agreeing with the decision. Because to this day I don't. But I knew deep down John never would have let him go if he thought it wouldn't be in Jax's best interest."

Joey frowned, her brain contemplating the areas of gray. "So even though you thought he was wrong, you didn't bash his head in with a frying pan?"

Phoebe nodded. "Exactly. Oh, I was furious with him when he came clean. To know that he'd driven Jax to the bus station and given him money and just sent him off into the unknown. Knowing he got to say goodbye and I didn't have that chance? There were many times I picked up the metaphorical frying pan. But what finally got through to me is the pain that John carried for that decision, even though he still believed he was right."

Joey gave a half-hearted "hmm."

"You and your mother and I would have solved the entire thing in seconds if they'd bothered to bring us into their testosterone fueled pow-wow of idiocy. Instead, we all had to live with the consequences of their decisions. But what it all boils down to is each of them thought they were doing the best they could for the people they loved."

Joey flopped back against the couch. "I get what you're saying. I do. But, my God, how do you forgive stupidity like that?"

"It takes a long, long time. And a lot of wine. But once you get to that point of understanding, everything starts to hurt just a little bit less. I honestly believe that they didn't do any of it to hurt you. They both thought they were protecting you in their own stupid, misguided way." Phoebe patted her leg.

Franklin entered the room carting a tray with steaming mugs, Mr. Snuffles on his heels. He'd sliced up lemon and added a little bowl of honey and a pitcher of cream.

"Thank you, handsome," Phoebe said, grinning up at her husband-to-be.

Franklin smiled sweetly back at her, and Joey wanted to

gag a little. Everyone was happy and in love except for her. Stupid Blue Moon.

"So what are you going to do?" Phoebe asked after Franklin left them again.

Mr. Snuffles jumped up next to her on the couch and cocked his head as if he were waiting for an answer too.

"I honestly don't know."

"Do you love Jax?"

Joey shrugged. "I guess. But that sure didn't get me very far either time with him. We're obviously missing something key to a successful relationship. Any ideas?"

"If I had to hazard a guess, I'd put my money on communication," Phoebe offered.

"Relationships would be so much easier if we didn't have to communicate," Joey grumbled. It was true. She and Jax rarely had a conversation that didn't begin or end with an argument. And if they weren't fighting, they were naked. Solid relationships couldn't be built on just sex, could they?

She hadn't realized she'd asked the question out loud until Phoebe snorted in her tea. "No, but they sure go better than the ones with terrible sex. And you know what? You can learn to communicate easier than you can learn to be more interesting in bed."

"You may have a point," Joey said, picking up her tea and sniffing it. "One last question. You knew all this time why Jax left. Why didn't you tell me?"

Phoebe sighed long and low. "I've been dreading this question for years. Not telling you makes me seem disloyal to you. Like I was protecting Jax over you."

"Maybe a little. I mean, he is your son and all, but you still should have told me."

"It was for Jax and your father to tell. Coming from anyone else, including me?" She shook her head. "The only way to save either or both of those relationships is for them to tell you the truth. Me telling you would have robbed them of that opportunity, and it would have quite possibly effectively ended one or both relationships."

"But my relationship with Jax was already over."

Phoebe smiled. "Honey, you two could run off and marry other people and have six kids apiece, and you still wouldn't be over. There are so many strings tying you two together I pity anyone who tries to keep you apart."

"John seemed to think that me loving Jax in high school was kind of like a prison."

"Leave it to a man to describe love as a prison." Phoebe sighed.

"Do you think I trapped him?"

"I think the decisions you both would have made together would have put you in different places than where you are now."

"So Jax wouldn't be a big-time Hollywood screenwriter?"

"And you wouldn't be a partner in the stables you helped build," Phoebe pointed out.

Joey couldn't imagine a life without her horses, without Pierce Acres, without her cozy home tucked away on a hill.

"Hmm. Well, you know there's really only one thing that's going to repair your relationship with me since you've been lying to me for all these years," Joey said, delicately sipping her tea.

Phoebe rolled her eyes and pulled a battered recipe card out from under the couch cushion. "Mercenary," she said.

"Thank you, Great-Aunt Felicia," Joey said, triumphantly holding up the raspberry cream cheese coffee cake recipe.

30

The day of Blue Moon's 45th Annual Sit-In And Good Cause Carnival dawned crisp and bright with temperatures promising a balmy high in the mid-forties.

To Joey it was both a ridiculous and entirely enjoyable tradition in town. Forty-five years ago, the town's library had faced a funding crisis, and shutdown had been imminent. The librarian at the time, Mrs. Manypenny, had somehow formed a bond with Blue Moon's newest flower child residents, allowing them to sell crafts in the library's basement, helping them with job applications, and pointing them toward the right resources for their many endeavors of the moment.

Mrs. Manypenny had helped Willa secure a loan to open Blue Moon Boots. She'd ordered beekeeping books when Elvira Eustace, then Elvira Sharpinski, wanted to start her own beekeeping enterprise. She'd arranged for guest speakers to address Blue Moon audiences on topics as vast and varied as raising growth-hormone-free livestock, hydroponics, transcendental meditation, and what to do when you hadn't paid income tax.

So when the library faced closure, the hippies decided to

show their support of the library and Mrs. Manypenny in the way they knew best. They staged a sit-in at the library with the highlight being two young lovers, Sheldon and Lenore Fitzsimmons—Fitz's parents— who handcuffed themselves to a shelving system of Nancy Drew books. The entire town showed up to see what all the fuss was about, and someone started passing a hat. The five o'clock news did a brief clip on the protest, and eleven hours after the sit-in started, the protestors had raised enough money to fund the library's operating budget for another year.

The townspeople had so much fun, they decided to do it again. And so every year since, they staged a sit-in for a different cause. And every year, the town chose a "lucky" couple to be handcuffed together as the Cuffed Lovers. Thankfully, the town had voted in favor of reducing the cuff time to two hours to better accommodate things like bathroom breaks.

This year, Furever Home Animal Rescue would be the recipient of the funds raised. The sit-in had outgrown its humble beginnings over the years. The library could no longer hold the crowds that invariably showed up, so the event was now hosted at the high school where booths, dancing, and food stands spilled over from the gymnasium into cafeteria and, in unseasonably warm years, the parking lot.

Joey had no intentions of attending this year's sit-in. Not since everyone in town knew she and Jax had imploded yet again. And especially not since there was barely a whisper of their breakup on Facebook. The Beautification Committee was probably hoping to cuff Moon Beam Parker to Jax to finally set their diabolical and horribly misguided plan into action.

Unsure of what her feelings actually were, she'd yet to reach out to Jax after reading his screenplay. She felt a softening around the edges of her anger. And he'd continued to give her space, staying out of her way. She hated that she missed him. On her couch, in her stables, in her bed. His absence was noticeable and uncomfortable. Jax might live in Blue Moon, but it was as if he had vanished from her life again. And this time it was at her request.

Jax would be there at the sit-in, she was sure of it. And as much as she missed him, she still wasn't ready to face him. She couldn't be sure that she wouldn't take out the metaphorical frying pan and bean him with it in front of witnesses. Nope. There was no way she was showing her face at the sit-in. At least, that's what she thought until Mrs. Penskee of Furever Home called her personally to invite Joey and Waffles to be their special guests of honor. Well, Waffles would be the guest of honor; Joey would hold the guest of honor's leash.

"It would be such great publicity for the rescue," Mrs. Penskee had told her. "And you and Waffles are one of our happiest stories. It would mean the world to us if you'll be there."

Joey had grudgingly agreed and then ordered Waffles a fire hydrant print bowtie for him to wear for his big day. And since the dog was dressing up, Joey thought she should take a little extra care with her appearance. It had nothing to do with the fact that Jax would probably be there. She didn't need to look extra good for him. She was doing this for herself. At least that's what she told herself as she traced eyeliner over each lash line. She pulled part of her hair back from her face so her dark curls fell down her back, and she chose a soft scoop neck sweater in a deep plum to go with her jeans and suede boots.

Armor in place, she gave a nod to her reflection in the mirror and marched out the door. At the high school, Waffles hopped out of the truck and pranced down the sidewalk with her as if he were walking the red carpet.

Several people called out greetings to her, and Joey realized she'd been avoiding town for quite a while now. It was kind of nice to be back around people... as long as none of them brought up a certain Pierce's name.

Gia and Summer flagged her down at the entrance.

"Hey! You came," Gia said, leaning down to pat Waffles.

"Waffles, I'm going to say hello from up here," Summer said, patting her belly. "I haven't been near my own shoes in weeks, so take a rain check on the petting."

"Are you okay?" Joey asked. Summer looked exhausted and uncomfortable.

"As okay as eight-plus months pregnant with twins can be," she said with a pained smile. "I'm here for the food, and then I'm going home to work from my couch."

"Where are the husbands?" Joey asked, hoping that the answer would be "on the farm with Jax."

"Oh, they're around here somewhere," Gia said, waving at the crowd around them. "I assume they followed Jax and the kids to some kind of deep-fried lard and sugar-by-the-ton stand."

Great. There was the J word. Well, at least she looked good.

She and Waffles followed the girls inside the school's gym where it looked like the entire town had congregated. The diehards dressed for the occasion in a rainbow of tie-dye, a sea of bellbottoms, and a mountain of fringe. There were retro Lennon sunglasses and faded bandanas everywhere.

Fran's band was playing again, this time without Gia's ex-husband, and Joey recognized nearly every couple on the dance floor. Games were set up carnival-style all over the polished gym floor. A giant inflatable obstacle course took up half the basketball court and looked like it was raking in the bucks.

"Fitz, isn't that just for kids?" Joey called out. Bill Fitzsimmons was finally in style. His strict adherence to sixties fashion worked for him one day of the year. He was wearing patched bellbottom jeans and a yellow, skintight Peace Love Music t-shirt. Both looked like original pieces, as was his scraggly rattail. Fitz was standing in line with a dozen kids under the age of seven. He was counting quarters in his hand.

"Grown-ups can play too," he yelled back. "Besides, I need a rematch with the Delroy boys." Two little blonde boys taunted him by sticking out their tongues.

They continued on, giving wide berth to the Higgenworth Communal Alternative Education Day Care stand that was selling what looked like hand-woven leashes. A script handwritten sign listed the prices for the colorful "child safety tethers."

Joey thought back to the annual daycare field trip to Pierce Acres and shivered. "There's something wrong with those kids," she whispered to Summer.

"Yeah, guess where these two aren't going to daycare," Summer whispered back.

There was no sign of Mrs. Penskee or the Pierce men in the gym, so they followed the long hallway of lockers to the cafeteria.

"There's Phoebe and Franklin with the kids," Summer said, pointing to a fried cauliflower stand. Phoebe and Franklin were both sporting colored sunglasses and matching tie-dye.

Gia grimaced. "Well, at least it's a vegetable. There's the rest of them," she said, pointing to the vegan eggroll stand.

Joey hazarded a guess that they were in line for Carter's lunch, seeing as how no one else in their right mind would willingly put that crap in their mouth.

Except maybe Jax who had just bitten off half of one of said eggrolls. Well, if he was eating garbage, that meant he too was suffering from their latest breakup. That made her feel marginally better.

God, he looked good. And the three of them together made quite the picture. Jax in his fitted long sleeve t-shirt. Carter in his flannel. And Beckett sporting his usual crisp button down.

Joey realized Gia and Summer had stopped next to her to admire the picture the Pierces presented.

"Damn," Summer sighed happily.

"Yeah, we have really excellent taste," Gia agreed.

"I'm gonna go find Mrs. Penskee," Joey said, pulling Waffles with her before she could be drawn in by Jax's sexiness like a tractor beam.

She finally found the woman in front of the stage. Mrs. Penskee was wearing some kind of bell-bottom pantsuit decorated with paisley pineapples and a matching headscarf. She was barking orders into a headset.

"I understand that he crawled under the bleachers himself, but that doesn't mean we can just leave him there... Well, then send a skinny ten-year-old in after him."

Between her tight, graying curls and her wire-rimmed glasses, she was a shoe-in for Mrs. Claus and always rode shotgun to Ernest Washington's Santa in the holiday parade.

"Those Higgenroth kids," Mrs. Penskee sighed. "Little Wahlon crawled under the bleachers and won't come out. There's got to be an easier way to raise money than this."

"Sounds like Wahlon's parents should have invested in one of those handy child safety tethers," Joey said.

"Next year, we should handcuff all the kids together and give their parents two hours of peace and quiet."

Joey was fairly certain Mrs. Penskee was joking, but the woman made a "hmm" noise and pulled out a little notebook from her back pocket. "Handcuff the children," she muttered to herself as she wrote.

"So, where would you like Waffles?" Joey asked, distracting Mrs. Penskee from a potential felony.

"Oh, up on stage, please."

"Now?"

"We can do our little announcement and ceremonial kickoff now and distract everyone's attention while someone fishes Wahlon out from under the bleachers." Mrs. Penskee ushered Joey and Waffles up the stairs onto the raised stage. Joey instantly felt conspicuous, and she could tell the exact second that Jax spotted her by the way her nipples came to attention. She saw him making his way through the crowd toward her, a shark scenting blood in the water.

Her pulse ratcheted up another notch as their eyes met. Waffles's tail thumped happily on the stage. *Traitor*, Joey thought. Jax climbed the stairs, and Joey's heart was thudding out of her chest. Shit. This wasn't just anger. This was deep-in-the-bone 'til-the-day-I-die love. And it hit her like a well-placed hoof to the heart.

She loved Jax. But when in their history had that ever been enough?

"Hey," he said, shoving his hands in the pockets of his jeans.

"Hey yourself," she said, crossing her arms in front of her chest. Waffles did his seated wiggle so he could lean lovingly against Jax's leg.

"Hey, buddy," Jax said, leaning down to ruffle Waffles's fur. The dog dissolved into a puddle of happiness and flopped over onto his back so Jax could rub his belly. "I missed you and your mom."

"He *may* have noticed your absence," Joey said grudgingly.

"What about you?"

Joey shook her head. "No, it's been party, party, party for me. Didn't even realize you weren't around the past few days."

His gray eyes warmed at her sarcasm. "Same with me. Too busy partying to miss you."

"You're missing me right now," she shot back.

"Okay, if the rest of you can just fill in behind them," Mrs. Penskee interrupted with a clipboard and a microphone. She directed Phoebe, Franklin, Carter, Summer, Gia, Beckett, and the kids to line up behind Joey and Waffles.

"Great. That's perfect. Ladies and gentlemen, if I can have your attention?" She tapped the microphone, which let out an ear-splitting shriek. Waffles buried his head in his paws and gave a short, sharp yip.

The crowd quieted.

"Whoops! Sorry about that. Anyway, I'd like to welcome you to the 45th Annual Blue Moon Sit-In and Good Cause Carnival. This year's proceeds are going to a very worthy cause if I do say so myself," she said, pointing at the Furever Home Rescue banner behind them.

Mrs. Penskee chattered on about the work her rescue had done over the years, and Joey tried to stay tuned in, but having Jax next to her, his shoulder resting against hers was too distracting. The back of his hand brushing her arm. Joey stared hard out into the sea of time-forgotten hippies as she tried to hold on to the hurt, the anger. Those feelings would protect her against future pain. Keeping her safe and separate.

But safe and separate left no room for Jax.

"As you all are well aware, thanks to the Pierce family, our little rescue had its most successful day ever with the adoption of six of our pets, one of which is on stage now."

Waffles seemed to understand that they were talking about him. He sat up straight with his ears perked and a happy doggy smile above his bowtie.

"We at the rescue couldn't think of a better way to thank you for your kindness and generosity than this."

Joey didn't even realize Donovan Cardona was on the stage until she felt the cold metal close over her wrist with a snap.

"No!" Joey's arm recoiled, and she stared in horror as Jax's arm went with it. They were cuffed together, and the crowd was cheering.

"Let's give a warm welcome to this year's Cuffed Lovers, Joey Greer and Jackson Pierce."

The applause drowned out Joey's expletive-laden gasp. She stared at Jax who didn't look remotely surprised. "You son of a bitch," she growled.

Jax grinned and raised their cuffed hands to wave to the crowd. Joey tried to yank her arm down to no avail. Anthony Berkowicz pushed through the front row and snapped a picture of them with an oversized digital camera. Between the camera flash and rage, Joey was temporarily blinded. Jax dragged her off stage and handed Waffles over to Mrs. Penskee.

"How about you take the guest of honor around?" he suggested to her.

Mrs. Penskee and Waffles happily trotted off into the crowd.

"I am going to murder you," Joey hissed at him.

"Then you'll be cuffed to my rotting body," Jax said amicably as he weaved a path through the crowd.

Joey accepted the congratulations with less enthusiasm than Jax, who was waving and shaking hands left and right as if he were Beckett.

He dragged her into a relatively quiet corner behind the goat milk soap booth.

"What's the plan here, Jax?" She held up their cuffed hands. "Kinky sex in public to win me back?"

The slow, knowing smile that spread across his face had her mouth going dry and her underwear going damp. She smacked him in the chest with her free hand. "Very funny. Why the hell am I handcuffed to you? There's a town-wide vote that picks the 'lucky' couple. And we're not even a couple."

"Congratulations, you guys," Ellery waved cheerfully from the front of the soap stand.

It hit Joey like a bolt of lightning. "You!" She pointed at Ellery, dragging Jax's hand up with hers. "This was all you!"

Ellery's purple lipstick spread into a wide grin. "I don't know what you're talking about." She skipped away before Joey could find anything to throw at her.

"Oh my God. Moon Beam." Joey paced, bringing Jax with her. "All of this 'you two are a huge mistake' crap was all a set up."

"Diabolical, right?" Jax laughed.

"What about Facebook? No one ever mentioned us in the group."

"Not in the Blue Moon group, but in the secret Jax and Joey Forever group there were a few mentions."

"I hate everything. I hate this town. I hate these cuffs. I hate your face."

"God, I love you, Jojo," Jax swiveled in front of her in mid-stride and brought his mouth to hers.

"I hate kissing," Joey muttered against his lips.

Jax brought his hands up to frame her face and succeeded in slapping her in the face with her own limp hand. "Oops. Sorry."

"You can't kiss me. We're broken up."

"We're fighting. That's different from breaking up," he corrected. "Tell me you read it," he said suddenly serious.

Joey raised her chin. "I read it."

"And?"

"How do you feel?"

"Pissed off and hungry."

"I'll feed you in a minute, but Joey, we have to start talking sooner or later. Our entire relationship can't happen in bed."

"You've been talking to your mother."

Jax grimaced. "I don't want to know what that segue is about. Focus on us right here, right now. Tell me why you're mad, right now."

"Besides the cuffs?" she asked, sarcastically jiggling the metal around her wrist.

"Besides the cuffs."

"I'm furious because you and my father made stupid decisions about my future without bothering to consult me."

"Let's talk about that," Jax said. "Put yourself in my shoes. If I do the only thing that I want to do, which is stay by your side, I'd be opening my family up to a lawsuit and forcing you to kiss your dreams at Centenary good-bye. Imagine how that felt. You'd lose everything you'd been working toward. My family would lose their home and their livelihood. And it was all because of me."

She shook her head, started to deny him.

"Just picture it, Jojo. How long had you spent researching schools, applying for scholarships, plotting out your courses? I knew what that school, that program meant to you. There's no way you could have afforded it on your own if your dad had cut you off."

"He wouldn't have actually done it—"

"And then imagine how scared I was thinking about my parents having to say goodbye to the land they'd worked for years. The house they'd raised their family in. Carter wouldn't have had a home to come back to. Would Beckett have stayed in Blue Moon if it wasn't for the farm? I saw all of that vanishing. Because of me. And I thought it would be selfish if I stayed."

Joey's eye was starting to twitch.

"When the father of the girl you love—a man she loves and respects—tells you that you're not good enough, a truth you're already wrestling with?" Jax shook his head. "It makes you want to be better. To be good enough. I never intended to leave permanently. I knew I would come back when I was good enough to be with you."

"That is the stupidest thing I've ever heard," Joey snapped. "You were always good enough."

"I didn't feel like I was," Jax countered. "And neither did your father. I felt like a teenage screw up compared to my brothers, to my dad. They were out doing things, trying to make the world and Blue Moon a better place. And I was skipping school and fantasizing about a certain brunette knockout who would come over and swim in our pond in a tiny red bikini."

"All teenagers feel that way. It's part of puberty. It could have been different. It should have been different," Joey argued.

"But, Jojo, it wasn't. And we can waste the next eight years of our lives arguing about what could have been done differently, but that still won't change it. I'm sorry. I'm sorry for hurting you. I'm sorry for everything, but I think I've been punished enough. It's time for us to start over."

"I don't know how to do that," Joey admitted. "Do you feel good enough now?"

Jax grinned. "Nope. But my plan is to spend the rest of my life showering you with love and presents so you forget how not good enough I am. What else are you mad about?"

"I'm a steaming hot ball of rage because you still didn't tell me when you came home. You said you came back for me, yet you still had no plans to tell me why you left in the first place."

"That's fair."

"I don't give a crap if it's fair," Joey shot back. "If you came back to rebuild this relationship, you should have started with the truth."

"Hear me out. Please," he added. "When I left, I didn't tell you because I was afraid it would force the choice of me or your father. And I didn't think I'd win. You looked up to him, trusted him, respected him. I worried that he'd pressure you to give me up. I didn't think you'd choose me over him."

"And when you came back?"

"When I came back and things started up again between us, I was so happy. Everything was falling into place, but I realized there was a chance that if I told you why I left you'd face that choice again. Me or your father. And I worried you'd choose me."

Joey shook her head in confusion. "So I should choose neither?"

"Jojo, I know what it's like to live without a dad. I don't want you to ever face that. Especially not while Forrest is alive and well."

"He hurt me just as badly as you did," Joey said stubbornly.

"Baby, I know." Jax brushed the fingers of his uncuffed hand over her cheek. "But now that you know the whole truth, you have to choose both of us or neither of us."

"You screwed up so bad."

"Oh, Joey, don't I know it," he said, wrapping his arm around her in an awkward one-armed hug. "I did it all for you."

"Do you think maybe in the future, you could do less

stupid things for me?" she asked, her voice muffled against his shoulder.

"That depends, are you saying we have a future?"

"Hey guys, how's it going?" Carter asked, leading Summer between the soap booth and the gluten-free funnel cake stand.

"I'm handcuffed. How do you think it's going?" Joey muttered.

"If it makes you feel better, the vote was unanimous for you two to be the Cuffed Lovers," Summer said, undeterred by Joey's general mood. "It was pretty cool. The B.C. posted a live video of their meeting, and everyone got to post their votes online."

"I've been betrayed by everyone," Joey said, bringing her hands—and one of Jax's—to her face. She'd been conspired against by an entire town for months and had neatly fallen into their trap.

The elementary school kazoo band took the stage and began a horrific rendition of "What a Wonderful World."

Beckett and Gia approached, hands over their ears to block out the racket.

"You guys back together yet?" Beckett bellowed over the noise.

"I hate all of you," Joey yelled back.

"I can't hear what they're yelling about," Summer shouted in Carter's ear.

Jax took matters into his own hands and, dragging Joey, led the way down a hallway. The first doorknob he tried turned, and he pulled her inside and flicked the light switch. The others piled in behind them.

"A janitor's closet. Seems appropriate for cleaning up messes," Beckett said shutting the door behind him.

"Sooo, are you getting back together?" Summer asked.

"You mean, are they going to go back to just casually

seeing each other," Gia corrected her with a wink at Joey.

At least she had one friend in the crowd.

"What's that smell?" Carter asked. "It's like old vomit and sawdust."

"Gross!"

"Can you guys just shut the hell up for a minute?" Jax said at a kazoo concert level.

A chorus of "sorries" sounded.

"Look, guys. I'm sorry. I can't just bounce back like the rest of you. I can't be like Carter and tell Summer it's fine that she ran away when it ripped his heart out. I can't be like Gia and just forget that Beckett tried to throw her at her ex-husband. I need time to process stuff like that."

They looked disappointed. "I'm sorry you're disappointed. But I'm just trying to be honest here. A pair of handcuffs and a screenplay isn't going to make me suddenly forgive. Maybe I'm starting to understand now. But it's going to take some time."

"Your honesty is appreciated," Gia said graciously.

"It's this new thing we're trying," Joey said, looking at Jax.

Carter shoved his hands into his pockets. "I'd like to make a motion that from this point on, we all come clean on any past lies or withheld truths, and in the future we don't bullshit each other."

Beckett looked guilty. Joey knew he had only recently revealed how close Phoebe had come to losing the farm after their father's death. It had been a shock to both Jax and Carter, who had been off busy living their lives. If it hadn't been for Blue Moon Bank President Rainbow Berkowicz giving Beckett a personal loan, the Pierces would be spending their family Christmas in Phoebe's cramped townhouse instead of the farmhouse Carter had lovingly renovated.

"I agree," Jax announced. "Just so we're all on the same page, I left town all those years ago because I thought Joey's dad was going to scrap Joey's college plans to keep her away from me and sue our family for the accident. I decided to stay away until I thought I was good enough for her."

"I am scared shitless about having twins," Carter said.

"I know the genders," Summer confessed.

"I freaking knew it!" Joey pointed victoriously at Summer.

"You lied to my face," Carter said.

"I know! I'm so sorry, but I couldn't stand not knowing. It was driving me insane, so I called the doctor and made her tell me. Please don't be mad!"

"Well, then in the bid for honesty, let me correct my statement," Carter said. "I'm scared shitless about having twins, so I thought maybe knowing what to expect would make me feel better, so I called the doctor—"

Summer brought her hands to her mouth. "You didn't! I was supposed to be the one to crack!"

"Sorry, honey. We both cracked under the pressure."

"So you know we're having—"

Carter nodded, a sweet smile spreading across his face. He pulled Summer in for a hug. "I love you."

"I love you too," Summer sighed against him.

"I pay Phoebe under the table to do the books for the studio so Beckett doesn't judge me." Gia continued the truth train with her confession.

Beckett snorted.

All eyes turned to Joey. "I may have trained Clementine to attack Jax."

"Well, that explains a lot," Jax said, baffled. "How in the hell did you do that?"

"Mostly by stuffing your old clothes with cookies. She figured it out pretty fast. That's why she always goes for your pants."

"I made out with Joey once," Beckett said.

Jax was on Beckett in less time than it took for the words to sink in to everyone else.

Joey was dragged right along into the fray. Jax tried to hit with his left hand, but Joey's weight stalled the blow. He fired off a quick jab with his right, catching Beckett in the face. They grappled and went to the floor, sending Gia and Summer jumping for cover.

"You made out with the woman I love?"

Jax slapped at Beckett with his cuffed hand. "Ow! You left. You were broken up. She was sad."

"So you shoved your tongue down her throat?" Two long-handled mops rained down on them, and a jug of organic multi-surface cleaner tumbled from a shelf.

Beckett snuck in a gut shot. "It wasn't like that. Get off of me!" His foot lashed out, denting a plastic bucket.

Jax made a grab for his brother's throat and dragged Joey down on top of them. "If one of you punches me, I am going to knee you both in the balls so hard you'll never have kids," she yelled.

Carter pried them apart with one of the mops. "Stop it. Both of you."

Jax grudgingly accepted Beckett's hand and let his brother pull him to his feet. "Not cool, man."

Beckett looked contrite. "I know. I'm sorry. It was a big mistake, and we both knew it right away."

"Well maybe by the third or fourth kiss," Joey put it. She enjoyed the sparks of rage she saw in Jax's eyes when he turned to look at her.

"Don't think you're not in trouble. We'll talk about this later," Jax decided.

"Does anyone else have anything to confess before we leave this closet of truth?" Carter asked.

Summer raised her hand. "I think I'm in labor."

31

———

 $\mathcal{W}$ hen the hospital staff hauled Summer away in a wheelchair, Carter running behind them clutching their perfectly packed and organized overnight bag, Summer was still shouting instructions to Gia and Joey. "Call Audrey and make sure she still has all the logins for the website. And call my parents! And make sure the posts are all scheduled for the next two days. And—" The automatic doors closed behind them cutting off Summer's to do list.

Gia sagged against Beckett. "You're going to be an uncle." She smiled.

"Aunt Gia," Beckett said, brushing a red curl back from her face. "Our kids are going to have playmates."

"Finally. Then maybe they'll leave us alone," Gia laughed.

Joey looked down at her still-cuffed hand and then at the man she was attached to. He was smiling at the closed doors like it was Christmas morning. "Carter's gonna be a dad," he said, his voice ripe with pride.

"Where's your mom?" Joey asked.

"Right behind you," Phoebe said, half-jogging through the

automatic doors. "The sheriff was kind enough to give me a ride. Franklin took the kids home to let the dogs out."

"You're like the best mother-in-law in the world," Gia said, hugging her. "You ready for two more grandkids?"

"I'm going to wear a hole in the waiting room carpet," Phoebe promised.

"Figured you two would need these," Donovan said, twirling the handcuff keys on his finger.

"Oh, thank God," Joey said, holding up their joined hands. She rubbed her wrist when the cuff slid off. "I'm still mad at you for that," she told Donovan.

"Yeah, well, I'm still not happy about you and Beckett making out," Jax said.

"Really? Exactly when did this make-out session happen?" Donovan asked.

"Oh man, don't start that shit again," Beckett said.

The nurse behind the desk shot Beckett a look.

"Sorry," he said.

"Geez, what happened to your face?" Donovan asked looking at the bruise Beckett was sporting on his cheekbone.

"This ass—guy here goes off on me for a kiss that happened eight years ago."

Gia bit her lip and tried not to laugh.

"It doesn't matter if it was eighteen years ago," Jax snapped.

Joey stepped in front of him and put her newly freed hand on his chest. "Not that I owe you an explanation since you'd left and we weren't together anymore, but it happened one night when Beckett drove me home from dinner. We knew it was a mistake immediately."

"And why was it a mistake?" Donovan wondered.

"Because Beckett wasn't Jax."

Beckett looked down at his wife. "And Joey wasn't you," he told her.

"You didn't even know me then."

"That doesn't mean I wasn't waiting for you."

"Oh, for Christ's sake, get a room," Joey muttered.

FOUR HOURS LATER, Jonathan and Meadow Pierce arrived within two minutes of each other. They were tiny pink bundles of health and dubbed the most perfect set of twins in the world by their parents. Joey thought they were pretty okay. Meadow looked at her with indigo eyes and the slightest frown as if she were trying to figure everything out. "You've got time, kid. Don't try to figure it all out at once," Joey whispered.

She glanced over at Jax who was holding Jonathan with Carter leaning over his shoulder. The looks of absolute adoration on their faces as they looked at the newborn did something funny to Joey's gut. She caught Summer's soft smile and wandered over to her bed to hand over her daughter.

"How do you feel?" Summer asked her.

"Shouldn't I be the one asking you?" Joey asked, depositing Meadow carefully in Summer's arms.

"I feel tired and pained and exhausted and completely in love right now. Now your turn."

"I feel most of those things too."

"It's going to be fine, Joey. You'll find your way through. You'll be able to forgive. And you'll be as nauseatingly happy as I am right now."

Joey shot another glance in Jax's direction. He was promising Jonathan that he'd teach him and his sister to ride their bikes off the dock into the pond. Summer rolled her eyes.

"Can you wait until they're at least a day or two old before you start teaching them to drive me insane?"

"Sorry, sis." Jax handed Jonathan over and kissed Summer on the forehead.

Phoebe snapped yet another picture on her phone. "Mom, enough already," Carter sighed sliding onto the bed next to Summer. "They're too young for paparazzi."

"I can't help it." Phoebe sighed. "They're just so perfect! And I need just the right picture for Facebook, and we promised Evan and Aurora we'd bring them pictures of their cousins."

"When will your parents be here?" Joey asked Summer.

"Dad said they'll be here before eight tonight. He has the pedal to the metal in the RV."

Jax glanced at his watch. "We should probably get going. The dogs are going to need let out soon."

"Yeah, Waffles is probably ready for his dinner soon."

"How about you? Hungry?" Jax asked.

Joey raised an eyebrow. "Is that really a question you ever have to ask?"

"I'm thinking steaks and baked potatoes."

Joey's mouth watered at the thought. "Where is this magical dinner you speak of?"

"Your house. We'll hit the grocery store on the way."

"Inviting yourself over?"

"The way to a Joey's heart is through her stomach."

They said their goodbyes to the exhausted new parents and enthusiastic grandparents. Joey led the way to her truck in the dusk. The visitors lot had cleared out considerably since they arrived, and her cherry red pickup sat by itself against a fence. Driving home would be easier without the handcuffs, she mused.

"I'm still mad at you, by the way," she said, shutting her door.

"I appreciate your honesty. I'm still not thrilled about you making out with my brother and not telling me about it."

"Well, it never came up in the eight years that you were living on the other side of the country."

"Touché," Jax sighed. "I'm better though, right?"

"Better?"

"You like making out with me better than Beckett."

"Beckett is like a big brother to me. He could be very good at making out, and I wouldn't know it because I couldn't get past the brother thing."

"You've never thought of me as a brother, have you?" Jax asked grabbing her hand.

Joey thought about lying but figured they'd both had enough of that. "No," she sighed. "I never thought of you like a brother."

"Good, because if you did, that would make what I'm about to do very wrong."

Before she could ask what it was that he was about to do, Jax grabbed her by the sweater and yanked her to him. The kiss was frantic, unforgiving. Joey forgot about the division between them, and together they scaled the slick cliffside of need.

His hands were under her sweater, skimming over her stomach. "I thought about doing this all day," he murmured against her. "You are never out of my mind."

Joey kissed him just to shut him up and only stopped when he yanked her sweater over her head.

"Here?" she whispered. A parking lot seemed reminiscent of their teenage trysts.

"Here." His fingers shoved her bra straps off her shoulders, and her bared nipples tightened at the cold. Any argument she'd planned disappeared the moment his mouth brushed the first aching bud. He pressed her down on the seat, his lips and tongue busy teasing her while his palm stroked her other breast.

"God I love bench seats," he groaned.

Joey levered her hips against him, and Jax shifted so he could press his erection against her.

"Too many layers," Joey muttered. While he sampled her other nipple, sucking it into the heat of his mouth, her fingers worked her jeans open before moving to his. With the zipper under the pressure of his erection, Joey cautioned herself to go slowly. But the second he sprang free, she gripped his shaft in her fist.

"Fuck," he moaned, releasing her nipple and dropping his head to her shoulder. He let her stroke him, let her grip him like a vice, and she felt the first bead of moisture when she dragged her fingers over his crown.

"Baby, this isn't going to be slow and sweet," he said, dragging her jeans down until he could free one of her legs.

"Good." She ground the word out.

When he saw the sheer lace of the red thong she wore, his eyes went glassy and then curious.

"Jesus, Jojo. What the hell is that?"

Joey, expecting a tarantula or something even worse, tried to sit up. Jax was staring at the hoof print bruise on her thigh.

"Oh, that. That's Calypso being a shithead."

Jax forced her non-imprinted leg up against the back of the seat and yanked her underwear to the side. He inserted two fingers in his mouth, and Joey stopped breathing when she watched him pull them out between his lips and bring them down to her exposed flesh.

"Everything about you gets me," he said, sliding his wet

fingers inside her. "I just look at you and need to be inside you."

Joey cried out as he brushed his thumb over that tiny bundle of nerves that demanded his attention. She braced her free leg against the dashboard, her foot touching the window.

"Every time. You get so wet for me, Joey," he murmured, leaning down to bite at her neck.

"Now, Jax. Now. I need you." She begged him for it and thanked God he didn't make her beg long. The second his fingers withdrew, Jax lined up his cock with her opening and surged into her. Joey groaned as she stretched to accommodate his girth. This felt good. This felt right. No matter what else was going on between them, she could always be sure that this was right. It was where they both belonged.

There was no time to get used to it. He was already moving in her. She wrapped her free leg around him, urging him deeper, and when he accommodated her, she bit into his shoulder.

Her breasts crushed against his chest as he thrust into her with a demand that bordered on violence. Jax buried his face in her neck, and Joey let him take her as he wanted. Fast, fierce, aggressive. The separation had made them both jagged and shaky with need.

He slammed into her again, and Joey was dimly aware that the truck was probably rocking on its tires, but she didn't care. Her entire world had shrunk to the cab of her pickup. There was nowhere else she wanted to be.

"Fuck. Baby, I can't hold on much longer." It was the rawness in his voice that set her off. Joey reared up to capture his mouth just as he drove inside her again and she felt that delicious tightening of release. It hit her like an explosion.

"Come, Jax." She gritted the words out. And on his next thrust, she felt him lose himself in her. She felt him come buried inside her to the hilt. His shout—her name—rang in her ears as she came around him in fitful waves of dark pleasure.

They owned each other in the moment, in the night.

~

BY THE TIME Joey found her sweater in the dark and they defrosted the windows, the promise of steak had lost out to more immediate need. They settled on drive-thru tacos, and Joey ate two of them while Jax drove home.

Exhaustion settled over her like a cloud, and she fell asleep with a bag of nachos on her lap. She didn't wake until Jax pulled up in front of her house. She could see Waffles's silhouette frantically pawing at the glass of the sidelight next to the door.

"I should get in there," she yawned.

"Yeah, I need to go let Valentina and Meatball out," Jax said, scrubbing his hands over his face.

She could have asked him to come back, was going to, but something stopped her. Things still felt unsettled between them, and spending the night together probably wasn't a good idea.

"Bring the truck back tomorrow, and I can run into town with you to pick up your car," Joey decided.

She felt his gaze on her and didn't turn to meet it. After a few seconds of silence, he sighed.

"If that works for you."

"Yeah, after feeding." Joey nodded. She waited another beat, but still the invitation to spend the night wouldn't come.

So she grabbed her nachos and opened the passenger door. "Congratulations on the whole uncle thing," she said sliding out of the truck.

"Thanks, Joey."

"There's another taco in the bag for you," she told him before shutting the door.

He waited until she walked into the house and shut the front door before driving away.

THE NEXT AFTERNOON, Jax pulled his Nova up to the painted brick ranch on the corner. It had navy trim and bright green ferns hanging from the rafters of the front porch. The postage stamp yard was neatly trimmed. He followed the concrete walkway up to the porch, planted his feet on the welcome mat, and stabbed his finger in the bell.

If last night in his lonely bed with his sad taco had told him anything, it was that as much as he and Joey wanted each other, there needed to be some kind of closure for her before they could move forward. And dammit, he was going to get it for her.

Forrest Greer answered the cheery yellow door wearing a New York Giants sweatshirt and a fierce frown. When he opened his mouth, Jax pushed the six-pack of beer he held into the man's hands.

"You've had more than your say. It's my turn. I'm going to marry your daughter, and you need to fix things with her."

Forrest turned a shade of fuchsia not often seen in nature.

"Before you say it, no. I'm not good enough for her. But no one is. I know that, and you know that. I'd hate for her to end up with someone who thinks he is good enough for her. You and I have had a shitty ass relationship before now, but I love your daughter more than anything on this planet, and I plan to spend the rest of my life earning my place next to her. That should count for something. You love her too. Otherwise, you wouldn't act like such an overprotective ass all the time."

The vein in Forrest's forehead was throbbing, but Jax pressed on.

"Now, I haven't asked her to marry me yet. I wanted to come to you first." He saw the triumphant gleam in Forrest's eyes and laughed. "No. I'm not asking you for your permission. It's not my style, and right now Joey is more inclined to marry me just to piss you off more."

"So why the hell are you here then?" Forrest grumbled, shifting the six-pack into one hand.

"You need to make things right with Joey. She needs you. She wants you to be proud of her, to treat her like an adult."

"Well, then she should act like an adult instead of running off pouting about things."

"The only two people who aren't acting like adults are you and me. I've apologized to Joey, and she seems to have reluctantly accepted it. I shouldn't have tried to make life-altering decisions for her without consulting her, and I know that now. I think you know that now too. I don't think either of us will make that mistake again."

Forrest grunted with what sounded like assent.

"I live without a father. I don't want her to do the same. Not when you're alive and well. You'd be an idiot to let things go on this way."

"An idiot, am I?"

"Yeah. And so am I, but she still loves us anyway. She wants to forgive you, but you've got to give her a reason to."

Forrest grunted again as he looked down at the beer. "Are you trying to bribe me with alcohol?"

"That is the first six pack of Joey's IPA. It's a new tradition of Pierce men to brew a beer for their bride. I figured since she was your girl first, you should have the first six."

Forrest pulled out a bottle to examine the label. "If you hurt my girl ever, in any way, I'm going to hunt you down," he said quietly as if talking to the bottle.

"Understood." Jax nodded. "And if you continue to hurt my girl, I'm going to drive here on the wedding day and tie you up and make you walk her down the aisle with a shotgun pointed between your shoulder blades."

Forrest harrumphed. "We'll see if it comes to that. She may say no to you."

Jax grinned. "She probably will. At first. But I've got nothing but time to wear her down."

"I suppose a man shouldn't drink an entire six-pack by himself," Forrest said. He turned around and walked back into the house, leaving the front door open.

JOEY WAS FROWNING FIERCELY at her monthly numbers on the computer screen. Adding two god-like horses to their stable had hiked her operating costs, and she knew it was just the beginning. Of course, once she had the breeding program up and running, the operational costs would be a drop in the bucket compared to what they'd be bringing in. But for now, she'd keep a close eye and tighten the belts where they could be tightened.

When the phone on her desk rang, she gladly abandoned her bookkeeping.

"Hey, Joey. It's Ellery."

"Oh, you mean old Two-Face Magee?"

"You can't be mad at me. You're the stubborn one who warranted pulling out the big guns. If we'd gone with our usual matchmaking approach, you probably would have left town."

"Or gone lesbian."

Ellery snorted. "Please, we're four for four on our gay matches. One way or another, the Beautification Committee will prevail in your love life."

"It's more like a tentative like life these days," Joey corrected.

"Give it time. Pierce men are awfully hard to ignore in the long-term."

"Is there a reason you called, or did you just want to rub salt in wounds?"

"Oh, right! I was wondering if you do private riding lessons?"

"Maybe," Joey said, wary of any request from a member of the Beautification Committee.

"Well my cousin's coming into town this week, and it's his birthday, and I thought a riding lesson would make up for last year's hand-dipped lilac candles that he was allergic to."

"Uh, sure. Why not?" Joey said. Taking on a few paying extras would help balance the books until Apollo and Calypso started doing the deed.

"Great! How about Wednesday at four?"

Joey flipped through her calendar. "That's fine. Does your cousin have any riding experience?"

Ellery's end was silent for a second. "Uh, can you hang on a second? Beckett needs something. I'm just going to put you on hold real quick."

"Okay." Joey drummed a rhythm on the desk with her pencil until Ellery came back on the line a minute later.

"He has some beginner riding experience, but he's been around horses a lot."

"Okay. And what size is he?"

"Size?"

"You know like height and weight."

"He's, you know, normal-sized?" Ellery's voice trailed up, reminding Joey of the L.A. question-askers.

"Good for him. What exactly does normal-sized mean?"

"Why do you need to know?"

"I don't want to put a three-hundred-pound man on a thirteen-hand pony."

"Can you hang on again?" Ellery asked. "Sorry, Beckett's really needy today."

"Sure. It's not like I have things to do or anything," Joey muttered.

"Thanks!" And then Ellery was gone. Joey jotted down a note to tell Beckett to get some kind of on-hold music.

Ellery came back on the line. "Sorry about that. Beckett needed stuff for some things. Anyway, my cousin is about two hundred and fifty pounds and six feet tall."

"Okay, no ponies. Got it."

"Thanks for doing this, Joey. He's really going to appreciate it."

"Wait until after the lesson. He may hate it," Joey told her. "What's your cousin's name?"

"It's, uh—"

"If you put me on hold again, I'm hanging up."

"Woods. His name is Woods."

32

_____

Wednesday afternoon Joey was in Carter's kitchen walking him through her predicted timeline of Calypso's heat cycles and swaying with one of the twins—she wasn't sure which one—in her arms when the alarm on her phone went off.

"Crap. I forgot I have a private lesson today."

Carter, who was holding the other baby, gestured at the infant seat on the island. "Just put him in there. If I can keep them quiet for another ten minutes, Summer should be awake and showered, or her parents will be back from the grocery store."

Joey put Jonathan down into the seat and watched as his little face scrunched up. "Well, good luck with that," she smirked as she headed toward the door.

"Who's your lesson with?" Carter called after her.

"Ellery's cousin Woods something. It's for his birthday. Guess the guy likes horses."

She caught Carter's weird look but didn't give it a second thought. Between twin babies and Meatball sleeping under the barstools he probably just smelled something ripe.

"I'm free after the lesson if you need any extra hands around the farm," she called over her shoulder as she headed out the side door.

The March air was still brisk, but it lacked the Arctic needles that stung the face in February. She tucked her hands into the pockets of her fitted down jacket and hunkered down into the wind. She probably should have driven over to the farm, but she was good and sick of winter. She wanted to force spring along. Spring would bring with it not just warmth but new beginnings. The first season of her breeding program for one. It was time to see if her gamble, the Pierce's gamble, would pay off. And warmer weather probably couldn't help but thaw some of the awkwardness that still surrounded her when it came to Jax.

She was still pondering that when she strode into the stable through the side door. It wasn't Ellery's cousin standing outside her office with his hands stuffed in his pockets. It was her father.

She'd been had yet again by the B.C., and this meant war.

"I didn't know you and Ellery were cousins," she said evenly.

"More like old friends," Forrest fibbed.

"Uh-huh. How old?"

"Oh, we go way back."

Joey crossed her arms. "She tracked you down didn't she? Diabolical B.C.," she muttered.

"She didn't come to me. Her services were recommended by... an acquaintance."

"What acquaintance?"

"I'd rather not say."

"I guess we're not past the whole lying to each other thing, huh?"

"Oh, for God's sake. Jax gave me her business card if I

needed help getting in touch with you. You haven't been taking my calls."

Joey added Jax back on to the shit list. "I haven't wanted to take your calls. And since when did you and Jax get so buddy-buddy that you're trading Ellery's business card?"

"We're not buddy-buddy." Her father seemed to take great offense to that.

"What are you doing here?"

"That's a fine greeting for your father. I thought I'd come by and maybe we could go for a ride," Forrest said, scuffing his boot in the dirt. "Never did get to see the new horses last time I was here."

"You mean when I found out that you'd betrayed me and our family friends by shipping off my high school boyfriend?"

Her father sighed heavily. "I'm no good at apologies. Ask your mother. Can't we just go back to the way things were?"

Joey's eye began to twitch wickedly. "The way things were, Dad? With you and Mom breathing down my neck over every life decision I've made since high school? Trying to keep me in some bubble of control—"

"If anything, it was a bubble of safety," Forrest interjected. "You'll understand when you have kids of your own. We could have lost you that night."

"But you didn't because Jax paid attention in health class and knew how to tie a damn tourniquet. And instead of thanking him for saving my life, you blamed him for almost losing it."

Forrest was shaking his head. "Maybe it wasn't one of my finest moments. But I thought I was doing the right thing. You never let on that you wished things had been different. You're happy now, aren't you?"

Was she? Was she really happy with her life, or was she

just sitting behind the safety of her walls waiting for the next shoe to drop? Just like her father.

Joey didn't have an answer for him, so she changed the subject. "So you want to go for a ride?"

Forrest was one who generally appreciated horses from a distance, usually on the racetrack, but he'd always given in to Joey when she'd offered to go riding with him. Her love of horses had always baffled him, but the talent she'd displayed even as a kid had persuaded him to support her hobby.

He nodded briskly. "If you're okay with it."

Joey stared at him a beat, debating whether she should just throw him out. But that would probably make Thanksgiving awkward, she decided.

"Ellery's paying me for it so I might as well deliver," Joey said. Ellery would indeed be paying a steep price for her scheming.

"Who do you want me on?"

"You can have Tucker," she said, nodding at the bay two stalls down. "He's a lesson horse and probably won't throw you."

"That's comforting," her father said with sarcasm.

"You remember how to tack up?" Joey asked, bringing Tucker out of his stall and hooking him in the crossties in the aisle.

"I can manage."

"Good. Try not to get kicked," Joey told him before heading down to the end to bring Apollo out. He'd keep her occupied with his need for constant supervision. Plus, she could let him run a bit after she sent her father back.

Her father gave Apollo an appreciative once over. "That your new stud?"

"Yep." Joey said hoping to quell any conversation.

Her father got the hint, and they groomed their mounts and tacked up in silence. Waffles came scurrying in and planted himself at Joey's feet. Apollo tossed his black head in greeting.

"There you are," Joey said, running her hands through Waffles's wiry fur. "You want to come along?"

Waffles spun in a happy circle before running over to sniff Forrest's boots.

"Who's this?" Forrest asked.

"That's Waffles."

"He yours?"

Joey gave a noncommittal "uh-huh" as she hefted the saddle onto Apollo's back.

"You always wanted a dog," her father ventured again.

"Yep. Jax got him for me from the rescue in town." She'd deliberately dropped Jax's name again, curious to see what her father's reaction was. It wasn't so long ago that the mere mention of the man's name had veins throbbing. She wondered if her twitchy eye was a genetic trait that she shared with her father.

Her father harrumphed a response but bent to let Waffles sniff his hand. Waffles gave his knuckles a tentative lick before scampering back to Joey.

"Lead out, and then we'll tighten the saddles in the yard," Joey instructed her father.

Apollo nipped at Joey's hand when she looped the reins over his head to lead him out. "Don't be a dick," she told the horse.

"What's that now?" Forrest asked over his shoulder.

"I was talking to my horse, but same goes," she warned.

Outside, the sun was slowly starting its late afternoon descent and taking with it its modest heat. Joey tightened the girth on the saddle and did the same for her father. No use having him slide off his mount and start bitching about a lawsuit, she decided.

She led them over to the mounting block next to the outdoor paddock and watched as Forrest swung into the saddle. Satisfied that his seat was steady, Joey swung up onto Apollo's back and pulled on her riding gloves. She nodded north. "We'll take a lap around the brewery and loop around the upper pasture," she told him, before kicking Apollo into motion. "Don't let Tucker get too close. Apollo's a kicker. And a biter," she instructed her father, smugly pleased that the distance would prevent most of the conversation she didn't want to be a part of.

They walked up the grassy slope dappled with small mounds of snow that had stubbornly refused to melt with the rest. Apollo's tail swished restlessly with the desire to run, but Joey kept his impulses in check. Waffles scampered out in front of them pausing to sniff whatever caught his attention.

"That's a fine-looking animal," her father said, breaking what Joey considered to be a comfortable silence.

"The dog or the horse?"

"Horse. But I guess the dog kind of grows on you too."

"You been to the brewery yet?" Joey asked when the building came into sight, knowing full well the answer was no.

"No. Not yet. Heard it's doing well. Maybe I'll have to bring your mother sometime for dinner."

Joey wheeled Apollo around. "All right. Just what exactly is going on? All of a sudden, you're the Pierces' number one fan?"

Forrest steered his mount to the left giving Apollo wide berth.

"Every once in a great while people can be not exactly right about something," he said grudgingly.

"Oh, for Pete's sake. Are you saying you were wrong?"

"I'm not saying that. And I'm not saying I'm sorry either."

Apologies and her father did not go hand-in-hand. They weren't even on a first name basis.

"Exactly what is it that you are trying to say?"

"It wasn't my intention to hurt you. I was trying to protect you," Forrest said. "That's what fathers do."

"Yeah, well, eventually you have to stop protecting, don't you?"

"Maybe when you're fifty. You should have it all figured out by then," Forrest predicted. Joey didn't think he was joking.

"You've hated Jax since we started dating a hundred years ago," she reminded him.

"I probably wouldn't have liked anyone you were dating them. Except maybe Beckett. He's a hard one not to like. He's a good man, good leader like his dad. Too bad he's married now."

Joey felt a blush creep up her cheeks. She was hoping Donovan Cardona hadn't broadcast that little tidbit about her ill-advised make-out session with the middle Pierce to the world.

"Anyway, Jax has grown up a lot since you were both eighteen. He sure loves you."

"Yeah, well, sometimes love isn't even close to enough," Joey said, her breath appearing before her in an angry cloud.

"I'd hate to think that you'd miss out on your chance at happiness with a guy who isn't so bad just because of me," Forrest said, keeping his eyes between Tucker's ears.

Joey sighed as they crested another hill. From here, it looked like they were miles away from civilization. "It's not just you. It's him too. You guys don't make it easy to trust you."

"I can't say a lot about that boy, but all either one of us have ever done is what we thought was best for you. Maybe you could help us all out and do what's best for you, and we can just follow your lead?"

Joey cast her eyes heavenward at her father's suggestion. He was trying, in his own special snowflake Forrest way. How her mother had not murdered him decades ago she'd never know.

They continued on in silence, the creaking of the saddles the only noise in the late afternoon silence.

"Shit." Joey said, bringing Apollo to a stop.

"What's wrong?" Forrest asked.

"Someone ripped up the chicken wire," she said, nodding at the pasture gate. "It keeps the horses from chewing up the wood. I need to fix that before one of them steps on it and gets hurt." She looked up at the sky and judged that she had enough daylight to get it done now. "Can you take Tucker back to the stables and get a hammer for me?"

"Sure, where do you keep 'em?"

Joey told him where to find her tools. "Just tie Tucker to the hitch outside. If you take him back in with you, he'll think it's dinnertime."

"Got it. Anything else?"

"The staple gun if you can find it."

She watched as he rode off at a peppier walk than what they started out on. He'd always had a decent seat. He wasn't a natural like Evan was, but he had an aptitude and usually ended up enjoying their rides when Joey had been able to talk him into going out. Her mother, on the other hand, was convinced that horses were domesticated monsters and didn't like getting any closer than a Facebook picture to one.

Waffles yipped happily at something halfway down the hill and chased after it.

Joey leaned over Apollo's neck to get a better look at the wire mess. She was already off balance when she spotted the groundhog waddle out of a hole at the tree line just a few feet away. It hissed.

Apollo reared, and without being steady in her seat, she felt herself slip.

"Fuc—"

She didn't even get the full word out. Her head struck something hard, and the world went bright white and then disappeared.

～

"SON OF A BITCH," Joey mumbled. She didn't know how long she'd been out, but judging by the sun in the sky, it hadn't been more than a few minutes. Her head was pounding, her arm felt like it was being yanked off her body, and there was an uncomfortable pressure in her ankle. She did not want to open her eyes and find herself skewered on a fence post or something gruesome like that. But she needed to grow a pair and look around. If there was a million-dollar horse running around free, she was going to be pissed.

Something licked her face, and she cranked open an eyelid. It was harder to do than she thought. Everything looked funny, including Waffles's face. The fur around his nose was matted and red. "Crap! Are you hurt, buddy?" Joey said, the words slurring together in an incoherent string. Had she landed on the poor dog?

She moved her hand toward him and saw the red on her glove. Confused, she brought her hand to her head. Even through the glove, she could feel the sticky wetness of blood. "Oh, man. That's not good."

Waffles whimpered and pawed her shoulder. Joey pried her other eye open and took a good look around. She was screwed. Apollo was not off gallivanting the countryside. He was standing stock still above her, his sides heaving nervously. Her foot was twisted in the stirrup, and the rest of her was crumpled on the ground half under the stallion.

"Not good. Really not good." If Apollo moved an inch, he'd trample her, and it wouldn't be pretty. "I hope that fucking groundhog left town," she said to herself.

What the hell was she going to do? Her dad would be at least another twenty minutes, especially if the hammer wasn't in the specially designated hammer spot. It could be a half an hour before he came back. She was out of sight of the brewery and the farm, and she was stuck under a nervous horse that, if he didn't trample her, would probably bite her out of spite.

She looked up.

"Oh my God, Apollo. Do not shit on me."

She tried to tug on her foot, but it was good and wedged in the stirrup. And the movement only caused Apollo to shift his weight, effectively scaring her into a motionless heap.

"Fuck. Fuck. Fuck."

She put her hand to her head again and looked at the fresh blood on the glove. "Why do head wounds have to bleed so much? It's like a freaking sieve."

Joey dropped her head back to the cold, hard ground and tried to brainstorm. It was like trying to solve world hunger while drunk on a merry-go-round. "Just whoa, okay, Apollo. Whatever you do, whoa."

Her head was pounding so loud it sounded like hoof beats in her skull.

She was so sleepy. That probably wasn't good. She was pretty sure sleepiness and head wounds were a bad combination, but she wasn't sure why.

She felt Waffles tugging on her glove. She wasn't in the mood to play though. "Not now, Waffles. Mommy's tired."

But Waffles wasn't there anymore, and neither was her

glove. It was just her and the twelve hundred pounds of anxiety-ridden stallion. It was as good a place as any to take a little nap.

~

JAX SPOTTED Forrest when the man rode up to the barn on Tucker.

Forrest gave him a curt nod. It was the friendliest greeting Jax had gotten out of him in the history of their relationship. "Joey sent me back for a hammer and staple gun. One of the horses pulled the wire off a gate in the back pasture."

"Probably Romeo," Jax said, holding Tucker's reins while Forrest dismounted. "He loves to chew on fence posts. I'll show you where the tools are."

Jax tied Tucker to a hitch, and they started toward the door. "How's it going?"

"Well, she hasn't thrown me off the property yet," Forrest answered. "But you might want to warn Ellery that Joey's none too pleased with her."

"I'll let her know to lay low for a few days."

Jax pushed the door open just as a gray and white blur of fur hurtled around the corner.

"Geez, Waffles," Jax said, as the dog ran a figure eight through his legs yipping.

"Waffles was with us on the ride. He must have followed me back," Forrest said. "What's that he's got in his mouth?"

Jax gave Waffles the "sit" signal and held out his hand. The dog dropped the item neatly into Jax's palm.

"It's a riding glove."

"Must be Joey's," Forrest said. "I think she was wearing a pair like that."

Jax examined the glove closer and stooped down to look at

Waffles who was yipping again. "Forrest, there's blood on the glove and on the dog."

Their eyes met, and understanding and fear bloomed sharp and bright between them. Jax was running for Tucker and shouting instructions over his shoulder. "Go to the brewery and get Carter's Jeep. Meet me where you left Joey and bring a cell phone."

He swung up onto the bay's back and kicked him into gear. Tucker, sensing the excitement, launched into a canter.

"Fuck. Fuck. Fuck," Jax chanted to himself. It was probably just a scrape. She was messing with the wire and cut herself.

Waffles was racing alongside him, and Jax knew that a cut on the hand was not what he'd find. He felt the cold fist of fear clutch at his gut and urged Tucker on. The big bay wasn't usually a sprinter, but he mustered everything he had for this uphill haul.

When Jax crested the hill, his heart stopped. He immediately reined Tucker in to a careful walk. He got as close as he dared with Tucker before pulling him to a stop.

"Joey?" Jax called out not loud enough to spook Apollo who looked like he was just looking for a reason to run.

He slid off Tucker's back and tied him to the post and walked as quickly as he could without freaking out the stallion.

"Joey," he said again, leaning over her. There was blood in her hair, over her forehead, drying in her eye. Her beautiful, pale face looked like a crime scene.

"What?" she grumbled. Waffles scooted over and curled up next to her, resting his head on her shoulder.

"Joey, open your eyes and look at me."

"I fell off my horse," she said on a sing-songy sigh. Some of the fear that had iced in his gut started to thaw.

"I can see that, Jojo. You're laying on the ground under Apollo."

"I told him not to crap on me. I think I have a concussion."

Jax shook his head. Joey never lost her cool in any situation, including this one.

"I think that's a pretty good bet. Good thing you hit your head and not something else."

"You're trying to make a hard-head joke, and I think that's highly inappropriate."

"You're right. I'm sorry. Listen, baby. I need to get your foot out of the stirrup, but first I have to make sure Apollo doesn't move, okay?"

"He bites."

Jax stood up and approached the stallion's head. The horse's brown eyes were wide with nervous energy. "It's okay, bud. You did good. Way to not trample the woman I love," Jax said, taking the horses reins and securing them to the gate. "Just let me get her out from under you, and you can go back to your nice, warm stall."

He traced a hand down Apollo's neck over the horse's shoulder so the mount knew where he was. "Joey?"

She didn't answer him.

"Joey," he said a little sharper and felt Apollo start to shift against him. "Sorry, boy. Didn't mean to yell."

Jax nudged Joey's free leg with his boot. "Joey, wake the fuck up."

"Jesus, I am awake," she said with a bad-tempered pout.

"Good. Listen to me. I'm going to pull your foot out of your boot, okay?"

"It's cold."

"I know it is. But I have to get your foot out of the stirrup."

"Gynecologists have stirrups too, you know."

"I was not aware of that," Jax said, gripping the heel of her boot in one hand while the other worked her foot free. He could have sworn that Apollo sighed with relief when her foot slid out.

He could feel some swelling in her ankle through the sock, probably a sprain, and was careful to place it gently on the ground.

"Okay, now I'm going to slide you out from under the crap and trample zone." It wasn't smart to move head wound victims, but it was even dumber to leave them under a horse that could crush them with one stomp of their bad-tempered hoof.

"I want a blanket," Joey muttered.

"I'll get you a blanket. Just let me move you a little this way." He gritted his teeth and slid one hand under her shoulders and one under her knees. "I'm going to pick you up, okay?"

Waffles sat up and wriggled out from under the horse.

"One, two, three." Jax picked her up as carefully as he could and carried her a few feet away. He tried to set her down against a fence post but found his arms just wouldn't let her go. He was shaking so bad his muscles had locked in place. He tried a second time, and she whimpered.

"Tell me what hurts, Jojo."

"Head. Foot. Arm. Hungry."

"My poor girl." Jax gave up trying to put her down when he spotted Carter's Jeep flying toward them through the adjoining pasture. "Here comes our ride."

"No!" She grumbled against his shoulder. "You need to put Apollo back. Can't have seven figures of horse running away."

"We'll have Carter put him back," Jax promised as Carter and Forrest jumped out of the Jeep and came running.

"No. You. Make sure he's safe."

"Fuck, Joey, come on."

"Do I have to go to the hospital?"

"Yes."

"Then you have to put Apollo back in his stall." There was no arguing with a non-head wound Joey so he deemed it completely useless to argue with her in this state. So they compromised. Jax rode Apollo back to the stables with Carter and Tucker on his heels while Forrest drove Joey and Waffles down in the Jeep.

The second they hit the yard, Jax slid off Apollo's back and handed the reins over to Carter. "If Joey asks, I put him away."

"You got it. Go take care of our girl," Carter said, his face carved with lines of worry.

Jax opened the passenger door of the Jeep. "I'm coming with you."

"I figured," Forrest said.

Waffles thumped his tail. "Sorry, Waffles. You can't go with us. You hold down the fort with Carter, okay?"

Jax thought it looked like Waffles's lower lip was trembling, but the dog hopped out of the Jeep and wandered into the stable after Carter.

Jax climbed in and shut the door. Forrest put the Jeep in gear, and they started down the slope toward the main road. "I promised her no ambulance," he said to Jax. His voice sounded calm, but his knuckles were white on the wheel. "Carter's calling the emergency department to let them know to expect us."

Jax leaned back between the seats and pressed a hand to Joey's forehead. "The bleeding looks like it's slowed down a lot. I think she hurt her arm or her shoulder, though."

"I didn't hurt it. The groundhog did," Joey muttered from the back.

"Groundhogs are jerks," Forrest said.

"Yeah," Joey agreed with a frown. "Jerks."

Forrest drove like a Frenchman at Le Mans and had them pulling up to the emergency department's doors in record time. There were two orderlies ready and waiting with a gurney. "Oh, she's going to hate that," Forrest predicted, worry still heavy in his eyes.

Jax had to tell Joey it was just a bed for her to agree to get out of the Jeep and onto the sterile sheets. He weighed his options as the orderlies got her strapped down to keep her steady.

"Listen, give me the keys. I'll go park the Jeep, and you go in with her," he offered.

Forrest looked relieved. "Okay, you should be able to find us inside. Just follow the cursing."

Jax thumped the man on the shoulder. "She's going to be okay. Just keep her sort of calm if you can."

Jax kept it together until he pulled the parking brake on the Jeep. He put his head on the steering wheel. He must have lost ten years off his life when he saw her lying there, crumpled on the ground like a forgotten flower. And the blood. The memories came back at him fast and sharp. Once again, he was walking into a hospital covered in a good deal of Joey Greer's blood.

She was going to be okay, he told himself. She was going to be just fine, and she'd be pissed off about all the worrying and the fussing. But she'd looked so helpless, so fragile just lying there.

He owed Apollo an unrepayable debt. Never in this century would he have thought that horse would have kept his head about him and not freaked the fuck out. But he hadn't. He'd stayed statue still, and Waffles, the little furry genius, had found the fastest way to bring help.

She was going to be fine. And damn it, she was going to love him again. And they were going to get married and have a family and breed horses and brew beer. No matter what anyone said. Even her.

He got out of the Jeep and stormed toward the doors.

He followed Forrest's advice and followed the sound of the f-bomb being dropped like confetti. He pulled back the curtain and saw Forrest standing near Joey's head while a doctor tried to explain to her that her shoulder was dislocated and they needed to put it back in its rightful place.

A nurse was cleaning up the gash on her hairline and another one was stripping off her sock so they could get a good look at her ankle.

"I'm sorry, sir. Are you family?" The nurse with the sock in her gloved hand was staring at him and probably the better portion of Joey's drying blood on his jacket and shirt.

Joey's eyes were closed. Frozen with old memories, Jax didn't respond.

"Sir?"

"Of course he's family," Forrest blustered. "He's my daughter's fiancé."

"This is your fiancé?" the nurse asked Joey, and those big, brown eyes slowly fluttered open. She gave Jax a lopsided smile and shrugged with her good shoulder.

"Sure, why not? He's pretty cute, isn't he?" she asked the nurse.

The nurse finally cracked a smile. "Set a date soon, honey. Men like that you need to lock down fast."

"'K." Joey smiled and closed her eyes.

"Okay, Joey, we're going to set your shoulder on three. One, two, th—"

And the f-bombs flew with abandon.

33

$\mathcal{B}$etween Phoebe humming while she cleaned the upstairs bathroom and her own mother puttering around the kitchen making a nice "hearty stew to put some meat back on her bones," Joey was over the whole convalescing thing.

She was forbidden from working at all for at least a week and not allowed to get on a horse for three. Lifting anything heavy like straw or saddles or a full water bucket? Forget it. She was good and screwed for at least six weeks.

She'd put up with the pampering and the mother henning as long as she could. Three whole days now. She was busting out of this joint. What would make her feel better? Seeing her damn horses, maybe swinging by Apollo's stall with some apple slices and a heartfelt "thank you very much for not murdering me with your hooves when you had the chance."

She waited until April wandered upstairs to the laundry room before she made her escape. Pulling on boots would take too long, so she slid her moccasins on her feet and grabbed Phoebe's down coat from the hook by the front door.

She snagged Jax's John Pierce Brews baseball hat and pulled it down over the gauze on her forehead.

Incognito, she limped out the front door and skirted the far side of the house to avoid detection. It felt like it had been weeks, not days, since she'd last walked through the door of the stables. Jax had spent every night with her but refused to have sex with her, saying that she needed to take it easy for a while. She'd offered to let him be on top, but he still wasn't biting.

She tucked her hands into the pockets of Phoebe's coat and hunched her shoulders against the March wind. Winter was hanging on to the bitter end in Blue Moon. The cold made the ache in her shoulder even more noticeable. But soon, spring would be here. And spring meant sunshine and flowers and impregnating horses. It was going to be a good year. She could feel it in her bones.

Joey glanced around her when she got to the stables to make sure the Joey police weren't making their rounds before she slipped inside. She limped around the corner, thankful that she'd been lucky with just a minor sprain, and glanced down the aisle. She spotted Gia, with her fiery red hair piled on top of her head, mucking out a stall with aplomb, if not a great deal of efficiency.

Beckett poked his head out of the office, and Joey ducked back so he wouldn't see her. "Babe, coffee's ready," he called to Gia.

"Oh, thank God. Listen, I think I can get one more stall done before I have to head in for my class."

"No problem," Beckett said, holding the door for her. "I'm finishing up some invoices here, and then I can take over. Evan said he'll help out Saturday."

Joey heard the door behind her open, and she limped into the tack room. Carter hauled in a fresh bale of straw and put it next to Gia's wheelbarrow before ducking into the office with them.

She heard voices and the soft trod of horses in the indoor ring. It sounded like someone was teaching her group lesson. She tiptoed out of the tack room and toward the ring. Her five o'clock students were all on their appropriate mounts working on a figure eight led by Jax and... her father?

Jax and Forrest stood shoulder to shoulder in the center of the ring. They took turns calling out instructions, some that were spot on and others that were a little more questionable.

Jax said something to her dad, and Forrest laughed and clapped him on the shoulder. Joey felt a lump build in her throat.

They were doing this for her. All of them. Because they loved her. And whether she understood or even appreciated what they were doing, she realized that they were doing their absolute best for her. And that's all anyone ever had done. Maybe they hadn't known better before. Maybe they knew better now. But what mattered is that they were putting their best efforts forward for her.

And she loved every single one of them for it.

She'd eat their damn stew and smile at the ridiculous pattern someone had raked in the ring. She'd praise the weird goat milk fabric softener Phoebe brought her. And she'd sure as hell tell each and everyone one of them how much she appreciated them. In her own way, of course. Baked goods most likely. Maybe a funny card. Not with actual words and hugs and stuff.

She snuck another peek at Jax and her father standing side by side and shook her head. Damned if she didn't love them both with a fierceness that scared her. Was this what forgiveness felt like? She felt lighter, happier. Jax had been so calm during "the incident" as her mother had taken to calling it.

And the tenderness he showed her after, well, that just choked her up with emotion. Despite her obvious durability and her impatience to get back to normal, he handled her as if she were something precious.

He'd stuck this time. And she knew now that he would always stick, always stay. They were tied up in each other, and there would be no untangling these knots ever again.

With her heart coming to life in her chest, she snuck back out of the stables and headed home to think.

That night, she waited until it was just she and Jax, relaxing on the couch. The fire was low, the dishes were done, and Waffles was curled up in a furry ball at her feet. Her head rested on his shoulder, his fingers stroking her bare arm. She watched the story unfold, carefully crafted and beautifully written.

"Jax?" she said.

His lips brushed the top of her head in a lazy kiss. "Yeah?"

"Seeing as how we're fake engaged and all, I think you should move in."

"Is this the head wound talking?" he asked lightly.

She shook her head and smiled. "No. It's the 'I think you should move in before we get married so we can make sure we won't murder each other living together' talking."

"Are you sure you didn't hit your head again?" He turned her chin this way and that to check her pupil dilation.

"Pretty sure."

"Marriage is a big deal," he told her.

"So I've heard. But now that I know what a big deal you are in Hollywood, I want to lock you down while I still can."

He pinched her, and she yelped. "Also, I get why you did what you did."

Jax stilled his hands on her. "You do?"

"And while I don't agree with some of the things you've

done," she said pointedly. "Everything you've ever done where I'm concerned came from a place of love. Sometimes stupidity and love. But the love part is what's important. And I'd be the biggest asshole in Blue Moon if I ignored that."

Jax tipped her chin up, brought his mouth within a whisper of hers. "I'm so glad you're not the biggest asshole in Blue Moon. I love you, Jojo."

"I love you back."

~

JAX MOVED in the next day. With all the troops at Joey's beck and call, it was easy work forming a vehicle convoy filled with Jax's limited possessions and distributing them all over Joey's house.

The first few days were a little rocky with Joey ceding so much of her own territory, but they soon found their rhythm. And just to make sure they both had enough elbow room, Jax put a call in to Calvin to see if the man's crew could handle yet another Pierce Acres project with an office, sunroom, and bedroom add-on to Joey's house. Calvin told him thanks to all the Pierce projects he was thinking about retiring... or at least taking his wife on that Hawaiian vacation she'd always wanted.

Spring finally sprung, chasing the last vestiges of winter north. Everyone's workloads on the farm doubled—those with twins found their workloads quadrupled—but the acres were never lonely. Grandparents, kids, neighbors, and friends were constant visitors. The dogs, enjoying the warm weather and muddy fields, spent their days romping between stables and barns giving chase to lazy barn cats and each other.

Business at the brewery was booming, and the need for a full-time manager was no longer just speculation. Joey's relationship with her parents had smoothed out to the point where she no longer felt like she was wearing a plastic bag over her head during conversations with them. Forrest had stopped treating Jax as a pariah, and April had only hinted around for a week or two after Joey's fall that maybe Joey should start working with livestock smaller than horses.

Joey and Jax agreed that Apollo and Calypso's first "experience" with each other seemed wildly successful after a few well-placed kicks from the mare reminding Apollo to mind his manners. In a few weeks they'd know for sure if there would be a baby Aplypso, as Jax had dubbed the potential foal.

Yes, life in Blue Moon was beautiful. Joey sighed, letting the spring air from the open car window rush through her fingers.

After some spectacular early morning sex, Jax had talked her into breakfast at Overly Caffeinated to celebrate their day off together. And after plates of growth-hormone- and cruelty-free bacon and eggs, they were heading home to do whatever the hell they felt like. Jax brought the knuckles of her hand to his lips, and she felt that familiar flutter in her stomach.

In his aviators and t-shirt, his hair carelessly tousled, he looked more movie star or model than writer and brewer. And he was all hers.

Suck it, Moon Beam Parker. Joey grinned. "Breakfast sure puts you in a good mood," she said.

"I was just thinking about a vacation with you."

"A vacation? Don't tell me you're back on road trips again."

The sun glinted off the glassy waters of Diller's pond as they cruised past.

"I was thinking more along the lines of passports and white sand, blue water, and a tiny bikini."

"If you think you can pull off a bikini, I'll be happy to post photographic evidence to Facebook," Joey teased.

Jax slowed and downshifted, bringing the Nova to a smooth stop on the side of the road.

"Oh, gee. Are we out of gas?" Joey smirked.

"Cute. Now get out," Jax said, reaching across her and pulling the door handle.

It wouldn't be the first time Jax had pretended to throw her out of a car. But when she looked around them, she realized where they were. The oak was still standing and, despite the scars it bore on its trunk, it looked stronger than ever.

She climbed out of the car and wandered over to it, fingers skimming the bark. She'd never revisited the site of the accident. She'd driven past it hundreds of times since but had never stopped. Never wanted to remember that night.

"What are we doing here?" she asked, wondering why Jax would want to put a damper on what had started off as the perfect day.

His fingers joined hers on the trunk of the tree. "Do you know what I see when I look at you, Joey?"

She faced him, arched an eyebrow. "I can't even imagine."

He brought his hands to her waist, and she felt the love in those gray eyes. "I see my past," he began, turning her wrist up and starting to trace her scar from the elbow. "I see my present." He skimmed a hand over her cheek, fingers dipping into her hair. "And I see my future." Jax looked her square in the eye and slowly began to sink down on one knee.

Goosebumps sprang up on her skin as Jax's hand left her face and traveled down her arm until he held her hand. Her breath caught in her throat.

"Joey, it's always been you for me. There's no home, no heart, without you. Marry me. Be my wife, my partner, my home."

She saw it then, the diamond glinting in the spring sunshine.

She bent at the waist, trying to catch her breath. "Are you sure about this?" she asked.

His slow, sexy-as-hell smile made her heart beat even faster. "Hell yes. Say yes."

"Are you asking or telling?" Joey's vision blurred with tears.

"There's only one answer here, Jojo."

She laughed and straightened. She knew it too. There had always been only one answer.

"Let's do it."

Jax whooped and picked her up around the waist, spinning her in a circle. Joey laughed as he let her slide down his body inch by inch until her toes touched the ground. He was hard before her lips met his, sealing the deal. When he pulled her against his hard-on, she put a hand on his chest. "Gimmie the ring, Ace. And then take me home and make love to me."

He slid it on her finger and pressed a kiss to her palm.

"It's freaking beautiful," Joey said admiring the glint and glitter. The platinum band rested snugly against her finger, and despite the fact that the diamond was the size of a car tire, it sat low enough in the setting that she might actually be able to wear it and not snag it on a horse.

"Beautiful and practical, just like my girl," he told her.

On the drive home, Joey made Jax promise he wouldn't say anything to anyone yet. She didn't want to deal with Summer and Gia showing up with their Pinterest wedding boards. If anyone asked her opinion on tablecloths and invitations, she'd tell them exactly where they could shove said tablecloths and invitations.

When she said as much to Jax as they pulled up to the house, he laughed. "I don't think that's going to be an issue."

She pulled him out of the car. "Come on, let's find out if engaged sex is different from dating sex." She planted a hot, fast kiss on his mouth, and he wrapped her legs around his waist carrying her up the porch steps.

"Door's open," she said, dipping her fingers into his hair and tugging just hard enough to elicit a groan from him.

"Wait, wait, wait, Jojo. Shit," he murmured against her mouth.

She bit his lower lip, and he growled.

"Wait?"

"We don't have time to find out what engaged sex is like."

"Why the hell not?" she demanded, squeezing him with her thighs.

"Because we're getting married in an hour."

JAX WASN'T KIDDING. One hour later, Joey walked down the grassy aisle on her father's arm in her Brigid Winston dress. All the pieces of her heart were there. There on the ridge where John Pierce's ashes were scattered.

The Pierces, Franklin, Evan, and Aurora, her parents, even her sister's family.

Jax waited for her at the end of the aisle looking model perfect in one of his tuxes. And as she walked toward him, he lay his hand over his heart.

"I'm still not going to apologize for wanting what's best for you," Forrest whispered gruffly.

"I wouldn't expect you to, Dad."

"Maybe I wasn't entirely right when it came to Jax. He's not so bad, I guess. But if you ever need someone to set him straight or come down to the police station with bail money, you call me, okay?"

"Thanks, Dad."

Ten minutes later, after Beckett officiated them through a

short and sweet ceremony, Joey wrapped her arms around her husband's neck, and they swayed from side to side in the meadow to Louis Armstrong crooning about the wonderful world.

"I can't believe you did this," she laughed as Jax dipped her low.

"No backing out now," Jax warned. "You legally belong to me."

"I'm not sure that's how marriage works."

"We'll figure it out," Jax said, spinning her around in a dizzying circle before reeling her back in.

"I can't believe we're married. How did you know I wouldn't have wanted to plan a wedding?"

"Because I'm not an idiot," Jax teased. "I think we've all heard your napkin-ring seating-chart rant before."

"Your deep knowledge and acceptance of me is very much appreciated," Joey told him, slipping a hand between their bodies to cup his crotch.

"Patience, wife. We have a picnic lunch, and then you can have your way with me."

"Mmm, lunch. Okay. Food then sex." Joey glanced around them at their family. Aurora and her nephew Isaiah took turns chasing Waffles in and out of the slowly swaying couples. Her parents were dancing next to her sister and brother-in-law and laughing about something. Gia was sitting on Beckett's lap holding one of the twins while Carter and Summer stole a quick dance.

Phoebe and Franklin shared a sweet kiss and a laugh about something.

"Isn't it amazing that your mom found a love like that twice in a lifetime?" Joey asked, nodding at them.

"I think it's amazing that we did," Jax said as he lowered his mouth tenderly to hers. She responded by biting his lip.

EPILOGUE
FATHER'S DAY

*B*eckett tore into the paper wrapping of Evan's gift.

"Geez, destroy my impeccable wrap job, why don't ya?" Evan grumbled from the picnic table. With as many events as they'd been hosting on the ridge where John Pierce's ashes had been spread, the Pierces finally decided to put up a small pavilion with picnic tables and a fireplace and grill. They christened it with a Father's Day picnic.

"Next time wrap it with duct tape," Jax suggested as he stole a bite of Joey's hot dog. "He hates that."

"Noted," Evan said with the amused smirk of an official teenager.

Beckett tossed the paper to the ground. He held a coffee mug that he couldn't stop staring at.

He turned it around so everyone could see it.

World's #1 Dad.

Evan paused, his brown eyes serious for a moment. "You're a really good dad. Aurora and me, we're pretty lucky."

Jax could see his brother's throat working furiously, knew it must be one hell of a lump in there.

Beckett pulled Evan to his feet, ruffled his hair, and then yanked the kid in for a hug.

"Oh, man. You're gonna cry, aren't you?" Evan's voice was muffled against Beckett's polo shirt.

"I'm not gonna cry. You're gonna cry," Beckett croaked, making a valiant effort to not choke on emotion.

"Happy Faver's Day, Bucket. I made you dis." Aurora scampered up behind him holding up a crayon drawing. "Dat's you, an dat's me," she said, pointing to one stick figure and then the other.

"Shit." Beckett swore brokenly.

From a glance at the paper, Jax assumed the one with the giant head was Beckett and the one with the big foot was Aurora. The art must have moved his brother because Beckett grabbed the little redhead and lifted both her and Evan off their feet in a bone-crushing hug.

"You're suffocating me." Evan sounded a little winded.

"Mama, Bucket said—"

"I know. I know," Gia sighed. "Bucket said 'shit.'" She laughed and launched herself into the hug, smashing the kids between her and Beckett.

Carter grinned up at them from his position on the blanket, a twin in each arm and Meatball curled up against his side. Jax had seen his brother angry and brittle after battle. He'd seen him ecstatic at his wedding to Summer. But he'd never seen contentment smooth out all of Carter's rough edges as it had now with his son and daughter in his arms.

Beckett finally released the kids and Gia in a pile on the ground. He furtively wiped a hand over his eyes. "It's just allergies," he muttered.

Evan swiped a hand under his nose. "Yeah. Allergies."

Gia pulled her husband in for another hug and wrapped

her arms around his waist. Beckett dropped a kiss on the top of her red hair.

"Great. Now Mom's crying too," Evan said, rolling his eyes.

"Shut your face," Gia ordered.

Summer rushed to Carter's side holding two bottles as if they were anti-venom. Valentina gamboled on her heels.

"I'm so sorry it took me so long! I didn't have any clean bottles," she gasped, flopping down on the blanket. "I hope they didn't cry too... Are they asleep?"

"About two minutes after you went back to the house," Carter sighed. "Our kids are jerks."

"Beautiful, amazing jerks," Summer leaned in to place a soft kiss on each baby's forehead.

Valentina shoved her giant spotted head into the happy family, and Summer threw her arms around the dog's neck. "Who could forget you, Valentina? You're Mommy's perfect angel."

Joey tossed the last bite of hot dog to Waffles and laughed as Diesel the gangly teenage puppy sniffed the ground for leftovers. Jax pulled his wife in and dropped a quick kiss on her mouth. Forrest, to his credit, didn't even bother rolling his eyes anymore. Their constant affection was slowly wearing the man down into a reasonable facsimile of tolerance toward their relationship.

"When are you going to hand out the b-o-o-k-ses?" Joey whispered, nodding conspicuously at the stack of brown paper packages on the end of the food table.

Jax laughed. "The only people who are getting them are the ones who can already spell," he teased.

"Your brothers are going to freak out," Joey predicted.

Jax had his father's essays printed up and turned into paperbacks for his brothers and his mother.

"I hope so. Then I won't have to get them anything for Christmas."

"What are you getting me for Christmas?" Joey asked, sliding her hands around his waist.

"I moved my production trip to very early spring so you can come with me and we both can be here if there's a baby Aplypso ready to be born."

"A, we're coming up with a better name than that; and B, thank you." Joey wrapped her arms around his neck and gave him a smacking kiss on the cheek. "Did anyone give you any problems on moving up the schedule?"

"The studio seems even more excited about the project than I am," Jax told her.

"Who are they going to get to play you?" Joey wondered.

"Probably someone really handsome and debonair. Maybe a James Bond-type?"

"I hope they pick Didi to play me."

"I would hate to see her on a horse," Jax said with a far-off look.

Joey smacked him good-naturedly. "Stop fantasizing about it, Ace."

"Are you sure everyone here can manage without you for two weeks, Jojo?" he asked, drawing her hand up to kiss her wedding band as had become his habit.

"Are you kidding? With a new full-time manager and two more part-timers to split between the farm and the stables, I don't have anything to do. Hell, I might take up writing screen-plays in my spare time."

Jax grinned. Joey's spare time was non-existent. With demand for Apollo through the roof, she was juggling breeding rights seasons in advance. Plus, she was working on putting together another proposal for the Pierces. This one for a therapeutic riding program. His Joey was never idle, and she pushed him to be just as tireless.

"Let's get a group picture," Phoebe said, clapping her hands. Jax and his brothers grumbled good-naturedly but lined up on the ridge where their wives directed them. Joey positioned Jax between her and her parents, and when Forrest put his hand on Jax's shoulder, he decided it wasn't a bad feeling.

Phoebe set the camera on the picnic table and fiddled with it.

"Okay, it's on timer and burst mode, so it's going to take a bunch of pictures in ten seconds. Try to behave like human beings for a few of those pictures!" She scurried back to the group, ducking under Franklin's arm and putting her hands on Evan's shoulders.

"Everyone smile!"

On the first shutter click, Jax heard Franklin and Gia gasp, and his grin widened. His surprise happened right on schedule. Gia's sister Emmaline strolled into the picture with a lemonade in one hand and a suitcase in the other.

"Well, aren't you going to welcome me home?" she asked with a grin just before Franklin nearly tackled her to the ground in a bear hug.

"What are you doing here?" Gia asked, clinging to her sister's shoulders.

"I heard there was a brewery that needed a manager."

Joey drilled a finger into Jax's shoulder. "Sneaky," she said.

"I thought you wouldn't mind having a little more time with your husband," he said, kissing her on the temple.

"When did you have time to arrange that?"

"Right after the closing on my house when we were in L.A. You were visiting that riding academy, and I met Emma at her restaurant and planted the seeds."

Joey watched Gia sob all over her sister. "It looks like you did good."

"Why are you crying, G?" Emma asked Gia, patting her back.

"Because I'm pregnant!"

One look at Beckett's stunned face told Jax this was the first he was hearing the news.

"What?" The question flew loud and fast from a dozen different directions at once.

"Speaking of growing families," Joey whispered in his ear.

"Don't even joke about that right now," Jax warned her. They'd already talked. Kids were definitely in their future, probably a lot of them. Loud, messy ones. Just not in their immediate future. He was just getting used to waking up next to his beautiful wife every morning. He wasn't ready to share quite yet.

"Get used to it because in ten to eleven months, we're going to be grandparents," she said, handing him a grainy picture.

"Eleven months? Grandparents? What the hell is this?" He peered at the picture.

"That's an ultrasound of Apollo and Calypso's baby."

"It took?" Jax grabbed Joey around the waist and lifted her up.

"Dr. Sammy was here yesterday and confirmed. The Pierce Stables breeding program has officially begun. We've got a very long list of parties interested in our Apollo's breeding rights."

Jax pulled his wife into his arms and lowered his forehead to hers. "What did you get me into, Joey Greer?"

Joey's brown eyes danced. "I have no idea. Probably the biggest mess of your life."

"I like getting messy with you, Jojo."

"Well, here's to a lifetime of messiness together."

Joey closed the gap and kissed him long and hard. When they broke apart and Joey put her head on his shoulder, Jax looked around them and saw circles within circles. Another baby for the new generation of family. Another venture for the farm that had sustained them all in one way or another. Marriages, promises, mended relationships. A love that just kept building on itself.

If home was where the heart is, Jax's heart was right here in the middle of chaos.

They were all so busy celebrating that no one noticed when Clementine meandered over to the picnic table and helped herself to the bowl of macaroni salad.

AUTHOR'S NOTE TO THE READER

Dear Reader,

Holy cow, you guys. Or goat, more accurately. Jax and Joey finally got their happily ever after. There was so much freaking history to wade through in their story, I hope you enjoyed how it all came together.

I was *really* nervous about including the essays from John Pierce in this story for three reasons. 1. He's dead. 2. His wife is engaged to another man. 3. The book was already super long. But I wanted to give Jax, the perpetual black sheep of the family, a connection to his father that made him feel like he really fit, so I went for it.

I also had a blast writing Joey. At first, I thought she was going to be a really unlikeable leading lady, but she ended up being one of my favorites to write. Joey's sarcasm and her abhorrence of socializing was oddly endearing to me, and I hope you felt the same about her.

Favorite scene: The rolling fart circus. I was almost hysterical while writing it.

Can't get enough Blue Moon? Sad the Pierce brothers' stories are over? But wait! There's more! *Not Part of the Plan* will take you back to Blue Moon when Summer's photographer friend Niko arrives for a much-needed sabbatical and decides to distract himself with Gia's sister Emma, manager of the brewery. The only problem is Emma's sworn off womanizing bad boys and has no interest in being anything but friends.

So did you fall hard for *The Last Second Chance*? Feel free to leave a review on Amazon or BookBub and visit me on social media and spoil me with compliments... or suggestions. Whatever floats your literary boat. If you think this book is just the beginning of a long-term love affair with all Lucy Score books, sign up for my newsletter and never miss a release. You can also find me on Facebook and Instagram.

Thank you for reading!

Xoxo,
 Lucy

ABOUT THE AUTHOR

Lucy Score is a *Wall Street Journal* and #1 Amazon bestselling author. She grew up in a literary family who insisted that the dinner table was for reading and earned a degree in journalism. She writes full-time from the Pennsylvania home she and Mr. Lucy share with their obnoxious cat, Cleo. When not spending hours crafting heartbreaker heroes and kick-ass heroines, Lucy can be found on the couch, in the kitchen, or at the gym. She hopes to someday write from a sailboat, or oceanfront condo, or tropical island with reliable Wi-Fi.

Sign up for her newsletter and stay up on all the latest Lucy book news.
And follow her on:
Website: Lucyscore.com
Facebook at: lucyscorewrites
Instagram at: scorelucy
Readers Group at: Lucy Score's Binge Readers Anonymous

LUCY'S TITLES

Standalone Titles

Undercover Love

Pretend You're Mine

Finally Mine

Protecting What's Mine

Mr. Fixer Upper

The Christmas Fix

Heart of Hope

The Worst Best Man

Rock Bottom Girl

The Price of Scandal

By a Thread

Forever Never

Things We Never Got Over

Riley Thorn

Riley Thorn and the Dead Guy Next Door

Riley Thorn and the Corpse in the Closet

Riley Thorn and the Blast from the Past

The Blue Moon Small Town Romance Series

No More Secrets

Fall into Temptation

The Last Second Chance

Not Part of the Plan

CPSIA information can be obtained
at www.ICGtesting.com
Printed in the USA
LVHW042228200323
742053LV00001B/42